John le Carré

John le Carré was born in 1931. After attending the universities
of Bern and Oxford, he taught at Eton and spent five years in
the British Foreign Service.

He is the author of seventeen novels and he lives in Cornwall.

SCEPTRE

Also by John le Carré

Call for the Dead
A Murder of Quality
The Spy Who Came in From the Cold
The Looking Glass War
A Small Town in Germany
The Naive and Sentimental Lover
Tinker Tailor Soldier Spy
The Honourable Schoolboy
Smiley's People
The Little Drummer Girl
A Perfect Spy
The Russia House
The Secret Pilgrim
The Night Manager
Our Game
The Tailor of Panama
Single & Single

John le Carré

THE CONSTANT GARDENER

SCEPTRE

First published in Great Britain in 2001 by Hodder and Stoughton
A division of Hodder Headline
Sceptre edition published 2002
A Sceptre Paperback

10 9 8 7 6 5 4 3 2 1

Grateful acknowledgement is made for permission to reprint
excerpts from the following copyrighted works:

Clinical Trials: A Practical Approach by Stuart J. Pocock.
1984 © John Wiley & Sons Ltd. Reproduced with permission.

'Drug Firm Put Patients at Risk in Hospital Trials' by Paul Nuki,
David Leppard, Gareth Walsh and Guy Dennis from *The Sunday Times*,
London © Times Newspapers Ltd, 14 May 2000

A CIP catalogue record for this title
is available from the British Library

ISBN 0 340 73353 5

Typeset in Monotype Baskerville by Rowland Phototypesetting Ltd,
Bury St Edmunds, Suffolk
Printed and bound in Great Britain by
Clays Ltd, St Ives plc

Hodder and Stoughton
A division of Hodder Headline Ltd
338 Euston Road
London NW1 3BH

For Yvette Pierpaoli
who lived and died giving a damn

'Ah, but a man's reach should exceed his grasp.
Or what's a heaven for?'

'Andrea del Sarto' by Robert Browning

CHAPTER ONE

The news hit the British High Commission in Nairobi at nine-thirty on a Monday morning. Sandy Woodrow took it like a bullet, jaw rigid, chest out, smack through his divided English heart. He was standing. That much he afterwards remembered. He was standing and the internal phone was piping. He was reaching for something, he heard the piping so he checked himself in order to stretch down and fish the receiver off the desk and say, '*Woodrow*.' Or maybe, 'Woodrow here.' And he certainly barked his name a bit, he had that memory for sure: of his voice sounding like someone else's, and sounding stroppy: '*Woodrow here*,' his own perfectly decent name, but without the softening of his nickname Sandy, and snapped out as if he hated it, because the High Commissioner's usual prayer meeting was slated to start in thirty minutes prompt, with Woodrow, as Head of Chancery, playing in-house moderator to a bunch of special-interest prima donnas, each of whom wanted sole possession of the High Commissioner's heart and mind.

In short, just another bloody Monday in late January, the hottest time in the Nairobi year, a time of dust and water shortages and brown grass and sore eyes and heat ripping off the city pavements; and the jacarandas, like everybody else, waiting for the long rains.

Exactly why he was standing was a question he never resolved. By rights he should have been crouched behind his desk, fingering his keyboard, anxiously reviewing guidance material from London and incomings from neighbouring African Missions. Instead of which he was standing in front of his desk and performing some unidentified vital act – such as straightening the photograph of his wife Gloria and two small sons, perhaps, taken last summer while the family was on home leave. The High Commission stood on a slope, and its continuing subsidence was enough to tilt pictures out of true after a weekend on their own.

Or perhaps he had been squirting mosquito spray at some Kenyan insect from which even diplomats are not immune. There had been a plague of 'Nairobi eye' a few months back, flies that when squidged and rubbed accidentally on the skin could give you boils and blisters, and even send you blind. He had been spraying, he heard his phone ring, he put the can down on his desk and grabbed the receiver: also possible, because somewhere in his later memory there was a colour-slide of a red tin of insecticide sitting in the out-tray on his desk. So, 'Woodrow here,' and the telephone jammed to his ear.

'Oh, Sandy, it's Mike Mildren. Good morning. You alone by any chance?'

Shiny, overweight, twenty-four-year-old Mildren, High Commissioner's private secretary, Essex accent, fresh out from England on his first overseas posting – and known to the junior staff, predictably, as Mildred.

Yes, Woodrow conceded, he was alone. Why?

'Something's come up, I'm afraid, Sandy. I wondered if I might pop down a moment actually.'

'Can't it wait till after the meeting?'

'Well, I don't think it can really – no, it can't,' Mildren replied, gathering conviction as he spoke. 'It's Tessa Quayle, Sandy.'

A different Woodrow now, hackles up, nerves extended. Tessa. 'What about her?' he said. His tone deliberately incurious, his mind racing in all directions. Oh Tessa. Oh Christ. What have you done now?

'The Nairobi police say she's been killed,' Mildren said, as if he said it every day.

'Utter nonsense,' Woodrow snapped back before he had given himself time to think. 'Don't be ridiculous. Where? When?'

'At Lake Turkana. The eastern shore. This weekend. They're being diplomatic about the details. In her car. An unfortunate accident, according to them,' he added apologetically. 'I had a sense that they were trying to spare our feelings.'

'*Whose* car?' Woodrow demanded wildly – fighting now, rejecting the whole mad concept – who, how, where and his other thoughts and senses forced down, down, down, and all his secret memories of her furiously edited out, to be replaced by the baked moonscape of Turkana as he recalled it from a field trip six months ago in the unimpeachable company of the military attaché. 'Stay where you are, I'm coming up. And don't talk to anyone else, d'you hear?'

Moving by numbers now, Woodrow replaced the receiver, walked round his desk, picked up his jacket from the back of his chair and pulled it on, sleeve by sleeve. He would not customarily have put on a jacket to go upstairs. Jackets were not mandatory for Monday meetings, let alone for going to the private office for a chat with chubby Mildren. But the professional in Woodrow was telling him he was facing a long journey. Nevertheless on his way upstairs he managed by a sturdy effort of self-will to revert to his first principles whenever a crisis appeared on his horizon, and assure himself, just as he had assured Mildren, that it was a lot of utter nonsense. In support of which, he summoned up the sensational case of a young Englishwoman who had been hacked to pieces in the African bush ten years ago. It's a sick hoax, of course it is. A replay in somebody's deranged imagination. Some wildcat African policeman stuck out in the desert, half loco on *bangi*, trying to bolster the dismal salary he hasn't been paid for six months.

The newly completed building he was ascending was austere

and well designed. He liked its style, perhaps because it corresponded outwardly with his own. With its neatly defined compound, canteen, shop, fuel pump and clean, muted corridors, it gave off a self-sufficient, rugged impression. Woodrow, to all appearances, had the same sterling qualities. At forty, he was happily married to Gloria – or if he wasn't, he assumed he was the only person to know it. He was Head of Chancery and it was a fair bet that, if he played his cards right, he would land his own modest Mission on his next posting, and from there advance by less modest Missions to a knighthood – a prospect to which he himself attached no importance, of course, but it would be nice for Gloria. There was a bit of the soldier about him, but then he was a soldier's son. In his seventeen years in Her Majesty's Foreign Service he had flown the flag in half a dozen overseas British Missions. All the same, dangerous, decaying, plundered, bankrupt, once-British Kenya had stirred him more than most of them, though how much of this was due to Tessa he dared not ask himself.

'All right,' he said aggressively to Mildren, having first closed the door behind him and dropped the latch.

Mildren had a permanent pout. Seated at his desk he looked like a naughty fat boy who has refused to finish up his porridge.

'She was staying at the Oasis,' he said.

'*What* oasis? Be precise, if you can.'

But Mildren was not as easily rattled as his age and rank might have led Woodrow to believe. He had been keeping a shorthand record, which he now consulted before he spoke. Must be what they teach them these days, thought Woodrow with contempt. How else does an Estuary upstart like Mildren find time to pick up shorthand?

'There's a lodge on the eastern shore of Lake Turkana, at the southern end,' Mildren announced, his eyes on the pad. 'It's called the Oasis. Tessa spent the night there and set off next morning in a four-track provided by the Lodge's owner. She said she wanted to see the birthplace of civilisation two hundred miles north. The Leakey dig.' He corrected himself. 'The site of Richard Leakey's excavation. In the Siboloi National Park.'

'Alone?'

'Wolfgang provided a driver. His body's in the four-track with hers.'

'Wolfgang?'

'The Lodge's owner. Surname to follow. Everyone calls him Wolfgang. He's German, apparently. A character. According to the police, the driver's been brutally murdered.'

'How?'

'Decapitated. Missing.'

'Who's missing? You said he was in the car with her.'

'The head's missing.'

I might have guessed that for myself, mightn't I? 'How's Tessa supposed to have died?'

'An accident. That's all they're saying.'

'Was she robbed?'

'Not according to the police.'

The absence of a theft, coupled with the driver's murder, had Woodrow's imagination racing. 'Just give it me exactly as you have it,' he ordered.

Mildren rested his big cheeks in his palms while he again consulted his shorthand. 'Nine-twenty-nine, incoming from Nairobi police headquarters flying squad asking for the High Commissioner,' he recited. 'I explained that H.E. was in town visiting ministries, due back ten a.m. latest. An efficient-sounding duty officer, name supplied. He said reports were coming in from Lodwar –'

'Lodwar? That's miles from Turkana!'

'It's the nearest police station,' Mildren replied. 'A four-track, property of the Oasis Lodge, Turkana, had been found abandoned on the east side of the lake, short of Allia Bay, on the way to the Leakey site. The bodies were thirty-six hours old at least. One dead white female, death unexplained, one headless African, identified as Noah the driver, married with four children. One Mephisto safari boot, size seven. One blue bush jacket, size XL, bloodstained, found on the floor of the car. The woman in her mid-to-late twenties, dark-haired, one gold ring on third finger of left hand. One gold necklace on the car floor.'

That necklace you're wearing, Woodrow heard himself saying in mock challenge as they danced.

My grandmother gave it to my mother on her wedding day, she answered. *I wear it with everything, even if it's out of sight.*

Even in bed?

Depends.

'Who found them?' Woodrow asked.

'Wolfgang. He radioed the police and informed his office here in Nairobi. Also by radio. The Oasis has no telephone.'

'If the driver was headless, how can they know it was the driver?'

'He had a crushed arm. That's why he took up driving. Wolfgang watched Tessa drive off with Noah on Saturday at five-thirty, in the company of Arnold Bluhm. That was the last time he saw them alive.'

He was still quoting from notes or if he wasn't he was pretending to. His cheeks were still in his hands and he seemed determined they should stay here, for there was a stubborn rigidity across his shoulders.

'Give me that again,' Woodrow ordered, after a beat.

'Tessa was accompanied by Arnold Bluhm. They checked into the Oasis Lodge together, spent Friday night there and set off in Noah's jeep next morning at five-thirty,' Mildren repeated patiently. 'Bluhm's body wasn't in the four-track and there's no trace of him. Or none reported so far. Lodwar police and the flying squad are on site but Nairobi headquarters want to know if we'll pay for a helicopter.'

'Where are the bodies now?' Woodrow was his soldier-father's son, crisp and practical.

'Not known. The police wanted the Oasis to take charge of them but Wolfgang refused. He said his staff would walk out and so would his guests.' A hesitation. 'She booked in as Tessa Abbott.'

'*Abbott?*'

'Her maiden name. "Tessa Abbott, care of a PO Box in Nairobi." Ours. We haven't got an Abbott so I ran the name across our records and got Quayle, maiden name Abbott, Tessa. I gather it's the name she uses for her relief work.' He was studying the last page of his notes. 'I've tried to raise the High Commissioner but he's doing the ministries and it's rush hour,' he said. By which he meant: this is President Moi's modern Nairobi, where a local call can take half an hour of listening to *I'm sorry, all lines are busy, please try again later*, repeated tirelessly by a complacent woman in middle age.

Woodrow was already at the door. 'And you've told nobody?'

'Not a soul.'

'Have the police?'

'They say no. But they can't answer for Lodwar and I shouldn't think they can answer for themselves.'

'And Justin's been told nothing as far as you know.'

'Correct.'

'Where is he?'

'In his office, I assume.'

'Keep him there.'

'He came in early. It's what he does when Tessa's on a field trip. Do you want me to cancel the meeting?'

'Wait.'

Aware by now, if he ever doubted it, that he was coping with a Force Twelve scandal as well as a tragedy, Woodrow darted up a back staircase marked Authorised Staff Only and entered a glum passage that led to a closed steel door with an eye-hole and a bell-button. A camera scanned him while he pressed the button. The door was opened by a willowy, red-headed woman in jeans and a flowered smock. Sheila, their number two, kiSwahili speaker, he thought automatically.

'Where's Tim?' he asked.

Sheila pressed a buzzer then spoke into a box. 'It's Sandy in a hurry.'

'Hold for figures *one* minute,' cried an expansive male voice. They held.

'Coast now *totally* clear,' the same voice reported as another door burped open.

Sheila stood back and Woodrow strode past her into the room. Tim Donohue, the six-foot-six Head of Station, was looming in front of his desk. He must have been clearing it, for there was not a paper in sight. Donohue looked even sicker than usual. Woodrow's wife Gloria insisted he was dying. Sunken, colourless cheeks. Nests of crumbling skin below the drooping yellowed eyes. The straggling moustache clawed downward in comic despair.

'Sandy. Greetings. What can we do you for?' he cried, peering down on Woodrow through his bifocals and grinning his skull's grin.

He comes too close, Woodrow remembered. He overflies your territory and intercepts your signals before you make them. 'Tessa Quayle seems to have been killed somewhere near Lake Turkana,' he said, feeling a vindictive urge to shock. 'There's a place called Oasis Lodge. I need to talk to the owner by radio.'

This is how they're trained, he thought. Rule one: never show your feelings, if you have any. Sheila's freckled features, frozen in pensive rejection. Tim Donohue still grinning his foolish grin – but then the grin hadn't meant anything in the first place.

'Been *what*, old boy? Say again?'

'Killed. Method unknown or the police aren't saying. The driver of her jeep had his head hacked off. That's the story.'

'Killed and robbed?'

'Just killed.'

'Near Lake Turkana.'

'Yes.'

'What the hell was she doing up there?'

'I've no idea. Visiting the Leakey site, allegedly.'

'Does Justin know?'

'Not yet.'

'Anyone else we know involved?'

'One of the things I'm trying to find out.'

Donohue led the way to a soundproofed communications booth that Woodrow had never seen before. Coloured telephones with cavities for code lozenges. A fax machine resting on what looked like an oil drum. A radio set made of stippled green metal boxes. A home-printed directory lying on top of them. So this is how our spies whisper to each other from inside our buildings, he thought. Overworld or underworld? He never knew. Donohue sat himself at the radio, studied the directory, then fumbled the controls with trembling white fingers while he intoned, 'ZNB 85, ZNB 85 calling TKA 60,' like a hero in a war film. 'TKA 60, do you read me, please? Over. Oasis, do you read me, Oasis? Over.'

A burst of atmospherics was followed by a challenging, 'Oasis here. Loud and clear, Mister. Who are you? Over' – spoken in a raffish German accent.

'Oasis, this is the British High Commission in Nairobi, I'm passing you to Sandy Woodrow. Over.'

Woodrow leaned both hands on Donohue's desk in order to come closer to the microphone.

'This is Woodrow, Head of Chancery. Am I speaking to Wolfgang? Over.'

'Chancellery like Hitler had one?'

'The political section. Over.'

'OK, Mr Chancery, I'm Wolfgang. What's your question? Over.'

'I want you to give me, please, your own description of the woman who checked into your hotel as Miss Tessa Abbott. That's correct, is it? That's what she wrote? Over.'

'Sure. Tessa.'

'What did she look like? Over.'

'Dark hair, no make-up, tall, late twenties, not British. Not for me. South German, Austrian or Italian. I'm a hotelier. I look at people. And beautiful. I'm a man too. Sexy like an animal, how she moves. And clothes like you could blow them off. That sound like your Abbott or somebody else's? Over.'

Donohue's head was a few inches from his own. Sheila was

standing at his other side. All three of them were gazing at the microphone.

'Yes. That sounds like Miss Abbott. Can you tell me, please: when did she make the reservation at your hotel, and how? I believe you have an office in Nairobi. Over.'

'She didn't.'

'I'm sorry?'

'Dr Bluhm made the reservation. Two persons, two cabins close to the pool, one night. We've only got one cabin free, I tell him. OK, he'll take it. That's some fellow. Wow. Everybody looks at them. The guests, the staff. One beautiful white woman, one beautiful African doctor. That's a nice sight. Over.'

'How many rooms does a cabin have?' Woodrow asked, feebly hoping to head off the scandal that was staring him in the face.

'One bedroom, two single beds, not too hard, nice and springy. One sitting room. Everybody signs the register here. No funny names, I tell them. People get lost, I got to know who they are. So that's her name, right? Abbott? Over.'

'Her maiden name. Over. The PO Box number she gave is the High Commission.'

'Where's the husband?'

'Here in Nairobi.'

'Oh boy.'

'So when did Bluhm make the reservation? Over.'

'Thursday. Thursday evening. Radios me from Loki. Tells me they expect to leave Friday first light. Loki like Lokichoggio. On the northern border. Capital of the aid agencies working South Sudan. Over.'

'I know where Lokichoggio is. Did they say what they were doing there?'

'Aid stuff. Bluhm's in the aid game, right? That's the only way you get to Loki. Works for some Belgian medical outfit, he told me. Over.'

'So he booked from Loki and they left Loki on Friday morning early. Over.'

'Tells me they expect to reach the west side of the lake around noon. Wants me to fix them a boat to bring them across the lake to the Oasis. "Listen," I tell him. "Lokichoggio to Turkana, that's a hairy drive. Best you ride with a food convoy. The hills are lousy with bandits, there's tribes stealing each other's cattle which is normal, except that ten years ago they had spears and today they all got AK47s." He laughs. Says he can handle it. And he can. They make it, no problem. Over.'

'So they check in, then sign the register. Then what? Over.'

'Bluhm tells me they want a jeep and a driver to go up to Leakey's place first light next morning. Don't ask me why he didn't mention it when he booked, I didn't ask him. Maybe they only just decided. Maybe they didn't like to discuss their plans over the radio. "OK," I tell him. "You're lucky. You can have Noah." Bluhm's pleased. She's pleased. They walk in the garden, swim together, sit at the bar together, eat together, tell goodnight to everybody, go to their cabin. In the morning they leave together. I watch them. You want to know what they had for breakfast?'

'Who saw them leave apart from you? Over.'

'Everybody who's awake sees them. Packed lunch, box of water, spare gas, emergency rations, medical supplies. All three of them in the front and Abbott in the middle, like one happy family. This is an oasis, OK? I got twenty guests, mostly they're asleep. I got forty staff, mostly they're awake. I got about a hundred guys I don't need hanging round my car park selling animal skins and walking sticks and hunting knives. Everyone who sees Bluhm and Abbott leave waves bye-bye. I wave, the skin sellers wave, Noah waves back, Bluhm and Abbott wave back. They don't smile. They're serious. Like they've got heavy business to do, big decisions, what do I know? What you want me to do, Mr Chancery? Kill the witnesses? Listen, I'm Galileo. Put me in prison, I'll swear she never came to the Oasis. Over.'

For a moment of paralysis Woodrow had no further questions, or perhaps he had too many. I'm in prison already, he thought. My life sentence started five minutes ago. He passed a hand across his eyes and when he removed it he saw Donohue and

Sheila watching him with the same blank expressions they had worn when he told them she was dead.

'When did you first get the idea something might have gone wrong? Over,' he asked lamely – 'like, do you live up there all year round? Over. Or, how long have you been running your nice hotel? Over.'

'The four-track has a radio. On a trip with guests, Noah is supposed to call and say he's happy. Noah doesn't call. OK, radios fail, drivers forget. To make a link it's boring. You got to stop the car, get out, set up the aerial. You still hearing me? Over.'

'Loud and clear. Over.'

'Except Noah never forgets. That's why he drives for me. But he doesn't call. Not in the afternoon, not in the evening. OK, I think. Maybe they camped somewhere, gave Noah too much to drink or something. Last thing in the evening before shut-down I radio the rangers up around the Leakey site. No sign. First thing next morning I go to Lodwar to report the loss. It's my jeep, OK? My driver. I'm not allowed to report the loss by radio, I've got to do it in person. It's a hell of a journey but that's the law. The Lodwar police really like helping citizens in distress. My jeep went missing? Tough shit. It had two of my guests and my driver in it? Then why don't I go look for them? It's a Sunday, they're not expecting to work today. They got to go to church. "Give us some money, lend us a car, maybe we help you," they tell me. I come home, I put a search party together. Over.'

'Consisting of whom?' Woodrow was getting back into his stride.

'Two groups. My own people, two trucks, water, spare fuel, medical supplies, provisions, Scotch in case I need to disinfect something. Over.' A cross-broadcast intervened. Wolfgang told it to get the hell off the air. Surprisingly, it did. 'It's pretty hot up here right now, Mr Chancery. We got a hundred and fifteen Fahrenheit plus jackals and hyenas like you got mice. Over.'

A pause, apparently for Woodrow to speak.

'I'm listening,' Woodrow said.

'The jeep was on its side. Don't ask me why. The doors were closed. Don't ask me why. One window open like five centimetres. Somebody closed the doors and locked them, took away the key. The smell unspeakable, just from the little gap. Hyena scratches all over, big dents where they'd tried to get in. Tracks all round while they went crazy. A good hyena smells blood ten kilometres away. If they'd been able to reach the bodies they'd have cracked them open one bite, got the marrow out the bones. But they didn't. Somebody locked the door on them and left the bit of window open. So they went crazy. So would you. Over.'

Woodrow struggled to get his words together. 'The police say Noah was decapitated. Is that right? Over.'

'Sure. He was a great guy. Family's worried crazy. They got people everywhere looking for his head. If they can't find the head they can't give him a decent funeral and his spirit will come back to haunt them. Over.'

'What about Miss Abbott? Over –' a vile vision of Tessa without her head.

'Didn't they tell you?'

'No. Over.'

'Throat cut. Over.'

A second vision, this time of her killer's fist as it ripped off her necklace to clear the way for the knife. Wolfgang was explaining what he did next.

'Number one, I tell my boys, leave the doors closed. Nobody's alive in there. Anybody opening the doors is going to have a very bad time. I leave one group to light a fire and keep watch. I drive the other group back to the Oasis. Over.'

'Question. Over.' Woodrow was struggling to hold on.

'What's your question, Mr Chancery? Come in, please. Over.'

'Who opened the jeep? Over.'

'The police. Soon as the police arrived, my boys get the hell out the way. No one likes police. No one likes to be arrested. Not up here. Lodwar police came first, now we've got the flying squad, plus some guys from Moi's personal Gestapo. My boys are locking the till and hiding the silver, except I haven't got any silver. Over.'

Another delay while Woodrow wrestled for rational words.

'Was Bluhm wearing a safari jacket when they set out for Leakey's place? Over.'

'Sure. Old one. More a waistcoat. Blue. Over.'

'Did anyone find a knife at the scene of the murder? Over.'

'No. And it was some knife, believe me. A panga with a Wilkinson blade. Went through Noah like butter. One swing. Same with her. Vump. The woman was stripped naked. Lot of bruising. Did I say that? Over.'

No, you didn't say that, Woodrow told him silently. You omitted her nakedness completely. The bruising also. 'Was there a panga in the four-track when they set out from your Lodge? Over.'

'I never knew an African yet who didn't take his panga on safari, Mr Chancery.'

'Where are the bodies now?'

'Noah, what's left of him, they give him to his tribe. Miss Abbott, the police sent a motor dinghy for her. Had to cut the jeep roof off. Borrowed our cutting equipment. Then strap her to the deck. No room for her downstairs. Over.'

'Why not?' But he was already wishing he hadn't asked.

'Use your imagination, Mr Chancery. You know what happens to corpses in this heat? You want to fly her down to Nairobi, you better cut her up or she won't get into the hold.'

Woodrow had a moment of mental numbness and when he woke from it he heard Wolfgang saying yes, he had met Bluhm once before. So Woodrow must have asked him the question, although he hadn't heard it himself.

'Nine months back. Bear-leading a party of fat-cats in the aid game. World food, world health, world expense accounts. Bastards spent a mountain of money, wanted receipts for twice the amount. I tell them to get fucked. Bluhm liked that. Over.'

22

'How did he seem to you this time? Over.'

'What's that mean?'

'Was he different in any way? More excitable or strange or anything?'

'What are you talking about, Mr Chancery?'

'I mean – do you think it possible he was *on* something? *High* on something, I mean?' He was floundering. 'Well, like – I don't know – cocaine or something. Over.'

'Sweetheart,' said Wolfgang, and the line went cold.

Woodrow was once more conscious of Donohue's probing stare. Sheila had disappeared. Woodrow had the impression she had gone to do something urgent. But what could that be? Why should Tessa's death require the urgent action of the spies? He felt chilly and wished he had a cardigan, yet the sweat was pouring off him.

'Nothing more we can do for you, old boy?' Donohue asked, with peculiar solicitude, still staring down at him with his sick, shaggy eyes. 'Little glass of something?'

'Thank you. Not at present.'

They knew, Woodrow told himself in fury as he returned downstairs. *They knew before I did that she was dead*. But that's what they want you to believe: we spies know more about everything than you do, and sooner.

'High Commissioner back yet?' he asked, shoving his head round Mildren's door.

'Any minute.'

'Cancel the meeting.'

Woodrow did not head directly for Justin's room. He looked in on Ghita Pearson, Chancery's most junior member, friend and confidante of Tessa. Ghita was dark-eyed, fair-haired, Anglo-Indian and wore a caste mark on her forehead. Locally employed, Woodrow rehearsed, but aspires to make the Service her career. A distrustful frown crossed her brow as she saw him close the door behind him.

'Ghita, this one's strictly for you, OK?' She looked at him steadily, waiting. 'Bluhm. Dr Arnold Bluhm. Yes?'

'What about him?'

'Chum of yours.' No response. 'I mean you're friendly with him.'

'He's a contact.' Ghita's duties kept her in daily touch with the relief agencies.

'And a chum of Tessa's, obviously.' Ghita's dark eyes made no comment. 'Do you know other people at Bluhm's outfit?'

'I ring Charlotte from time to time. She's his office. The rest are field people. Why?' The Anglo-Indian lilt to her voice that he had found so alluring. But never again. Never anybody again.

'Bluhm was in Lokichoggio last week. Accompanied.'

A third nod, but a slower one, and a lowering of the eyes.

'I want to know what he was doing there. From Loki he drove across to Turkana. I need to know whether he's made it back to Nairobi yet. Or maybe he returned to Loki. Can you do that without breaking too many eggs?'

'I doubt it.'

'Well, try.' A question occurred to him. In all the months he had known Tessa, it had never presented itself till now. 'Is Bluhm married, d'you know?'

'I would imagine so. Somewhere down the line. They usually are, aren't they?'

They meaning Africans? Or *they* meaning lovers? *All* lovers?

'But he hasn't got a wife here? Not in Nairobi. Or not so far as you've heard. Bluhm hasn't.'

'Why?' – softly, in a rush. 'Has something happened to Tessa?'

'It may have done. We're finding out.'

Reaching the door to Justin's room, Woodrow knocked and went in without waiting for an answer. This time he did not lock the door behind him but, hands in pockets, leaned his broad shoulders against it, which for as long as he remained there had the same effect.

Justin was standing with his elegant back to him. His neatly groomed head was turned to the wall and he was studying a graph, one of several ranged around the room, each with a caption of initials in black, each marked in steps of different colours, rising or descending. The particular graph that held his attention was titled RELATIVE INFRA-STRUCTURES 2005–2010 and purported, so far as Woodrow could make out from where he stood, to predict the future prosperity of African nations. On the window sill at Justin's left stood a line of pot plants that he was nurturing. Woodrow identified jasmine and balsam, but only because Justin had made gifts of these to Gloria.

'Hi, Sandy,' Justin said, drawing out the *Hi*.

'Hi.'

'I gather we're not assembling this morning. Trouble at mill?'

The famous golden voice, thought Woodrow, noticing every detail as if it were fresh to him. Tarnished by time but guaranteed to enchant, as long as you prefer tone to substance. Why am I despising you when I'm about to change your life? From now until the end of your days there will be before this moment and after it and they will be separate ages for you, just as they are for me. Why don't you take your bloody jacket off? You must be the only fellow left in the Service who goes to his tailor for tropical suits. Then he remembered he was still wearing his own jacket.

'And you're all *well*, I trust?' Justin asked in that same studied drawl of his. 'Gloria not languishing in this awful heat? The boys both flourishing and so forth?'

'We're fine.' A delay, of Woodrow's manufacture. 'And Tessa is up-country,' he suggested. He was giving her one last chance to prove it was all a dreadful mistake.

Justin at once became lavish, which was what he did when Tessa's name was spoken at him. 'Yes, indeed. Her relief work is absolutely non-stop these days.' He was hugging a United Nations tome to himself, all of three inches thick. Stooping again, he laid it to rest on a side table. 'She'll have saved all Africa by the time we leave, at this rate.'

'What's she gone up-country *for*, actually?' – still clutching at straws – 'I thought she was doing stuff down here in Nairobi. In the slums. Kibera, wasn't it?'

'Indeed she is,' said Justin proudly. 'Night and day, the poor girl. Everything from wiping babies' bottoms to acquainting paralegals with their civil rights, I'm told. Most of her clients are women, of course, which appeals to her. Even if it doesn't appeal quite so much to their menfolk.' His wistful smile, the one that says *if only*. 'Property rights, divorce, physical abuse, marital rape, female circumcision, safe sex. The whole menu, every day. You can see why their husbands get a little touchy, can't you? I would, if I was a marital rapist.'

'So what's she doing up-country?' Woodrow persisted.

'Oh, goodness knows. Ask Doc Arnold,' Justin threw out, too casually. 'Arnold's her guide and philosopher up there.'

This is how he plays it, Woodrow remembered. The cover story that covers all three of them. Arnold Bluhm, MD, her moral tutor, black knight, protector in the aid jungle. Anything but her tolerated lover. 'Up where exactly?' he asked.

'Loki. *Lokichoggio.*' Justin had propped himself on the edge of his desk, perhaps in unconscious imitation of Woodrow's careless posture at the door. 'The World Food Programme people are running a *gender awareness workshop* up there, can you imagine? They fly unaware village women down from South Sudan, give them the crash course in John Stuart Mill and fly them back aware. Arnold and Tessa went up to watch the fun, lucky dogs.'

'Where is she now?'

Justin appeared not to like this question. Perhaps it was the moment when he realised there was purpose to Woodrow's small talk. Or perhaps – thought Woodrow – he didn't take kindly to being pinned down on the subject of Tessa, when he couldn't pin her down himself.

'On her way back, one assumes. Why?'

'With Arnold?'

'Presumably. He wouldn't just leave her there.'

'Has she been in touch?'

'With me? From Loki? How could she be? They haven't got telephones.'

'I thought she might have used one of the aid agencies' radio links. Isn't that what other people do?'

'Tessa's not other people,' Justin retorted, as a frown collected on his brow. 'She has strong principles. Such as not spending donors' money unnecessarily. What's going on, Sandy?'

Justin scowling now, shoving himself away from the desk and placing himself upright at the centre of the room with his hands behind his back. And Woodrow, observing his studiously handsome face and greying black hair in the sunlight, remembered Tessa's hair, the same colour exactly, but without the age in it, or the restraint. He remembered the first time he saw them together, Tessa and Justin our glamorous newly wedded arrivals, honoured guests of the High Commissioner's welcome-to-Nairobi party. And how, as he had stepped forward to greet them, he had imagined to himself that they were father and daughter, and he was the suitor for her hand.

'So you haven't heard from her since when?' he asked.

'Tuesday when I drove them to the airport. What is this, Sandy? If Arnold's with her she'll be all right. She'll do what she's told.'

'Do you think they could have gone on to Lake Turkana, she and Bluhm – Arnold?'

'If they had transport and felt like it, why not? Tessa loves the wild places, she has a great regard for Richard Leakey, both as an archaeologist and as a decent white African. Surely Leakey's got a clinic up there? Arnold probably had work to do and took her along. Sandy, what *is* this?' he repeated indignantly.

Delivering the death blow, Woodrow had no option but to observe the effect of his words on Justin's features. And he saw how the last remnants of Justin's departed youth drained out of him as, like some kind of sea creature, his pretty face closed and hardened, leaving only seeming coral.

'We're getting reports of a white woman and an African driver found on the eastern shore of Lake Turkana. Killed,' Woodrow began deliberately, avoiding the word 'murdered'. 'The car and driver were hired from the Oasis Lodge. The Lodge's owner claims to have identified the woman as Tessa. He says she and Bluhm spent the night at the Oasis before setting out for the Richard Leakey site. Bluhm's still missing. They've found her necklace. The one she always wore.'

How do I know that? Why, in God's name, do I choose this moment to parade my intimate knowledge of her necklace?

Woodrow was still watching Justin. The coward in him wanted to look away, but to the soldier's son it would have been like sentencing a man to be executed and not showing up for his hanging. He watched Justin's eyes widen in injured disappointment, as if he had been hit from behind by a friend, then dwindle to almost nothing, as if the same friend had knocked him unconscious. He watched his nicely carved lips part in a spasm of physical pain, then gather themselves into a muscular line of exclusion turned pale by pressure.

'Good of you to tell me, Sandy. Can't have been pleasant. Does Porter know?' Porter was the High Commissioner's improbable first name.

'Mildren's chasing him up. They found a Mephisto boot. Size seven. Does that figure?'

Justin was having difficulty coordinating. First he had to wait for the sound of Woodrow's words to catch up with him. Then he hastened to respond in brisk, hard-won sentences. 'There's this shop off Piccadilly. She bought three pairs last home leave. Never seen her splash out like that. Not a spender as a rule. Never had to think about money. So she didn't. Dress at the Salvation Army shop. Given half a chance.'

'And some kind of safari tunic. Blue.'

'Oh she absolutely hated the beastly things,' Justin retorted, as the power of speech came back to him in a flood. 'She said if I ever caught her wearing one of those khaki contraptions with pockets on the thighs I should burn it or give it to Mustafa.'

Mustafa, her houseboy, Woodrow remembered. 'The police say blue.'

'She *detested* blue' – now apparently on the verge of losing his temper – 'she absolutely loathed anything paramilitary.' The past tense already, Woodrow noticed. 'She once owned a *green* bush jacket, I grant you. She bought it at Farbelow's in Stanley Street. I took her, don't know why. Probably made me. Hated shopping. She put it on and promptly had a fit. "Look at me," she said. "I'm General Patton in drag." No, sport, I told her, you're not General Patton. You're a very pretty girl wearing a bloody awful green jacket.'

He began packing up his desk. Precisely. Packing to leave. Opening and shutting drawers. Putting his file trays into his steel cupboard and locking it. Absently smoothing back his hair between moves, a tic that Woodrow had always found particularly irritating in him. Gingerly switching off his hated computer terminal – stabbing at it with his forefinger as if he was afraid it would bite him. Rumour had it that he got Ghita Pearson to switch it on for him every morning. Woodrow watched him give the room a last sightless look round. End of term. End of life. Please leave this space tidy for the next occupant. At the door Justin turned and glanced back at the plants on the window sill, perhaps wondering whether he should bring them with him, or at least give instructions for their maintenance, but he did neither.

Walking Justin along the corridor, Woodrow made to touch his arm, but some kind of revulsion caused him to withdraw his hand before it made contact. All the same he was careful to walk close enough to catch him if he sagged or stumbled in some way, because by now Justin had the air of a well-dressed sleepwalker who had abdicated his sense of destination. They were moving slowly and without much sound, but Ghita must have heard them coming because as they passed her door she opened it and tiptoed alongside Woodrow for a couple of paces while she murmured in his ear, holding back her golden hair so that it didn't brush against him.

'He disappeared. They're searching high and low for him.'

But Justin's hearing was better than either of them could have anticipated. Or perhaps, in the extremity of emotion, his perceptions were abnormally acute.

'You're worrying about Arnold, I expect,' he told Ghita, in the helpful tone of a stranger indicating the way.

*   *   *

The High Commissioner was a hollowed, hyper-intelligent man, an eternal student of something. He had a son who was a merchant banker and a small daughter called Rosie who was severely brain-damaged, and a wife who, when she was in England, was a Justice of the Peace. He adored them all equally and spent his weekends with Rosie strapped to his stomach. Yet Coleridge himself had somehow remained stranded on the brink of manhood. He wore a young man's braces with baggy Oxford trousers. A matching jacket hung behind the door on a hanger with his name on it: P. Coleridge, Balliol. He stood poised at the centre of his large office, his tousled head tipped angrily to Woodrow as he listened. There were tears in his eyes and on his cheeks.

'*Fuck*,' he announced furiously, as if he had been waiting to get the word off his chest.

'I know,' said Woodrow.

'That poor girl. How old was she? Nothing!'

'Twenty-five.' *How did I know that?* 'About,' he added, for vagueness.

'She looked about eighteen. That poor bugger Justin with his flowers.'

'I know,' Woodrow said again.

'Does Ghita know?'

'Bits.'

'What the hell will he do? He hasn't even got a career. They were all set to throw him out at the end of this tour. If Tessa

30

hadn't lost her baby, they'd have ditched him in the next cull.' Sick of standing in one place, Coleridge swung away to another part of the room. 'Rosie caught a two-pound trout on Saturday,' he blurted accusingly. 'What do you make of *that*?'

Coleridge had this habit of buying time with unannounced diversions.

'Splendid,' Woodrow murmured dutifully.

'Tessa'd have been thrilled to bits. Always said Rosie would make it. And Rosie adored her.'

'I'm sure she did.'

'Wouldn't eat it, mind. We had to keep the sod on life-support all weekend, then bury it in the garden.' A straightening of the shoulders indicated that they were in business again. 'There's a back story to this, Sandy. A bloody messy one.'

'I'm well aware of that.'

'That shit Pellegrin's already been on the line bleating about limiting the damage' – Sir Bernard Pellegrin, Foreign Office mandarin with special responsibility for Africa and Coleridge's arch-enemy – 'how the hell are we supposed to limit the damage when we don't know what the fucking damage is? Ruined his tennis for him too, I expect.'

'She was with Bluhm for four days and nights before she died,' Woodrow said, glancing at the door to make sure it was still shut. 'If that's damage. They did Loki, then they did Turkana. They shared a cabin and Christ knows what. A whole raft of people saw them together.'

'Thanks. Thanks very much. Just what I wanted to hear.' Plunging his hands deep into his baggy pockets, Coleridge waded round the room. 'Where the fuck *is* Bluhm, anyway?'

'They're hunting high and low for him, they say. Last seen sitting at Tessa's side in the jeep when they set out for the Leakey site.'

Coleridge stalked to his desk, flopped into his chair and leaned back with his arms splayed. 'So the butler did it,' he declared. 'Bluhm forgot his education, went berserk, topped the two of them, bagged Noah's head as a souvenir, rolled the jeep on its side, locked it and did a runner. Well, wouldn't we all? *Fuck.*'

'You know him as well as I do.'

'No, I don't. I keep clear of him. I don't like film stars in the aid business. Where the hell did he go? Where is he?'

Images were playing in Woodrow's mind. Bluhm the Westerner's African, bearded Apollo of the Nairobi cocktail round, charismatic, witty, beautiful. Bluhm and Tessa side by side, glad-handing guests while Justin the old debutantes' delight purrs and smiles and pushes out the drinks. Arnold Bluhm MD, sometime hero of the war in Algeria, discoursing from the rostrum of the United Nations lecture hall on medical priorities in disaster situations. Bluhm when the party's nearly over, slumped in a chair and looking lost and empty, with everything worth knowing about him hidden five miles down.

'I couldn't send them home, Sandy,' Coleridge was saying in the sterner voice of a man who has visited his conscience and come back reassured. 'I never saw it as my job to ruin a man's career just because his wife likes to get her leg over. It's the new millennium. People must be allowed to screw up their lives as they see fit.'

'Of course.'

'She was doing a bloody good job out there in the slums, whatever anybody said about her up at the Muthaiga Club. She may have got up the noses of Moi's Boys but Africans who mattered loved her to a man.'

'No question,' Woodrow agreed.

'All right, she was into all that gender crap. So she should be. Give Africa to the women and the place might work.'

Mildren entered without knocking.

'Call from Protocol, sir. Tessa's body's just arrived at the hospital morgue and they're asking for an immediate identification. And the press agencies are screaming for a statement.'

'How the hell did they get her to Nairobi so fast?'

'Flew her,' Woodrow said, recalling Wolfgang's repulsive image of slicing up her body to get it into the hold.

'No statement till she's been identified,' Coleridge snapped.

*   *   *

Woodrow and Justin went there together, crouching on the slatted bench of a High Commission Volkswagen van with tinted windows. Livingstone drove, with Jackson his massive fellow Kikuyu squeezed beside him on the front seat for added muscle in case they needed it. With the air-conditioning on high the van was still a furnace. The city traffic was at its demented worst. Crammed Matutu minibuses hurtled and honked to either side of them, poured out fumes and hurled up dust and grit. Livingstone negotiated a roundabout and pulled up outside a stone doorway surrounded by chanting, swaying groups of men and women. Mistaking them for demonstrators Woodrow let out an exclamation of anger, then realised they were mourners waiting to collect their bodies. Rusted vans and cars with red cortège ribbons were parked expectantly along the kerb.

'There is really no need for you to do this, Sandy,' Justin said.

'Of course there's a need,' said the soldier's son nobly.

A gaggle of police and medical-looking men in spattered white overalls waited on the doorstep to receive them. Their one aim was to please. An Inspector Muramba presented himself and, smiling delightedly, shook hands with the two distinguished gentlemen from the British High Commission. An Asian in a black suit introduced himself as Surgeon Doctor Banda Singh at their service. Overhead pipes accompanied them down a weeping concrete corridor lined with overflowing dustbins. The pipes supply the refrigerators, thought Woodrow, but the refrigerators don't work because there's a power cut and the morgue has no generators. Dr Banda led the way, but Woodrow could have found it on his own. Turn left, you lose the smell. Turn right, it gets stronger. The unfeeling side of him had taken over again. A soldier's duty is to be here, not to feel. *Duty*. Why did she always make me think of duty? He wondered whether there was some ancient piece of superstition about what happened to aspiring adulterers when they gazed on the dead bodies of the women they had coveted. Dr Banda was leading them up a short staircase. They emerged in an unventilated reception hall where the stench of death was all-pervading.

A rusting steel door stood closed against them and Banda hammered on it in a commanding manner, leaning back on his heels and rapping four or five times at calculated intervals as if a code were being transmitted. The door creaked open partway to reveal the haggard, apprehensive heads of three young men. But at the sight of the surgeon doctor they reeled back, enabling him to slither past them, with the result that Woodrow, left standing in the stinking hall, was treated to the hellish vision of his school dormitory given over to the Aids-dead of all ages. Emaciated corpses lay two-a-bed. More corpses lay on the floor between them, some dressed, some naked on their backs or sides. Others had their knees drawn up in futile self-protection and their chins flung back in protest. Over them, in a swaying, muddy mist, hung the flies, snoring on a single note.

And at the centre of the dormitory, parked by itself in the passage between the beds, stood matron's ironing board, on wheels. And on the ironing board, an arctic mass of winding sheet, and two monstrous semi-human feet protruding from it, reminding Woodrow of the duck-feet bedroom slippers he and Gloria had given to their son Harry last Christmas. One distended hand had somehow contrived to remain outside the sheet. Its fingers were coated in black blood and the blood was thickest at the joints. Its fingertips were aquamarine blue. *Use your imagination, Mr Chancery. You know what happens to corpses in this heat?*

'Mr Justin Quayle, please,' Dr Banda Singh called, with the portent of a barker at a royal reception.

'I'm coming with you,' Woodrow muttered and, with Justin at his side, stepped bravely forward in time to see Dr Banda roll back the sheet and reveal Tessa's head, grossly caricatured and bound chin-to-skull in a strip of grimy cloth which had been led round the throat where her necklace had once hung. A drowning man rising to the surface for the last time, Woodrow recklessly took in the rest: her black hair plastered to her skull by some undertaker's comb. Her cheeks puffed out like a cherub's blowing up a wind. Her eyes closed and eyebrows raised and mouth open in lolling disbelief, black blood caked inside as if she'd had all her teeth pulled at the same time. *You?* she is blowing stupidly as they kill her, her mouth formed into an *oo*. *You?* But who does she say it to? Who is she ogling through her stretched white eyelids?

'You know this lady, sir?' Inspector Muramba enquired delicately of Justin.

'Yes. Yes, I do, thank you,' Justin replied, each word carefully weighed before it was delivered. 'It's my wife Tessa. We must fix her funeral, Sandy. She'll want it to be here in Africa as soon as possible. She's an only child. She has no parents. There is no one apart from me who needs to be consulted. Better make it as soon as possible.'

'Well, I suppose that will have to depend a bit on the police,' said Woodrow gruffly and was barely in time to make it to a cracked handbasin where he vomited his heart out while Justin the ever-courteous stood at his shoulder with his arm round him, murmuring condolences.

*   *   *

From the carpeted sanctuary of the Private Office, Mildren slowly read aloud to the blank-voiced young man on the other end of the line:

> The High Commission is sad to announce the death by murder of Mrs Tessa Quayle, the wife of Justin Quayle, First Secretary in Chancery. Mrs Quayle died on the shores of Lake Turkana, close to Allia Bay. Her driver Mr Noah Katanga was also killed. Mrs Quayle will be remembered for her devotion to the cause of women's rights in Africa, as well as for her youth and beauty. We

wish to express our deep sympathy to Mrs Quayle's husband Justin and her many friends. The High Commission flag will be flown at half-mast until further notice. A book of condolence will be placed in the High Commission reception lobby.

'When will you be running that?'
'I just did,' said the young man.

CHAPTER TWO

The Woodrows lived in a suburban house of quarried stone and leaded mock-Tudor windows, one of a colony set in large English gardens in the exclusive hilltop suburb of Muthaiga, a stone's throw from the Muthaiga Club and the British High Commissioner's Residence and the ample residences of ambassadors from countries you may never have heard of till you ride the closely guarded avenues and spot their nameplates planted among warnings in kiSwahili of dangerous dogs. In the wake of the bomb attack on Nairobi's US Embassy, the Foreign Office had supplied all staff of Woodrow's rank and upwards with crash-proof iron front gates and these were conscientiously manned day and night by shifts of exuberant Baluhya and their many friends and relatives. Round the garden's perimeter, the same inspired minds had provided an electrified fence crowned with coils of razor wire and intruder lights that blazed all night. In Muthaiga there is a pecking order about protection, as there is about many other things. The humblest houses have broken bottles on stone walls, the middle-rankers razor wire. But for diplomatic gentry, nothing less than iron gates, electric fences, window sensors and intruder lights will secure their preservation.

The Woodrow house stood three floors high. The two upper floors comprised what the security companies called a safe haven protected by a folding steel screen on the first landing, to which the Woodrow parents alone had a key. And in the ground-floor guest suite which the Woodrows called the lower ground because of the slope of the hillside there was a screen on the garden side to protect the Woodrows from their servants. There were two rooms to the lower ground, both severe and white-painted and, with their barred windows and steel grilles, distinctly prison-like. But Gloria in anticipation of her guest's arrival had decked them out with roses from the garden and a reading light from Sandy's dressing room, and the staff television set and radio because it would do them good to be without them for a change. It wasn't exactly *five star* even then – she confided to her bosom friend Elena, English wife to a soft-palmed Greek official at the United Nations – but at least the poor man would have his aloneness, which everybody absolutely *had* to have when they lost someone, El, and Gloria herself had been *exactly* the same when Mummy died but then of course Tessa and Justin did have – well, they did have an *unconventional* marriage if one could call it that – though speaking for herself Gloria had never doubted there was real fondness there, at least on Justin's side, though what there was on Tessa's side – frankly, El darling, God alone knows, because none of *us* ever will.

To which Elena, much divorced and worldly wise where Gloria was neither, remarked, 'Well, you just watch your sweet arse, honey. Freshly widowed playboys can be *very* raunchy.'

*   *   *

Gloria Woodrow was one of those exemplary Foreign Service wives who are determined to see the good side of everything. If there wasn't a good side in sight, she would let out a jolly good laugh and say, 'Well, here we all are!' – which was a bugle call to all concerned to band together and shoulder life's discomforts without complaint. She was a loyal old-girl of the private schools that had produced her and she sent them regular bulletins of her progress, avidly devouring news of her contemporaries. Each Founder's Feast she sent them a witty telegram of congratulation or, these days, a witty e-mail, usually in verse, because she never wanted them to forget that she had won the school poetry prize. She was attractive in a forthright way, and famously loquacious, especially when there wasn't much to say. And she had that tottery, extraordinarily ugly walk that is affected by English women of the royal class.

Yet Gloria Woodrow was not naturally stupid. Eighteen years ago at Edinburgh University she had been rated one of the better brains of her year and it was said of her that if she hadn't been so taken up with Woodrow, she would have landed a decent 2:1 in Politics and Philosophy. However, in the years between, marriage and motherhood and the inconstancies of diplomatic life had replaced whatever ambitions she might have had. Sometimes, to Woodrow's private sadness, she appeared to have deliberately put her intellect to sleep in order to fulfil her wifely rôle. But he was also grateful to her for this sacrifice, and for the restful way in which she failed to read his inner thoughts, yet pliantly shaped herself to fit his aspirations. 'When I want a life of my own, I'll let you know,' she would assure him when, seized by one of his bouts of guilt or boredom, he pressed her to take a higher degree, read Law, read Medicine – or at least read *something*, for God's sake. 'If you don't like me as I am, that's different,' she would reply, deftly shifting his complaint from the particular to the general. 'Oh but I do, I do, I *love* you as you are!' he would protest, earnestly embracing her. And more or less he believed himself.

Justin became the secret prisoner of the lower ground on the evening of the same black Monday on which the news of Tessa's death had been brought to him, at the hour when limousines in ambassadorial driveways were starting to champ and stir inside their iron gates before processing towards the evening's mystically elected watering hole. Is it Lumumba Day? Merdeka Day? Bastille Day? Never mind: the national flag will be flying in the garden, the sprinklers will be turned off, the red carpet will be laid out, black servants in white gloves will be hovering, just as they did in the colonial times we all piously disavow. And the appropriate patriotic music will be issuing from the host's marquee.

Woodrow rode with Justin in the black Volkswagen van. From the hospital morgue, Woodrow had escorted him to police head-quarters and watched him compose, in his immaculate academic hand, a statement identifying his wife's corpse. From head-quarters Woodrow had called ahead to inform Gloria that, traffic permitting, he would be arriving in fifteen minutes with their *special guest* – 'and he'll be keeping his head down, darling, and we've got to make sure it stays that way' – though this did not prevent Gloria from putting through a crash call to Elena, dial-ling repeatedly till she got her, to discuss menus for dinner – did poor Justin love fish or hate it? she forgot, but she had a feeling he was *faddish* – and God, El, what *on earth* do I talk to him about while Sandy's off manning the fort and I'm stuck with the poor man alone for hours on end? I mean all the *real* subjects are off limits.

'You'll think of something, don't worry, darling,' Elena assured her, not altogether kindly.

But Gloria still found time to give Elena a rundown of the absolutely *harrowing* phone calls she'd taken from the press, and others she'd refused to take, preferring to have Juma, her Wakamba houseboy, say that Mr or Mrs Woodrow are not available to come to the telephone at present – except that there was this frightfully well-spoken young man from the *Telegraph* whom she would have *adored* to talk to, but Sandy had said no on pain of death.

'Perhaps he'll write, darling,' said Elena consolingly.

The Volkswagen van with tinted windows pulled up in the Woodrow driveway, Woodrow sprang out to check for journal-ists and immediately afterwards Gloria was treated to her first sight of Justin the widower, the man who had lost his wife and baby son in the space of six months, Justin the deceived husband

40

who would be deceived no longer, Justin of the tailored light-weight suit and soft gaze that were habitual to him, her secret fugitive to be hidden in the lower ground, removing his straw hat as he climbed out of the tailgate with his back to the audience, and thanking everybody – which meant Livingstone the driver, and Jackson the guard, and Juma who was hovering uselessly as per usual – with a distracted bow of his handsome dark head as he moved gracefully along the line of them to the front door. She saw his face first in black shadow, then in the short-lived evening twilight. He advanced on her, and said, 'Good evening, Gloria, how very good of you to have me,' in a voice so bravely mustered that she could have wept and later did.

'We're just *so* relieved to be able to do *anything* to help, Justin darling,' she murmured, kissing him with cautious tenderness.

'And there's no word of Arnold, one takes it? Nobody rang while we were on the road?'

'I'm sorry, dear, not a peep. We're all on tenterhooks, of course.' *One takes it*, she thought. I'll say one does. Like a hero.

Somewhere in the background Woodrow was advising her in a bereaved voice that he needed another hour in the office, sweet, he'd ring, but she barely bothered with him. Who's *he* lost? she thought scathingly. She heard car doors clunk and the black Volkswagen drive away but paid it no attention. Her eyes were with Justin, her ward and tragic hero. Justin, she now realised, was as much the victim of this tragedy as Tessa was, because Tessa was dead while Justin had been lumbered with a grief he would have to cart with him to his grave. Already it had greyed his cheeks and changed the way he walked and the things he looked at as he went along. Gloria's cherished herbaceous borders, planted to his specification, passed him by without a glance. So did the rhus and two malus trees he had so sweetly refused to let her pay for. Because it was one of the *marvellous* things about Justin that Gloria had never *really* got used to – this to Elena in a lengthy résumé the same evening –

that he was *hugely* knowledgeable about plants and flowers and gardens. And I mean, where on earth did *that* come from, El? His mother probably. Wasn't she half a Dudley? Well, *all* the Dudleys gardened like mad, they'd done it for aeons. Because we're talking classic English *botany* here, El, not what you read in the Sunday papers.

Ushering her treasured guest up the steps to the front door, across the hall and down the servants' stairs to the lower ground, Gloria gave him the tour of the prison cell that would be home to him for the duration of his sentence: the warped plywood wardrobe for hanging up your suits, Justin – why on earth had she never given Ebediah another fifty shillings and told him to paint it? – the worm-eaten chest of drawers for your shirts and socks – why had she never thought to line it?

But it was Justin, as usual, who was doing the apologising. 'I'm afraid I haven't much in the way of clothes to put in them, Gloria. My house is besieged by news hounds and Mustafa must have taken the phone off the hook. Sandy kindly said he'd lend me whatever I need until it's safe to smuggle something round.'

'Oh Justin, how *stupid* of me,' Gloria exclaimed, flushing.

But then, either because she didn't want to leave him, or didn't know how to, she insisted on showing him the awful old fridge crammed with bottles of drinking water and mixers – why had she never had the rotting rubber replaced? – and the ice *here*, Justin, just run it under the tap to break it up – and the plastic electric kettle that she'd always hated, and the bumble-bee pot from Ilfracombe with Tetley tea bags and a crack in it, and the battered Huntley & Palmer's tin of sugared biscuits in case he liked a nibble last thing at night, because Sandy always does, although he's been told to lose weight. And finally – thank God she'd got *something* right – the splendid vase of many-coloured snapdragons that she had raised from seed on his instructions.

'Well, good, I'll leave you in peace then,' she said – until, reaching the door, she realised to her shame that she had still not spoken her words of commiseration. 'Justin darling –' she began.

'Thanks, Gloria, there's really no need,' he cut in with surprising firmness.

Deprived of her tender moment, Gloria struggled to recover a tone of practicality. 'Yes, well, you'll come up whenever you want, won't you, dear? Dinner at eight, theoretically. Drinkies before if you feel like it. Just do whatever you wish. Or nothing. *Heaven* knows when Sandy will be back.' After which she went gratefully upstairs to her bedroom, showered and changed and did her face, then looked in on the boys at their prep. Quelled by the presence of death, they were working diligently, or pretending to.

'Does he look terrifically sad?' asked Harry, the younger one.

'You'll meet him tomorrow. Just be very polite and serious with him. Mathilda's making you hamburgers. You'll eat them in the playroom, not the kitchen, understood?' A postscript popped out of her before she had even thought about it: 'He's a very courageous fine man, and you're to treat him with *great* respect.'

Descending to the drawing room she was surprised to find Justin ahead of her. He accepted a hefty whisky and soda, she poured herself a glass of white wine and sat in an armchair, actually Sandy's, but she wasn't thinking of Sandy. For minutes – she'd no idea how many in real time – neither of them spoke, but the silence was a bond that Gloria felt more keenly the longer it went on. Justin sipped his whisky, and she was relieved to note that he had not caught Sandy's thoroughly irritating new habit of closing his eyes and pouting as if the whisky had been given him to test. Glass in hand, he moved himself to the french window, looking out into the floodlit garden – twenty 150-watt bulbs hooked up to the house generator, and the blaze of them burning one half of his face.

'Maybe that's what everyone thinks,' he remarked suddenly, resuming a conversation they had not had.

'What is, dear?' Gloria asked, not certain she was being addressed, but asking anyway because he clearly needed to talk to someone.

'That you were loved for being someone you weren't. That you're a sort of fraud. A love-thief.'

Gloria had no idea whether this was something everyone thought, but she had no doubts at all that they shouldn't. 'Of *course* you're not a fraud, Justin,' she said stoutly. 'You're one of the most genuine people I know, you always were. Tessa adored you and so she should have done. She was a very lucky young girl indeed.' As for *love-thief*, she thought – well, no prizes for guessing who did the love-thieving in *that* duo!

Justin did not respond to this glib assurance, or not that she could see, and for a spell all she heard was the chain reaction of barking dogs – one started, then all the others did, up and down Muthaiga's golden mile.

'You were always *good* to her, Justin, you know you were. You mustn't go castigating yourself for crimes you didn't commit. A lot of people do that when they lose someone, and they're not being fair on themselves. We can't go round treating people as if they were going to drop dead any minute, or we'd never get anywhere. Well, would we? You were loyal to her. Always,' she asserted, thereby incidentally implying that the same could not be said for Tessa. And the implication was not lost on him, she was sure of it: he was on the brink of talking about that wretched Arnold Bluhm when to her vexation she heard the clunk of her husband's latchkey in the door and knew the spell was broken.

'Justin, you poor chap, how's it going?' Woodrow cried, pouring himself an unusually modest glass of wine before crashing onto the sofa. 'No more news, I'm afraid. Good or bad. No clues, no suspects, not as yet. No trace of Arnold. The Belgians are supplying a helicopter, London's coming up with a second. Money, money, curse of us all. Still, he's a Belgian citizen, so why not? How very pretty you're looking, sweet. What's for dins?'

He's been drinking, Gloria thought in disgust. He pretends to work late and he sits there in his office drinking while I make the boys do their homework. She heard a movement from the window and saw to her dismay that Justin had braced himself to take his leave – scared off, no doubt, by her husband's elephantine flat-footedness.

'No food?' Woodrow protested. 'Got to keep your strength up, you know, old boy.'

'You are very kind but I fear I have no appetite. Gloria, thank you again. Sandy, goodnight.'

'And the Pellegrin sends strong supporting messages from London. Whole Foreign Office struck down with grief, he says. Didn't want to intrude personally.'

'Bernard was always very tactful.'

She watched the door close, she heard his footsteps descend the concrete staircase, she saw his empty glass resting on the bamboo table beside the french window, and for a frightening moment she was convinced she would never see him again.

Woodrow bolted his dinner clumsily, not tasting it as usual. Gloria, who like Justin had no appetite, watched him. Juma their houseboy, tiptoeing restlessly between them, watched him too.

'How we faring?' Woodrow murmured with a conspiratorial slur, keeping his voice down and pointing at the floor to warn her to do the same.

'Been fine,' she said, playing his game. 'Considering.' What are you doing down there? she wondered. Are you lying on your bed, flailing yourself in the darkness? Or are you staring through your bars into the garden, talking to her ghost?

'Anything of any significance come out?' Woodrow was asking, stumbling a bit on the word significance, but still contriving to keep their conversation allusive on account of Juma.

'Like what?'

'About our lover-boy,' he said and, leering shamefully, jabbed a thumb at her begonias and mouthed *bloom*, at which Juma hurried off to get a jug of water.

For hours Gloria lay awake beside her snoring husband until, fancying she heard a sound from downstairs, she crept to the landing and peered out of the window. The power cut was over. An orange glow from the city lifted to the stars. But no Tessa lurked in the lighted garden, and no Justin either. She returned to bed to find Harry diagonally asleep with his thumb in his mouth and one arm across his father's chest.

*   *   *

The family rose early as usual, but Justin was ahead of them, dressed in his crushed suit and hovering. He looked flushed, she thought, a little over-busy, too much colour under the brown eyes. The boys shook his hand, gravely as instructed, and Justin meticulously returned their greetings.

'Oh Sandy, yes, good morning,' he said as soon as Woodrow appeared. 'I wondered whether we might have a quick word.'

The two men withdrew to the sun lounge.

'It's about my house,' Justin began, as soon as they were alone.

'House here or house in London, old boy?' Woodrow countered, in a fatuous effort to be cheerful. And Gloria, listening to every word through the serving hatch to the kitchen, could have brained him.

'Here in Nairobi. Her private papers, lawyers' letters. Her family trust material. Documents that are precious to both of us. I can't leave her personal correspondence sitting there for the Kenyan police to plunder at will.'

'So what's the solution, old boy?'

'I'd like to go there. At once.'

So firm! Gloria rhapsodised. So forceful, in spite of everything!

'My dear chap, that's impossible. The hacks would eat you alive.'

'I don't believe that's true, actually. They can try and take my photograph, I suppose. They can shout at me. If I don't reply to them, that's about as far as they can go. Catch them while they're shaving.'

Gloria knew her husband's prevarications inside out. In a minute he'll call Bernard Pellegrin in London. That's what he always does when he needs to bypass Porter Coleridge and get the answer he wants to hear.

'Look here, tell you what, old boy. Why not write me a list of what you want and I'll pass it to Mustafa somehow and have him bring the stuff here?'

Typical, thought Gloria furiously. *Dither, haver, look for the easy way out every time.*

'Mustafa would have no idea what to select,' she heard Justin reply, as firmly as before. 'And a list would be no good to him at all. Even shopping lists defeat him. I *owe* it to her, Sandy. It's a debt of honour and I must discharge it. Whether or not you come along.'

Class will out! Gloria applauded silently from her touchline. *Well played, that man!* But even then it did not occur to her, though her mind was opening up in all sorts of unexpected directions, that her husband might have his own reasons for wishing to visit Tessa's house.

*   *   *

The press were not shaving. Justin had that wrong. Or if they were, they were doing it on the grass verges outside Justin's house, where they had been camping all night in hire cars, dumping their garbage in the hydrangea bushes. A couple of African vendors in Uncle Sam pants and top hats had opened a tea stand. Others were cooking maize on charcoal. Lacklustre policemen hung around a beaten-up patrol car, yawning and smoking cigarettes. Their leader, an enormously fat man in a polished brown belt and gold Rolex, was sprawled in the front passenger seat with his eyes shut. It was half past seven in the morning. Low cloud cut off the city. Large black birds were changing places on the overhead wires, waiting for their moment to swoop for food.

'Drive past, then stop,' Woodrow the soldier's son ordered from the back of the van.

It was the same arrangement as the day before: Livingstone and Jackson up front, Woodrow and Justin hunkered on the rear seat. The black Volkswagen had CD plates but so had every second vehicle in Muthaiga. An informed eye might have spotted the British prefix to the licence number, but no such eye was present, nobody showed any interest as Livingstone drove sedately past the gates and up the gentle slope. Easing the van to a halt, he put on the handbrake.

'Jackson, get out of the van, walk slowly down the hill to the gates of Mr Quayle's house. What's the name of your gate-keeper?' This to Justin.

'Omari,' Justin said.

'Tell Omari that as the van approaches he is to open the gates at the last minute, and close them as soon as it's through. Stay with him to make sure he does exactly what he's told. Now.'

Born to the part, Jackson clambered out of the van, stretched, fiddled with his belt and finally ambled down the hill to Justin's iron security gates where, under the eye of police and journalists, he took up a place beside Omari.

'All right, back down,' Woodrow ordered Livingstone. 'Very slowly. Take your time.'

Livingstone released the handbrake and, with the engine still running, allowed the van to curl gently backward down the slope until the tailgate was tucked into the opening to Justin's drive. He's turning round, they may have thought. If so, they can't have thought it long, because in the next moment he had slammed down the accelerator and was racing backwards to the gates, scattering astonished journalists to left and right of him. The gates flew open, pulled on one side by Omari and on the other by Jackson. The van passed through, the gates slammed shut again. Jackson on the house side leaped back into the van while Livingstone kept it rolling all the way to Justin's porch and up the two steps, to rest inches from the front door, which Justin's houseboy Mustafa, with exemplary prescience, flung open from inside while Woodrow bundled Justin ahead of him, then sprang after him into the hall, slamming the front door shut behind them as he went.

*　　*　　*

The house was in darkness. Out of respect for Tessa or the news hounds, the staff had drawn the curtains. The three men stood in the hall, Justin, Woodrow, Mustafa. Mustafa was weeping silently. Woodrow could make out his crumpled face, the grimace of white teeth, the tears set wide on the cheeks, almost underneath the ears. Justin was holding Mustafa's shoulders, comforting him. Startled by this un-English demonstration of affection on Justin's part, Woodrow was also offended by it. Justin drew Mustafa against him until Mustafa's clenched jaw rested on his shoulder. Woodrow looked away in embarrassment. Down the passage other shadows had appeared from the servants' area: the one-armed illegal Ugandan shamba boy who helped Justin in the garden and whose name Woodrow had never managed to retain, and the illegal South Sudanese refugee called Esmeralda who was always having boy-trouble. Tessa could no more resist a sob-story than she could bow to local regulations. Sometimes her household had resembled a pan-African hostel for disabled down-and-outs. More than once, Woodrow had remonstrated with Justin on the subject but met a blank wall. Only Esmeralda was not weeping. Instead she wore that wooden look that whites mistake for churlishness or indifference. Woodrow knew it was neither. It was familiarity. This is how *real* life is constituted, it said. This is grief and hatred and people hacked to death. This is the everyday we have known since we were born and you Wazungu have not.

Gently pushing Mustafa away, Justin received Esmeralda in a double handshake during which she laid the side of her braided

49

forehead against his. Woodrow had the sensation of being admitted to a circle of affection he had not dreamed of. Would Juma weep like this if Gloria got her throat cut? Like hell he would. Would Ebediah? Would Gloria's new maid, whatever her name is? Justin pressed the Ugandan outdoor boy against him, fondled his cheek, then turned his back on all of them and with his right hand took a grasp of the handrail on the staircase. Looking for a moment like the old man he soon would be, he began hauling himself upward. Woodrow watched him gain the shadows of the landing and vanish into the bedroom Woodrow had never entered, though he had imagined it in countless furtive ways.

Finding he was alone, Woodrow hovered, feeling threatened, which was how he felt whenever he entered her house: a country boy come to town. If it's a cocktail party, why don't I know these people? Whose cause are we being asked to espouse tonight? Which room will she be in? Where's Bluhm? At her side, most likely. Or in the kitchen, reducing the servants to paroxysms of helpless laughter. Remembering his purpose, Woodrow edged his way along the twilit corridor to the drawing room door. It was unlocked. Blades of morning sunlight thrust their way between the curtains, illuminating the shields and masks and frayed hand-woven throw-rugs made by paraplegics, with which Tessa had succeeded in enlivening her dreary government furnishings. How did she make everything so pretty with this junk? The same brick fireplace as ours, the same boxed-in iron girders masquerading as oak beams of Merrie England. Everything like ours but smaller, because the Quayles were childless and a rank lower. Then why did Tessa's house always seem to be the real thing, and ours its unimaginative ugly sister?

He reached the middle of the room and stopped, arrested by the power of memory. This is where I stood and lectured her, the contessa's daughter, from beside this pretty inlaid table that she said her mother had loved, while I clutched the back of this flimsy satinwood chair and pontificated like a Victorian father. Tessa standing over there in front of the window, and the

50

sunlight cutting straight through her cotton dress. Did she know that I was talking to a naked silhouette? That just to look at her was to see my dream of her come true, my girl on a beach, my stranger on a train?

'I thought the best thing I could do was call by,' he begins sternly.

'Now why did you think that, Sandy?' she asks.

Eleven in the morning. Chancery meeting over, Justin safely despatched to Kampala, attending some useless three-day conference on Aid & Efficiency. I have come here on official business, but I have parked my car in a side street like a guilty lover calling on a brother officer's beautiful young wife. And God, is she beautiful. And God, is she young. Young in the high, sharp breasts that never move. How can Justin let her out of his sight? Young in the grey, wide-angry eyes, in the smile too wise for her age. Woodrow can't see the smile because she is backlit. But he can hear it in her voice. Her teasing, foxing, classy voice. He can retrieve it in his memory any time. As he can retrieve the line of her waist and thighs in the naked silhouette, the maddening fluidity of her walk, no wonder she and Justin fell for one another – they're from the same thoroughbred stable, twenty years apart.

'Tess, honestly, this can't go on.'

'Don't call me Tess.'

'Why not?'

'That name's reserved.'

Who by? he wonders. Bluhm, or another of her lovers? Quayle never called her Tess. Nor did Ghita, as far as Woodrow knew.

'You simply can't go on expressing yourself so freely. Your opinions.'

And then the passage he has prepared in advance, the one that reminds her of her duty as the responsible wife of a serving diplomat. But he never reaches the end of it. The word *duty* has stung her into action.

'Sandy, my *duty* is to Africa. What's yours?'

He is surprised to have to answer for himself. 'To my country,

51

if you'll allow me to be pompous. As Justin's is. To my Service and my Head of Mission. Does that answer you?'

'You know it doesn't. Not nearly. It's *miles* off.'

'How would I know anything of the kind?'

'I thought you might have come to talk to me about the riveting documents I gave you.'

'No, Tessa, I did not. I came here to ask you to stop shooting your mouth off about the misdoings of the Moi government in front of every Tom, Dick and Harry in Nairobi. I came here to ask you to be one of the team for a change, instead of – oh, finish the sentence for yourself,' he ends rudely.

Would I have talked to her like that if I'd known she was pregnant? Probably not so baldly. But I would have talked to her. Did I guess that she was pregnant while I tried not to notice her naked silhouette? No. I was wanting her beyond bearing, as she could tell by the altered state of my voice and the stiltedness of my movements.

'So you mean you haven't read them?' she says, sticking determinedly to the subject of the documents. 'You'll be telling me in a minute that you haven't had time.'

'Of course I've read them.'

'And what did you make of them when you'd read them, Sandy?'

'They tell me nothing I don't know, and nothing I can do anything about.'

'Now Sandy, that's very negative of you. It's worse. It's pusillanimous. *Why* can't you do anything about them?'

Woodrow, hating how he sounds: 'Because we are diplomats and not policemen, Tessa. The Moi government is terminally corrupt, you tell me. I never doubted it. The country is dying of Aids, it's bankrupt, there is not a corner of it, from tourism to wildlife to education to transport to welfare to communications, that isn't falling apart from fraud, incompetence and neglect. Well observed. Ministers and officials are diverting lorry-loads of food aid and medical supplies earmarked for starving refugees, sometimes with the connivance of aid agency employees, you say. Of course they are. Expenditure on the country's health runs at five dollars per head per year and that's before everybody from the top of the line to the bottom has taken his cut. The police routinely mishandle anybody unwise enough to bring these matters to public attention. Also true. You have studied their methods. They use water torture, you say. They soak people, then beat them, which reduces visible marks. You are right. They do. They are not selective. And we do not protest. They also rent out their weapons to friendly murder gangs, to be returned by first light or you don't get your deposit back. The High Commission shares your disgust, but still we do not protest. Why not? Because we are here, mercifully, to represent *our* country, not *theirs*. We have thirty-five thousand indigenous Britons in Kenya whose precarious livelihood depends on President Moi's whim. The High Commission is not in the business of making life harder for them than it already is.'

'And you have British business interests to represent,' she reminds him playfully.

'That is not a sin, Tessa,' he retorts, trying to wrest the lower half of his gaze from the shadow of her breasts through the puff of dress. 'Commerce is not a sin. Trading with emerging countries is not a sin. Trade helps them to emerge, as a matter of fact. It makes reforms possible. The kind of reforms we all want. It brings them into the modern world. It enables *us* to help *them*. How can we help a poor country if we're not rich ourselves?'

'Bullshit.'

'I *beg* your pardon?'

'Specious, unadulterated, pompous Foreign Office bullshit, if you want its full name, worthy of the inestimable Pellegrin himself. Look around you. Trade isn't making the poor rich. Profits don't buy reforms. They buy corrupt government officials and Swiss bank accounts.'

'I dispute that absolutely –'

She cuts him short. 'So it's file and forget. Right? No action at this time, signed Sandy. Great. The mother of democracies is once more revealed as a lying hypocrite, preaching liberty and human rights for all, except where she hopes to make a buck.'

'That's not fair at all! All right, Moi's Boys are crooks and the old man still has a couple of years to run. But good things are on the horizon. A word in the right ear – the collective withholding of donor nations' aid – quiet diplomacy – they're all having their effect. And Richard Leakey is being drafted into the Cabinet to put a brake on corruption and reassure donors that they can start giving again without financing Moi's rackets.' He is beginning to sound like a guidance telegram, and knows it. Worse, she knows it too, as evidenced by a very big yawn. 'Kenya may not have much of a present but it has a future,' he ends bravely. And waits for a reciprocal sign from her to indicate that they are moving towards some kind of cobbled truce.

But Tessa, he remembers too late, is not a conciliator, neither is her bosom pal Ghita. They are both young enough to believe there is such a thing as simple truth. 'The document I gave you supplies names and dates and bank accounts,' she insists remorselessly. 'Individual ministers are identified and incriminated. Will that be a word in the right ear too? Or is nobody listening out there?'

'Tessa.'

She is slipping away from him when he came here to be closer to her.

'Sandy.'

'I take your point. I hear you. But for Heaven's sake – in the name of sanity – you can't seriously be suggesting that HMG in the person of Bernard Pellegrin should be conducting a witch hunt against named ministers of the Kenyan government! I mean, my God – it's not as if we Brits were above corruption ourselves. Is the Kenyan High Commissioner in London about to tell *us* to clean up *our* act?'

'Sheer bloody humbug and you know it,' Tessa snaps, eyes flaming.

He has not reckoned with Mustafa. He enters silently, at the stoop. First with great accuracy he sets a small table midway between them on the carpet, then a silver tray with a silver coffee pot and her late mother's silver sweetmeat basket filled with shortbread. And the intrusion clearly stimulates Tessa's ever-present sense of theatre, for she kneels upright before the little table, shoulders back, dress stretched across her breasts while she punctuates her speech with humorously barbed enquiries about his tastes.

'Was it black, Sandy, or just a touch of the cream – I forget?' she asks with mock gentility. *This is the Pharisaic life we lead* – she is telling him – *a continent lies dying at our door, and here we stand or kneel drinking coffee off a silver tray while just down the road children starve, the sick die and crooked politicians bankrupt the nation that was tricked into electing them.* 'A witch hunt – since you mention it – would make an excellent beginning. Name 'em, shame 'em, chop their heads off and spike 'em on the city gates, says I. The trouble is, it doesn't work. The same List of Shame is published every year in the Nairobi newspapers, and the same Kenyan politicians feature in it every time. Nobody is sacked, nobody is hauled up before the courts.' She hands him a cup, swivelling on her knees to reach him. 'But it doesn't bother you, does it? You're a status quo man. That's a decision you've taken. It hasn't been thrust upon you. You took it. You, Sandy. You looked in the mirror one day and you thought: "Hullo, me, from now on I'll treat the world as I find it. I'll get the best deal I can for Britain, and I'll call it my duty. Never mind if it's a duty that accounts for the survival of some of the foulest governments on the globe. I'll do it anyway."' She offers him sugar. He silently declines it. 'So I'm afraid we can't agree, can we? I want to speak up. You want me to bury my head where yours is. One woman's duty is another man's cop-out. What's new?'

'And Justin?' Woodrow asks, playing his last useless card. 'Where does he come into this, I wonder?'

She stiffens, sensing a trap. 'Justin is Justin,' she replies warily. 'He has made his choices as I have made mine.'

'And Bluhm's Bluhm, I suppose,' Woodrow sneers, driven by jealousy and anger to speak the name he has promised himself he will on no account utter. And she, apparently, has sworn not to hear it. By some bitter inner discipline she keeps her lips tightly closed while she waits for him to make an even bigger fool of himself. Which he duly does. Royally. 'You don't think you're prejudicing Justin's career, for instance?' he enquires haughtily.

'Is that why you came to see me?'

'Basically, yes.'

'I thought you'd come here to save me from myself. Now it turns out you've come to save Justin from me. How very laddish of you.'

'I had imagined Justin's interests and yours were identical.'

A taut, humourless laugh, as her anger returns. But unlike Woodrow she does not lose her self-control. 'Good Heavens, Sandy, you must be the only person in Nairobi who imagines any such thing!' She stands up, the game over. 'I think you'd better go now. People will begin to talk about us. I won't send you more documents, you'll be relieved to hear. We can't have you wearing out the High Commissioner's shredder, can we? You might lose promotion points.'

Reliving this scene as he had relived it repeatedly in the twelve months since it had taken place, feeling again his humiliation and frustration and her scornful gaze burning his back as he took his leave, Woodrow surreptitiously pulled open a slim drawer of the inlaid table that her mother had loved and swept his hand round the inside, gathering together anything he found. I was drunk, I was mad, he told himself in extenuation of this act. I had a craving to do something rash. I was trying to bring the roof tumbling round my head so that I would see clear sky.

One piece of paper – that's all he asked as he frantically slewed and skimmed his way through drawers and shelves – one insignificant sheet of Her Majesty's Stationery Office blue, with one side of writing, mine, saying the unsayable in words that for once do not equivocate, do not say *On the one hand this, but*

on the other hand there's nothing I can do about it – signed not S or
SW but *Sandy* in good, legible script and very nearly the name
WOODROW in block capitals after it to show the whole world
and Tessa Quayle that, for five deranged minutes back in his
office that same evening, with her naked silhouette still taunting
his memory, and a king-sized glass of hospitality whisky at his
timid lover's elbow, one Sandy Woodrow, Head of Chancery
at the British High Commission in Nairobi, performed an act
of unique, deliberate, calculated lunacy, putting at risk career,
wife and children in a doomed effort to bring his life closer to
his feelings.

And, having written as he wrote, had enclosed said letter in
Her Majesty's envelope and sealed said envelope with a whisky-
flavoured tongue. Had carefully addressed it and – ignoring all
sensible internal voices urging him to wait an hour, a day,
another lifetime, have himself another Scotch, apply for home
leave or at the very least send the letter tomorrow morning after
he has slept on it – had borne it aloft to the High Commission
mail room where a locally employed Kikuyu clerk named Jomo
after the great Kenyatta, not troubling to enquire why a Head
of Chancery might be sending a hand-delivered letter marked
PERSONAL to the naked silhouette of the beautiful young wife
of a colleague and subordinate, had slung it in a bag marked
LOCAL UNCLASSIFIED, while obsequiously chanting, 'Night, Mr
Woodrow, sir,' to his departing back.

*   *   *

Old Christmas cards.

Old invitation cards marked with a cross for 'no' in Tessa's
hand. Others, more emphatically marked, 'never'.

Old get-well card from Ghita Pearson, portraying Indian
birds.

A twist of ribbon, a wine cork, a bunch of diplomats' calling
cards held together with a bulldog clip.

But no small, single sheet of HM Stationery Office blue

ending with the triumphant scrawl: 'I love you, I love you and I love you, Sandy.'

Woodrow sidled swiftly along the last shelves, flipping open books at random, opening trinket boxes, acknowledging defeat. Take a grip on yourself, man, he urged, as he fought to turn bad news into good. All right: no letter. Why *should* there be a letter? *Tessa?* After *twelve months?* Probably chucked it in the waste-paper basket the day she got it. A woman like that, compulsive flirt, husband a wimp, she gets a pass made at her twice a month. Three times! Weekly! Daily! He was sweating. In Africa, sweat broke out on him in a greasy shower, then dried up. He stood head forward, letting the torrent fall, listening.

What's the bloody man doing up there? Softly back and forth? Private papers, he had said. Lawyers' letters. What papers did she keep upstairs that were too private for the ground floor? The drawing room telephone was ringing. It had been ringing non-stop ever since they entered the house, but he had only now noticed it. Journalists? Lovers? Who cares? He let it ring. He was plotting the upstairs layout of his own house and applying it to this one. Justin was directly above him, left of the stairwell as you went up. There was a dressing room and there was the bathroom and there was the main bedroom. Woodrow remembered Tessa telling him she had converted the dressing room into a workroom: *It's not only men who have dens, Sandy. Us girls have them too*, she had told him provocatively, as if she were instructing him in body parts. The rhythm changed. Now you're collecting stuff from round the room. What stuff? *Documents that are precious to both of us.* To me too maybe, thought Woodrow, in a sickening reminder of his folly.

Discovering he was now standing at the window overlooking the back garden, he poked aside the curtain and saw festoons of flowering shrubs, the pride of Justin's 'open days' for junior staff when he served strawberries and cream and cold white wine and gave them the tour of his Elysium. 'One year's gardening in Kenya is worth ten in England,' he liked to claim as he made his comic little pilgrimages round Chancery, handing out his flowers to the boys and girls. It was the only subject, come to think of it, on which he had been known to boast. Woodrow squinted sideways along the shoulder of the hill. The Quayle house was no distance from his own. The way the hill ran, they could see one another's lights at night. His eye homed on the very window from which too often he had been moved to stare in this direction. Suddenly he was as near as he ever came to weeping. Her hair was in his face. He could swim in her eyes, smell her perfume and the scent of warm sweet grass you got from her when you were dancing with her at Christmas at the Muthaiga Club and by sheer accident your nose brushed against her hair. It's the curtains, he realised, waiting for his half-tears to recede. They've kept her scent and I'm standing right up against them. On an impulse he grabbed the curtain in both hands, about to bury his face in it.

'Thank you, Sandy. Sorry to have kept you waiting.'

He swung round, shoving the curtain away from him. Justin was looming in the doorway, looking as flustered as Woodrow felt and clutching a long, orange, sausage-shaped leather Gladstone bag, fully laden and very scuffed, with brass screws, brass corners and brass padlocks either end.

'All set then, old man? Debt of honour discharged?' Woodrow asked, taken aback but, as a good diplomat, recovering his charm immediately. '*Jolly* good. That's the way then. And you've got everything you came for, all that?'

'I believe so. Yes. To a point.'

'You sound unsure.'

'Really? I don't mean to. It was her father's,' he explained, making a gesture with the bag.

'Looks more like an abortionist's,' said Woodrow, to be chummy.

He offered a hand to help him, but Justin preferred to carry his booty for himself. Woodrow climbed into the van, Justin climbed after him, to sit with one hand curled over its old leather carrying handles. The taunts of journalists came at them through the thin walls:

'*Do you reckon Bluhm topped her, Mr Quayle?*'

'*Hey, Justin, my proprietor is offering mega-mega-bucks.*'

From the direction of the house, above the ringing of the telephone, Woodrow thought he heard a baby crying, and realised it was Mustafa.

CHAPTER THREE

Press coverage of Tessa's murder was at first not half as dire as Woodrow and his High Commissioner had feared. Arseholes who are expert at making something out of nothing, Coleridge cautiously observed, appeared equally capable of making nothing out of something. To begin with, that was what they did. 'Bush Killers Slay British Envoy's Wife' ran the first reports, and this robust approach, written upwards for the broadsheets and downwards for the tabloids, served a discerning public well. The increasing hazards to aid workers around the globe were dwelled upon, there were stinging editorials on the failure of the United Nations to protect its own and the ever-rising cost of humanitarians brave enough to stand up and be counted. There was high talk of lawless tribesmen seeking whom they might devour, ritual killings, witchcraft and the gruesome trade in human skins. Much was made of the presence of roving gangs of illegal immigrants from Sudan, Somalia and Ethiopia. But nothing at all of the irrefutable fact that Tessa and Bluhm, in full view of staff and guests, had shared a cabin on the night before her death. Bluhm was 'a Belgian aid official' – right – 'a United Nations medical consultant' – wrong – 'an expert in tropical diseases' – wrong – and was feared abducted by the murderers, to be held for ransom or killed.

The bond between the experienced Dr Arnold Bluhm and his beautiful young protégée was commitment, it was humanitarian. And that was all it was. Noah only made it to the first editions, then died a second death. Black blood, as every Fleet Street schoolboy knows, is not news, but a decapitation is worth a mention. The searchlight was remorselessly on Tessa, the Society Girl Turned Oxbridge Lawyer, the Princess Diana of the African Poor, the Mother Teresa of the Nairobi Slums and the FO Angel Who Gave a Damn. An editorial in the *Guardian* made much of the fact that the Millennium's New Woman Diplomat [sic] should have met her death at Leakey's cradle of mankind, and drew from this the disquieting moral that, though racial attitudes may change, we cannot plumb the wells of savagery that are to be found at the heart of every man's darkness. The piece lost some of its impact when a sub-editor unfamiliar with the African continent set Tessa's murder on the shores of Lake Tanganyika rather than Turkana.

There were photographs of her galore. Cheerful baby Tessa in the arms of her father the judge in the days when His Honour was a humble barrister struggling along on half a million a year. Ten-year-old Tessa in plaits and jodhpurs at her rich-girl's private school, docile pony in background. (Though her mother was an Italian contessa, it was noted approvingly, the parents had wisely settled for a British education.) Teenaged Golden Girl Tessa in bikini, her uncut throat artfully highlighted by the photographic editor's airbrush. Tessa in saucily pitched mortarboard, academic gown and miniskirt. Tessa in the ludicrous garb of a British barrister, following in her father's footsteps. Tessa on her wedding day, and Old Etonian Justin already smiling his older Etonian's smile.

Towards Justin, the press showed an unusual restraint, partly because they wished nothing to tarnish the shining image of their instant heroine, partly because there was precious little to say about him. Justin was 'one of the FO's loyal middle-rankers'

– read 'pen-pusher' – a long-term bachelor 'born into the diplomatic tradition' who before his marriage had flown the flag in some of the world's least favoured hot-spots, among them Aden and Beirut. Colleagues spoke kindly of his coolness in crisis. In Nairobi he had headed a 'high-tech international forum' on aid. Nobody used the word 'backwater'. Rather comically, there turned out to be a dearth of photographs of him either before or after his wedding. A 'family snap' showed a clouded, inward-looking youth who with hindsight seemed marked down for early widowhood. It was abstracted, Justin confessed under pressure from his hostess, from a group picture of the Eton rugby team.

'I didn't know you were a rugger man, Justin! How very plucky of you,' cried Gloria, whose self-appointed task each morning after breakfast was to take him his letters of commiseration and newspaper cuttings sent up by the High Commission.

'It wasn't plucky at all,' he retorted in one of those flashes of spirit that Gloria so relished. 'I was press-ganged into it by a thug of a housemaster who thought we weren't men till we'd been kicked to pieces. The school had no business releasing that photograph.' And cooling down: 'I'm most grateful, Gloria.'

As he was for everything, she reported to Elena: for his drinks and meals and for his prison cell; for their turns together in the garden and their little seminars on bedding plants – he was particularly complimentary about the alyssum, white and purple, that she had *finally* persuaded to spread underneath the bombax tree – for her help in handling details of the approaching funeral, including going with Jackson to inspect the grave site and funeral home, since Justin by edict of London was to remain gated till the hue and cry died down. A faxed Foreign Office letter to this effect, addressed to Justin at the High Commission and signed 'Alison Landsbury, Head of Personnel', had produced an almost violent effect on Gloria. She could not afterwards remember an occasion when she so nearly lost control of herself.

'Justin, you are being *outrageously* misused. "Surrender the keys to your house until the appropriate steps have been taken by the authorities," my Aunt Fanny! *Which* authorities? *Kenyan* authorities? Or those flat-feet from Scotland Yard who still haven't even bothered to call on you?'

'But Gloria, I have already *been* to my house,' Justin insisted, in an effort to soothe her. 'Why fight a battle that is won? Will the cemetery have us?'

'At two-thirty. We are to be at Lee's Funeral Parlour at two. A notice goes to the newspapers tomorrow.'

'And she's next to Garth' – Garth his dead son, so named after Tessa's father the judge.

'As near as we can be, dear. Under the same jacaranda tree. With a little African boy.'

'You're very kind,' he told her for the umpteenth time and, without further word, removed himself to the lower ground and his Gladstone bag.

The bag was his comforter. Twice now Gloria had glimpsed him through the bars of the garden window, seated motionless on his bed, head in hands and the bag at his feet, staring down at it. Her secret conviction – shared with Elena – was that it contained Bluhm's love letters. He had rescued them from prying eyes – no thanks to Sandy – and he was waiting till he was strong enough to decide whether to read them or burn them. Elena agreed, though she thought Tessa a stupid little tart to have kept them. 'Read 'em and sling 'em is my motto, darling.' Noticing Justin's reluctance to stray from his room for fear of leaving the bag unguarded, Gloria suggested he put it in the wine store which, having an iron grille for a door, added to the prison-like grimness of the lower ground.

'And you shall keep the key, Justin' – grandly entrusting it to him. 'There. And when Sandy wants a bottle he'll have to come and ask you for it. Then perhaps he'll drink less.'

*　　*　　*

Gradually, as one press deadline followed another, Woodrow and Coleridge almost persuaded themselves that they had held the dam. Either Wolfgang had silenced his staff and guests, or the press was so obsessed with the scene of the crime that nobody bothered to check out the Oasis, they told each other. Coleridge personally addressed the assembled elders of the Muthaiga Club entreating them, in the name of Anglo-Kenyan solidarity, to stem the flow of gossip. Woodrow delivered a similar homily to the staff of the High Commission. Whatever we may think privately we must do nothing that could fan the flames, he urged, and his wise words, earnestly delivered, had their effect.

But it was all illusion, as Woodrow in his rational heart had known from the start. Just as the press was running out of steam, a Belgian daily ran a front-page story accusing Tessa and Bluhm of 'a passionate liaison' and featuring a page photocopied from the registration book at the Oasis and eye-witness accounts of the loving couple dining head to head on the eve of Tessa's murder. The British Sundays had a field day; overnight Bluhm became a figure of loathing for Fleet Street to snipe at as it wished. Until now, he had been Arnold Bluhm MD, the adopted Congolese son of a wealthy Belgian mining couple, educated Kinshasa, Brussels and the Sorbonne, medical monk, denizen of war zones, selfless healer of Algiers. From now on he was Bluhm the seducer, Bluhm the adulterer, Bluhm the maniac. A page-three feature about murderous doctors down the ages was accompanied by lookalike photographs of Bluhm and O. J. Simpson over the catchy heading 'Which Twin is the Doctor?' Bluhm, if you were that kind of newspaper reader, was your archetypal black killer. He had ensnared a white man's wife, cut her throat, decapitated the driver and run off into the bush to seek new prey or do whatever those salon blacks do when they revert to type. To make the comparison more graphically, they had airbrushed out Bluhm's beard.

All day long Gloria kept the worst away from Justin, fearing it would unhinge him. But he insisted on seeing everything, warts and all. So come the evening hour and before Woodrow returned, she took him a whisky and reluctantly presented him with the whole garish bundle. Entering his prison space, she was outraged to discover her son Harry sitting opposite him at the rickety pine table, and both of them frowning in concentration over a game of chess. A wave of jealousy seized her.

'Harry, dear, that's *most* inconsiderate of you, badgering poor Mr Quayle for *chess* when –'

But Justin interrupted her before she could finish her sentence.

'Your son has a most serpentine mind, Gloria,' he assured her. 'Sandy will have to watch himself, believe me.' Taking the bundle from her, he sat himself languidly on the bed and flicked through it. 'Arnold has a pretty good notion of our prejudices, you know,' he went on in the same remote tone. 'If he's alive, he won't be surprised. If he's not, he's not going to care, is he?'

But the press had a far more lethal shot in its locker which Gloria at her most pessimistic could not have foreseen.

*   *   *

Among the dozen or so maverick newsletters to which the High Commission subscribed – coloured local broadsheets, pseudonymously written and printed on the hoof – one in particular had shown a remarkable capacity for survival. It was called, without adornment, AFRICA CORRUPT, and its policy, if such a word could be applied to the turbulent impulses that drove it, was to rake mud regardless of race, colour, truth or the consequences. If it exposed alleged acts of larceny perpetrated by ministers and bureaucrats of the Moi administration, it was equally at home laying bare the 'grafting, corruption and pigs-in-clover lifestyle' of the aid bureaucrats.

But the newsletter in question – known ever after as Issue 64 – was devoted to none of these matters. It was printed on both sides of a single sheet of shocking-pink paper a yard square. Folded small, it fitted nicely in the jacket pocket. A thick black border signified that Issue 64's anonymous editors were in mourning. The headline consisted of the one word TESSA in black letters three inches high, and Woodrow's copy was delivered to him on the Saturday afternoon by none other than the sickly, shaggy, bespectacled, moustached, six-foot-six Tim Donohue in person. The front door bell rang as Woodrow was playing tip-and-run cricket with the boys in the garden. Gloria, normally a tireless wicketkeeper, was grappling with a headache upstairs; Justin was hull-down in his cell with the curtains closed. Woodrow walked through the house and, suspecting some journalist's ruse, peered through the fish-eye. And there stood Donohue on the doorstep, a sheepish smile on his long sad face, flapping what looked like a pink table napkin back and forth.

'*Frightfully* sorry to disturb you, old boy. Holy Saturday and all that. Spot of shit seems to have hit the proverbial fan.'

With undisguised distaste Woodrow led him to the drawing room. What on earth's the bloody man up to now? What on earth was he *ever* up to, come to think of it? Woodrow had always disliked the Friends, as the spies were unaffectionately known to the Foreign Office. Donohue wasn't smooth, he had no known linguistic skills, he didn't charm. He was to all outward purposes past his sell-by date. His day hours appeared to be spent on the Muthaiga Club golf course with the fleshier members of Nairobi's business community, his evenings at bridge. Yet he lived high, in a grand hiring with four servants and a faded beauty called Maud who looked as ill as he did. Was Nairobi a sinecure for him? A kiss-off at the end of a distinguished career? Woodrow had heard the Friends did that sort of thing. Donohue was in Woodrow's judgment surplus ballast in a profession that was by definition parasitic and out of date.

'One of my boys just happened to be loafing in the market place,' Donohue explained. 'A couple of chaps were handing out free copies in a shifty sort of way, so my lad thought he might as well have one.'

The front page consisted of three separate eulogies of Tessa, each purportedly written by a different African woman friend. The style was Afro-English vernacular: a little of the pulpit, a little of the soapbox, disarming flourishes of feeling. Tessa, each of the writers claimed in her different way, had broken the mould. With her wealth, parentage, education and looks she should have been up there dancing and feasting with the worst of Kenya's white supremacists. Instead she was the opposite of all they stood for. Tessa was in revolt against her class, race and whatever she believed was tying her down, whether it was the colour of her skin, the prejudice of her social equals or the bonds of a conventional Foreign Service marriage.

'How's Justin holding up?' Donohue asked, while Woodrow read.

'Well, thank you, considering.'

'I heard he was over at his house the other day.'

'Do you want me to read this or not?'

'Pretty smart footwork, I must say, old boy, dodging those reptiles on the doorstep. You should join our lot. Is he around?'

'Yes, but not receiving.'

If Africa was Tessa Quayle's adopted country, Woodrow read, Africa's women were her adopted religion.

Tessa fought for us no matter where the battleground, no matter what the taboos. She fought for us at posh champagne parties, posh dinner parties and any other posh party that was crazy enough to invite her, and her message was always the same. Only the emancipation of African women could save us from the blunderings and corruption of our menfolk. And when Tessa discovered she was pregnant, she insisted on bearing her African child among the African women she loved.

'Oh my Christ,' Woodrow exclaimed softly.

'Bit what I felt, actually,' Donohue agreed.

The last paragraph was printed in capitals. Mechanically, Woodrow read it also:

GOODBYE MAMA TESSA. WE ARE THE CHILDREN OF YOUR COURAGE. THANK YOU, THANK YOU, MAMA TESSA, FOR YOUR LIFE. ARNOLD BLUHM MAY LIVE ON BUT YOU ARE DEAD WITHOUT QUESTION. IF THE BRITISH QUEEN EVER AWARDS MEDALS POSTHUMOUSLY, THEN INSTEAD OF ELEVATING MR PORTER COLERIDGE TO A KNIGHTHOOD FOR HIS SERVICES TO BRITISH COMPLACENCY, LET'S HOPE SHE'LL GIVE THE VICTORIA CROSS TO YOU, MAMA TESSA, OUR FRIEND, FOR YOUR OUTSTANDING GALLANTRY IN THE FACE OF POST-COLONIAL BIGOTRY.

'Best bit's on the back, actually,' Donohue said.

Woodrow turned the paper round.

✝

MAMA TESSA'S AFRICAN BABY

Tessa Quayle believed in putting her body and her life wherever her convictions led her. She expected others to do the same. When Tessa was confined in the Uhuru Hospital, Nairobi, her very close friend Dr Arnold Bluhm visited her every day and, according to some reports, most nights as well, even taking a folding bed with him so that he could sleep beside her in the ward.

Woodrow folded the broadsheet and put it in his pocket. 'Think I'll just run this round to Porter, if it's all right by you. I can keep it, presumably?'

'All yours, old boy. Comps of the Firm.'

Woodrow was moving towards the door but Donohue showed no sign of following him.

'Coming?' Woodrow asked.

'Thought I'd just hang on, if you didn't mind. Say my piece to poor old Justin. Where is he? Upstairs?'

'I thought we agreed you wouldn't do that.'

'Did we, old boy? No problem at all. Another time. Your house, your guest. You haven't got Bluhm tucked away too, have you?'

'Don't be ridiculous.'

Undeterred, Donohue loped to Woodrow's side, dipping at the knees, making a party piece of it. 'Care for a lift? Only round the corner. Save you getting the car out. Too hot to walk.'

Still half fearing Donohue might nip back to make another attempt on Justin, Woodrow accepted the lift and watched his car safely over the brow. Porter and Veronica Coleridge were sunning themselves in the garden. Behind them lay the High Commission's Surrey mansion, before them the faultless lawns and weedless flower beds of a rich stockbroker's garden. Coleridge had the swing seat and was reading documents from a despatch case. His blonde wife Veronica, in corn-blue skirt and floppy straw hat, was sprawled on the grass beside a padded playpen. Within it, their daughter Rosie rolled to and fro on her back, admiring the foliage of an oak tree through the gaps between her fingers while Veronica hummed to her. Woodrow handed Coleridge the broadsheet and waited for the expletives. None came.

'Who reads this crap?'

'Every hack in town, I would imagine,' said Woodrow tonelessly.

'What's their next stop?'

'The hospital,' he replied with a sinking heart.

Slumped in a corduroy armchair in Coleridge's study, one ear listening to him trading guarded sentences with his detested superior in London over the digital telephone that Coleridge kept locked inside his desk, Woodrow in the recurrent dream he would not shake off until his dying day watched his white man's body striding at colonial speed through the immense crowded halls of Uhuru Hospital, pausing only to ask anybody in uniform for the right staircase, the right floor, the right ward, the right patient.

'The shit Pellegrin says, shove the whole thing under the carpet,' Porter Coleridge announced, slamming down the telephone. 'Shove it far and fast. Biggest bloody carpet we can find. Typical.'

Through the study window, Woodrow watched as Veronica lifted Rosie from her playpen and carried her towards the house.

'I thought we were doing that already,' he objected, still lost in his reverie.

'What Tessa did in her spare time was her own business. That includes having it off with Bluhm and any noble causes she may have been into. Off the record and only if asked, we respected her crusades but considered them under-informed and screwball. And we don't comment on irresponsible claims by the gutter press.' A pause while he wrestled with his self-disgust. 'And we're to put it about that she was crazy.'

'Why on earth should we do that?' – waking sharply.

'Ours not to reason why. She was unhinged by her dead baby and unstable before it. She went to a shrink in London, which helps. It stinks and I hate it. When's the funeral?'

'Middle of next week is the earliest.'

'Can't it be sooner?'

'No.'

'Why not?'

'We're waiting for the post-mortem. Funerals have to be booked in advance.'

'Sherry?'

'No thanks. Think I'll get back to the ranch.'

'The Office wants long-suffering. She was our cross but we bore her bravely. Can you do long-suffering?'

'I don't think I can.'

'Neither can I. It makes me absolutely fucking *sick*.'

The words had slipped from him so fast, with such subversiveness and conviction, that Woodrow at first doubted whether he had heard them at all.

'The shit Pellegrin says it's a three-line whip,' Coleridge continued in a tone of mordant contempt. 'No doubters, no defectors. Can you accept that?'

'I suppose so.'

'Well done, you. I'm not sure I can. Any outside representations she made anywhere – she and Bluhm – together or separately – to *anyone*, including you or me – any bees she had in her bonnet – about matters animal, vegetable, political *or pharmaceutical* –' a long unbearable pause while Coleridge's eyes rested on him with the fervour of a heretic enjoining him to treason – 'are outside our bailiwick and we know absolutely and completely fuck all about them. Have I made myself clear or would you like me to write it on the wall in secret ink?'

'You've made yourself clear.'

'Because Pellegrin made *him*self clear, you see. Unclear he was not.'

'No. He wouldn't be.'

'Did we keep copies of that stuff she never gave you? The stuff we never saw, touched or otherwise sullied our lily-white consciences with?'

'Everything she gave us went to Pellegrin.'

'How clever of us. And you're in good heart, are you, Sandy? Tail up and all that, given that times are trying and you've got her husband in your guest room?'

'I think so. How about you?' asked Woodrow who for some time, with Gloria's encouragement, had been looking with favour on the growing rift between Coleridge and London, and wondering how best to exploit it.

'Not sure I *am* in good heart, actually,' Coleridge replied, with more frankness than he had shown to Woodrow in the past. 'Not sure at all. In fact, come to think of it, I'm bloody *un*sure that I can subscribe to any of it. I can't, in fact. I refuse. So scupper Bernard bloody Pellegrin and all his works. Bugger them in fact. And he's a bloody awful tennis player. I shall tell him.'

On any other day Woodrow might have welcomed such evidence of schism and done his modest best to foment it, but his memories of the hospital were hounding him with a vividness he could not escape, filling him with hostility towards a world that held him prisoner against his will. To walk from the High Commissioner's Residence to his own took no more than ten minutes. Along the way he became a moving target for barking dogs, begging children calling 'five shillings, five shillings' as they ran after him, and well-intentioned motorists who slowed down to offer him a lift. Yet by the time he walked into his drive he had relived the most accusing hour of his life.

* * *

There are six beds in the ward at the Uhuru Hospital, three to either wall. None has sheets or pillows. The floor is concrete. There are skylights but they are unopened. It is winter, but no breeze passes through the room, and the stench of excreta and disinfectant is so fierce that Woodrow seems to ingest as well as smell it. Tessa lies in the middle bed of the left-hand wall, breastfeeding a child. He sees her last, deliberately. The beds either side of her are empty except for perished sheets of rubber buttoned to the mattresses. Across the room from her, one very young woman huddles on her side, her head flat on the mattress, one bare arm dangling. A teenaged boy crouches on the floor close beside her, his wide beseeching gaze turned unflinchingly to her face as he fans it with a piece of cardboard. Next to them a dignified old woman with white hair perches sternly upright reading a Mission Bible through horn-rimmed spectacles. She wears a kanga cloth of cotton, the type sold to tourists as a cover-up. Beyond her, a woman with earphones scowls at whatever she is hearing. Her face is etched in pain, and deeply devout. All this Woodrow takes in like a spy, while out of the corner of his eye he watches Tessa and wonders whether she has seen him.

But Bluhm has seen him. Bluhm's head has lifted as soon as Woodrow steps awkwardly into the room. Bluhm has risen from his place at Tessa's bedside, then stooped to whisper something in her ear, before coming silently towards him to take his hand and murmur, 'Welcome,' man to man. Welcome to *what* precisely? Welcome to Tessa, courtesy of her lover? Welcome to this reeking hell-hole of lethargic suffering? But Woodrow's only response is a reverent, 'Good to see you, Arnold,' as Bluhm slips discreetly into the corridor.

English women feeding children, in Woodrow's limited experience of the species, exercised a decent restraint. Certainly Gloria had done so. They open their fronts as men open theirs, then use their arts to obscure whatever lies within. But Tessa in the stifling African air feels no need of modesty. She is naked to her waist which is covered in a kanga cloth similar to the old woman's, and she is cradling the child to her left breast, her right breast free and waiting. Her upper body is slender and translucent. Her breasts, even in the aftermath of childbirth, are as light and flawless as he has so often imagined them. The child is black. Blue-black against the marble whiteness of her skin. One tiny black hand has found the breast that is feeding it, and is working it with eerie confidence while Tessa watches. Then slowly she raises her wide grey eyes and looks into Woodrow's. He reaches for words but hasn't any. He leans over her and past the child and, with his left hand resting on her bedhead, kisses her brow. As he does so he is surprised to see a notebook on the side of the bed where Bluhm has been sitting. It is balanced precariously on a tiny table, together with a glass of stale-looking water and a couple of ballpoint pens. It is open, and she has been writing in it in a vague, spidery hand that is like a bad memory of the privately tutored italic script he associates with her. He lowers himself side-saddle onto the bed while he thinks of something to say. But it is Tessa who speaks first. Weakly, a voice drugged and strangled after pain yet unnaturally composed, still managing to strike the mocking note she always has for him.

'His name is Baraka,' she says. 'It means blessing. But you knew that.'

'Good name.'

'He's not mine.' Woodrow says nothing. 'His mother can't feed him,' she explains. Her voice is slow and dreamy.

'Then he's lucky to have you,' Woodrow says handsomely. 'How are you, Tessa? I've been terribly worried for you, you can't imagine. I'm just so sorry. Who's looking after you, apart from Justin? Ghita and who else?'

'Arnold.'

'I mean apart from Arnold too, obviously.'

'You told me once that I court coincidences,' she says, ignoring his question. 'By putting myself in the front line, I make things happen.'

'I was admiring you for it.'

'Do you still?'

'Of course.'

'She's dying,' she says, shifting her eyes from him and staring across the room. 'His mother is. Wanza.' She is looking at the woman with the dangling arm, and the mute boy hunched on the floor beside her. 'Come on, Sandy. Aren't you going to ask what of?'

'What of?' he asks obediently.

'Life. Which the Buddhists tell us is the first cause of death. Overcrowding. Undernourishment. Filthy living conditions.' She is addressing the child. 'And greed. Greedy men in this case. It's a miracle they didn't kill you too. But they didn't, did they? For the first few days they visited her twice a day. They were terrified.'

'Who were?'

'The coincidences. The greedy ones. In fine white coats. They watched her, prodded her a bit, read her numbers, talked to the nurses. Now they've stopped coming.' The child is hurting her. She tenderly adjusts it and resumes. 'It was all right for Christ. Christ could sit at dying people's bedsides, say the magic words, the people lived and everybody clapped. The coincidences couldn't do that. That's why they went away. They've killed her and now they don't know the words.'

'Poor things,' Woodrow says, humouring her.

'No.' She turns her head, wincing as pain hits her, and nods across the room. 'They're the poor things. Wanza. And him down on the floor there. Kioko, her brother. He walked eighty kilometres from his village to keep the flies off you, didn't he, your uncle?' she says to the baby and, settling it on her lap, gently taps its back until it blindly belches. She places her palm beneath her other breast for it to suck.

'Tessa, listen to me.' Woodrow watches her eyes measure him. She knows the voice. She knows all his voices. He sees the shadow of suspicion fall across her face and not move on. She sent for me because she had a use for me, but now she's remembered who I am. 'Tessa, please, hear me out. Nobody's dying. Nobody's killed anyone. You're fevered, you're imagining things. You're dreadfully tired. Give it a rest. Give yourself a rest. Please.'

She returns her attention to the child, buffing its tiny cheek with her fingertip. 'You're the most beautiful thing I ever touched in my life,' she whispers to it. 'And don't you go forgetting it.'

'I'm sure he won't,' says Woodrow heartily, and the sound of his voice reminds her of his presence.

'How's the hothouse?' she asks – her word for the High Commission.

'Thriving.'

'You could all pack up and go home tomorrow. It wouldn't make the slightest difference,' she says vaguely.

'So you always tell me.'

'Africa's over here. You're over there.'

'Let's argue about that when you're stronger,' Woodrow suggests in his most placatory voice.

'Can we?'

'Of course.'

'And you'll listen?'

'Like a hawk.'

'And then we can tell you about the greedy coincidences in white coats. And you'll believe us. It's a deal?'

'Us?'

'Arnold.'

The mention of Bluhm brought Woodrow back to earth. 'I'll do whatever I can in the circumstances. Whatever it is. Within reason. I promise. Now try to get some rest. Please.'

She reflects on this. 'He promises to do whatever he can in the circumstances,' she explains to the child. 'Within reason. Well, there's a man. How's Gloria?'

'Deeply concerned. She sends her love.'

Tessa lets out a slow sigh of exhaustion and, with the child still at her breast, slumps back in the pillows and closes her eyes. 'Then go home to her. And don't write me any more letters,' she says. 'And leave Ghita alone. She won't play either.'

He gets up and turns, for some reason expecting to see Bluhm in the doorway, in the posture he detests most: Bluhm propped nonchalantly against the door frame, hands wedged cowboy-style into his arty belt, grinning his white-toothed grin inside his pretentious black beard. But the doorway is empty, the corridor windowless and dark, lit like an air-raid shelter by a line of underpowered lights. Making his way past broken-down trolleys laden with recumbent bodies, smelling the blood and excrement mingling with the sweet, horsy scent of Africa, Woodrow wonders whether this squalor is part of what makes her attractive to him: I have spent my life in flight from reality, but because of her I am drawn to it.

He enters a crowded concourse and sees Bluhm engaged in a heated conversation with another man. First he hears Bluhm's voice – though not the words – strident and accusing, echoing in the steel girders. Then the other man speaks back. Some people, once seen, live for ever in our memories. For Woodrow this is one of them. The other man is thickly built and paunchy, with a glistening, meaty face that is cast in an expression of abject despair. His hair, blond to ginger, is spread sparsely over his scalded pate. He has a pinched, rosebud mouth that pleads and denies. His eyes, round with hurt, are haunted by a horror that both men seem to share. His hands are mottled and very strong, his khaki shirt stained with tramlines of sweat around the collar. The rest of him is concealed under a white medical coat.

And then we can tell you about the greedy coincidences in white coats.

Woodrow moves stealthily forward. He is almost upon them, but neither head turns. They are too intent on arguing. He strides past them unnoticed, their raised voices lost in the din.

*   *   *

Donohue's car was back in the drive. The sight of it moved Woodrow to sick fury. He stormed upstairs, showered, put on a fresh shirt and felt no less furious. The house was unusually silent for a Saturday and when he glanced out of his bathroom window he saw why. Donohue, Justin, Gloria and the boys were seated at the table in the garden playing Monopoly. Woodrow loathed all board games but for Monopoly he had an unreasoning hatred not unlike his hatred of the Friends and all the other members of Britain's overblown Intelligence community. What the devil does he mean by coming back here minutes after I told him to keep his bloody distance? And what kind of weird husband is it who sits down to a jolly game of Monopoly just days after his wife is hacked to death? House guests, Woodrow and Gloria used to tell each other, quoting the Chinese proverb, were like fish and stank on the third day. But Justin was becoming more fragrant to Gloria with each day that passed.

Woodrow went downstairs and stood in the kitchen, looking out of the window. No staff on Saturday afternoons, of course. So much nicer to be just ourselves, darling. Except that it's not *our*selves, it's *your*selves. And you look a bloody sight happier with two middle-aged men fawning on you than you ever look with *me*.

At the table, Justin had landed on somebody's street and was paying out a stack of money in rent while Gloria and the boys hooted with delight and Donohue protested that it was about time too. Justin was wearing his stupid straw hat, and as with everything else he wore, it became him perfectly. Woodrow filled a kettle and set it on the gas. I'll take out tea to them, let them know I'm back – assuming they aren't too tied up with one another to notice. Changing his mind, he stepped smartly into the garden and marched up to the table.

'Justin. Sorry to butt in. Wondered if we could have a quick word.' And to the others – my own family, staring at me as if I've raped the housemaid – 'Didn't mean to break this up, gang. Only be a few minutes. Who's winning?'

'Nobody,' said Gloria with edge, while Donohue from the wings grinned his shaggy grin.

The two men stood in Justin's cell. If the garden hadn't been occupied, Woodrow would have preferred the garden. As it was, they stood facing each other across the drab bedroom, with Tessa's Gladstone bag – Tessa's *father's* Gladstone bag – reclining behind the grille. *My* wine store. *His* bloody key. *Her illustrious father's* bag. But as he started to speak, he was alarmed to see his surroundings change. Instead of the iron bedstead, he saw the inlaid desk her mother had loved. And behind it, the brick fireplace with invitations on it. And across the room where the bogus beams appeared to converge, Tessa's naked silhouette in front of the french window. He willed himself back to time present and the illusion passed.

'Justin.'

'Yes, Sandy.'

But for the second time in as many minutes he veered away from the confrontation he had planned. 'One of the local broadsheets is running a sort of *liber amicorum* about Tessa.'

'How nice of them.'

'There's a lot of rather unambiguous stuff about Bluhm in it. A suggestion that he personally delivered her child. Sort of not very hidden inference that the baby might be his as well. Sorry.'

'You mean Garth.'

'Yes.'

Justin's voice was taut and, to Woodrow's ear, as dangerously pitched as his own. 'Yes, well, that is an inference that people have drawn from time to time in recent months, Sandy, and no doubt in the present climate there will be more of it.'

Though Woodrow allowed space for him to do so, Justin did

not suggest that the inference was wrong. And this impelled Woodrow to press harder. Some guilty inner force was driving him.

'They also suggest that Bluhm went so far as to take a camp bed to the ward so that he could sleep close to her.'

'We shared it.'

'I beg your pardon?'

'Sometimes Arnold slept on it, sometimes I did. We took turns, depending on our respective workloads.'

'So you don't mind?'

'Mind what?'

'That this should be said of them – that he was devoting this amount of attention to her – with your consent, apparently – while she was acting as your wife here in Nairobi.'

'*Acting?* She *was* my wife, damn you!'

Woodrow hadn't reckoned with Justin's anger any more than he'd reckoned with Coleridge's. He'd been too busy quelling his own. He'd got his voice down, and in the kitchen he'd managed to shrug some of the tension out of his shoulders. But Justin's outburst came at him out of a clear sky, and startled him. He had expected contrition and, if he was honest, humiliation, but not armed resistance.

'What are you asking me precisely?' Justin enquired. 'I don't think I understand.'

'I need to know, Justin. That's all.'

'Know what? Whether I controlled my wife?'

Woodrow was pleading and backing away at the same time. 'Look, Justin – I mean, see it my way – just for a moment, OK? The whole world's press is going to pick this up. I have a right to know.'

'Know what?'

'What else Tessa and Bluhm got up to that's going to be headlines – tomorrow and for the next six weeks,' he ended, on a note of self-pity.

'Such as what?'

'Bluhm was her guru. Well, wasn't he? Whatever else he was.'

'So?'

'So they shared causes together. They sniffed out abuses. Human rights stuff. Bluhm has some kind of watchdog rôle – right? Or his employers have. So Tessa –' he was losing his way and Justin was watching him do it – 'she helped him. Perfectly natural. In the circumstances. Used her lawyer's head.'

'D'you mind telling me where this is leading?'

'Her papers. That's all. Her possessions. Those you collected. We did. Together.'

'What of them?'

Woodrow pulled himself together: I'm your superior, for God's sake, not some bloody petitioner. Let's get our rôles straight, shall we?

'I need your assurance, therefore – that any papers she assembled for her causes – in her capacity as your wife here – with diplomatic status – here on HMG's ticket – will be handed to the Office. It was on that understanding that I took you to your house last Tuesday. We would not have gone there otherwise.'

Justin had not moved. Not a finger, not an eyelid flickered while Woodrow delivered himself of this untruthful afterthought. Backlit, he remained as still as Tessa's naked silhouette.

'The other assurance I'm to obtain from you is self-evident,' Woodrow went on.

'What other assurance?'

'Your own discretion in the matter. Whatever you know of her activities – her agitations – her so-called aid work that spun out of control.'

'Whose control?'

'I simply mean that wherever she ventured into official waters, you are as much bound by the rules of confidentiality as the rest of us. I'm afraid that's an order from on high.' He was trying to make a joke of it but neither of them smiled. 'Pellegrin's order.'

And you're in good heart, are you, Sandy? Given that times are trying and you've got her husband in your guest room?

Justin was speaking at last. 'Thank you, Sandy. I'm appreciative of all you've done for me. I'm grateful that you enabled me to visit my own house. But now I must collect the rent on Piccadilly, where I seem to own a valuable hotel.'

At which to Woodrow's astonishment he returned to the garden and, resuming his place next to Donohue, took up the game of Monopoly where he had left it.

CHAPTER FOUR

The British police were absolute lambs. Gloria said so, and if Woodrow didn't agree with her, he didn't show it. Even Porter Coleridge, though parsimonious in describing his dealings with them, declared them 'surprisingly civilised considering they were shits'. And the *nicest* thing about them was – Gloria reported to Elena from her bedroom after she had escorted them to the living room for the start of their second day with Justin – the nicest thing *ever* was, El, that you really felt they were here to *help*, not heap more pain and embarrassment onto poor dear Justin's shoulders. Rob the boy was dishy – well, *man* really, El, he must be twenty-five if a day! A bit of an actor in a non-flashy way, and awfully good at taking off the Nairobi Blue Boys they had to work alongside. And Lesley – who's a *woman*, darling, nb, which took *everybody* by surprise, and shows you how little we know about the real England these days – clothes a *little* bit last season but, apart from that, well, frankly you'd never have guessed she didn't have our sort of education. Not by the voice, of course, because *nobody* speaks the way they're brought up any more, they daren't. But *totally* at home in one's drawing room, *very* composed and self-assured, and *cosy*, with a nice warm smile and a bit of early grey in her hair which she very sensibly *leaves*, and what Sandy calls a *decent quiet*, so that you don't have to think of things to say all the time when they're having their pit-stops and giving poor Justin a rest. The only problem was, Gloria had absolutely *no* idea what went on between them all, because she could hardly stand in the kitchen all day with her ear glued to the serving hatch, well, certainly not with the servants watching her, well, could she, El?

But if the matter of the discussions between Justin and the two police officers eluded her, Gloria knew even less about their dealings with her husband, for the good reason that he did not tell her they were taking place.

*   *   *

The opening exchanges between Woodrow and the two officers were courtesy itself. The officers said they understood the delicacy of their mission, they were not about to lift the lid on the white community in Nairobi, et cetera. Woodrow in return pledged the cooperation of his staff and all appropriate facilities, amen. The officers promised to keep Woodrow abreast of their investigations, so far as this was compatible with their instructions from the Yard. Woodrow genially pointed out that they were all serving the same Queen; and if first names were good enough for Her Majesty, they were good enough for us.

'So what's Justin's job description here in the High Commission then, Mr Woodrow?' Rob the boy asked politely, ignoring this call to intimacy.

Rob was a London Marathon runner, all ears and knees and elbows and true grit. Lesley, who could have been his smarter elder sister, carried a useful bag which Woodrow facetiously imagined to contain the things Rob needed at the track-side – iodine, salt tablets, spare laces for his running shoes – but which actually, so far as he could see, contained nothing but a tape recorder, cassettes and a colourful array of shorthand pads and notebooks.

Woodrow affected to consider. He wore the judicious frown that told you he was the professional. 'Well, he's our in-house Old Etonian for a start,' he said, and everybody enjoyed this good joke. '*Basically*, Rob, he's our British representative on the East African Donors' Effectiveness Committee known otherwise by the acronym EADEC,' he went on, speaking with the clarity owed to Rob's limited intelligence. 'The second E was originally for Efficacy but that wasn't a word many people were familiar with round here, so we changed it to something more user-friendly.'

'It does what, this committee?'

'EADEC is a relatively *new* consultative body, Rob, based here in Nairobi. It comprises representatives of all donor nations who provide aid, succour and relief to East Africa, in whatever form. Its members are drawn from the Embassies and High Commissions of each donor; the committee meets weekly and renders a fortnightly report.'

'To?' said Rob, writing.

'All member countries, obviously.'

'On?'

'On what the title says,' said Woodrow patiently, making allowances for the boy's manners. 'It fosters *efficacy*, or *effectiveness*, in the aid field. In aid work, *effectiveness* is pretty much the gold standard. Compassion's a given,' he added with a disarming smile that said we were all compassionate people. 'EADEC addresses the thorny question of how much of each dollar from each donor nation actually reaches its target, and how much wasteful overlap and unhelpful competition exists between agencies on the ground. It grapples, as we all do, alas, with the aid world's three Rs: Reduplication, Rivalry, Rationalisation. It balances overheads against productivity and – ' the smile of one bestowing wisdom – 'makes the odd *tentative* recommendation, given that – unlike you chaps – it has no executive powers and no powers of enforcement.' A gracious tilting of the head announced the little confidence. 'I'm not sure it was the greatest idea on earth, between ourselves. But it was the brainchild of our very own dear Foreign Secretary, it sat well with calls for greater transparency and an ethical foreign policy and other questionable nostrums of the day, so we pushed it for all it was worth. There are those who say the UN should do the job. Others say the UN already does it. Others again say the UN is part of the disease. Take your pick.' A deprecating shrug invited them to do just that.

'What disease?' said Rob.

'EADEC is not empowered to investigate at field level. Nevertheless, corruption is a major factor that has to be costed in as soon as you start to relate what is spent to what is achieved. Not to be confused with natural wastage and incompetence, but akin to them.' He reached for a common man's analogy. 'Take our dear old British water grid, built 1890 or thereabouts. Water leaves the reservoir. Some of it, if you're lucky, comes out of your tap. But there are some very leaky pipes along the way. Now when that water is donated out of the goodness of the general public's heart, you can't just let it seep away into nowhere, can you? Certainly not if you're dependent on the fickle voter for your job.'

'Who does this committee job bring him into contact with?' Rob asked.

'Ranking diplomats. Drawn from the international community here in Nairobi. Mostly counsellor and above. The odd first secretary, but not many.' He seemed to think this required some explanation. 'EADEC had to be *exalted*, in my judgment. Head in the clouds. Once it allowed itself to be dragged down to field level, it would end up as some kind of super Non-Governmental Organisation – NGO to you, Rob – and be tarred with its own brush. I argued that strongly. All right: EADEC must be here in Nairobi, on the ground, locally aware. Obviously. But it's still a think-tank. It must preserve the dispassionate overview. Absolutely vital that it remains – if you'll allow me to quote myself – an *emotion-free zone*. And Justin is the committee secretary. Nothing he's earned: it's our turn. He takes the minutes, collates the research and drafts the fortnightlies.'

'Tessa wasn't an emotion-free zone,' Rob objected after a moment's thought. 'Tessa was emotion all the way, from what we hear.'

'I'm afraid you've been reading too many newspapers, Rob.'

'No, I haven't. I've been looking at her field reports. She was right in there with her sleeves rolled up. Shit up to her elbows, day and night.'

'And very necessary, no doubt. Very laudable. But hardly conducive to objectivity, which is the committee's first responsibility as an international consultative body,' said Woodrow graciously, ignoring this descent into gutter language, as – at a different level entirely – he ignored it in his High Commissioner.

'So they went their different ways,' Rob concluded, sitting back and tapping his teeth with his pencil. 'He was objective, she was emotional. He played the safe centre, she worked the dangerous edges. I get it now. As a matter of fact, I think I knew that already. So where does Bluhm fit in?'

'In what sense?'

'Bluhm. Arnold Bluhm. Doctor. Where does he fit into the scheme of things in Tessa's life and yours?'

Woodrow gave a little smile, forgiving this quirkish formulation. *My* life? What did *her* life have to do with *mine*? 'We have a great variety of donor-financed organisations here, as I'm sure you know. All supported by different countries and funded by all sorts of charitable and other outfits. Our gallant President Moi detests them *en bloc*.'

'Why?'

'Because they do what his government would do if it was doing its job. They also bypass his systems of corruption. Bluhm's organisation is modest, it's Belgian, it's privately funded and medical. That's all I can tell you about it, I'm afraid,' he added, with a candour that invited them to share his ignorance of these things.

But they were not so easily won.

'It's a watchdog outfit,' Rob informed him shortly. 'Its physicians tour the other NGOs, visit clinics, check out diagnoses and correct them. Like "maybe this isn't malaria, doctor, maybe it's liver cancer". Then they check out the treatment. They also deal in epidemiology. What about Leakey?'

'What about him?'

'Bluhm and Tessa were on their way to his site – correct?'

'Purportedly.'

'Who is he exactly? Leakey? What's his bag?'

'He's by way of being a white African legend. An anthropologist and archaeologist who worked alongside his parents on the eastern shores of Turkana exploring the origins of mankind. When they died he continued their work. He directed the National Museum here in Nairobi and later took over wildlife and conservation.'

'But resigned.'

'Or was pushed. The story is complex.'

'Plus he's a thorn in Moi's breeches, right?'

'He opposed Moi politically and was badly beaten up for his pains. He is now undergoing some kind of resurrection as the scourge of Kenyan corruption. The International Monetary Fund and the World Bank are effectively demanding his presence in the gôvernment.' As Rob sat back and Lesley took her turn, it was clear that the distinction Rob had applied to the Quayles also defined the police officers' separate styles. Rob spoke in jerks, with the thickness of a man fighting to hold back his emotions. Lesley was the model of dispassion.

'So what sort of *man* is this Justin?' she mused, observing him as a distant character in history. 'Away from his place of work and this committee of his? What are his interests, appetites, what's his lifestyle, who *is* he?'

'Oh my *God*, who are *any* of us?' Woodrow declaimed, perhaps a little too theatrically, at which Rob again rattled his pencil against his teeth, Lesley smiled patiently and Woodrow, with charming reluctance, recited a checklist of Justin's meagre attributes: a keen gardener – though, come to think of it, not so keen since Tessa lost her baby – loves nothing better than toiling in the flower beds on a Saturday afternoon – a *gentleman*, whatever that means – the *right sort* of Etonian – courteous to a fault in his dealings with locally employed staff, of course – kind of chap who can be relied on to dance with the wallflowers at the High Commissioner's annual bash – bit of an old bachelor in ways Woodrow couldn't immediately call to mind – not a golfer or a tennis player to his knowledge, not a shooter or a fisher, not an outdoor man at all, apart from his gardening. And, of course, a first-rate, meat-and-potatoes professional diplomat – bags of field experience, two or three languages, safe pair of hands, *totally* loyal to London guidance. And – here's the cruel bit, Rob – by no fault of his own, caught in the promotion bulge.

'And he doesn't keep low company or anything?' Lesley asked, consulting her notebook. 'You wouldn't see him whooping it up in the shady nightclubs while Tessa was out on her field trips?' The question was already a bit of a joke. 'That wouldn't be his thing, I take it?'

'*Nightclubs?* Justin? What a wonderful thought! Annabel's maybe, twenty-five years ago. Whatever gave you that idea?' Woodrow exclaimed with a heartier laugh than he had had for days.

Rob was happy to enlighten him. 'Our Super, actually. Mr Gridley, he did a spell in Nairobi on liaison. He says the nightclubs are where you'd hire a hit-man if you had a mind to. There's one on River Road, a block away from the New Stanley, which is handy if you're staying there. Five hundred US and they'll whack out anyone you want. Half down, half afterwards. Less in some clubs, according to him, but then you don't get the quality.'

'Did Justin *love* Tessa?' Lesley asked, while Woodrow was still smiling.

In the relaxed spirit that was growing up between them, Woodrow threw up his arms and offered a muted cry to Heaven. 'Oh my God! Who loves whom in this world and why?' And when Lesley did not immediately relieve him of the question: 'She was beautiful. Witty. Young. He was forty-something when he met her. Menopausal, heading for injury time, lonely, infatuated, wanting to settle down. *Love?* That's your call, not mine.'

But if this was an invitation to Lesley to chime in with her own opinions, she ignored it. She appeared, like Rob beside her, more interested in the subtle transfiguration of Woodrow's features; in the tightening of the skin lines in the upper cheeks, the faint blotches of colour that had appeared at the neck; in the tiny, involuntary puckerings of the lower jaw.

'And Justin wasn't angry with her – like about her aid work for instance?' Rob suggested.

'Why should he be?'

'It didn't get up his nose when she banged on about how certain Western companies, British included, were ripping off the Africans – overcharging them for technical services, dumping overpriced out-of-date medicines on them? Using Africans as human guinea pigs to try out new drugs, which is sometimes implied if seldom proved, so to speak?'

'I'm sure Justin was very proud of her aid work. A lot of our wives here tend to sit back. Tessa's involvement redressed the balance.'

'So he wasn't angry with her,' Rob pressed.

'Justin is simply *not* given to anger. Not in the normal way. If he was anything at all, he was embarrassed.'

'Were *you* embarrassed? I mean, you here at the High Commission?'

'What on earth by?'

'Her aid work. Her special interests. Did they conflict at all with HM interests?'

Woodrow composed his most puzzled and disarming frown. 'Her Majesty's government could never be embarrassed by acts of humanity, Rob. You should know that.'

'We're learning it, Mr Woodrow,' Lesley cut in quietly. 'We're new.' And having examined him for a while without for one second relaxing her nice smile, she loaded her notebooks and tape recorder back into her bag and, pleading engagements in the town, proposed they resume their deliberations tomorrow at the same hour.

'Did Tessa confide in anyone, do you know?' Lesley asked, in a by-the-by tone as they all three moved in a bunch towards the door.

'Apart from Bluhm, you mean?'

'I meant women friends, actually.'

Woodrow ostentatiously searched his memory. 'No. No, I don't *think* so. Nobody comes specifically to mind. But I don't suppose I'd know really, would I?'

'You might if it were someone on your staff. Like Ghita Pearson or somebody,' said Lesley helpfully.

'Ghita? Oh well, obviously, yes, Ghita. And they're looking after you all right, are they? You've got transport and everything? Good.'

A whole day passed, and a whole night, before they came again.

*   *   *

This time it was Lesley not Rob who opened the proceedings, and she did so with a freshness that suggested encouraging things had happened since they last met. 'Tessa had had recent intercourse,' she announced in a bright start-the-day sort of voice as she set out her properties like court exhibits – pencils, notebooks, tape recorder, a piece of india rubber. 'We suspect rape. That's not for publication, though I expect we'll all be reading it in tomorrow's newspapers. It's only a vaginal swab they've taken at this stage and peeked through a microscope to see whether the sperm was alive or dead. It was dead, but they still think it may be more than one person's sperm. Maybe a whole cocktail. Our view is they've got no way to tell.'

Woodrow sank his head into his hands.

'We'll have to wait for our own boffins to pronounce before it's a hundred per cent,' Lesley said, watching him.

Rob, as yesterday, was nonchalantly tapping his pencil against his big teeth.

'And the blood on Bluhm's tunic was Tessa's,' Lesley continued in the same frank tone. 'Only provisional, mind. They only do the basic types here. Anything else, we'll have to do back home.'

Woodrow had risen to his feet, a thing he did quite often at informal meetings to put everyone at their ease. Strolling languidly to the window he took up a position at the other end of the room and affected to study the hideous city skyline. There was freak thunder about, and that indefinable smell of tension that precedes the magical African rain. His manner, by contrast, was repose itself. Nobody could see the two or three drops of hot sweat that had left his armpits and were crawling like fat insects down his ribs.

'Has anyone told Quayle yet?' he asked, and wondered, as perhaps they did, why a raped woman's widower suddenly becomes a Quayle and not a Justin.

'We thought it would be better coming from a friend,' Lesley replied.

'You,' Rob suggested.

'Of course.'

'Plus it *is* just possible – like Les here said – that she and Arnold had one last one for the road. If you want to mention that to him. It's up to you.'

What's my last straw? he wondered. What more has to happen before I open this window and jump out? Perhaps that was what I wanted her to do for me: take me beyond the limits of my own acceptance.

'We really *like* Bluhm,' Lesley broke out in chummy exasperation, as if she needed Woodrow to like Bluhm too. 'All right, we've got to be on the lookout for the *other* Bluhm, the beast in human shape. And where we come from, the most peaceable people will do the most terrible things when they're pushed. But who pushed him – if he *was* pushed? Nobody, unless she did.'

Lesley paused here, inviting Woodrow's comment, but he was exercising his right to remain silent.

'Bluhm's as close as you'll ever get to a *good man*,' she insisted, as if *good man* were a finite condition like *Homo sapiens*. 'He's done a lot of really, really good things. Not for display, but because he wanted to. Saved lives, risked his own, worked in awful places for no money, hidden people in his attic. Well, don't you agree, sir?'

Was she goading him? Or merely seeking enlightenment from a mature observer of the Tessa–Bluhm relationship?

'I'm sure he has a fine record,' Woodrow conceded.

Rob gave a snort of impatience, and a disconcerting writhe of his upper body. 'Look. Forget his record. Personally: do you like him, yes or no? Simple as that.' And flung himself into a fresh position on his chair.

'My God,' said Woodrow over his shoulder, careful this time not to overdo the histrionics, but allowing nonetheless a note of exasperation to enter his voice. 'Yesterday it was define *love*, today it's define *like*. We do rather chase our absolute definitions in Cool Britannia these days, don't we?'

'We're asking your opinion, sir,' said Rob.

Perhaps it was the *sirs* that turned the trick. At their first meeting it was Mr Woodrow, or when they felt bold, Sandy. Now it was sir, advising Woodrow that these two junior police officers were not his colleagues, not his friends, but lower-class outsiders poking their noses into the exclusive club that had given him standing and protection these seventeen years. He linked his hands behind his back and braced his shoulders, then turned on his heel until he faced his interrogators.

'Arnold Bluhm is persuasive,' he declared, lecturing them down the length of the room. 'He has looks, charm of a sort. Wit if you like that type of humour. Some sort of aura – perhaps it's that neat little beard. To the impressionable, he's an African folk hero.' After which he turned away from them, as if waiting for them to pack and leave.

'And to the unimpressionable?' asked Lesley, taking advantage of his turned back to reconnoitre him with her eyes: the hands nonchalantly comforting one another behind him, the unweighted knee lifted in self-defence.

'Oh, we're in the minority, I'm sure,' Woodrow replied silkily.

'Only I imagine it could be very worrying for you – vexing too, in your position of responsibility as Head of Chancery – seeing all this happening under your nose and knowing there's nothing you can do to stop it. I mean you can't go up to Justin, can you, and say, "Look at that bearded black man over there, he's carrying on with your wife," can you? Or can you?'

'If scandal threatens to drag the good name of the Mission into the gutter, I'm entitled – indeed obliged – to interpose myself.'

'And did you?' – Lesley speaking.

'In a general way, yes.'

'With Justin? Or with Tessa directly?'

'The problem was, obviously, that her relationship with Bluhm had *cover*, as one might say,' Woodrow replied, contriving to ignore the question. 'The man's a ranking doctor. He's well regarded in the aid community. Tessa was his devoted volunteer. On the surface, all perfectly above-board. One can't just sail in and accuse them of adultery on no evidence. One can only say – look here, this is giving out the wrong signals, so please be a little more circumspect.'

'So who did you say it to?' Lesley asked while she jotted in a notebook.

'It's not as simple as that. There was more to it than just one episode – one dialogue.'

Lesley leaned forward, checking as she did so that the spool was turning in her tape recorder. 'Between you and Tessa?'

'Tessa was a brilliantly designed engine with half the cogs missing. Before she lost her baby boy, she was a bit wild. All right.' About to make his betrayal of Tessa absolute, Woodrow was remembering Porter Coleridge seated in his study furiously quoting Pellegrin's instructions. 'But *afterwards* – I have to say this – with enormous regret – she struck more than a few of us as pretty much unhinged.'

'Was she nympho?' Rob asked.

'I'm afraid that question is a little above my pay grade,' Woodrow replied icily.

'Let's just say she flirted outrageously,' Lesley suggested. 'With everyone.'

'If you insist' – no man could have sounded more detached – 'it's hard to tell, isn't it? Beautiful girl, belle of the ball, older husband – is she flirting? Or is she just being herself, having a good time? If she wears a low dress and flounces, people say she's fast. If she doesn't, they say she's a bore. That's white Nairobi for you. Perhaps it's anywhere. I can't say I'm an expert.'

'Did she flirt with *you*?' asked Rob, after another infuriating tattoo of the pencil on his teeth.

'I've told you already. It was impossible to tell whether she was flirting or merely indulging her high spirits,' said Woodrow, reaching new levels of urbanity.

'So, er, did you by any chance have a bit of a flirt back?' Rob enquired. 'Don't look like that, Mr Woodrow. You're forty-something, menopausal, heading for injury time, same as Justin is. You had the hots for her, why not? I'll bet I would have.'

Woodrow's recovery was so quick that it had happened almost before he was aware of it. 'Oh my dear chap. Thought of nothing else. Tessa, Tessa, night and day. Obsessed by her. Ask anyone.'

'We did,' said Rob.

* * *

Next morning, it seemed to the beleaguered Woodrow, his interrogators were indecent in their haste to get at him. Rob set the tape recorder on the table, Lesley opened a large red notebook at a double page marked by an elastic band and led the questioning.

'We have reason to believe you visited Tessa in the Nairobi hospital soon after she lost her baby, sir, is that correct?'

Woodrow's world rocked. Who in God's name told them *that*? Justin? He can't have done, they haven't seen him yet, I'd know.

'Hold everything,' he ordered sharply.

Lesley's head came up. Rob unravelled himself and, as if about to flatten his face with his palm, extended one long hand and laid it upright against his nose, then studied Woodrow over the tips of his extended fingers.

'Is this to be our topic for the morning?' Woodrow demanded.

'It's one of them,' Lesley conceded.

'Then can you tell me, please – given that time is short for all of us – what on earth visiting Tessa in hospital has to do with tracking down her murderer – which I understand is the purpose of your being here?'

'We're looking for a motive,' said Lesley.

'You told me you had one. Rape.'

'Rape doesn't fit any more. Not as motive. Rape was a side-effect. Maybe a blind, to make us think we're looking at a random killing, not a planned one.'

'Premeditation,' Rob explained, his big brown eyes fixing Woodrow in a lonely stare. 'What we call a corporate job.'

At which, for a brief but terrifying moment, Woodrow thought of absolutely nothing at all. Then he thought *corporate*. Why did he say *corporate*?

Corporate as performed by a corporation? Outrageous! Too far-fetched to be worthy of consideration by a reputable diplomat!

After that his mind became a blank screen. No words, not even the most banal and meaningless, came to rescue him. He saw himself, if at all, as some kind of computer, retrieving, assembling and then rejecting a train of heavily encrypted connections from a cordoned-off area of his brain.

Corporate nothing. It was random. Unplanned. A blood feast, African style.

'So what took you to the hospital?' he heard Lesley saying, as he caught up with the soundtrack. 'Why did you go and see Tessa after she lost her baby boy?'

'Because she asked me to. Through her husband. In my capacity as Justin's superior.'

'Anyone else invited to the party?'

'Not to my knowledge.'

'Maybe Ghita?'

'You mean Ghita Pearson?'

'D'you know a different one?'

'Ghita Pearson was not present.'

'So just you and Tessa,' Lesley noted aloud, writing in her notebook. 'What's you being his superior got to do with it?'

'She was concerned for Justin's welfare and wished to reassure herself that all was well with him,' Woodrow replied, deliberately taking his time rather than respond to her quickening rhythm. 'I had tried to persuade Justin to take leave of absence, but he preferred to remain at his post. The EADEC annual conference of ministers was coming up and he was determined to prepare for it. I explained this to her and promised to continue to keep an eye on him.'

'Did she have her laptop with her?' Rob cut in.

'I beg your pardon?'

'Why's that so difficult? Did she have her laptop with her? – beside her, on a table, under the bed, in it? Her laptop. Tessa loved her laptop. She e-mailed people with it. She e-mailed Bluhm. She e-mailed Ghita. She e-mailed a sick kid in Italy she was looking after, and some old boyfriend she had in London. She e-mailed half the world all the time. Did she have the laptop with her?'

'Thank you for being so explicit. No, I saw no laptop.'

'What about a notebook?'

A hesitation while he searched his memory and composed the lie. 'None that I *saw*.'

'Any you didn't?'

Woodrow did not deign to answer. Rob leaned back and studied the ceiling in a falsely leisured way.

'So how was she in herself?' he enquired.

'Nobody's at her best after producing a stillborn baby.'

'So how was she?'

'Weak. Rambling. Depressed.'

'And that was all you talked about. Justin. Her beloved husband.'

'So far as I remember, yes.'

'How long were you with her?'

'I didn't time myself, but I would imagine something in the region of twenty minutes. Obviously I didn't want to tire her.'

'So you talked about Justin for twenty minutes. Whether he's eating his porridge and that.'

'The conversation was intermittent,' Woodrow replied, colouring. 'When someone is feverish and exhausted and has lost her child, it is not easy to have a lucid exchange.'

'Anyone else present?'

'I told you already. I went alone.'

'That's not what I asked you. I asked whether anyone else was present?'

'Such as who?'

'Such as whoever else was present. A nurse, a doctor. Another visitor, a friend of hers. Girlfriend. Man friend. African friend. Like Dr Arnold Bluhm, for instance. Why do I have to drag it out of you, sir?'

As evidence of his annoyance, Rob unwound himself like a javelin-thrower, first flinging a hand in the air, then tortuously repositioning his long legs. Woodrow meanwhile was again visibly consulting his memory: bringing his eyebrows together in an amused and rueful frown.

'Now you come to mention it, Rob, you're right. How very clever of you. Bluhm was there when I arrived. We greeted each other and he left. I would imagine we overlapped by the better part of twenty seconds. For you, twenty-five.'

But Woodrow's careless demeanour was hard won. Who the devil told him Bluhm was at her bedside? But his apprehension went further. It reached into the darkest crevices of his other mind, touching again on that chain of causality he refused to acknowledge, and Porter Coleridge had furiously ordered him to forget.

'So what was Bluhm doing there, do you suppose, sir?'

'He offered no explanation, neither did she. He's a doctor, isn't he? Apart from anything else.'

'What was Tessa doing?'

'Lying in the bed. What did you expect her to be doing?' he retorted, losing his head for a moment. 'Playing tiddlywinks?'

Rob stretched his long legs in front of him, admiring his huge feet down the length of them in the manner of a sunbather. '*I* don't know,' he said. 'What *do* we expect her to be doing, Les?' he asked of his fellow officer. 'Not tiddlywinks, for sure. There she is lying in bed. Doing what? we ask ourselves.'

'Feeding a black baby, I should think,' Lesley said. 'While its mother died.'

For a while the only sounds in the room came from passing footsteps in the corridor, and cars racing and fighting in the town across the valley. Rob reached out a gangly arm and switched off the tape recorder.

'As you pointed out, sir, we're all short of time,' he said courteously. 'So kindly don't fucking waste it by dodging questions and treating us like shit.' He switched the tape recorder back on. 'Be so good as to tell us in your own words about the dying woman in the ward and her little baby boy, Mr Woodrow, sir,' he said. 'Please. And what she died of, and who was trying to cure her of it and how, and anything else you happen to know in that regard.'

Cornered and resentful in his isolation, Woodrow reached instinctively for the support of his Head of Mission, only to be reminded that Coleridge was playing hard to get. Last night, when Woodrow had tried to reach him for a private word, Mildren had advised that his master was cloistered with the

American Ambassador and could be reached only in emergency. This morning Coleridge was reportedly 'conducting business from the Residence'.

CHAPTER FIVE

Woodrow was not easily unmanned. In his diplomatic career he had been obliged to carry off any number of humiliating situations, and had learned by experience that the soundest course was to refuse to recognise that anything was amiss. He applied this lesson now as, in curt sentences, he gave a minimalist's rendering of the scene in the hospital ward. Yes, he agreed – mildly surprised that they should be so interested in the minutiae of Tessa's confinement – he distantly remembered that a fellow patient of Tessa's was asleep or comatose. And that since she was not able to feed her own baby, Tessa was acting as the child's wet-nurse. Tessa's loss was the child's gain.

'Did the sick woman have a name?' Lesley asked.

'Not that I recall.'

'Was there anybody with the sick woman – a relative or friend?'

'Her brother. A teenaged boy from her village. That is how Tessa told it, but given her state, I do not regard her as a reliable witness.'

'D'you know the brother's name?'

'No.'

'Or the name of the village?'

'No.'

'Did Tessa tell you what was wrong with the woman?'

'Most of what she said was incoherent.'

'So the rest was coherent,' Rob pointed out. An eerie forbearance was settling over him. His gangling limbs had found a resting place. He suddenly had all day to kill. 'In her coherent moments, what did Tessa tell you about the sick woman across the ward from her, Mr Woodrow?'

'That she was dying. That her illness, which she did not name, derived from the social conditions in which she lived.'

'Aids?'

'That's not what she said.'

'Makes a change, then.'

'Indeed.'

'Was anyone treating the woman for this unnamed illness?'

'Presumably. Why else would she be in hospital?'

'Was Lorbeer?'

'Who?'

'Lorbeer.' Rob spelled it. 'Lor like Lor' help us, beer like Heineken. Dutch mongrel. Red-haired or blond. Mid-fifties. Fat.'

'I've never heard of the man,' Woodrow retorted with absolute facial confidence while his bowels churned.

'Did you see anyone treat her?'

'No.'

'Do you know *how* she was being treated? What with?'

'No.'

'You never saw anybody give her a pill or inject her with anything?'

'I told you already: no hospital staff appeared in the ward during my presence.'

In his new-found leisure Rob found time to contemplate this reply, and his response to it. 'How about *non*-hospital staff?'

'Not in my presence.'

'Out of it?'

'How should I know that?'

'From Tessa. From what Tessa told you when she was being coherent,' Rob explained, and smiled so broadly that his good humour became a disturbing element, the precursor of a joke they had yet to share. 'Was the sick woman in Tessa's ward – whose baby she was feeding – receiving any medical attention from *anyone*, according to Tessa?' he asked patiently, composing his words to fit some unspecified parlour game. 'Was the sick woman being visited – or examined – or observed – or treated – by anyone, male or female, black or white, be they doctors, nurses, non-doctors, outsiders, insiders, hospital sweepers, visitors or plain *people*?' He sat back: wriggle out of that one.

Woodrow was becoming aware of the scale of his predicament. How much more did they know that they weren't revealing? The name Lorbeer had sounded in his head like a death knell. What other names were they about to throw at him? How much more could he deny and stay upright? What had Coleridge told them? Why was he withholding comfort, refusing to collude? Or was he confessing all, behind Woodrow's back?

'She had some story about the woman being visited by little men in white coats,' he replied disdainfully. 'I assumed she had dreamed it. Or was dreaming it while she related it. I gave it no credence.' And nor should you, he was saying.

'Why were the white coats visiting her? According to Tessa's story. In what you call her dream.'

'Because the men in white coats had killed the woman. At one point she called them the *coincidences*.' He had decided to tell the truth and ridicule it. 'I think she also called them greedy. They wished to cure her, but were unable to do so. The story was a load of rubbish.'

'Cure her how?'

'That was not revealed.'

'Killed her how, then?'

'I'm afraid she was equally unclear on that point.'

'Had she written it down at all?'

'The story? How could she?'

'Had she made notes? Did she read to you from notes?'

'I told you. To my knowledge she had no notebook.'

Rob tilted his long head to one side in order to observe Woodrow from a different angle, and perhaps a more telling one. 'Arnold Bluhm doesn't think the story was a load of rubbish. He doesn't think she was incoherent. Arnold reckons she was bang on target with everything she said. Right, Les?'

*   *   *

The blood had drained from Woodrow's face, he could feel it. Yet even in the aftershock of their words he remained as steady under fire as any other seasoned diplomat who must hold the fort. Somehow he found the voice. And the indignation. 'I'm sorry. Are you saying you've *found* Bluhm? That's utterly outrageous.'

'You mean you don't want us to find him?' Rob enquired, puzzled.

'I mean nothing of the kind. I mean that you're here on terms, and that if you have found Bluhm or spoken to him, you're under a clear obligation to share that knowledge with the High Commission.'

But Rob was already shaking his head. 'No way we've found him, sir. Wish we had. But we've found a few papers of his. Useful bits and pieces, as you might say, lying around his flat. Nothing sensational, unfortunately. A few case notes, which I suppose might interest someone. Copies of the odd rude letter the doctor sent to this or that firm, laboratory, or teaching hospital around the world. And that's about it, isn't it, Les?'

'Lying around's a bit of an exaggeration, actually,' Lesley admitted. 'Stashed is more like. There was one batch pasted to the back of a picture frame, another underneath the bathtub. Took us all day. Well, most of one, anyway.' She licked her finger and turned a page of her notebook.

'Plus the whoevers had forgotten his car,' Rob reminded her.

'More like a rubbish tip than a flat by the time they'd finished with it,' Lesley agreed. 'No art to it. Just smash and grab. Mind you, we get that in London these days. Someone's posted missing or dead in the papers, the villains are round there the same morning, helping themselves. Our crime prevention people are getting quite bothered about it. Mind if we bounce a couple more names off you a minute, Mr Woodrow?' she enquired, raising her grey eyes and turning them steadily upon him.

'Make yourselves at home,' said Woodrow, as if they hadn't.

'Kovacs – believed Hungarian – woman – young. *Raven*-black hair, *long* legs – he'll be giving us her vital statistics next – first name unknown, researcher.'

'You'd remember *her* all right,' said Rob.

'I'm afraid I don't.'

'Emrich. Medical doctor, research scientist, first qualified in Petersburg, took a German degree at Leipzig, did research work in Gdansk. Female. No description available. Name to you?'

'I've never heard of such a person in my life. Nobody of that description, nobody of that name, nobody of that origin or qualification.'

'Blimey. You really *haven't* heard of her, have you?'

'And our old friend Lorbeer,' Lesley came in apologetically. 'First name unknown, origins unknown, probably half Dutch or Boer, qualifications also a mystery. We're quoting from Bluhm's notes, that's the problem, so we're at his mercy, as you might say. He's got the three names ringed together like a flow chart, with itsy-bitsy descriptions inside each balloon. Lorbeer and the two women doctors. Lorbeer, Emrich, Kovacs. Quite a mouthful. We'd have brought you a copy but we're a bit queasy about using copiers at the moment. You know what the local police are like. And copy-shops – well, we wouldn't trust them to copy the Lord's Prayer, frankly, would we, Rob?'

'Use ours,' said Woodrow too quickly.

A ruminative silence followed, which to Woodrow was like a deafness where no cars went by, and no birds sang, and nobody walked down the corridor outside his door. It was broken by

Lesley doggedly describing Lorbeer as the man they would most like to question.

'Lorbeer's a floater. He's *believed* to be in the pharmaceutical business. He's *believed* to have been in and out of Nairobi a few times in the last year but the Kenyans can't trace him, surprisingly. He's *believed* to have visited Tessa's ward in the Uhuru Hospital when she was confined there. *Bullish*, that's another description we've had. I thought that was the Stock Exchange. And you're sure you've never come across a reddish-haired medical Lorbeer of bullish appearance at all, may be a doctor? Anywhere in your travels?'

'Never heard of the man. Or anyone like him.'

'We're getting that quite a lot, actually,' Rob commented from the wings.

'Tessa knew him. So did Bluhm,' said Lesley.

'That doesn't mean I knew him.'

'So what's the white plague when it's at home?' Rob asked.

'I've absolutely no idea.'

They left as they had left before: on an ever-growing question mark.

*   *   *

As soon as he was safely clear of them, Woodrow picked up the internal phone to Coleridge and, to his relief, heard his voice.

'Got a minute?'

'I suppose so.'

He found him sitting at his desk, one splayed hand to his brow. He was wearing yellow braces with horses on them. His expression was wary and belligerent.

'I need to be assured that we have London's backing in this,' Woodrow began, without sitting down.

'*We* being who exactly?'

'You and I.'

'And by London, you mean Pellegrin, I take it.'

'Why? Has anything changed?'

'Not to my knowledge.'

'Is it going to?'

'Not to my knowledge.'

'Well, does Pellegrin have backing? Put it that way.'

'Oh, Bernard *always* has backing.'

'So *do* we go on with this, or *don't* we?'

'Go on lying, you mean? Of course we do.'

'Then why can't we agree on – on what we say?'

'Good point. I don't know. If I were a God man, I'd sneak off and pray. But it's not as fucking easy as that. The girl's dead. That's one part of it. And we're alive. That's another part.'

'So have you told them the truth?'

'No, no, good Lord no. Memory like a sieve, me. Terribly sorry.'

'Are you *going* to tell them the truth?'

'Them? No, no. Never. Shits.'

'Then why can't we agree our stories?'

'That's it. Why not? Why not indeed. You've put your finger on it, Sandy. What's stopping us?'

* * *

'It's about your visit to the Uhuru Hospital, sir,' Lesley began crisply.

'I thought we'd rather *done* that one in our last session.'

'Your other visit. Your second one. A bit later. More a follow-up.'

'*Follow-up?* Follow-up of what?'

'A promise you made to her, apparently.'

'What *are* you talking about? I don't understand you.'

But Rob understood her perfectly, and said so. 'Sounded pretty good English to me, sir. Did you have a second meeting with Tessa at the hospital? Like four weeks after she'd been discharged, for instance? Like meet her in the ante-room to the post-natal clinic where she had an appointment? Because that's what it says you did in Arnold's notes, and he hasn't been wrong so far, not from what us ignorant folk can understand of them.'

Arnold, Woodrow recorded. Not Bluhm any more.

The soldier's son was debating with himself, and he was doing so with the glacial calculation that in crisis was his muse, while in his memory he was following the scene in the crowded hospital as if it had happened to someone else. Tessa is carrying a tapestry bag with cane handles. It is the first time he has seen it, but from now on and for the rest of her short life it is part of the tough image that she had formed of herself while she was lying in hospital with her dead baby in the morgue and a dying woman in the bed opposite her and the dying woman's baby at her breast. It goes with the less make-up and the shorter hair and the glower that is not so very different from the disbelieving stare that Lesley was bestowing on him this minute, while she waited for his edited version of the event. The light, as every-where in the hospital, is fickle. Huge shafts of sunlight bisect the half-dark of the interior. Small birds glide among the rafters. Tessa is standing with her back against a curved wall, next to an ill-smelling coffee shop with orange chairs. There is a crowd milling in and out of the sunbeams but he sees her immediately. She is holding the tapestry bag in both hands across her lower belly and standing the way tarts used to stand in doorways when he was young and scared. The wall is in shadow because the sunbeams don't reach the edges of the room and perhaps that's why Tessa has chosen this particular spot.

'You said you would listen to me when I was stronger,' she reminds him in a low, harsh voice he scarcely recognises.

It is the first time they have spoken since his visit to the ward. He sees her lips, so fragile without the discipline of lipstick. He sees the passion in her grey eyes, and it scares him as all passion scares him, his own included.

'The meeting you are referring to was not social,' he told Rob, avoiding Lesley's unrelenting gaze. 'It was professional. Tessa claimed to have stumbled on some documents which, if genuine, were politically sensitive. She asked me to meet her at the clinic so that she could hand them over.'

'Stumbled how?' asked Rob.

'She had outside connections. That's all I know. Friends in the aid agencies.'

'Such as Bluhm?'

'Among others. It was not the first time she had approached the High Commission with stories of high scandal, I should add. She made quite a habit of it.'

'By High Commission, you mean you?'

'If you mean me in my capacity as Head of Chancery, yes.'

'Why didn't she give them to Justin to hand over?'

'Justin must remain out of the equation. That was her determination, and presumably his.' Was he explaining too much, another peril? He plunged on. 'I respected that in her. To be frank, I respected any sign of scruple in her at all.'

'Why didn't she give them to Ghita?'

'Ghita is new and young and locally employed. She would not have been a suitable messenger.'

'So you met,' Lesley resumed. 'At the hospital. In the anteroom to the post-natal clinic. Wasn't that a rather conspicuous meeting place: two whites among all those Africans?'

You've been there, he thought, with another lurch into near-panic. You've visited the hospital. 'It wasn't Africans she was afraid of. It was whites. She was not to be reasoned with. When she was among Africans she felt safe.'

'Did she say that?'

'I deduced it.'

'What from?' – Rob.

'Her attitude during those last months. After the baby. To me, to the white community. To Bluhm. Bluhm could do no wrong. He was African and handsome and a doctor. And Ghita's half Indian' – a little wildly.

'How did Tessa make the appointment?' Rob asked.

'Sent a note to my house, by hand of her houseboy Mustafa.'

'Did your wife know you were meeting her?'

'Mustafa gave the note to my houseboy, who passed it to me.'

'And you didn't tell your wife?'

'I regarded the meeting as confidential.'

'Why didn't she phone you?'

'My wife?'

'Tessa.'

'She distrusted diplomatic telephones. With reason. We all do.'

'Why didn't she simply send the documents with Mustafa?'

'There were assurances she required of me. Guarantees.'

'Why didn't she bring the papers to you here?' Still Rob, pressing, pressing.

'For the reason I have already given you. She had reached a point where she did not trust the High Commission, did not wish to be tainted by it, did not wish to be seen entering or leaving it. You speak as if her actions were logical. It's hard to apply logic to Tessa's final months.'

'Why not Coleridge? Why did it have to be you all the time? You at her bedside, you at the clinic? Didn't she know anyone else here?'

For a perilous moment, Woodrow joined forces with his inquisitors. Why me indeed? he demanded of Tessa in a surge of angry self-pity. Because your bloody vanity would never let me go. Because it pleased you to hear me promise my soul away, when both of us knew that on the day of reckoning I wouldn't deliver it and you wouldn't accept it. Because grappling with me was like meeting head-on the English sicknesses you loved to hate. Because I was some kind of archetype for you, 'all ritual and no faith' – your words. We are standing face to face and half a foot apart and I am wondering why we are the same height till I realise that a raised step runs round the base of the curved wall and that, like other women there, you have climbed onto it, waiting to be spotted by your man. Our faces are at the same level and, despite your new austerity, it is Christmas again and I am dancing with you, smelling the sweet warm grass in your hair.

'So she gave you a bundle of papers,' Rob was saying. 'What were they about?'

I am taking the envelope from you and feeling the maddening

contact of your fingers as you give it to me. You are deliberately reviving the flame in me, you know it and can't help it, you are taking me over the edge again, although you know you will never come with me. I am wearing no jacket. You watch me while I undo my shirt buttons, slide the envelope against my naked skin and work it downward until its lower edge is stuck between the waistband of my trousers and my hip. You watch me again as I refasten the buttons, and I have the same shameful sensations that I would have if I had made love to you. As a good diplomat I offer you a cup of coffee in the shop. You decline. We stand face to face like dancers waiting for music to justify our proximity.

'Rob asked you what the papers were about,' Lesley was reminding Woodrow from outside his field of consciousness.

'They purported to describe a major scandal.'

'Here in Kenya?'

'The correspondence was classified.'

'By Tessa?'

'Don't be damn silly. How could she classify anything?' Woodrow snapped, and too late regretted his heat.

You must force them to act, Sandy, you are urging me. Your face is pale with suffering and courage. Your theatrical impulses have not been dimmed by the experience of real tragedy. Your eyes are brimming with the tears that, since the baby, swim in them all the time. Your voice urges, but it caresses too, working the scales the way it always did. *We need a champion, Sandy. Someone outside us. Someone official and capable. Promise me. If I can keep faith with you, you can keep faith with me.*

So I say it. Like you, I am carried away by the power of the moment. *I believe. In God. In love. In Tessa.* When we are on stage together, *I believe.* I swear myself away, which is what I do every time I come to you, and what you want me to do because you also are an addict of impossible relationships and theatrical scenes. *I promise*, I say, and you make me say it again. *I promise, I promise. I love you and I promise.* And that is your cue to kiss me on the lips that have spoken the shameful promise: one kiss to silence me and seal the contract; one quick hug to bind me and let me smell your hair.

'The papers were sent by bag to the relevant under-secretary in London,' Woodrow was explaining to Rob. 'At which point, they were classified.'

'Why?'

'Because of the serious allegations they contained.'

'Against?'

'Pass, I'm afraid.'

'A company? An individual?'

'Pass.'

'How many pages in the document, d'you reckon?'

'Fifteen. Twenty. There was an annexe of some sort.'

'Any photographs, illustrations, exhibits at all?'

'Pass.'

'Any tape recordings? Disks – taped confessions, statements?'

'Pass.'

'Which under-secretary did you send them to?'

'Sir Bernard Pellegrin.'

'Did you keep a copy locally?'

'It is a matter of policy to keep as little sensitive material here as possible.'

'Did you keep a copy or not?'

'No.'

'Were the papers typed?'

'By whom?'

'Were they typed or written by hand?'

'Typed.'

'What by?'

'I am not an expert on typewriters.'

'Electronic type? Off a word processor? A computer? Do you remember the *sort* of type? The font?'

Woodrow gave an ill-tempered shrug that was close to violence.

'It wasn't italicised, for instance?' Rob persisted.

'No.'

'Or that fake, half-joined-up handwriting they do?'

'It was perfectly ordinary roman type.'

'Electronic.'

'Yes.'

'Then you do remember. Was the annexe typed?'

'Probably.'

'The same type?'

'Probably.'

'So fifteen to twenty pages, give or take, of perfectly ordinary electronic roman type. Thank you. Did you hear back from London?'

'Eventually.'

'From Pellegrin?'

'It may have been Sir Bernard, it may have been one of his subordinates.'

'Saying?'

'No action was required.'

'Any reason given at all?' Still Rob, throwing his questions like punches.

'The so-called evidence offered in the document was tendentious. Any enquiries on the strength of it would achieve nothing and prejudice our relations with the host nation.'

'Did you tell Tessa that was the answer – no action?'

'Not in as many words.'

'What *did* you tell her?' Lesley asked.

Was it Woodrow's new policy of truth-telling that made him reply as he did – or some weaker instinct to confess? 'I told her what I felt would be acceptable to her, given her condition – given the loss she had suffered, and the importance she attached to the documents.'

Lesley had switched off the tape recorder and was packing away her notebooks. 'So what lie was acceptable to her, sir? In your judgment?' she asked.

'That London was on the case. Steps were being taken.'

For a blessed moment Woodrow believed the meeting was over. But Rob was still in there, slugging away.

'One more thing, if you don't mind, Mr Woodrow. Bell, Barker & Benjamin. Known otherwise as ThreeBees.'

Woodrow's posture did not alter by a fraction.

'Ads all over town. "ThreeBees, Busy for Africa." "Buzzing for You, Honey! I Love ThreeBees." Headquarters up the road. Big new glass building, looks like a Dalek.'

'What of them?'

'Only we pulled out their company profile last night, didn't we, Les? Quite an amazing outfit, you don't realise. Finger in every African pie but British to the core. Hotels, travel agencies, newspapers, security companies, banks, extractors of gold, coal and copper, importers of cars, boats and trucks – I could go on for ever. Plus a fine range of drugs. "ThreeBees Buzzing for Your Health." We spotted that one as we drove here this morning, didn't we, Les?'

'Just back down the road,' Lesley agreed.

'And they're hugger-mugger with Moi's Boys too, from all we hear. Private jets, all the girls you can eat.'

'I assume this is getting us somewhere.'

'Not really. I just wanted to watch your face while I talked about them. I've done it now. Thank you for your patience.'

Lesley was still busy with her bag. For all the interest she had shown in this exchange, she might not have heard it at all.

'People like you should be stopped, Mr Woodrow,' she mused aloud, with a puzzled shake of her wise head. 'You think you're solving the world's problems but actually you're the problem.'

'She means you're a fucking liar,' Rob explained.

This time, Woodrow did not escort them to the door. He remained at his post behind the desk, listening to the fading footsteps of his departing guests, then he called the front desk and asked, in the most casual tone, to be advised when they had cleared the building. On learning they had, he made his way swiftly to Coleridge's private office. Coleridge, he well knew, was away from his desk, conferring with the Kenyan Ministry of External Affairs. Mildren was speaking on the internal telephone, looking unpleasantly relaxed.

'This is urgent,' Woodrow said, in contrast to whatever Mildren thought he was doing.

Seated at Coleridge's empty desk, Woodrow watched Mildren extract a white lozenge from the High Commissioner's personal safe and insert it officiously in the digital phone.

'Who do you want, anyway?' Mildren asked, with the insolence peculiar to lower-class private secretaries to the great.

'Get out,' Woodrow said.

And as soon as he was alone, dialled the direct number of Sir Bernard Pellegrin.

*   *   *

They sat on the verandah, two Service colleagues enjoying an after-dinner nightcap under the relentless glare of intruder lights. Gloria had taken herself to the drawing room.

'There's no good way of saying this, Justin,' Woodrow began. 'So I'll say it anyway. The very strong probability is, she was raped. I'm terribly, terribly sorry. For her and for you.'

And Woodrow *was* sorry, he *must* be. Sometimes you don't have to feel something to know you feel it. Sometimes your senses are so trampled that another appalling piece of news is just one more tiresome detail to administer.

'This is ahead of the post-mortem of course, so it's premature and off the record,' he went on, avoiding Justin's eye. 'But they seem to have no doubt.' He felt a need to offer practical consolation. 'The police feel it's actually quite thought-clearing – to have a motive at least. It helps them with the broad thrust of the case, even if they can't point a finger yet.'

Justin was sitting to attention, holding his brandy glass in front of him with both hands, as if someone had handed it to him as a prize.

'Only a *probability*?' he objected at last. 'How very strange. How can that be?'

Woodrow had not imagined that, once again, he would be

subjected to questioning but in some ghastly way he welcomed it. A devil was driving him.

'Well, obviously they do have to ask themselves whether it could have been consensual. That's routine.'

'Consensual with whom?' Justin enquired, puzzled.

'Well, whoever – whoever they have in mind. We can't do their job for them, can we?'

'No. We can't. Poor you, Sandy. You seem to get all the dirty jobs. And now I am sure we should pay attention to Gloria. How right she was to leave us to ourselves. Sitting outside with the entire insect kingdom of Africa would be more than that fair English skin of hers could bear.' Developing a sudden aversion to Woodrow's proximity, he had stood up and pushed open the french window. 'Gloria, my dear, we have been neglecting you.'

CHAPTER SIX

Justin Quayle buried his much-murdered wife in a beautiful African cemetery called Langata under a jacaranda tree between her stillborn son Garth and a five-year-old Kikuyu boy who was watched over by a plaster-cast kneeling angel with a shield declaring he had joined the saints. Behind her lay Horatio John Williams of Dorset, with God, and at her feet Miranda K. Soper, loved for ever. But Garth and the little African boy, who was called Gitau Karanja, were her closest companions, and Tessa lay shoulder to shoulder with them, which was what Justin had wanted, and what Gloria, after an appropriate distribution of Justin's largesse, had obtained for him. Throughout the ceremony Justin stood apart from everyone, Tessa's grave to his left and Garth's to his right, and a full two paces forward of Woodrow and Gloria who until then had hovered protectively to either side of him, in part to give him comfort, in part to shield him from the attentions of the press which, ever mindful of its duty to the public, was relentless in its determination to obtain pictures and copy concerning the cuckolded British diplomat and would-be father whose butchered white wife – thus the bolder tabloids – had borne a baby by her African lover and now lay beside it in a corner of a foreign field – to quote no less than three of them on the same day – that was for ever England.

Beside the Woodrows and well clear of them stood Ghita Pearson in a sari, head forward and hands joined before her in the ageless attitude of mourning, and beside Ghita stood the deathly pale Porter Coleridge and his wife Veronica, and to Woodrow's eye it was as if they were lavishing on her the protection they would otherwise have lavished on their absent daughter Rosie.

Langata graveyard stands on a lush plateau of tall grass and red mud and flowering ornamental trees, both sad and joyful, a couple of miles from the town centre and just a short step from Kibera, one of Nairobi's larger slums, a vast brown smear of smoking tin houses overhung with a pall of sickly African dust, crammed into the Nairobi river valley without a hand's width between them. The population of Kibera is half a million and rising, and the valley is rich in deposits of sewage, plastic bags, colourful strands of old clothing, banana and orange peel, corn cobs, and anything else the city cares to dump in it. Across the road from the graveyard are the dapper offices of the Kenyan Tourist Board and the entrance to the Nairobi Game Park, and somewhere behind them the ramshackle hutments of Wilson airport, Kenya's oldest.

To both of the Woodrows and many of Tessa's mourners there was something ominous as well as heroic in Justin's solitude as the moment of interment approached. He seemed to be taking leave not just of Tessa but of his career, of Nairobi, of his stillborn son, and of his entire life till now. His perilous proximity to the grave's edge appeared to signal this. There was the inescapable suggestion that a good deal of the Justin they knew, and perhaps all of it, was going with her to the hereafter. Only one living person seemed to merit his attention, Woodrow noticed, and that was not the priest, it was not the sentinel figure of Ghita Pearson, it was not the reticent and white-faced Porter Coleridge his Head of Mission, nor the journalists who jockeyed with each other for a better shot, a better view, nor the long-jawed English wives locked in empathetic grief for their departed sister whose fate could so easily have been their own, nor the dozen overweight Kenyan policemen who tugged at their leather belts.

It was Kioko. It was the boy who had been sitting on the floor of Tessa's ward in the Uhuru Hospital, watching his sister die; who had walked ten hours from his village to be with her at the end, and had walked ten more to be with Tessa today. Justin and Kioko saw each other at the same time and, having done so, held each other's gaze in a complicitous exchange. Kioko was the youngest person present, Woodrow noticed. In response to tribal tradition, Justin had requested that young people stay away.

White gateposts marked the graveyard's entrance as Tessa's cortège arrived. Giant cacti, red mud tracks and docile sellers of bananas, plantain and ice-creams lined the path to her grave. The priest was black and old and grizzled. Woodrow had a recollection of shaking his hand at one of Tessa's parties. But the priest's love of Tessa was effusive, and his belief in the afterlife so fervent, and the din of road and air traffic so persistent – not to mention the proximity of other funerals and the blare of spiritual music from mourners' lorries and the competing orators with bullhorns who harangued the rings of friends and family picnicking on the grass around their loved ones' coffins – that it was not surprising that only a few of the holy man's winged words reached the ear of his audience. And Justin, if he heard them at all, showed no sign of having done so. Dapper as ever in the dark double-breasted suit he had mustered for the occasion, he kept his gaze fixed on the boy Kioko who, like Justin, had sought out his own bit of space apart from everyone, and appeared to have hanged himself in it, for his spindly feet scarcely touched the ground and his arms swung raggedly at his side and his long crooked head was craned in a posture of permanent enquiry.

Tessa's final journey had not been a smooth one, but neither

Woodrow nor Gloria would have wished it to be. Each tacitly found it fitting that her last act should contain the element of unpredictability that had characterised her life. The Woodrow household had risen early although there was nothing to rise early for, except that in the middle of the night Gloria realised she had no dark hat. A crack-of-dawn phone call established that Elena had two, but they were both a bit twenties and aviator-like, did Gloria mind? An official Mercedes was despatched from her Greek husband's residence, conveying a black hat in a Harrod's plastic carrier. Gloria returned it, preferring a black lace headscarf of her mother's: she would wear it like a *mantilla*. After all, Tessa *was* half Italian, she explained.

'Spanish, darling,' Elena replied.

'Nonsense,' Gloria riposted. 'Her mother was a Tuscan contessa, it said so in the *Telegraph*.'

'The *mantilla*, darling,' Elena patiently corrected her. '*Mantillas* are Spanish, not Italian, I'm afraid.'

'Well, her *mother* was bloody well Italian,' Gloria snapped – only to ring again five minutes later, blaming her temper on the stress.

By then the Woodrow boys had been bundled off to school and Woodrow himself had left for the High Commission and Justin was hovering in the dining room wearing his suit and tie and wanting flowers. Not flowers from Gloria's garden, but his own. He wanted the yellow scenting freesias he grew for her all year round, he said, and always had waiting for her in the living room when she came back from her field trips. He wanted two dozen of them at the least for Tessa's coffin. Gloria's deliberations on how best to obtain these were interrupted by a confused call from a Nairobi newspaper purporting to announce that Bluhm's corpse had been found in a dried-up river bed fifty miles east of Lake Turkana, and had anyone anything to say about it? Gloria bawled 'No comment' into the receiver and slammed it down. But she was shaken, and in two minds whether or not to share the news with Justin now, or wait till the funeral was over. She was therefore greatly relieved to receive a call from Mildren not five minutes later saying that Woodrow was in a meeting but rumours about Bluhm's corpse were drivel: the body, for which a tribe of Somali bandits was demanding ten thousand dollars, was at least a hundred years old, and more like a thousand, and was it possible for him to have a tiny word with Justin?

Gloria brought Justin to the telephone and remained officiously at his side while he said yes – that suited him – you're very kind, and he would make sure he was prepared. But what Mildren was being kind about and what Justin would prepare himself for remained obscure. And no thank you – Justin said emphatically to Mildren, adding to the mystery – he did not wish to be met on arrival, he preferred to make his own arrangements. After which he rang off and asked – rather pointedly, considering everything she had done for him – to be left alone in the dining room to make a reverse-charge call to his solicitor in London, a thing he had done twice before in the last few days, also without admitting Gloria to his deliberations. With a show of discretion she therefore removed herself to the kitchen in order to listen at the hatch – only to find a grief-stricken Mustafa, who had arrived unbidden at the back door with a basketful of yellow freesias which on his own initiative he had picked from Justin's garden. Armed with this excuse Gloria marched into the dining room, hoping at least to catch the end of Justin's conversation, but he was ringing off as she entered.

Suddenly, without more time passing, everything was late. Gloria had finished dressing but hadn't *touched* her face, nobody had eaten a *thing* and it was past lunchtime, Woodrow was waiting outside in the Volkswagen, Justin was standing in the hall clutching his freesias – now bound into a posy – Juma was waving a plate of cheese sandwiches at everyone and Gloria was trying to decide whether to tie the *mantilla* under her chin or drape it over her shoulders like her mother.

Seated on the rear seat of the van next to Justin with Woodrow on the other side of her, Gloria privately acknowledged what Elena had been telling her for several days: that she had fallen head over heels in love with Justin, a thing that hadn't happened to her for years, and it was an absolute agony to think he would be gone any day. On the other hand, as Elena had pointed out, his departure would at least allow her to get her head straight and resume normal marital services. And if it should turn out that absence only made the heart grow fonder, well, as Elena had daringly suggested, Gloria could always do something about it in London.

The drive through the city struck Gloria as more than usually bumpy and she was too conscious for her comfort of the warmth of Justin's thigh against her own. By the time the Volkswagen pulled up at the funeral home, a lump had formed in her throat, her handkerchief was a damp ball in the palm of her hand and she no longer knew whether she was grieving for Tessa or Justin. The rear doors of the van were opened from outside, Justin and Woodrow hopped out, leaving her alone on the back seat with Livingstone in the front. No journalists, she recorded gratefully, struggling to regain her composure. Or none yet. She watched her two men through the windscreen as they climbed the front steps of a single-storey granite building with a touch of the Tudors about the eaves. Justin with his tailored suit and perfect mane of grey-black hair that you never saw him brush or comb, clutching yellow freesias – and that cavalry officer's walk he had, and for all she knew all half-Dudleys had, right shoulder forward. Why did Justin always seem to lead and Sandy follow? And why was Sandy so *menial* these days, so *butler*-like? she complained to herself. And it's time he bought himself a new suit; that serge thing makes him look like a private detective.

They disappeared into the entrance lobby. 'Papers to sign, sweet,' Sandy had said in a superior voice. 'Releases for the deceased's body and that kind of nonsense.' Why does he treat me like his Little Woman suddenly? Has he forgotten I arranged the whole bloody funeral? A gaggle of black-clad bearers had formed at the side entrance of the funeral home. Doors were opening, a black hearse was backing towards them, the word HEARSE gratuitously painted in white letters a foot high on its

122

side. Gloria caught a glimpse of honey-varnished wood and yellow freesias as the coffin slid between black jackets into the open back. They must have taped the posy to the lid; how else did you get freesias to sit tight on a coffin lid? Justin thought of everything. The hearse pulled out of the forecourt, bearers aboard. Gloria had a big sniff, then blew her nose.

'It is bad, madam,' Livingstone intoned from the front. 'It is very, very bad.'

'It is indeed, Livingstone,' said Gloria, grateful for the formality of the exchange. You are about to be watched, young woman, she warned herself firmly. Time to chin up and set an example. The back doors slammed open.

'All right, girl?' Woodrow asked cheerfully, crashing down beside her. 'They were marvellous, weren't they, Justin? Very sympathetic, very professional.'

Don't you *dare* call me girl, she told him furiously – but not aloud.

*   *   *

Entering St Andrew's Church, Woodrow took stock of the congregation. In a single sweep he spotted the pallid Coleridges and behind them Donohue and his weird wife Maud looking like an ex-Gaiety Girl fallen on hard times, and next to them Mildren alias Mildred and an anorexic blonde who was held to be sharing his flat. The Heavy Mob from the Muthaiga Club – Tessa's phrase – had formed a military square. Across the aisle he picked out a contingent from the World Food Programme and another that consisted entirely of African women, some in hats, others in jeans, but all with the determined glower of combat that was the hallmark of Tessa's radical friends. Behind them stood a cluster of lost, Gallic-looking, vaguely arrogant young men and women, the women with their heads covered, the men in open necks and designer stubble. Woodrow, after some puzzlement, concluded that they were fellow members of Bluhm's Belgian organisation. Must be wondering whether they're going to be back here next week for Arnold, he thought brutally. The Quayles' illegal servants were ranged alongside them: Mustafa the houseboy, Esmeralda from South Sudan and the one-armed Ugandan, name unknown. And in the front row, towering over her furtive little Greek husband, stood the upholstered, carrot-haired figure of Darling Elena herself, Woodrow's bête noire, decked out in her grandmother's funereal jet jewellery.

'Now, darling, should I wear the jet or is it over the top?' she had needed to know of Gloria at eight this morning. Not without mischief, Gloria had counselled boldness.

'On other people, frankly El, it might be a tad too much. But with *your* colouring, darling – go for it.'

And no policemen, he noticed with gratification, neither Kenyan nor British. Had Bernard Pellegrin's potions worked their magic? Whisper who dares.

He stole another look at Coleridge, so whey-faced, so martyred. He remembered their bizarre conversation in the Residence last Saturday, and cursed him for an indecisive prig. His gaze returned to Tessa's coffin lying in state before the altar, Justin's yellow freesias safely aboard. Tears filled his eyes, to be sharply returned to where they came from. The organ was playing the Nunc Dimittis and Gloria, word-perfect, was singing lustily along. House evensong at her boarding school, Woodrow was thinking. Or mine. He hated both establishments equally. Sandy and Gloria, born unfree. The difference is, I know it and she doesn't. *Lord, now lettest thou thy servant depart in peace.* Sometimes I really wish I could. Depart and never come back. But where would the peace be? His eye again rested on the coffin. I loved you. So much easier to say, now it's in the past tense. I loved you. I was the control freak who couldn't control himself, you were good enough to tell me. Well, now look what's happened to you. And look *why* it's happened to you.

And no, I never heard of Lorbeer. I know no long-legged Hungarian beauties called Kovacs and I do not, *will* not listen to any more unproven, unspoken theories that are tolling like tower bells inside my head, and I am *totally* uninterested in the sleek olive shoulders of the spectral Ghita Pearson in her sari. What I do know is: after you, nobody need ever know again what a timorous child inhabits this soldier's body.

*   *   *

Needing to distract himself, Woodrow embarked on an energetic study of the church windows. Male saints, all white, no Bluhms. Tessa would go ballistic. Memorial window commemorating one pretty white boy in a sailor suit symbolically surrounded by adoring jungle animals. *A good hyena smells blood ten kilometres away.* Tears again threatening, Woodrow forced his attentions on dear old St Andrew himself, a dead ringer for Macpherson the gillie that time we drove the boys to Loch Awe to fish the salmon. The fierce Scottish eye, the rusty Scottish beard. What must they make of us? he marvelled, transferring his misty gaze to the black faces in the congregation. What did we imagine we were doing here, back in those days, plugging our white British God and our white Scottish saint while we used the country as an adventure playground for derelict upper-class swingers?

'Personally, I'm trying to make amends,' you reply when flirtatiously I put the same question to you on the floor of the Muthaiga Club. But you never answer a question without turning it round and using it in evidence against me: 'And what are *you* doing here, Mr Woodrow?' you demand. The band is boisterous and we are having to dance close to hear each other at all. Yes, those are my breasts, your eyes say when I dare to look down. Yes, those are my hips, gyrating while you hold me by the waist. You may look at them too, feast your eyes on them. Most men do, and you needn't try to be the exception.

'I suppose what I'm really doing is helping *Kenyans* to husband the things we've given them,' I yell pompously above the music and feel your body stiffen and slip away almost before I've finished the sentence.

125

'We didn't bloody *give* them a thing! They *took* it! At the end of a bloody gun! We gave them nothing – nothing!'

Woodrow swung sharply round. Gloria beside him did the same and so, from the other side of the aisle, did the Coleridges. A scream from outside the church had been followed by the smash of something big and glassy breaking. Through the open doorway Woodrow saw the forecourt gates being dragged shut by two frightened vergers in black suits as helmeted police formed a cordon along the railings, brandishing metal-tipped riot sticks in both hands, like baseball players limbering for a strike. In the street where the students had gathered a tree was burning and a couple of cars lay belly-up beneath it, their occupants too terrified to clamber out. To roars of encouragement from the crowd, a glistening black limousine, a Volvo like Woodrow's, was rising shakily from the ground, borne aloft by a swarm of young men and women. It rose, it lurched, it flipped, first to its side, then onto its back, before falling with a huge bang, dead beside its fellows. The police charged. Whatever they had been waiting for till then, it had happened. One second they were lounging, the next they were hacking themselves a red path through the fleeing rabble, only pausing to rain more blows on those they had brought down. An armoured van drew up, half a dozen bleeding bodies were tossed into it.

'University's an absolute tinderbox, old chap,' Donohue had advised when Woodrow had consulted him on risk. 'Grants have stopped dead, staff aren't being paid, places going to the rich and stupid, dormitories and classrooms packed out, loos all blocked, doors all pinched, fire risk rampant and they're cooking over charcoal in the corridors. They've no power, and no electric light to study by, and no books to study in. The poorest students are taking to the streets because the government is privatising the higher education system without consulting anyone and education is strictly for the rich, plus the exam results are rigged and the government is trying to force students to get their education abroad. And yesterday the police killed a couple of students, which for some reason their friends refuse to take lightly. Any more questions?'

The church gates opened, the organ struck up again. God's business could resume.

*　　*　　*

In the cemetery the heat was aggressive and personal. The grizzled old priest had ceased speaking but the clamour had not subsided and the sun beat through it like a flail. To one side of Woodrow a ghetto-blaster was playing a rock version of Hail Mary at full throttle to a group of black nuns in grey habits. To the other, a football squad of blazers was gathered round a coconut shy of empty beer cans while a soloist sang goodbye to a team-mate. And Wilson airport must have been holding some kind of air day, because brightly painted small planes were zooming overhead at twenty-second intervals. The old priest lowered his prayer book. The bearers stepped to the coffin. Each grasped an end of webbing. Justin, still alone, seemed to sway. Woodrow started forward to support him but Gloria restrained him with a gloved claw.

'He wants her to *himself*, idiot,' she hissed through her tears.

The press showed no such tact. This was the shot they had come for: black bearers lower murdered white woman into African soil, watched by husband she deceived. A pock-faced man with a crew-cut and cameras bouncing on his belly offered Justin a trowel laden with earth, hoping for a shot of the widower pouring it on the coffin. Justin brushed it aside. As he did so, his gaze fell on two ragged men who were trundling a wooden wheelbarrow with a flat tyre to the grave's edge. Wet cement was slopping over its gunwales.

'What are you doing, please?' he demanded of them, so sharply that every face turned to him. 'Will somebody kindly find out from these gentlemen what they are intending to do with their cement? Sandy, I need an interpreter, please.'

Ignoring Gloria, Woodrow the general's son strode quickly

to Justin's side. Wiry Sheila from Tim Donohue's department spoke to the men, then to Justin.

'They say they do it for all rich people, Justin,' Sheila said.

'Do what exactly? I don't understand you. Please explain.'

'The cement. It's to keep out intruders. Robbers. Rich people are buried in wedding rings and nice clothes. Wazungu are a favourite target. They say the cement's an insurance policy.'

'Who instructed them to do this?'

'No one. It's five thousand shillings.'

'They're to go, please. Kindly tell them that, will you, Sheila? I do not wish their services and I shall pay them no money. They're to take their barrow and leave.' But then, perhaps not trusting her to impart his message with sufficient vigour, Justin marched over to them and, placing himself between their barrow and the grave's edge, struck out an arm, Moses-like, pointing over the heads of the mourners. 'Go, please,' he ordered. 'Leave at once. Thank you.'

The mourners parted to make a path along the line his out-stretched arm commanded. The men with their barrow scuttled down it. Justin watched them out of sight. In the vibrating heat the men seemed to ride straight into the blank sky. Justin turned his body round, stiffly like a toy soldier, until he was addressing the press pack.

'I would like you all to go, please,' he said in the silence that had formed inside the din. 'You have been very kind. Thank you. Goodbye.'

Quietly, and to the amazement of the rest, the journalists stowed their cameras and their notebooks and, with mumbles like 'See you, Justin,' quit the field. Justin returned to his place of solitude at Tessa's head. As he did so, a group of African women trooped forward and arranged themselves in a horseshoe round the foot of the grave. Each wore the same uniform: a blue-flowered frilly dress and headscarf of the same material. Separately they might have looked lost, but as a group they looked united. They began singing, at first softly. Nobody conducted them, there were no instruments to sing to, most of the choir were weeping but they didn't let their tears affect their voices. They sang in harmony, in English and kiSwahili alternately, gathering power in the repetition: *Kwa heri, Mama Tessa . . . Little Mama, goodbye . . .* Woodrow tried to catch the other words. *Kwa heri, Tessa . . . Tessa our friend, goodbye . . . You came to us, Mama Tessa, Little Mama, you gave us your heart . . . Kwa heri, Tessa, goodbye.*

'Where the hell did they spring from?' he asked Gloria out of the corner of his mouth.

'Down the hill,' Gloria muttered, nodding her head towards Kibera slum.

The singing swelled as the coffin was lowered into the ground. Justin watched it descend, then winced as it struck bottom, then winced again as the first shovel-load of earth clattered onto the lid and a second crashed into the freesias, dirtying the petals. A frightful howl went up, as short as the shriek of a rusty hinge when a door is flung back, but long enough for Woodrow to watch Ghita Pearson collapse to her knees in slow motion, then roll onto one shapely hip as she buried her face in her hands; then, just as improbably, rise again on the arm of Veronica Coleridge and resume her mourner's pose.

Did Justin call out something to Kioko? Or did Kioko act of his own accord? Light as a shadow, he had moved to Justin's side and, in an unashamed gesture of affection, grasped his hand. Through a fresh flood of tears, Gloria saw their linked hands fidget till they found a mutually comfortable grip. Thus joined, the bereaved husband and bereaved brother watched Tessa's coffin disappear beneath the soil.

*   *   *

Justin left Nairobi the same night. Woodrow, to Gloria's eternal hurt, had given her no warning. The dinner table was laid for three, Gloria herself had uncorked the claret and put a duck in the oven to cheer us all up. She heard a footfall from the hall and assumed to her pleasure that Justin had decided on pre-dinner drinkies, just the two of us while Sandy reads *Biggles* to the boys upstairs. And suddenly there stood his scruffy Gladstone bag, accompanied by a mossy grey suitcase that Mustafa had brought for him, parked in the hall with labels on them, and Justin standing beside them with his raincoat over his arm and a night-bag on his shoulder, wanting to give her back the wine-store key.

'But Justin, you're not *off*!'

'You've all been immensely kind to me, Gloria. I shall never know how to thank you.'

'Sorry about this, darling,' Woodrow sang cheerfully, tripping down the stairs two at a time. 'Bit cloak and dagger, I'm afraid. Didn't want the servants gossiping. Only way to play it.'

At which moment there came a ping on the doorbell, and it was Livingstone the driver with a red Peugeot he'd borrowed from a friend to avoid telltale diplomatic licence plates at the airport. And slumped in the passenger seat, Mustafa, glowering ahead of him like his own effigy.

'But we must come with you, Justin! We must see you off! I insist! I've got to give you one of my watercolours! What's going to happen to you the other end?' Gloria cried miserably. 'We can't just let you go off into the night like this – *darling*! –'

The *darling* was technically addressed to Woodrow, but it might as well have been meant for Justin, for as she blurted it she dissolved into uncontrollable tears, the last of a long and tearful day. Sobbing wretchedly, she grasped Justin against her, punching his back and rolling her cheek against him and whispering, 'Oh don't go, oh please, oh Justin,' and other less decipherable exhortations before bravely thrusting herself free of him, elbowing her husband out of the light and charging up the stairs to her bedroom and slamming the door.

'Bit overwrought,' Woodrow explained, grinning.

'We all are,' said Justin, accepting Woodrow's hand and shaking it. 'Thank you again, Sandy.'

'We'll be in touch.'

'Indeed.'

'And you're quite sure you don't want a reception party the other end? They're all busting to do their stuff.'

'Quite sure, thank you. Tessa's lawyers are preparing for my arrival.'

And the next minute Justin was walking down the steps to the red car, with Mustafa one side of him with the Gladstone bag, and Livingstone carrying his grey suitcase on the other.

'I have left envelopes for you all with Mr Woodrow,' Justin told Mustafa as they drove. 'And this is to be handed privately to Ghita Pearson. And you know I mean privately.'

'We know you will always be a good man, Mzee,' said Mustafa prophetically, consigning the envelope to the recesses of his cotton jacket. But there was no forgiveness in his voice for leaving Africa.

*   *   *

The airport, despite its recent face-lift, was in chaos. Travel-weary groups of scalded tourists made long lines, harangued tour guides and frantically bundled huge rucksacks into X-ray machines. Check-in clerks puzzled over every ticket and murmured interminably into telephones. Incomprehensible loud-speaker announcements spread panic while porters and policemen looked idly on. But Woodrow had arranged everything. Justin had barely emerged from the car before a male British Airways representative spirited him to a small office, safe from public gaze.

'I'd like my friends to come with me, please,' Justin said.

'No problem.'

With Livingstone and Mustafa hovering behind him, he was handed a boarding pass in the name of Mr Alfred Brown. He looked on passively while his grey suitcase was similarly labelled.

'And I shall take this one into the cabin with me,' he announced, as an edict.

The representative, a blond New Zealand boy, affected to

weigh the Gladstone in his hand and let out an exaggerated grunt of exertion. 'Family silver, is it, sir?'

'My host's,' said Justin, duly entering into the joke, but there was enough in his face to suggest that the issue was not negotiable.

'If *you* can carry it, sir, so can *we*,' said the blond representative, passing the bag back to him. 'Have a nice flight, Mr Brown. We'll be taking you through the arrivals side, if it's all the same to you.'

'You're very kind.'

Turning to say his last goodbyes, Justin seized Livingstone's enormous fists in a double handshake. But for Mustafa the moment was too much. Silently as ever, he had slipped away. The Gladstone firmly in his grasp, Justin entered the arrivals hall in the wake of his guide, to find himself staring at a giant buxom woman of no definable race grinning down at him from the wall. She was twenty feet tall and five feet across her widest point and she was the only commercial advertisement in the entire hall. She was dressed in nurse's uniform and had three golden bees on each shoulder. Three more were prominently displayed on the breast pocket of her white tunic, and she was offering a tray of pharmaceutical delicacies to a vaguely multiracial family of happy children and their parents. The tray held something for each of them: bottles of gold-brown medicine that looked more like whisky for the dad, chocolate-coated pills just right for munching by the kiddies, and for the mum beauty products decorated with naked goddesses reaching for the sun. Blazoned across the top and bottom of the poster, violent puce lettering proclaimed the joyous message to all mankind:

ThreeBees

BUZZY FOR THE HEALTH OF AFRICA!

The poster held him.

Exactly as it had held Tessa.

Staring rigidly up at it, Justin is listening to her joyous protestations at his right side. Dizzy from travel, laden with last-

132

minute hand luggage, the two of them have minutes earlier arrived here from London for the first time. Neither has set foot on the African continent before. Kenya – all Africa – awaits them. But it is this poster that commands Tessa's excited interest.

'Justin, *look*! You're not *looking*.'

'What is it? Of course I am.'

'They've hijacked our bloody bees! Somebody thinks he's Napoleon! It's absolutely brazen. It's an outrage. You must do something!'

And so it was. An outrage. A hilarious one. Napoleon's three bees, symbols of his glory, treasured emblems of Tessa's beloved island of Elba where the great man had whittled away his first exile, had been shamelessly deported to Kenya and sold into commercial slavery. Pondering the same poster now, Justin could only marvel at the obscenity of life's coincidence.

CHAPTER SEVEN

Perched stiffly in his upgraded seat at the front of the plane, the Gladstone bag above him in the overhead locker, Justin Quayle stared past his reflection into the blackness of space. He was free. Not pardoned, not reconciled, not comforted, not resolved. Not free of the nightmares that told him she was dead, and waking to discover they were true. Not free of the survivor's guilt. Not free of fretting about Arnold. But free at last to mourn in his own way. Free of his dreadful cell. Of the gaolers he had learned to detest. Of circling his room like a convict, driven half crazy by the dazzlement of his mind and the squalor of his confinement. Free of the silence of his own voice, of sitting on the edge of his bed asking *why?* on and on. Free of the shameful moments when he was so low and tired and drained that he almost succeeded in convincing himself that he didn't give a damn, the marriage had been a madness anyway and was over, so be thankful. And if grief, as he had read somewhere, was a species of idleness, then free of the idleness that thought of nothing but its grief.

Free also of his interrogation by the police, when a Justin he didn't recognise strode to the centre of the stage and, in a series of immaculately sculpted sentences, laid his burden at the feet of his bemused interrogators – or as much of it as a puzzled instinct told him it was prudent to reveal. They began by accusing him of murder.

'There's a scenario hanging over us here, Justin,' Lesley explains apologetically, 'and we have to put it to you straight away, so that you're aware of it, although we know it's hurtful. It's called a love triangle, and you're the jealous husband and you've organised a contract killing while your wife and her lover are as far away from you as possible, which is always good for the alibi. You had them both killed, which was what you wanted for your vengeance. You had Arnold Bluhm's body taken out of the jeep and lost so that we'd think Arnold Bluhm was the killer and not you. Lake Turkana's full of crocodiles, so losing Arnold wouldn't be a problem. Plus there's a nice inheritance coming your way by all accounts, which doubles up the motive.'

They are watching him, he is well aware, for signs of guilt or innocence or outrage or despair – for signs of *something* anyway – and watching him in vain, because, unlike Woodrow, Justin at first does absolutely nothing. He sits groomed and pensive and remote on Woodrow's reproduction carving chair, his fingertips set to the table as if he has just played a chord of music and is listening to it fade away. Lesley is accusing him of murder, yet all she gets is a small frown linking him to his inner world.

'I had rather understood, from the little Woodrow has been good enough to tell me of the progress of your enquiries,' Justin objects, more in the plaintive manner of an academic than a grieving husband, 'that your prevailing theory was of a *random* killing, not a planned affair.'

'Woodrow's full of shit,' says Rob, keeping his voice down in deference to their hostess.

There is no tape recorder on the table yet. The notebooks of many colours lie untouched in Lesley's useful bag. There is nothing to hurry or formalise the occasion. Gloria has brought a tray of tea and, after a lengthy dissertation on the recent demise of her bull terrier, reluctantly departed.

'We found the marks of a second vehicle parked five miles from the scene of the murder,' Lesley explains. 'It was lying up in a gully south-west of the spot where Tessa was murdered. We found an oil patch, plus the remains of a fire.' Justin blinks, as if the daylight is a bit too bright, then politely inclines his head to show he is still listening. 'Plus freshly buried beer bottles and cigarette ends,' she goes on, laying all this at Justin's door. 'When Tessa's jeep drove by, the mystery wagon pulled out behind and tailed it. Then it pulled alongside. One of the front wheels of Tessa's jeep was shot off with a hunting rifle. That doesn't look like a random killing to us.'

'More like corporate murder, as we like to call it,' Rob explains. 'Planned and executed by paid professionals at the behest of a person or persons unknown. Whoever tipped them off knew Tessa's plans inside out.'

'And the rape?' Justin enquires with feigned detachment, keeping his eyes fixed on his folded hands.

'Cosmetic or incidental,' Rob retorts crisply. 'Villains lost their heads or did it with forethought.'

'Which brings us back to motive, Justin,' Lesley says.

'Yours,' says Rob. 'Unless you've got a better idea.'

Their two faces are trained on Justin's like cameras, one to either side of him, but Justin remains as impervious to their double stare as he is to innuendo. Perhaps in his internal isolation he is not aware of either. Lesley lowers one hand to her useful bag in order to locate the tape recorder, but thinks better of it. The hand remains caught in flagrante, while the rest of her is turned to Justin, to this man of impeccably drafted sentences, this sitting committee of one.

'But I know no killers, you see,' he is objecting – pointing out the flaw in their argument as he peers ahead of him with emptied eyes. 'I hired nobody, instructed nobody, I'm afraid. I had nothing whatever to do with my wife's murder. Not in the sense you are implying. I did not wish it, I did not engineer it.'

His voice falters, and strikes an embarrassing kink. 'I regret it beyond words.'

And this with such finality that for an instant the police officers appear to have nowhere to go, preferring to study Gloria's watercolours of Singapore, which hang in a row across the brick fireplace, each priced at '£199 and NO BLOODY VAT!', each with the same scrubbed sky and palm tree and flock of birds and her name in lettering loud enough to read across the road, plus a date for the benefit of collectors.

Until Rob, who has the brashness, if not the self-assurance of his age, throws up his long thin head and blurts, 'So you didn't mind your wife and Bluhm sleeping together, I suppose? A lot of husbands could get a bit ratty about a thing like that.' Then snaps his mouth shut, waiting for Justin to do whatever Rob's righteous expectations require deceived husbands to do in such cases: weep, blush, rage against their own inadequacies or the perfidy of their friends. If so, Justin disappoints him.

'That is simply not the point,' he replies, with such force that he takes himself by surprise, and sits upright, and peers round him as if to see who has spoken out of turn, and reprimand the fellow. 'It may be the point for the newspapers. It may be the point for you. It was never the point for me, and it is not the point now.'

'So what *is* the point?' Rob demands.

'I failed her.'

'How? Not up to it, you mean?' – a male sneer – 'failed her in the bedroom, did you?'

Justin is shaking his head. 'By detaching myself.' His voice fell to a murmur. 'By letting her go it alone. By emigrating from her in my mind. By making an immoral contract with her. One that I should never have allowed. And nor should she.'

'What was that then?' Lesley asks sweet as milk after Rob's deliberate roughness.

'She follows her conscience, I get on with my job. It was an immoral distinction. It should never have been made. It was like sending her off to church and telling her to pray for both of us. It was like drawing a chalk-line down the middle of our house and saying see you in bed.'

Unfazed by the frankness of these admissions, and the nights and days of self-recrimination suggested by them, Rob makes to challenge him. His lugubrious face is set in the same incredulous sneer, his mouth round and open like the muzzle of a large gun. But Lesley is quicker than Rob today. The woman in her is wide awake and listening to sounds that Rob's aggressively male ear can't catch. Rob turns to her, seeking her permission for something: to challenge him again with Arnold Bluhm perhaps, or with some other telling question that will bring him nearer to the murder. But Lesley shakes her head and, lifting her hand from the region of the bag, surreptitiously pats the air, meaning 'slowly, slowly'.

'So how did the two of you get together in the first place, anyway?' she asks Justin, as one might ask a chance acquaintance on a long journey.

And this is genius on Lesley's part: to offer him a woman's ear and a stranger's understanding; to call a halt like this, and lead him from his present battlefield to the unthreatened meadows of his past. And Justin responds to her appeal. He relaxes his shoulders, half closes his eyes and in a distant, deeply private tone of recollection tells it the way it was, exactly as he had told it to himself a hundred times in as many tormented hours.

*   *   *

'So when is a state not a state, in your opinion, Mr Quayle?' Tessa enquired sweetly, one idle midday in Cambridge four years ago, in an ancient attic lecture-room with dusty sunbeams sloping through the skylight. They are the first words she ever addressed to him, and they trigger a burst of laughter from the languid audience of fifty fellow lawyers who, like Tessa, had enrolled themselves for a two-week summer seminar on Law and the Administered Society. Justin repeats them now. How he came to be standing alone on the daïs, in a three-piece grey flannel suit by Hayward, clutching a lectern in both hands, is the story of his life so far, he explains, speaking away from both of them, into the fake Tudor recesses of the Woodrow dining room. 'Quayle will do it!' some acolyte in the permanent under-secretary's private office had cried, late last night, not eleven hours before the lecture was due to be given. 'Get me Quayle!' Quayle the professional bachelor, he meant, postable Quayle, the ageing debs' delight, last of a dying breed, thank God, just back from bloody Bosnia and marked for Africa but not yet. Quayle the *spare male*, worth knowing if you're giving a dinner party and stuck, perfect manners, probably gay – except he wasn't, as a few of the better-looking wives had reason to know, even if they weren't telling.

'Justin, is that you? – Haggarty. You were in College a couple of years ahead of me. Look here, the PUS is delivering a speech at Cambridge tomorrow to a bunch of aspiring lawyers, except he can't. He's got to leave for Washington in an hour –'

And Justin the good chap already talking himself into it with: 'Well, if it's already *written*, I suppose – if it's only a matter of *reading* it –'

And Haggarty cutting him short with, 'I'll have his car and driver standing outside your house at the stroke of nine, not a minute later. The lecture's crap. He wrote it himself. You can sap it up on the way down. Justin, you're a brick.'

So here he was, a fellow-Etonian brick, having delivered himself of the dullest lecture he had read in his life – patronising, puffy and verbose like its author, who by now presumably was relaxing in the lap of under-secretarial luxury in Washington DC. It had never occurred to him that he would be required to take questions from the floor, but when Tessa piped out hers, it never occurred to him to refuse her. She was positioned at the geometric centre of the room, which was where she belonged. Locating her, Justin formed the foolish impression that her colleagues had deliberately left a space round her in deference to her beauty. The high neck of her legal-white blouse reached, like a blameless choirgirl's, to her chin. Her pallor and spectral slimness made a waif of her. You wanted to roll her up in a blanket and make her safe. The sunbeams from the skylight shone so brightly on her dark hair that to begin with he couldn't make out the face inside. The most he got was a broad, pale brow, a pair of solemn wide eyes and a fighter's pebble jaw. But the jaw came later. In the meantime she was an angel. What he didn't know, but was about to discover, was that she was an angel with a cudgel.

'Well – I *suppose* the answer to your question is – ' Justin began – 'and you must please correct me if you think differently – ' bridging the age gap and the gender gap and generally imparting an egalitarian air – 'that a state ceases to be a state when it ceases to deliver on its essential responsibilities. Would that be *your* feeling, basically?'

'Essential responsibilities being *what?*' the angel-waif rapped back.

'*Well –*' said Justin again, not certain where he was heading any more, and therefore resorting to those non-mating signals with which he imagined he was securing protection for himself, if not some kind of outright immunity – '*Well –*' troubled gesture of the hand, dab of the Etonian forefinger at greying sideburn, down again – 'I would suggest to you that, these days, very roughly, the qualifications for being a *civilised state* amount to – electoral suffrage, ah – protection of life and property – um, justice, health and education for all, at least to a certain level – then the maintenance of a sound administrative infrastructure – and roads, transport, drains, et cetera – and – what else is there? – ah yes, the equitable collection of taxes. If a state fails to deliver on at least a quorum of the above – then one *has* to say that the contract between state and citizen begins to look pretty *shaky* – and if it fails on *all* of the above, then it's a *failed state*, as we say these days. An un-state.' Joke. 'An ex-state.' Another joke, but still no one laughed. 'Does that answer your question?'

He had assumed that the angel would require a moment's

reflection to ponder this profound reply, and was therefore rattled when, barely allowing him time to bring the paragraph home, she struck again.

'So can you imagine a situation where you personally would feel obliged to *undermine* the state?'

'I *personally*? In this country? Oh my goodness me, certainly not,' Justin replied, appropriately shocked. 'Not when I've just come home.' Disdainful laughter from the audience, which was firmly on Tessa's side.

'In no circumstances?'

'None that I can envisage, no.'

'How about other countries?'

'Well, I'm not a citizen of other countries, am I?' – the laughter beginning to go his way now – 'Believe me, it is really quite enough work trying to speak for *one* country –' greeted by more laughter, which further heartened him – 'I *mean* more than one is simply not –'

He needed an adjective but she threw her next punch before he found one: a salvo of punches, as it turned out, delivered in a rat-a-tat to face and body.

'Why do you have to be a citizen of a country before you make a judgment about it? You *negotiate* with other countries, don't you? You cut *deals* with them. You legitimise them through *trading* partnerships. Are you telling us there's one ethical standard for *your* country and another for the rest? What *are* you telling us, actually?'

Justin was first embarrassed, then angry. He remembered, a little late, that he was still deeply tired after his recent sojourn in bloody Bosnia and theoretically recuperating. He was reading for an African posting – he assumed, as usual, a gruesome one. He had not come back to Mother England to play whipping boy for some absentee under-secretary, let alone read his lousy speech. And he was damned if Eternally Eligible Justin was going to be pilloried by a beautiful harridan who had cast him as some kind of archetypal chinless wonder. There was more laughter in the air, but it was laughter on a knife-edge, ready to fall either way. Very well: if she was playing to the gallery, so would he. Hamming it like the best of them, he raised his sculpted eyebrows and kept them raised. He took a step forward and flung up his hands, palms outward in self-protection.

'Madam,' he began – as the laughter swung in his favour. 'I *think*, madam – I very much *fear* – that you are attempting to lure me into a discussion about my *morals*.'

At which the audience sent up a veritable thunder of applause – everyone but Tessa. The sun that had been shining down on her had disappeared and he could see her beautiful face and it was hurt and fugitive. And suddenly he knew her very well – better in that instant than he knew himself. He understood the burden of beauty and the curse of always being an event, and he realised he had scored a victory that he didn't want. He knew his own insecurities and recognised them at work in her. She felt, by reason of her beauty, that she had an obligation to be heard. She had set out on a dare and it had gone wrong for her, and now she didn't know how to get back to base, wherever base was. He remembered the awful drivel he had just read, and the glib answers he had given, and he thought: she's absolutely right and I'm a pig, I'm worse, I'm a middle-aged Foreign Office smoothie who's turned the room against a beautiful young girl who was doing what was natural to her. Having knocked her down, he therefore rushed to help her to her feet:

'However, if we are being *serious* for a moment,' he announced in an altogether stiffer voice, across the room to her, as the laughter obediently died, 'you *have* put your finger on precisely the issue that literally none of us in the international community knows how to answer. Who *are* the white hats? What *is* an ethical foreign policy? All right. Let's agree that what joins the better nations these days is some notion of humanistic liberalism. But what *divides* us is precisely the question you ask: when does a supposedly humanistic state become unacceptably repressive? What happens when it threatens our national interests? Who's the humanist then? When, in other words, do we press the panic button for the United Nations – assuming they show up, which is another question entirely? Take Chechnya – take Burma – take Indonesia – take three-quarters of the countries in the so-called developing world –'

And so on, and so on. Metaphysical fluff of the worst kind, as he would have been the first to admit, but it got her off the hook. A debate of sorts developed, sides were formed and facile points thrashed out. The meeting overran, and was therefore judged a triumph.

'I'd like you to take me for a walk,' Tessa told him as the meeting broke up. 'You can tell me about Bosnia,' she added, by way of an excuse.

They walked in the gardens of Clare College and, instead of telling her about bloody Bosnia, Justin told her the name of every plant, first name and family name, and how it earned its living. She held his arm and listened in silence except for the odd 'Why do they do *that*?' or 'How does *that* happen?' And this had the effect of keeping him talking, for which he was at first grateful, because talking was his way of putting up screens against people – except that with Tessa on his arm he found himself thinking less of screens than how frail her ankles were inside her modish heavy boots as she set them one after the other along the narrow path they shared. He was convinced she had only to fall forwards in them to snap her shin-bones. And how lightly she bobbed against him, as if they weren't so much walking as sailing. After the walk they had a late lunch at an Italian restaurant, and the waiters flirted with her, which annoyed him, until it transpired that Tessa was half Italian herself, which somehow made it all right, and incidentally enabled Justin to show off his own Italian, of which he was proud. But then he saw how grave she had become, how pensive, and how her hands faltered, as if her knife and fork were too heavy for her, the way her boots had been in the garden.

'You protected me,' she explained, still in Italian, face down inside her hair. 'You always will protect me, won't you?'

And Justin, polite to a fault as always, said yes, well, if called upon he would, of course. Or he'd certainly do his best, put it that way. As far as he ever remembered, those were the only words that passed between them during lunch, although later to his amazement she assured him that he talked brilliantly about the threat of future conflict in the Lebanon, a place he hadn't thought about for years, and about the Western media's demonisation of Islam and the ludicrous posture of Western liberals who did not allow their ignorance to stand in the way of their intolerance; and that she was greatly impressed by how much feeling he brought to this important theme, which again puzzled Justin because so far as he knew he was totally divided on the issue.

But then something was happening to Justin that, to his excitement and alarm, he was unable to control. He had been drawn completely by accident into a beautiful play, and was captivated by it. He was in a different element, acting a part, and the part was the one he had often wanted to play in life, but never till now quite brought off. Once or twice, it was true, he had sensed the onset of a similar sensation, but never with such heady confidence or abandon. And all this while the practised womaniser in him sent out dire warning signals of the most emphatic kind: abort, this one's trouble, she's too young for you, too real, too earnest, she doesn't know how the game is played.

It made no odds. After lunch, with the sun still shining on them, they went on the river, and he demonstrated to her what all good lovers are supposed to demonstrate to their womenfolk on the Cam – notably, how deft he was, and how polished, and how at ease, balanced up there in his waistcoat on the precarious stern of a punt, wielding a pole and making witty bilingual conversation – which again she swore was what he did, though all he could ever afterwards remember was her long waif's body in its white blouse and her horsewoman's black skirt with a slash in it, and her grave eyes watching him with some kind of recognition he could not reciprocate, since he had never in his life been possessed by such a strong attraction or been so helpless in its spell. She asked him where he had learned his gardening, and he replied, 'From our gardeners.' She asked him who his parents were, and he was obliged to admit – reluctantly, certain it would offend her egalitarian principles – that he was well born and well heeled, and that the gardeners were paid for by his father, who had also paid for a long succession of nannies and boarding schools and universities and foreign holidays, and whatever else was needed to ease his path into the 'family firm', which was what his father called the Foreign Office.

But to his relief she seemed to find this a perfectly reasonable description of his provenance, and matched it with a few confidences of her own. She too had been born into privilege, she confessed. But both her parents had died within the last nine months, both from cancer. 'So I'm an orphan,' she declared, with fake levity, 'free to good home.' After which they sat apart for a while, still in close communion.

'I've forgotten the car,' he told her at some point, as if this in some way put a bar on further business.

'Where did you park it?'

'I didn't. It's got a driver. It's a government car.'

'Can't you ring it up?'

And amazingly she had a telephone in her handbag and he had the driver's mobile number in his pocket. So he moored the boat and sat beside her while he told the driver to go back to London on his own, which was like throwing away the compass, an act of shared self-marooning that was lost on neither of them. And after the river she took him back to her rooms and made love to him. And why she did that, and who she thought *he* was when she did it, and who he thought *she* was, and who either of them was by the end of that weekend, such mysteries, she told him as she peppered him with kisses at the railway station, would be solved by time and practice. The fact was, she said, she loved him, and everything else would fall into place when they were married. And Justin, in the madness that had seized him, made similar heedless declarations, repeated them and enlarged upon them, all on the wave of the folly that was conveying him – and he let it gladly, even if, in some recess of his consciousness, he knew that each hyperbole would one day have its price.

She made no secret of wanting an older lover. Like many beautiful young women he had known, she was sick of the sight of men her own age. In language that secretly repelled him, she described herself as a tramp, a tart with a heart and a bit of a little devil, but he was too smitten to correct her. The expressions, he later discovered, stemmed from her father, whom he thereafter detested, while taking pains to disguise this from her since she spoke of him as a saint. Her need for Justin's love, she explained, was an unappeasable hunger in her, and Justin could only protest that the same went for him, no question. And at the time he believed himself.

His first instinct, forty-eight hours after returning to London, was to bolt. He had been hit by a tornado, but tornadoes, he knew from experience, did a lot of damage, some of it collateral, and moved on. His posting to an African hell-hole, still pending, suddenly looked inviting. His protestations of love alarmed him the more he rehearsed them: this is not true, this is me in the wrong play. He had had a string of affairs and hoped to have a few more – but only on the most contained and premeditated lines, with women as disinclined as he was to abandon common sense for passion. But more cruelly: he feared her faith because, as a fully paid-up pessimist, he knew he had none. Not in human nature, not in God, not in the future, and certainly not in the universal power of love. Man was vile and evermore would be so. The world contained a small number of reasonable souls of whom Justin happened to be one. Their job, in his simple view, was to head off the human race from its worst excesses – with the proviso that when two sides were determined to blow each other to smithereens, there was precious little a reasonable person could do about it, however ruthless he might be in his efforts to stave off ruthlessness. In the end, the master of lofty nihilism told himself, all civilised men are Canutes these days, and the tide is coming in faster all the time. It was therefore doubly unfortunate that Justin, who regarded any form of idealism with the deepest scepticism, should have involved himself with a young woman who, though delightfully uninhibited in many ways, was unable to cross the road without first taking a moral view. Escape was the only sensible recourse.

But as the weeks went by and he embarked on what was intended to be the delicate process of disengagement, the wonder of what had happened gained ground in him. Little dinners planned for the regretful parting scene turning out instead to be feasts of enchantment followed by ever headier sexual delights. He began to feel ashamed of his secret apostasy. He was amused, not deterred, by Tessa's kooky idealism – and in an untroubled way fired by it. Somebody should feel these things and say them. Until now he had regarded strongly held convictions as the natural enemies of the diplomat, to be ignored, humoured or, like dangerous energy, diverted into harmless channels. Now to his surprise he saw them as emblems of courage and Tessa as their standard-bearer.

And with this revelation came a new perception of himself. He was no longer the ageing debs' delight, the nimble bachelor forever sidestepping the chains of marriage. He was the droll, adoring father-figure to a beautiful young girl, indulging her every whim as the saying goes, letting her have her head any time she needed it. But her protector nonetheless, her rock, her steadying hand, her adoring elder gardener in a straw hat. Abandoning his plan of escape, Justin set course firmly towards her, and this time – or so he would wish the police officers to believe – he never regretted it, never looked back.

*   *   *

'Not even when she became an embarrassment to you?' Lesley asks after she and Rob, covertly astonished by his frankness, have sat in respectful silence for the regulation period.

'I told you. There were issues where we stayed apart. I was waiting. Either for her to moderate herself or for the Foreign Office to provide rôles for us that were not at odds. The status of wives in the Foreign Service is in constant flux. They can't earn pay in the countries where they're posted. They're obliged to move when their husbands move. One moment they're being offered all the freedoms of the day. The next they're expected to behave like diplomatic geisha.'

'Is that Tessa speaking or you?' Lesley asks with a smile.

'Tessa never waited to be given her freedom. She took it.'

'And Bluhm didn't embarrass you?' asks Rob roughly.

'It is neither here nor there, but Arnold Bluhm was not her lover. They were joined by quite other things. Tessa's darkest secret was her virtue. She loved to shock.'

This is too much for Rob. 'Four nights on the trot, Justin?' he objects. 'Sharing a cottage on Turkana? A girl like Tessa? And you're seriously asking us to believe they didn't have it off?'

'You'll believe whatever you want,' Justin replies, the apostle of unsurprise. 'I have no doubt of it whatever.'

'Why?'

'Because she told me.'

And to this they had no answer at all. But there was something more that Justin needed to say and, bit by bit, assisted by Lesley's prompting, he managed to get it out.

'She had married convention,' he began awkwardly. 'Me. Not some high-minded do-gooder. Me. You really mustn't see her as somebody exotic. I never doubted – nor did she when we arrived here – that she would be anything other than a member of the diplomatic geisha she derided. In her own way. But toeing the line.' He deliberated, conscious of their disbelieving stares. 'After her parents' death she had scared herself. Now, with me to steady her, she wanted to pull back from too much freedom. It was the price she was prepared to pay for not being an orphan any more.'

'So what changed that?' Lesley asked.

'*We* did,' Justin retorted with fervour. He meant the other *we*. We her survivors. We the guilty ones. 'With our complacency,' he said, lowering his voice. 'With *this*.' And here he

148

made a gesture that embraced not just the dining room and Gloria's hideous watercolours impaled along the chimney breast, but the whole house round them, and its occupants, and by inference the other houses in the street. 'We who are paid to see what's going on, and prefer not to. We who walk past life with our eyes down.'

'Did she say that?'

'I did. It's how she came to regard us. She was born rich but that never impressed her. She had no interest in money. She needed far less of it than the aspiring classes. But she knew she had no excuse for being indifferent to what she saw and heard. She knew she owed.'

And Lesley on this note calls a break until tomorrow at the same time, Justin, if that's all right by you. It is.

And British Airways seemed to have come to much the same conclusion, for they were dousing the lights in the first-class cabin and taking last orders for the night.

CHAPTER EIGHT

Rob lounges while Lesley again unpacks her toys: the coloured notebooks, pencils, the little tape recorder that yesterday remained untouched, the piece of india rubber. Justin has a prison pallor and a web of hairline cracks around his eyes, which is how the mornings take him now. A doctor would prescribe fresh air.

'You said you had nothing to do with your wife's murder *in the sense we're implying*, Justin,' Lesley reminds him. 'What other sense is there, if you don't mind us asking?' And has to lean across the table to catch his words.

'I should have gone with her.'

'To Lokichoggio?'

He shook his head.

'To Lake Turkana?'

'To anywhere.'

'Is that what she told you?'

'No. She never criticised me. We never told each other what to do. We had one argument, and it was to do with method, not substance. Arnold was never an obstruction.'

'What was the argument about, exactly?' Rob demands, clinging determinedly to his literal view of things.

'After the loss of our baby, I begged Tessa to let me take her back to England or Italy. Take her anywhere she wanted. She wouldn't think of it. She had a mission, thank God, a reason to survive, and it was here in Nairobi. She had come upon a great social injustice. A great crime; she called it both. That was all I was allowed to know. In my profession, studied ignorance is an art form.' He turns to the window and peers out sightlessly. 'Have you seen how people live in the slums here?'

Lesley shakes her head.

'She took me once. In a weak moment, she said later, she wanted me to inspect her workplace. Ghita Pearson came with us. Ghita and Tessa were naturally close. The affinities were ridiculous. Their mothers had both been doctors, their fathers lawyers, they'd both been brought up Catholic. We went to a medical centre. Four concrete walls and a tin roof and a thousand people waiting to get to the door.' For a moment he forgets where he is. 'Poverty on that scale is a discipline of its own. It can't be learned in an afternoon. Nevertheless, it was hard for me, from then on, to walk down Stanley Street without –' he broke off again – 'without the other image in my mind.' After Woodrow's sleek evasions, his words ring out like the true gospel. 'The great injustice – the great crime – was what kept her alive. Our baby was five weeks dead. Left alone in the house, Tessa would stare vacantly at the wall. Mustafa would telephone me at the High Commission – "Come home, Mzee, she is ill, she is ill." But it wasn't I who revived her. It was Arnold. Arnold understood. Arnold shared the secret with her. She'd only to hear his car in the drive and she became a different woman. "What have you got? What have you got?" She meant news. Information. Progress. When he'd gone, she'd retreat to her little workroom and toil into the night.'

'At her computer?'

A moment's wariness on Justin's part. Overcome. 'She had her papers, she had her computer. She had the telephone, which she used with the greatest circumspection. And she had Arnold, whenever he was able to get away.'

'And you didn't mind that then?' Rob sneers, in an ill-judged return to his hectoring tone. 'Your wife sitting about mooning, waiting for Dr Wonderful to show up?'

'Tessa was desolate. If she'd needed a hundred Bluhms, as far as I was concerned, she could have them all and on whatever terms she wished.'

'And you didn't know anything about the great crime,' Lesley resumed, unwilling to be persuaded. 'Nothing. What it was about, who the victims and the main players were. They kept it all from you. Bluhm and Tessa together, and you stuck out there in the cold.'

'I gave them their distance,' Justin confirmed doggedly.

'I just don't see how you could *survive* like that,' Lesley insists, putting down her notebook and opening her hands. 'Apart, but together – the way you describe it – it's like – not being on speaking terms – worse.'

'We didn't survive,' Justin reminds her simply. 'Tessa's dead.'

*　　*　　*

Here they might have thought that the time for intimate confidences had run its course and a period of sheepishness or embarrassment would follow, even recantation. But Justin has only begun. He jolts himself upright, like a man raising his game. His hands fall to his thighs and stay there until otherwise ordered. His voice recovers its power. Some deep interior force is driving it to the surface, into the unfresh air of the Woodrows' fetid dining room, still rank with last night's gravy.

'She was so *impetuous*,' he declares proudly, once more reciting from speeches he has made to himself for hours on end. 'I loved that in her from the start. She was so desperate to have our child at once. The death of her parents must be compensated as soon as possible! Why wait till we were married? I held her back. I shouldn't have done. I pleaded convention – God knows why. "Very well," she said, "if we must be married in order to have a baby, let's get married immediately." So we went off to

152

Italy and married immediately, to the huge entertainment of my colleagues.' He is entertained himself. ' "Quayle's gone mad! Old Justin's married his daughter! Has Tessa passed her A-levels yet?" When she became pregnant, after three years of trying, she wept. So did I.'

He breaks off, but no one interrupts his flow.

'With pregnancy she changed. But only for the good. Tessa grew into motherhood. Outwardly she remained lighthearted. But inwardly a deep sense of responsibility was forming in her. Her aid work took on new meaning. I am told that's not unusual. What had been important now became a vocation, practically a destiny. She was seven months pregnant and still tending the sick and dying, then coming back for some fatuous diplomatic dinner party in town. The nearer the baby came, the more determined she was to make a better world for it. Not just for *our* child. For *all* children. By then she'd set her heart on an African hospital. If I'd forced her to go to some private clinic, she'd have done it, but I'd have betrayed her.'

'How?' Lesley murmurs.

'Tessa distinguished absolutely between pain observed and pain shared. Pain observed is journalistic pain. It's diplomatic pain. It's television pain, over as soon as you switch off your beastly set. Those who watch suffering and do nothing about it, in her book, were little better than those who inflicted it. They were the bad Samaritans.'

'But she *was* doing something about it,' Lesley objects.

'Hence the African hospital. In her extreme moments she talked of bearing her child in the slums of Kibera. Mercifully, Arnold and Ghita between them were able to restore her sense of proportion. Arnold has the authority of suffering. He not only treated torture victims in Algeria, he was tortured himself. He had earned his pass to the wretched of the earth. I hadn't.'

Rob seizes on this, as if the point has not been made a dozen times before. 'A bit hard to see where you came in, then, isn't it? Bit of a spare wheel, you were, sitting up there in the clouds with your diplomatic pain and your high-level committee, weren't you?'

But Justin's forbearance is limitless. There are times when he is simply too well bred to disagree. 'She exempted me from active service, as she put it,' he assents with a shameful dropping of the voice. 'She invented specious arguments to put me at my ease. She insisted that the world needed both of us: me inside the System, pushing; herself outside it, in the field, pulling. "I'm the one who believes in the moral state," she would say. "If you lot don't do your job, what hope is there for the rest of us?" It was sophistry and we both knew it. The System didn't need my job. Neither did I. What was the point of it? I was writing reports no one looked at and suggesting action that was never taken. Tessa was a stranger to deceit. Except in my case. For me, she deceived herself totally.'

'Was she ever afraid?' Lesley asks, softly in order not to violate the atmosphere of confession.

Justin reflects, then allows himself a half-smile of recollection. 'She once boasted to the American Ambassadress that fear was the only four-letter word she didn't know the meaning of. Her Excellency was not amused.'

Lesley smiles too, but not for long. 'And this decision to have her baby in an African hospital,' she asks, her eye on her notebook. 'Can you tell us when and how it was taken, please?'

'There was a woman from one of the slum villages up north that Tessa regularly visited. Wanza, surname unknown. Wanza was suffering from a mystery illness of some sort. She had been singled out for special treatment. By coincidence they found themselves in the same ward at the Uhuru Hospital and Tessa befriended her.'

Do they hear the guarded note that has entered his voice? Justin does.

'Know what illness?'

'Only the generality. She was ill and might become dangerously so.'

'Did she have Aids?'

'Whether her illness was Aids-related I have no idea. My impression was that the concerns were different.'

'That's pretty unusual, isn't it, a woman from the slums giving birth in a hospital?'

'She was under observation.'

'*Whose* observation?'

It is the second time that Justin censors himself. Deception does not come naturally to him. 'I assume one of the health clinics. In her village. In a shanty town. As you see, I'm hazy. I marvel at how much I managed not to know.'

'And Wanza died, didn't she?'

'She died on the last night of Tessa's stay at the hospital,' Justin replies, gratefully abandoning his reserve in order to reconstruct the moment for them. 'I'd been in the ward all evening but Tessa insisted I go home for a few hours' sleep. She'd told the same to Arnold and Ghita. We were taking alternate watches at her bedside. Arnold had supplied a safari bed. At four in the morning, Tessa telephoned me. There was no telephone in her ward so she used the Sister's. She was distressed. Hysterical is the more accurate description, but Tessa, when she is hysterical, does not raise her voice. Wanza had disappeared. The baby also. She had woken to find Wanza's bed empty and the baby's cot vanished. I drove to Uhuru Hospital. Arnold and Ghita arrived at the same moment. Tessa was inconsolable. It was as if she'd lost a second child in the space of a few days. Between the three of us, we persuaded her that it was time for her to convalesce at home. With Wanza dead and the baby removed, she felt no obligation to remain.'

'Tessa didn't get to see the body?'

'She asked to see it but was told it was not appropriate. Wanza was dead and her baby had been taken to the mother's village by her brother. So far as the hospital was concerned, that was an end to the matter. Hospitals do not care to dwell on death,' he adds, speaking with the experience of Garth.

'Did Arnold get to see the body?'

'He was too late. It had been sent to the morgue and lost.'

Lesley's eyes widen in unfeigned astonishment while, on the other side of Justin, Rob leans quickly forward, grabs the tape recorder and makes sure the tape is turning in the little window.

'Lost? You don't *lose* bodies!' Rob exclaims.

'To the contrary, I'm assured that in Nairobi it happens all the time.'

'What about the death certificate?'

'I can only tell you what I learned from Arnold and Tessa. I know nothing of a death certificate. None was mentioned.'

'And no post-mortem?' Lesley is back.

'To my knowledge, none.'

'Did Wanza receive visitors at the hospital?'

Justin ponders this but evidently sees no reason not to reply. 'Her brother Kioko. He slept beside her on the floor when he wasn't keeping the flies off her. And Ghita Pearson would make a point of sitting with her when she called on Tessa.'

'Anyone else?'

'A white male doctor, I believe. I can't be sure.'

'That he was white?'

'That he was a doctor. A white man in a white coat. And a stethoscope.'

'Alone?'

The reserve again, falling like a shadow across his voice. 'He was accompanied by a group of students. Or so I took them to be. They were young. They wore white coats.'

With three golden bees embroidered on the pocket of each coat, he might have added, but his resolve held him back.

'Why do you say students? Did Tessa say they were students?'

'No.'

'Did Arnold?'

'Arnold made no judgment about them in my hearing. It is pure presumption on my part. They were young.'

'How about their leader? Their doctor, if that's what he was. Did Arnold say anything about him?'

'Not to me. If he had concerns, he addressed them to the man himself – the man with the stethoscope.'

'In your presence?'

'But not in my hearing.' Or almost not.

Rob like Lesley is craning forward to catch his every word. 'Describe.'

Justin is already doing so. For a brief truce he has joined their team. But the reserve has not left his voice. Caution and circumspection are written round his tired eyes. 'Arnold took the man to one side. By the arm. The man with the stethoscope. They spoke to each other as doctors do. In low voices, apart.'

'In English?'

'I believe so. When Arnold speaks French or kiSwahili he acquires a different body language.' And when he speaks English he is inclined to raise his pitch a little, he might have added.

'Describe him – the bloke with the stethoscope,' Rob commands.

'He was burly. A big man. Plump. Unkempt. I have a memory of suède shoes. I remember thinking it peculiar that a medical doctor should wear suède shoes, I am not sure why. But the memory of the shoes endures. His coat was grimy from nothing very particular. Suède shoes, a grimy coat, a red face. A show-man of some kind. If it had not been for his white coat, an impresario.' And three golden bees, tarnished but distinct, embroidered on his pocket, just like the nurse in the poster at the airport, he was thinking. 'He seemed ashamed,' he added, taking himself by surprise.

'What of?'

'Of his own presence there. Of what he was doing.'

'Why do you say that?'

'He wouldn't look at Tessa. At either of us. He'd look any-where else. Just not at us.'

'Colour of hair?'

'Fair. Fair to ginger. There was drink in his face. The reddish hair set it off. Do you know of him? Tessa was most curious about him.'

'Beard? Moustache?'

'Clean-shaven. No. He was not. He had a day's stubble at

157

least. It had a golden colour to it. She asked him his name repeatedly. He declined to give it.'

Rob comes crashing in again. 'What *kind* of conversation did it look like?' he insists. 'Was it an argument? Was it friendly? Were they inviting each other to lunch? What was going on?'

The caution back. I heard nothing. I only saw. 'Arnold appeared to be protesting – reproaching. The doctor was deny-ing. I had the impression –' he pauses, giving himself time to choose his words. Trust nobody, Tessa had said. Nobody but Ghita and Arnold. Promise me. I promise. 'My impression was, this was not the first time a disagreement had taken place between them. What I was witnessing was part of a continuing argument. So I thought afterwards, at least. That I had witnessed a resumption of hostilities between adversaries.'

'You've thought about it a lot, then.'

'Yes. Yes, I have,' Justin agrees dubiously. 'My other im-pression was that English was not the doctor's first language.'

'But you didn't discuss any of this with Arnold and Tessa?'

'When the man had gone, Arnold returned to Tessa's bedside, took her pulse and spoke in her ear.'

'Which again you didn't hear?'

'No and I was not intended to.' Too thin, he thinks. Try harder. 'It was a part I had become familiar with,' he explains, avoiding their gaze. 'To remain outside their circle.'

'What medication was Wanza on?' Lesley asks.

'I've no idea.'

He had every idea. Poison. He had fetched Tessa from the hospital and was standing two steps below her on the staircase to their bedroom, holding her night-bag in one hand and the bag of Garth's first clothes and bedclothes and nappies in the other, but he was watching her like a wrestler because, being Tessa, she had to manage on her own. As soon as she started to crumple he let go the bags and caught her before her knees gave way, and he felt the awful lightness of her, and the shaking and despair as she broke into her lament, not about dead Garth, but about dead Wanza. *They killed her!* she blurted, straight into his face because he was holding her so close. *Those bastards killed Wanza, Justin! They killed her with their poison.* Who did, darling? he asked, smoothing her sweated hair away from her cheeks and forehead. Who killed her? Tell me. With his arm across her emaciated back he manhandled her gently up the stairs. What bastards, darling? Tell me who the bastards are. *Those bastards in ThreeBees. Those phoney bloody doctors. The ones that wouldn't look at us!* What sort of doctors are we talking about? – lifting her up and laying her on the bed, not giving her the slightest second chance to fall. Do they have names, the doctors? Tell me.

From deep in his inner world, he hears Lesley asking him the same question in reverse. 'Does the name Lorbeer mean anything to you, Justin?'

If in doubt, lie, he has sworn to himself. If in hell, lie. If I trust nobody – not even myself – if I am to be loyal only to the dead, lie.

'I fear not,' he replies.

'Not overheard anywhere – on the phone? Bits of chit-chat between Arnold and Tessa? Lorbeer, German, Dutch – Swiss perhaps?'

'Lorbeer is not a name to me in any context.'

'Kovacs – Hungarian woman? Dark hair, said to be a beauty?'

'Does she have a first name?' He means no again, but this time it's the truth.

'Nobody does,' Lesley replies in a kind of desperation. 'Emrich. Also a woman. But blonde. No?' She tosses her pencil onto the table in defeat. 'So Wanza dies,' she says. 'Official. Killed by a man who wouldn't look at you. And today, six months later, you still don't know what of. She just died.'

'It was never revealed to me. If Tessa or Arnold knew the cause of her death, I did not.'

Rob and Lesley flop in their chairs like two athletes who have agreed to take time out. Leaning back, stretching his arms wide, Rob gives a stage sigh while Lesley stays leaning forward, cupping her chin in her hand, an expression of melancholy on her wise face.

'And you haven't made this up, then?' she asks Justin through her knuckles. 'This whole pitch about the dying woman Wanza, her baby, the so-called doctor who was ashamed, the so-called students in white coats? It's not a tissue of lies from end to end, for example?'

'What a perfectly ridiculous suggestion! Why on earth should I waste your time inventing such a story?'

'The Uhuru Hospital's got no record of Wanza,' Rob explains, equally despondent, from his half-recumbent position. 'Tessa existed, so did your poor Garth. Wanza didn't. She was never there, she was never admitted, she was never treated by a doctor, pseudo or otherwise, no one observed her, no one prescribed for her. Her baby was never born, she never died, her body was never lost because it never existed. Our Les here had a go at speaking to a few of the nurses but they don't know nuffink, do they, Les?'

'Somebody had a quiet word with them before I did,' Lesley explains.

*   *   *

Hearing a man's voice behind him, Justin swung round. But it was only the flight steward enquiring after his bodily comforts. Did Mr Brown require a spot of help with the controls on his seat at all? Thank you, Mr Brown preferred to remain upright. Or his video machine? Thank you, no, I have no need of it. Then would he like to have the blind across his window drawn at all? No, thank you – emphatically – Justin preferred his window open to the cosmos. Then what about a nice warm blanket for Mr Brown? Out of incurable politeness, Justin accepted a blanket and returned his gaze to the black window in time to see Gloria barging into the dining room without knocking, carrying a tray of paste sandwiches. Setting it on the table, she sneaks a look at whatever Lesley has written in her notebook: fruitlessly, as it happens, for Lesley has deftly turned to a fresh page.

'You won't overwork our poor house guest, will you, darlings? He's got *quite* enough on his plate as it is, haven't you, Justin?'

And a kiss on the cheek for Justin, and a music-hall exit for everyone, as the three of them with one mind spring to open the door for their gaoler as she departs with the spent tea-tray.

*   *   *

For a while after Gloria's intrusion the talk is piecemeal. They munch their sandwiches, Lesley opens a different notebook, a blue one, while Rob with his mouth full fires off a seemingly unrelated stream of questions.

'Know anyone who smokes Sportsman cigarettes incessantly, do we?' – in a tone to suggest that smoking Sportsmans is a capital offence.

'Not that I'm aware of, no. We both detested cigarette smoke.'

'I meant out and about, not just at home.'

'Still no.'

'Know anyone owns a green long wheelbase safari truck, good condition, Kenyan plates?'

'The High Commissioner boasts an armoured jeep of some sort, but I don't imagine that's what you have in mind.'

'Know any blokes in their forties, well-built military types, polished shoes, tanned complexions?'

'Nobody who comes to mind, I'm afraid,' Justin confesses, smiling in his relief to be clear of the danger zone.

'Ever heard of a place called Marsabit, at all?'

'Yes, I think so. Yes, Marsabit. Of course. Why?'

'Oh. Right. Good. We *have* heard of it. Where is it?'

'On the edge of the Chalbi desert.'

'East of Lake Turkana then?'

'As memory serves, yes. It's an administrative centre of some sort. A meeting place for wanderers from all over the northern region.'

'Ever been there?'

'Alas, no.'

'Know anyone who has?'

'No, I don't believe so.'

'Any idea of the facilities available to the careworn traveller at Marsabit?'

'I believe there is accommodation there. And a police post. And a national reserve.'

'But you've never been there.' Justin has not. 'Or sent anyone there? *Two* anyones, for instance?' Justin has not. 'So how come you know all about the place then? Psychic, are you?'

'When I am posted to a country I make it my business to study the map.'

'We're getting stories of a green long wheelbase safari truck that stopped over at Marsabit two nights before the murder, Justin,' Lesley explains, when this ritual display of aggression has run its course. 'Two white men aboard. They sound like white hunters. Fit, your sort of age, khaki drills, shiny shoes, like Rob says. Didn't talk to anyone except each other. Didn't flirt with a bevy of Swedish girls at the bar. Bought stores from the shop. Fuel, fags, water, beer, rations. The fags were Sportsmans, the beer was Whitecap in bottles. Whitecap only comes in bottles. They left next morning, headed west across the desert. If they kept driving they could have hit Turkana shore next evening. They might even have made it to Allia Bay. The empty beer bottles we found near the murder scene were Whitecaps. The fag-ends were Sportsmans.'

'Is it simplistic of me to ask whether the hotel at Marsabit keeps a register?' Justin enquires.

'Page missing,' Rob declares triumphantly, barging his way back. 'Untimely ripp'd. Plus the Marsabit staff don't remember them from shit. They're so scared they can't remember their own names. Someone had a quiet word with them too, we assume. Same people as had a word with the staff at the hospital.'

But this is Rob's swansong in his rôle of Justin's hangman, a truth that he himself seems to recognise, for he scowls and yanks at his ear and very nearly looks apologetic, but Justin meanwhile is quickening. His gaze travels restlessly from Rob to Lesley and back again. He waits for the next question and, when none is forthcoming, asks one of his own.

'What about the vehicle registration office?'

The suggestion drew a hollow laugh from the two officers.

'In Kenya?' they ask.

'The motor insurance companies, then. The importers, the suppliers. There can't be *that* many long wheelbase green safari trucks in Kenya. Not if you sift through them.'

'The Blue Boys are working on it flat-out,' says Rob. 'By the next millennium, if we're very nice, they may come up with an answer. The importers haven't been all that clever either, to be frank,' he goes on, with a sly look at Lesley. 'Little firm called Bell, Barker & Benjamin, known otherwise as ThreeBees – heard of them? President for Life, one Sir Kenneth K. Curtiss, golfer and crook, Kenny K to his friends?'

'Everyone in Africa has heard of ThreeBees,' says Justin, pulling himself sharply back into line. If in doubt, lie. 'And of Sir Kenneth, obviously. He's a character.'

'Loved?'

'Admired, I suppose is the word. He owns a popular Kenyan football team. And wears a baseball cap back to front,' he adds, with a distaste that makes them laugh.

'ThreeBees have shown a lot of what I'd call alacrity all right, but not a lot of results,' Rob resumes. 'Very *helpful*, not a lot of help. "No problem, officer! You'll have it by lunchtime, officer!" But that was lunchtime a week ago.'

'I'm afraid that's the way with quite a few people round here,' Justin laments with a weary smile. 'Have you tried the motor insurance companies?'

'ThreeBees do the motor insurance too. Well, they would, wouldn't they? Free Third Party cover when you buy one of their vehicles. Still, that hasn't been a lot of help either. Not when it comes to green safari trucks in good condition.'

'I see,' says Justin blandly.

'Tessa never had them in her sights at all, did she?' Rob asks, in his ever-so-casual tone. 'ThreeBees? Kenny K does seem rather close to the Moi throne, which can usually be relied on to get her dander up. Did she?'

'Oh I expect so,' says Justin with equal vagueness. 'At one time or another. Bound to have.'

'Which might account for why we're not getting that extra bit of help we're after from the noble House of ThreeBees on the matter of the mystery vehicle and one or two other matters not directly related to it. Only they're big in other fields too, aren't they? Everything from cough syrup to executive jets, they told us, didn't they, Les?'

Justin smiles distantly, but does not advance the topic of conversation – not even, though he is tempted, with an amusing reference to the borrowed glory of Napoleon, or the absurd coincidence of Tessa's connection with the Island of Elba. And he makes no reference whatever to the night he brought her home from the hospital, and to those bastards in ThreeBees who killed Wanza with their poison.

'But they weren't on Tessa's blacklist, you say,' Rob continues. 'Which is surprising really, considering what's been said about them by their many critics. "The iron fist in the iron glove," was how one Westminster MP recently described them if I remember rightly, apropos some forgotten scandal. I don't expect *he'll* be getting a free safari in a hurry, will he, Les?' Les said no way. 'Kenny K and his ThreeBees. Sounds like a rock group. But Tessa hadn't declared one of her *fatwas* against them, as far as you know?'

'Not to my knowledge, no,' says Justin, smiling at *fatwa*.

Rob doesn't let it go. 'Based on – I don't know – some bad experience she and Arnold had in their fieldwork, say – malpractice of some kind – of the pharmaceutical sort? Only she was pretty big on the medical side of things, wasn't she? And so's Kenny K, when he's not on the golf course with Moi's Boys or buzzing round in his Gulfstream buying a few more companies.'

'Oh indeed,' says Justin – but with such an air of detachment, if not downright disinterest, that there is clearly no prospect of further enlightenment.

'So if I told you that Tessa and Arnold had made repeated representations to numerous departments of the far-flung House of ThreeBees over recent weeks – had written letters, made phone calls and appointments and had persistently been given the run-around for their trouble – you would still be saying this was not something that had come to your notice in any shape or form. That's a question.'

'I'm afraid I would.'

'Tessa writes a string of furious letters to Kenny K personally. They're hand-delivered or registered. She phones his secretary three times a day and bombards him with e-mails. She attempts to doorstep him at his farm at Lake Naivasha and at the entrance to his illustrious new offices, but his boys tip him off in time and he uses the back stairs, to the great entertainment of his staff. All this would be total news to you, so help you God?'

'With or without God's help, it is news to me.'

'Yet you don't seem surprised.'

'Don't I? How odd. I thought I was astonished. Perhaps I am not betraying my emotions as I should,' Justin retorts, with a mixture of anger and reserve that catches the officers off their guard, for their heads lift to him, almost in salute.

*   *   *

But Justin is not interested in their responses. His deceptions come from an entirely different stable to Woodrow's. Where Woodrow was busily forgetting, Justin is being assailed from all sides by half-recovered memories: shreds of conversation between Bluhm and Tessa that in honour he had compelled himself not to hear, but now come drifting back to him; her exasperation, disguising itself as silence, whenever the omnipresent name of Kenny K is spoken in her hearing – for example, his imminent elevation to the House of Lords, which in the Muthaiga Club is predicted as a racing certainty – for example, the persistent rumours of a giant merger between ThreeBees and a multinational conglomerate even vaster than itself. He is remembering her implacable boycott of all ThreeBees products – her anti-Napoleonic crusade, as she ironically dubbed it – from the household foods and detergents that Tessa's domestic army of down-and-outs was not allowed to buy on pain of death, to the ThreeBees roadside cafeterias and gasoline stations, car batteries and oils that Justin was forbidden to make use of when they were out driving together – and her furious cursing whenever a ThreeBees billboard with Napoleon's stolen emblem leered at them from the hoardings.

'We're hearing *radical* a lot, Justin,' Lesley announces, emerging from her notes to break into his thoughts once more. '*Was* Tessa radical? Radical's like militant where we come from. "If you don't like it, bomb it", sort of thing. Tessa wasn't into that stuff, was she? Nor was Arnold. Or were they?'

Justin's answer has the weary ring of repeated drafting for a pedantic Head of Department.

'Tessa believed that the irresponsible quest for corporate profit is destroying the globe, and the emerging world in particular. Under the guise of investment, Western capital ruins the native environment and favours the rise of kleptocracies. So ran her argument. It is scarcely a radical one these days. I have heard it widely canvassed in the corridors of the international community. Even in my own committee.'

He pauses again while he recalls the unlovely sight of the vastly overweight Kenny K driving off from the first tee of the Muthaiga Club in the company of Tim Donohue, our over-aged head spy.

'By the same argument, aid to the Third World is exploitation under another name,' he resumes. 'The beneficiaries are the countries that supply the money on interest, local African politicians and officials who pocket huge bribes, and the Western contractors and arms suppliers who walk away with huge profits. The victims are the man-in-the-street, the uprooted, the poor and the very poor. And the children who will have no future,' he ends, quoting Tessa and remembering Garth.

'Do *you* believe that?' Lesley asks.

'It's a little late for me to believe anything,' Justin replies meekly, and there is a moment's quiet before he adds – less meekly – 'Tessa was that rarest thing: a lawyer who believes in justice.'

'Why were they heading for Leakey's place?' Lesley demands when she has silently acknowledged this statement.

'Perhaps Arnold had business up there for his NGO. Leakey is not one to disregard the welfare of native Africans.'

'Perhaps,' Lesley agrees, writing thoughtfully in a green-backed notebook. 'Had she met him?'

'I do not believe so.'

'Had Arnold?'

'I have no idea. Perhaps you should put the question to Leakey.'

'Mr Leakey never heard of either one of them till he turned on his television set last week,' Lesley replies, in a tone of gloom. 'Mr Leakey spends most of his time in Nairobi these days, trying to be Moi's Mr Clean and having a hard time getting his message over.'

Rob glances at Lesley for her approval and receives a veiled nod. He cranes himself forward and gives the tape recorder an aggressive shove in Justin's direction: speak into this thing.

'So what's the white plague then, when it's at home?' he demands, implying by his hectoring tone that Justin is personally responsible for its spread. 'The white plague,' he repeats, when Justin hesitates. 'What is it? Come on.'

A stoical immobility has once more settled over Justin's face. His voice retreats into its official shell. Paths of connection are again opening before him, but they are Tessa's and he will walk them alone.

'The white plague was once a popular term for tuberculosis,' he pronounces. 'Tessa's grandfather died of the disease. As a child she witnessed his death. Tessa possessed a book of the same title.' But he didn't add that the book had been lying at her bedside until he had transferred it to the Gladstone bag.

Now it is Lesley's turn to be cautious. 'Did she take a special interest in TB for that reason?'

'Special I don't know. As you have just said, her work in the slums gave her an interest in a range of medical matters. Tuberculosis was one of them.'

'But if her grandfather *died* of it, Justin –'

'Tessa particularly disliked the sentimentalism that attaches to the disease in literature,' Justin goes on severely, talking across her. 'Keats, Stevenson, Coleridge, Thomas Mann – she used to say that people who found TB romantic should have tried sitting at her grandfather's bedside.'

Rob again consults Lesley with his eyes, and again receives her silent nod. 'So would it surprise you to hear that in the course of an unauthorised search of Arnold Bluhm's apartment we found a copy of an old letter he had sent to the head of ThreeBees' marketing operation, warning him of the side-effects of a new short-course, anti-tuberculosis drug that ThreeBees are peddling?'

Justin does not hesitate for a second. The perilous line of questioning has reactivated his diplomatic skills. 'Why should it surprise me? Bluhm's NGO takes a close professional interest in Third World drugs. Drugs are the scandal of Africa. If any one thing denotes the Western indifference to African suffering, it's the miserable shortage of the right drugs, and the disgracefully high prices that the pharmaceutical firms have been exacting over the last thirty years' – quoting Tessa but without attribution. 'I'm sure Arnold has written dozens of such letters.'

'This one was hidden away by itself,' says Rob. 'Rolled up with a lot of technical data that's beyond us.'

'Well, let's hope you can ask Arnold to decipher it for you when he comes back,' says Justin primly, not bothering to conceal his distaste at the notion that they had been foraging through Bluhm's possessions and reading his correspondence without his knowledge.

Lesley takes over again. 'Tessa had a laptop, right?'

'Indeed she did.'

'What make?'

'The name escapes me. Small, grey and Japanese is about all I can tell you.'

He is lying. Glibly. He knows it, they know it. To judge by their faces, an air of loss has entered the relationship, of friendship disappointed. But not on Justin's side. Justin knows only stubborn refusal, concealed within diplomatic grace. This is the battle he has steeled himself for over days and nights, while praying it may never be joined.

'She kept it in her workroom, right? Where she kept her noticeboard and her papers and research material.'

'When she was not taking it with her, yes.'

'Did she use it for her letters – documents?'

'I believe so.'

'And e-mails?'

'Frequently.'

'And she'd print out from it, right?'

'Sometimes.'

'She wrote a long document about five or six months ago – around eighteen pages of letter and annexe. It was some kind of protest about malpractice, we think medical or pharmaceutical or both. A case history, describing something very serious that was going on here in Kenya. Did she show it to you?'

'No.'

'And you didn't read it – for yourself, without her knowledge?'

'No.'

'You know nothing about it then. Is that what you're saying?'

'I'm afraid it is.' Washed down with a regretful smile.

'Only we were wondering whether this was to do with the great crime she thought she'd got on to.'

'I see.'

'And whether ThreeBees might have something to do with that great crime.'

'It's always possible.'

'But she didn't show it to you?' Lesley insists.

'As I have told you several times, Lesley: no.' He almost adds, 'dear lady.'

'Do you think it might have involved ThreeBees in any way?'

'Alas, I have absolutely no idea.'

But he has every idea. It is the terrible time. It is the time when he feared he might have lost her; when her young face grew harder by the day and her young eyes acquired a zealot's light; when she crouched, night after night, at her laptop in her little office, surrounded by heaps of papers flagged and cross-referred like a lawyer's brief; the time when she ate her food without noticing what she was eating, then hurried back to her labours without even a goodbye; the time when shy villagers from the countryside came soundlessly to the side door of the house to visit her, and sat with her on the verandah, eating the food that Mustafa brought to them.

'So she never even *discussed* the document with you?' Lesley, acting incredulous.

'Never, I'm afraid.'

'Or in front of you – with Arnold or Ghita, say?'

'In the last months, Tessa and Arnold kept Ghita at arm's length, I assume, for her own good. As for myself, it was my perception that they actually mistrusted me. They believed that, if I was caught in a conflict of interest, I would owe my first allegiance to the Crown.'

'And would you?'

Never in a thousand years, he is thinking. But his answer reflects the ambivalence they expect of him. 'Since I am not familiar with the document you refer to, I fear that is not a question I can answer.'

'But the document would have been printed from her laptop, right? This eighteen-page job – even if she didn't show it to you.'

'Possibly. Or Bluhm's. Or a friend's.'

'So where is it now – the laptop? This minute?'

Seamless.

Woodrow could have learned from him.

No body language, no tremor in the voice or exaggerated pause for breath.

'I looked in vain for her laptop in the inventory of her possessions presented to me by the Kenyan police and, like a number of other things, regrettably it does not feature.'

'Nobody at Loki saw her with a laptop,' Lesley says.

'But then I don't suppose they inspected her personal luggage.'

'Nobody at the Oasis saw her with one. Did she have it with her when you drove her to the airport?'

'She had the rucksack that she always carried on her field trips. That too has disappeared. She had an overnight bag which may also have contained her laptop. Sometimes it did. Kenya does not encourage lone women to display expensive electronic equipment in public places.'

'But then she wasn't alone, was she?' Rob reminds him, after which a long silence intervenes – so long that it becomes a matter of suspense to see who breaks it first.

'Justin,' says Lesley finally. 'When you visited your house with Woodrow last Tuesday morning, what did you take away with you?'

Justin affects to assemble a mental list. 'Oh . . . family papers . . . private correspondence relating to Tessa's family trust . . . some shirts, socks . . . a dark suit for the funeral . . . a few trinkets of sentimental value . . . a couple of ties.'

'Nothing else?'

'Nothing that immediately springs to mind. No.'

'Anything that doesn't?' asks Rob.

Justin smiles wearily but says nothing.

'We talked to Mustafa,' says Lesley. 'We asked him: Mustafa, where's Miss Tessa's laptop? He gave out conflicting signals. One minute she'd taken it away with her. The next she hadn't. After that, the journalists had stolen it. The one person who *hadn't* taken it was you. We thought he might be trying to front for you and not succeeding very well.'

'I'm afraid that's rather what you get when you bully domestic staff.'

'We didn't bully him,' Lesley comes back, angry at last. 'We were extremely gentle. We asked him about her noticeboard. Why was it full of pins and pinholes but didn't have any notices on it? He'd tidied it, he said. Tidied it all by himself with no help from anyone. He can't read English, he's not allowed to touch her possessions or anything in the room, but he'd tidied the noticeboard. What had he done with the notices? we asked him. Burned them, he said. Who told him to burn them? Nobody. Who told him to tidy the noticeboard? Nobody. Least of all Mr Justin. We think he was covering for you, not very well. We think *you* took the notices, not Mustafa. We think he's covering for you on the laptop too.'

Justin has lapsed once more into that state of artificial ease that is the curse and virtue of his profession. 'I fear you do not take into account our cultural differences here, Lesley. A more likely explanation is that the laptop went with her to Turkana.'

'Plus the notices off her noticeboard? I don't think so, Justin. Did you help yourself to any disks during your visit?'

And here for a moment – but only here – Justin drops his guard. For while one side of him is engaged in bland denial, another is as anxious as his interrogators to obtain answers.

'No, but I confess I searched for them. Much of her legal correspondence was contained in them. She was in the habit of e-mailing her solicitor on a range of matters.'

'And you didn't find them.'

'They were *always* on her desk,' Justin protests, now lavish in his desire to share the problem. 'In a pretty lacquer box given her by the very same solicitor last Christmas – they're not just cousins but old friends. The box has Chinese lettering on it. Tessa had a Chinese aid worker translate it. To her delight, it turned out to be a tirade against loathsome Westerners. I can only suppose that it went the same way as the laptop. Perhaps she took the disks to Loki too.'

'Why should she do that?' asks Lesley sceptically.

'I'm not literate in information technology. I should be, but

I'm not. The police inventory said nothing of disks either,' he adds, waiting for their help.

Rob reflects on this. 'Whatever was on the disks, chances are it's on the laptop too,' he pronounces. 'Unless she downloaded onto a disk, then wiped the hard disk clean. But why would anyone do that?'

'Tessa had a highly developed sense of security, as I told you.'

Another ruminative silence, shared by Justin.

'So where are her papers now?' asks Rob roughly.

'On their way to London.'

'By diplomatic bag?'

'By whatever route I choose. The Foreign Office is being most supportive.'

Perhaps it is the echo of Woodrow's evasions that brings Lesley to the edge of her chair in an outburst of unfeigned exasperation.

'*Justin.*'

'Yes, Lesley.'

'Tessa *researched*. Right? Forget the disks. Forget the laptop. Where are her papers – *all* her papers – *physically and at this moment?*' she demands. 'And where are the notices off that board?'

Playing his artificial self again, Justin vouchsafes her a tolerant frown, implying that although she is being unreasonable, he will do his best to humour her. 'Among my effects, no doubt. If you ask me which particular suitcase, I might be a little stumped.'

Lesley waits, letting her breathing settle. 'We'd like you to open all your luggage for us, please. We'd like you to take us downstairs *now*, and show us *everything* you took from your house on Tuesday morning.'

She stands up. Rob does the same, and stations himself beside the door in readiness. Only Justin remains seated. 'I'm afraid that it not possible,' he says.

'Why not?' Lesley snaps.

'For the reason that I took the papers in the first place. They are personal and private. I do not propose to submit them to

173

your scrutiny, or anybody else's, until I have had a chance to read them myself.'

Lesley flushes. 'If this was England, Justin, I'd slap a subpoena on you so fast you wouldn't even feel it.'

'But this is not England, alas. You have no warrant and no local powers that I'm aware of.'

Lesley ignores him. 'If this was England, I'd get a warrant to search this house from top to bottom. And I'd take every trinket, piece of paper and disk that you lifted from Tessa's workroom. And the laptop. I'd go through them with a toothcomb.'

'But you've already searched *my* house, Lesley,' Justin protests calmly from his chair. 'I don't think Woodrow would take kindly to your searching his as well, would he? And I certainly cannot give you permission to do to me what you have done to Arnold without his consent.'

Lesley is scowling and pink like a woman wronged. Rob, very pale, stares longingly at his clenched fists.

'We'll see about that tomorrow then,' Lesley says ominously as they leave.

But tomorrow never comes. Not for all her fiery words. Throughout the night and late into the morning Justin sits on the edge of his bed, waiting for Rob and Lesley to return as they have threatened, armed with their warrants, their subpoenas and their writs, and a posse of Kenyan Blue Boys to do their dirty work for them. He fruitlessly debates options and hiding-places as he has done for days. Thinks like a prisoner of war, contemplating floors and walls and ceilings: *where*? Makes plans to recruit Gloria, drops them. Makes others involving Mustafa and Gloria's houseboy. Others again involving Ghita. But the only word of his inquisitors is a phone call from Mildren saying the police officers are required elsewhere, and no, there is no news of Arnold. And when the funeral comes, the police officers are still required elsewhere – or so it appears to Justin, when now and then he scans the mourners, counting absent friends.

*   *   *

The plane had entered a land of eternal pre-dawn. Outside his cabin window, wave after wave of frozen sea rolled towards a colourless infinity. All round him, white-shrouded passengers slept in the unearthly postures of the dead. One had her arm thrown upwards as if she had been shot while waving to someone. Another had his mouth open in a silent scream, and his dead man's hand across his heart. Upright and alone, Justin returned his gaze to the window. His face floated in it beside Tessa's, like the masks of people he once knew.

CHAPTER NINE

'It's just bloody horrible!' cried a balding figure in a voluminous brown overcoat, prising Justin free of his luggage trolley and blinding him with a bear-hug. 'It's absolutely foul and fucking unfair and bloody horrible. First Garth, now Tess.'

'Thank you, Ham,' said Justin, returning the embrace as best he could, given that his arms were pinned to his sides. 'And thank you for turning out at this ungodly hour. No, I'll take that, thank you. You carry the suitcase.'

'I'd have come to the funeral if you'd let me! Christ, Justin!'

'It was better to have you holding the fort,' said Justin kindly.

'That suit warm enough? Bit brass monkeys, isn't it, after sunny Africa?'

Arthur Luigi Hammond was sole partner of the law firm of Hammond Manzini of London and Turin. Ham's father had devilled with Tessa's father at law school at Oxford, and afterwards at law school in Milan. At a single ceremony in a tall church in Turin they had married two aristocratic Italian sisters, both fabled beauties. When Tessa was born to the one, Ham was born to the other. As the children grew they spent holidays together on Elba, skied together in Cortina and, as de facto brother and sister, graduated together at university, Ham with a rugger Blue and a hard-won Third, Tessa with a First. Since the death of Tessa's parents Ham had played the part of Tessa's wise uncle, zealously administering her family trust, making ruinously prudent investments for her and, with all the authority of his prematurely bald head, curbing his cousin's generous instincts while forgetting to render his own fees. He was big and pink and shiny, with twinkly eyes and liquid cheeks that frowned or smiled with every inner breeze. When Ham plays gin rummy, Tessa used to say, you know his hand before he does, just by the width of his grin when he picks up each card.

'Why not shove that thing in the back?' Ham roared as they clambered into his tiny car. 'All right, on the floor then. What's it got in it? Heroin?'

'Cocaine,' said Justin as he discreetly scanned the ranks of frosted cars. At immigration, two woman officers had nodded him through with conspicuous indifference. In the luggage hall, two dull-faced men in suits and identification tags had looked at everyone but Justin. Three cars down from Ham's, a man and woman sat head to head in the front of a beige Ford saloon studying a map. In a civilised country, you can never tell, gentlemen, the jaded instructor on the security course liked to say. The most comfortable thing you can do is assume they're with you all the time.

'All set?' Ham asked shyly, buckling his seat belt.

England was beautiful. Low rays of morning sun gilded the frozen Sussex plough. Ham drove as he always drove, at sixty-five miles an hour in a seventy speed limit, ten yards behind the belching exhaust pipe of the nearest convenient lorry.

'Meg sends love,' he announced gruffly, in a reference to his very pregnant wife. 'Blubbed for a week. So did I. Blub now if I'm not bloody careful.'

'I'm sorry, Ham,' said Justin simply, accepting without bitterness that Ham was one of those mourners who look to the bereaved for consolation.

'I just wish they'd find the bugger, that's all,' Ham burst out

177

some minutes later. 'And when they've strung him up, they can toss those Fleet Street bastards into the Thames for good measure. She's doing time with her bloody mother,' he added. '*That* should bring it on.'

They drove once more in silence, Ham glowering at the belching lorry in front of him, Justin staring in perplexity at the foreign country he had represented half his life. The beige Ford had overtaken them, to be replaced by a tubby motorcyclist in black leathers. In a civilised country, you can never tell.

'You're rich, by the by,' Ham blurted, as open fields gave way to suburbia. 'Not that you were exactly a pauper before, but now you're stinking. Her father's, mother's, the trust, whole shooting match. Plus you're sole trustee of her charity. She said you'd know what to do with it.'

'When did she say that?'

'Month before she lost the baby. Wanted to make sure everything was kosher in case she snuffed it. Well, what the hell was *I* supposed to do, for Christ's sake?' he demanded, mistaking Justin's silence for reproach. 'She was my client, Justin. I was her solicitor. Talk her out of it? Ring you up?'

His eye on the wing mirror, Justin made appropriate soothing noises.

'And Bluhm's the other bloody Executor,' Ham added in furious parenthesis. 'Executioner more like.'

The hallowed premises of Messrs Hammond Manzini were situated in a gated cul-de-sac called Ely Place on two wormy upper floors with panelled walls hung with disintegrating images of the illustrious dead. In two hours' time, bilingual clerks would be murmuring into grimy telephones while Ham's ladies-in-twinsets grappled with the modern technology. But at seven in the morning, Ely Place was deserted except for a dozen cars parked along the kerbside and a yellow light burning in the crypt of St Etheldreda's Chapel. Labouring under the weight of Justin's luggage, the two men clambered up four rickety flights to Ham's office, then up a fifth to his monkish attic flat. In the tiny living-dining-kitchen hung a photograph of a slimmer Ham kicking a goal, to the jubilation of an undergraduate crowd. In Ham's tiny bedroom where Justin was supposed to change, Ham and his bride Meg were cutting a three-tier wedding cake to the fanfares of Italian trumpeters in tights. And in the tiny bathroom where he took a shower hung a primitive oil painting of Ham's ancestral home in coldest Northumbria which accounted for Ham's penury.

'Bloody roof blew clean off the north wing,' he was yelling proudly through the kitchen wall while he smashed eggs and clattered pans. 'Chimney stacks, tiles, weathervane, clock, buggered to a man. Meg was out on Rosanne, thank God. If she'd been in the vegetable garden, she'd have caught the bell tower slap in the withers, whatever they are.'

Justin turned the hot tap and at once scalded his hand. 'How very alarming for her,' he commiserated, adding cold.

'Sent me this *extraordinary* little book for Christmas,' Ham boomed, to the sizzle of bacon. 'Not Meg. Tess. Happen to show it to you at all? Little book she sent me? For Christmas?'

'No, Ham, I don't think she did –' rubbing soap into his hair in the absence of shampoo.

'Some Indian mystic chap. Rahmi Whoosit. Ring any bells? I'll get the rest of him in a minute.'

'Afraid not.'

'All about how we should love each other without attachment. Struck me as a pretty tall order.'

Blinded with soap, Justin emitted a sympathetic growl.

'*Freedom, Love and Action* – that's the title. Hell she expect me to do with freedom, love and action? I'm married, for fuck's sake. Got a baby in the pipeline. Plus I'm a bloody Roman. Tess was a Roman herself before she jacked it in. Hussy.'

'I expect she wanted to thank you for all that running around you did for her,' Justin suggested, picking his moment, yet careful to preserve the casual note of their exchange.

Temporary disconnection from other side of wall. More sizzling, followed by heretical expletives and smells of burning.

'What *running around* was that then?' Ham bawled suspiciously.

'Thought you weren't supposed to *know* about any running around. Deadly secret, according to Tess, the running around was. "To be kept strictly out of reach of all Justins." Health warning. Put it as the subject in every e-mail.'

Justin had found a towel, but rubbing his eyes made the smarting worse. 'I didn't *know* about it exactly, Ham. I sort of *divined* it,' he explained through the wall with the same casualness. 'What did she want you to do? Blow up Parliament? Poison the reservoirs?' No answer. Ham was engrossed in his cooking. Justin groped for a clean shirt. 'Well, don't tell me she had you handing out subversive leaflets about Third World debt,' he said.

'Bloody company records,' he heard back, over more clashing of saucepans. 'Two eggs right for you or one? They're our hens.'

'One will be fine, thanks. Whatever records were they?'

'All she cared about. Any time she thought I was getting fat and comfortable: *pow*, in there with another e-mail about company records.' More crashing of pans deflected Ham to other paths. 'Cheated at tennis, know that? In Turin. Oh yes. Little minx and self were partnered in a kiddywink knockout competition. Lied like a trooper all through the match. Every line call: *out*. Could be a yard in, didn't make a blind bit of difference. *Out*. "I'm Italian," she said, "I'm allowed to." "Like hell you're Italian," I said. "You're English to your boots, same as me." God alone knows what I'd have done if we'd won. Given the cup back, I suppose. No, I wouldn't. She'd have killed me. Oh Christ. Sorry.'

Justin stepped into the drawing room to take his place before a greasy slag-heap of bacon, egg, sausages, fried bread and tomatoes. Ham was standing with one hand crammed to his mouth, dazed by his unhappy choice of metaphor.

'What *sort* of companies exactly, Ham? Don't look like that. You'll put me off my breakfast.'

'Ownership,' said Ham through his knuckles, as he sat down opposite Justin at the tiny table. 'Whole thing was about ownership. Who owned two pissy little companies in the Isle of Man. Anyone else call her Tess, d'you know?' he asked, still chastened. 'Apart from me?'

'Not in my hearing. And certainly not in hers. Tess was your sole copyright.'

'Loved her rotten, you see.'

'And she loved you. What *sort* of companies?'

'Intellectual property. Never had it off with her, mind. Too close.'

'And in case you were wondering, it was the same with Bluhm.'

'Is that official?'

'He didn't kill her, either. Any more than you or I did.'

'Sure?'

'Sure.'

Ham brightened. 'Old Meg wasn't convinced. Didn't know Tess the way I did, you see. Special thing. Can't be replicated. "Tess has *chums*," I told her. "Buddies. The demon sex doesn't come into it." I'll tell her what you said, if you don't mind. Cheer her up. All that shit in the press. Sort of rebounded on me.'

'So where were these companies registered? What were their names? Do you remember?'

''Course I remember. Couldn't help bloody remembering, with old Tess hammering away at me every other day.'

Ham was pouring tea, clutching the teapot in both hands, one for the pot, one to keep the lid from falling off while he grumbled. The operation completed, he sat back, still nursing the teapot, then lowered his head as if he were about to charge.

'All right,' he demanded aggressively. 'Name me the *most* secretive, duplicitous, mendacious, hypocritical bunch of corporate wide-boys it's been my dubious pleasure to encounter.'

'Defence,' Justin suggested disingenuously.

'Wrong. Pharmaceutical. Beats Defence into a cocked hat. I've got it now. Knew I would. Lorpharma and Pharmabeer.'

'*Who?*'

'It was in some medical rag. Lorpharma discovered the molecule and Pharmabeer owned the process. Knew I would. How those chaps come up with names like that, God knows.'

'Process to do what?'

'Produce the molecule, arsehole, what do you think?'

'What molecule?'

'God knows. Same as the law but worse. Words I've never seen before, hope never to see 'em again. Blind the punters with science. Keep 'em in their place.'

After breakfast they went downstairs together and put the Gladstone in Ham's strongroom next door to his office. Lips pursed for discretion, eyes lifted to the heavens, Ham spun the combination and hauled back the steel door for Justin to go in alone. Then watched from the doorway while Justin laid the bag on the floor close to a pile of age-honoured leather boxes with the firm's Turin address embossed on the lid.

'That was only the beginning, mark you,' Ham warned darkly, affecting indignation. 'A canter round the course before the real thing. After that it was names of directors of all companies owned by Messrs Karel Vita Hudson of Vancouver, Seattle, Basel plus every city you've heard of from Oshkosh to East Pinner. And "What's the state of play regarding the much-publicised rumours of an imminent collapse of the noble and ancient house of Balls, Birmingham & Bumfluff Limited or whatever they're called, known otherwise as ThreeBees, President for Life and Master of the Universe one Kenneth K. Curtiss, Knight?" Did she have any more questions? you wonder. Yes, she bloody did. I told her to get it off the Internet but she said half the stuff she wanted was X-rated or whatever they do if they don't want Joe Public looking over their shoulders. I said to her – "Tess, old thing, Christ's sake, this is going to take me *weeks*. Months, old girl." Did she give a tinker's? Did she hell. It was Tess, for Christ's sake. I'd have jumped out of a balloon without the parachute if she'd told me to.'

'And the sum of it was?'

Ham was already beaming with innocent pride. 'KVH Vancouver and Basel own fifty-one per cent of the pissy Isle of Man biotechnology companies, Lor-hoojamy and Pharma-whatnot. ThreeBees Nairobi have sole import and distribution rights of said molecule plus all derivatives for the whole of the African continent.'

'Ham, you're incredible!'

'Lorpharma and Pharmabeer are both owned by the same gang of three. Or were till they sold their fifty-one per cent. One chap, two hags. The chap is called Lorbeer. Lor plus Beer plus pharma gives you Lorpharma and Pharmabeer. The hags are both doctors. Address care of a Swiss gnome who lives in a letter box in Liechtenstein.'

'Names?'

'Lara Somebody. She's in my notes. Lara Emrich. Got it.'

'And the other one?'

'Forget. No, I don't. Kovacs. No first name given. It was Lara I fell in love with. My favourite song. Used to be. From Zhivago. Old Tess's too in those days. *Fuck.*' A natural break while Ham blew his nose and Justin waited.

'So what did you do with these nuggets of intelligence when you'd landed them, Ham?' Justin enquired tenderly.

'Read the whole lot to her over the telephone to Nairobi. Chuffed to bits, she was. Called me her hero –' he broke off, alarmed by Justin's expression – 'not *your* telephone, idiot. Some mate of hers up-country. "You're to go to a phone box, Ham, and you're to call me straight back on the following number. Got a pen?" Bossy little cow, always was. Bloody cagey about telephones, though. Bit paranoid in my view. Still, some paranoids have real enemies, don't they?'

'Tessa did,' Justin agreed, and Ham gave him a queer look, which got queerer the longer it lasted.

'You don't think that's what happened, do you?' Ham asked, in a subdued voice.

'In what way?'

'Old Tess fell foul of the pharmaceutical chaps?'

'It's conceivable.'

'But I mean, Christ – old sport – you don't think they shut her mouth for her, do you? I mean, I know they're not Boy Scouts.'

'I'm sure they're all dedicated philanthropists, Ham. Right down to their last millionaire.'

A very long silence followed, broken by Ham.

'Mother. Oh Christ. Well. Tread gently, what?'

'Exactly.'

'I dropped her in the shit by making that phone call.'

'No, Ham. You broke an arm and a leg for her and she loved you.'

'Well. Christ. Anything I can do?'

'Yes. Find me a box. A stout brown cardboard box would do. Got such a thing?'

Glad of an errand Ham charged off and, after much cursing, returned with a plastic draining tray. Crouching to the Gladstone, Justin opened the padlocks, released the leather straps and, masking Ham's view with his back, transferred the contents to the tray.

'And now, if you would, a wad of your dullest files on the Manzini estate. Back-numbers. Stuff you keep but never look at. Enough to fill up this bag.'

So Ham found him files too: as old and dog-eared as Justin seemed to want. And helped him load them into the empty bag. And watched him buckle the bag up, and lock it. Then from his window watched him again, as he strode down the cul-de-sac, bag in hand, to hail a cab. And as Justin disappeared from view, Ham breathed 'Holy Mother!' in an honest invocation to the Virgin.

*   *   *

'Good *morning*, Mr Quayle, sir. Take your bag, sir? I'll have to run it under the X-ray, if you don't mind. It's the new regulations. Wasn't like that in our day, was it? Or your father's. Thank you, sir. And here's your ticket, all shipshape and above-board as they say.' A dropping of the voice. 'Very sorry, sir. We're all greatly affected.'

'Good morning, sir! Nice to have you back with us.' Another dropped voice. 'Deepest condolences, sir. From the wife also.'

'Our very deepest commiserations, Mr Quayle' – another voice, breathing beer fumes in his ear – 'Miss Landsbury says please to go straight on up, sir. Welcome home.'

But the Foreign Office was no longer home. Its preposterous hall, built to strike terror into the hearts of Indian princes, imparted only strutting impotence. The portraits of disdainful buccaneers in periwigs no longer tipped him their familial smile.

'Justin. I'm Alison. We haven't met. What a terrible, *terrible* way to get to know each other. How are you?' said Alison Landsbury, appearing with posed restraint in the twelve-foot-tall doorway of her office, and pressing his right hand in both of hers before leaving it to swing. 'We're all *so, so* sad, Justin. So utterly *horrified*. And you're so brave. Coming here so soon. Are you *really* able to talk sensibly? I don't see how you *could*.'

'I was wondering whether you had any news of Arnold.'

'Arnold? – ah, the mysterious Dr Bluhm. Not a murmur, I'm afraid. We must fear the worst,' she said, without revealing what the worst might be. 'Still, he's not a British subject, is he?' – cheering up – 'we must let the good Belgians look after their own.'

Her room was two floors high, with gilded friezes and black wartime radiators and a balcony overlooking very private gardens. There were two armchairs and Alison Landsbury kept a cardigan over the back of hers so that you didn't sit in it by mistake. There was coffee in a thermos so that their tryst need not be interrupted. There was the mysteriously thick atmosphere of other bodies just departed. Four years Minister in Brussels, three years Defence Counsellor in Washington, Justin rehearsed, quoting from the form book. Three more back in London on attachment to the Joint Intelligence Committee. Appointed Head of Personnel six months ago. Our only recorded communications: one letter suggesting I trim my wife's wings – ignored.

One fax ordering me not to visit my own house – too late. He wondered what Alison's house was like, and awarded her a red-brick mansion flat behind Harrod's, handy for her bridge club at weekends. She was wiry and fifty-six and dressed in black for Tessa. She wore a man's signet ring on the middle finger of her left hand. Justin assumed it was her father's. A photograph on the wall showed her driving off at Moor Park. Another – somewhat ill-advisedly, in Justin's view – had her shaking hands with Helmut Kohl. Soon you'll get your women's college and be Dame Alison, he thought.

'I've spent the *whole* morning thinking of all the things I *won't* say to you,' she began, projecting her voice to the back of the hall for the benefit of latecomers. 'And all the things we simply mustn't agree on yet. I'm *not* going to ask you how you see your future. Or tell you how *we* see it. We're all *far* too upset,' she ended, with didactic satisfaction. 'By the way, I'm a Madeira cake. Don't expect me to be multi-layered. I'm the same wherever you slice me.'

She had set a laptop on the table in front of her, and it could have been Tessa's. As she spoke she prodded at the screen with a grey baton hooked at the end like a crochet needle. 'There are some things I *must* tell you, and I'll do that straight away.' Prod. 'Ah. Indefinite sick leave is the first thing. Indefinite because obviously it's subject to medical reports. Sick because you're in trauma, whether you know it or not.' So there. Prod. 'And we do counselling, and I'm afraid that with experience we're getting rather good at it.' Sad smile and another prod. 'Dr Shand. Emily outside will give you Dr Shand's *coordonnées*. You've got a provisional appointment tomorrow at eleven, but change it if you need to. Harley Street, where else? Do you mind a woman?'

'Not at all,' Justin replied hospitably.

'Where are you staying?'

'At our house. My house. In Chelsea. Will be.'

She frowned. 'But that isn't the family house?'

'Tessa's family.'

'Ah. But your father has a house in Lord North Street. Rather a beautiful one, I remember.'

'He sold it before he died.'

'Do you intend remaining in Chelsea?'

'At present.'

'Then Emily outside should have the *coordonnées* of *that* house as well, please.'

Back to the screen. Was she reading from it or hiding in it?

'Dr Shand isn't a one-night stand, she's a course. She counsels individuals, she counsels groups. And she encourages interaction between patients with similar problems. Where security permits, obviously.' Prod. 'And if it's a priest you'd like, instead of or as well, we have representatives of every denomination who've been cleared for most things so just ask. Our view here is, give *anything* a chance, provided it's secure. If Dr Shand doesn't fit, come back and we'll look for someone who does.'

Perhaps you also do acupuncture, thought Justin. But elsewhere in his head he was wondering why she was offering him security-cleared confessors when he had no secrets to confess.

'Ah. Now would you like a *haven*, Justin?' Prod.

'I'm sorry?'

'A quiet-house.' The emphasis on *quiet*, like *green*house. 'An away-from-it-all until the hue and cry dies down. Where you can be *totally* anonymous, recover your balance, take long country walks, pop up to London to see us when we need you or vice versa, pop back again. Because it's on offer. Not *wholly* free of charge in your case, but heavily subsidised by HMG. Discuss with Dr Shand before deciding?'

'If you say so.'

'I do.' Prod. 'You've suffered an awful amount of humiliation in public. How has this affected you, to your knowledge?'

'I'm afraid I haven't been in public very much. You had me hidden away, if you remember.'

'All the same you suffered it. Nobody likes to be portrayed as a deceived husband, nobody likes to have their sexuality raked over in the press. Anyway, you don't hate us. You don't feel

187

angry or resentful or demeaned. You're not about to take revenge. You're surviving. Of course you are. You're old Office.'

Uncertain whether this was a question, a complaint or merely a definition of durability, Justin let it alone, fixing his attention instead on a doomed peach-coloured begonia in a pot too close to the wartime radiator.

'I seem to have a memo here from the pay people. Do you want all this now or is it too much?' She gave it to him anyway. 'We're keeping you on full pay of *course*. Married allowances, I'm afraid, discontinued, effective from the day you became single. These are nettles one has to grasp, Justin, and in my experience they're best grasped now and accepted. And the usual return-to-UK cushioning allowances pending a decision about your eventual destination, but again obviously at single rates. Now Justin, is that *enough*?'

'Enough money?'

'Enough information for you to function for the time being.'

'Why? Is there more?'

She put down her baton and turned her gaze full on him. Years ago, Justin had had the temerity to complain at a grand store in Piccadilly, and had faced the same frigid managerial stare.

'Not as yet, Justin. Not that we're aware of. We live on tenterhooks. Bluhm's not accounted for, and the whole grisly press story will run and run until the case is cleared up one way or the other. And you're having lunch with the Pellegrin.'

'Yes.'

'Well, he's *awfully* good. You've been steadfast, Justin, you've shown grace under pressure and it's been noted. You've suffered appalling strain, I'm sure. Not only *after* Tessa's death but *before* it. We should have been firmer and brought you both home while there was time. Erring on the side of tolerance looks in retrospect very like the easy way out, I'm afraid.' Prod, and scrutinise screen with growing disapproval. 'And you've given no press interviews, have you? Not talked *at all*, on or off the record?'

'Only to the police.'

She let this go. 'And you won't. Obviously. Don't even say "no comment". In your state, you're perfectly entitled to put the phone down on them.'

'I'm sure that won't be hard.'

Prod. Pause. Study screen again. Study Justin. Return eyes to screen. 'And you've no papers or materials that belong to us? That are – how shall I say it? – our *intellectual property*? You've been asked, but I'm to ask you again in case something has come up, or comes up in the future. *Has* anything come up?'

'Of Tessa's?'

'I'm referring to her extramarital activities.' She took her time before defining what these might be. And while she did so, it dawned on Justin, a little late perhaps, that Tessa was some kind of monstrous insult to her, a disgrace to their schools and class and sex and country and the Service she had defiled; and that by extension Justin was the Trojan horse who had smuggled her into the citadel. 'I'm thinking of any research papers she may have acquired, legitimately or otherwise, in the course of her investigations or whatever she called them,' she added with frank distaste.

'I don't even know what I'm supposed to be looking for,' Justin complained.

'Neither do we. And really it's very hard for us here to understand how she ever got into this position in the first place.' Suddenly the anger that had been simmering was forcing its way out of her. She hadn't meant it to, he was sure; she had gone to great lengths to contain it. But it had evidently slipped from her control. 'It's really quite *extraordinary*, looking at what's since come to light, that Tessa was ever allowed to become *that person*. Porter has been an excellent Head of Mission in his way but I can't help feeling he must share a good deal of the blame for this.'

'For what exactly?'

Her dead stop took him by surprise. It was as if she had hit the buffers. She came to a halt, her eyes firmly on her screen.

She held the crochet needle at the ready, but made no move with it. She laid it softly on the table as if grounding her rifle at a military funeral.

'Yes, well, Porter,' she conceded. But he had made no point for her to concede.

'What's happened to him?' Justin asked.

'I think it's absolutely marvellous the way the two of them sacrificed everything for that poor child.'

'I do too. But what have they sacrificed now?'

She seemed to share his bewilderment. To need him as an ally, if only while she was denigrating Porter Coleridge. 'Terribly, terribly hard, in this job, Justin, to know where to put one's foot down. One *wants* to treat people as individuals, one *longs* to be able to fit each person's circumstances into the general picture.' But if Justin thought she was tempering her assault on Porter, he was dead wrong. She was simply reloading. 'But Porter – we have to face it – was on the spot and we weren't. We can't act if we're kept in the dark. It's no good asking us to pick up the pieces *ex post facto* if we haven't been informed *a priori*. Is it?'

'I suppose not.'

'And if Porter was too starry-eyed, too tied up with his *awful* family problems – nobody disputes that – to see what was developing under his nose – the Bluhm thing and so on, I'm sorry – he had an absolutely first-class lieutenant in Sandy, with a very safe pair of hands, *at* his elbow, *any* time, to spell it out for him in words a foot high. Which Sandy did. Ad nauseam, one gathers. But to no effect. So I mean it's perfectly clear that the child – obviously – the poor girl – Rosie or whatever its name is – claims *all* their out-of-hours attention. Which isn't *necessarily* what one appoints a High Commissioner for. Is it?'

Justin made a meek face, indicating his sympathy with her dilemma.

'I'm not prying, Justin. I'm asking you. How is it possible – how *was* it possible – forget Porter for a moment – for your wife to engage in a *range* of activities of which, by your account,

190

you knew nothing? All right. She was a modern woman. Jolly good luck to her. She led her life, she had her relationships.' Pointed silence. 'I'm not suggesting you should have restrained her, that would be sexist. I'm asking you *how*, in reality, you remained *totally* ignorant of her *activities* – her enquiries – her – how shall I put it? I'd like to say *meddling*, actually.'

'We had an arrangement,' Justin said.

'Of course you did. Equal and parallel lives. But in the same *house*, Justin! Are you really saying she told you nothing, *showed* you nothing, *shared* nothing? I find that awfully hard to believe.'

'I do too,' Justin agreed. 'But I'm afraid it's what happens when you put your head in the sand.'

Prod. 'So now did you share her computer?'

'Did I what?'

'The question is perfectly clear. Did you share, or otherwise have access to, Tessa's laptop computer? You may not know it, but she addressed some very strong documents to the Office, among others. Raising grave allegations about certain people. Accusing them of awful things. Making trouble of a potentially very damaging kind.'

'Potentially damaging to whom, actually, Alison?' Justin asked, delicately fishing for any free gifts of information she might care to bestow.

'It's not a matter of *whom*, Justin,' she replied severely. 'It's whether you have Tessa's laptop computer in your possession and, if not, where is it, physically at this moment in time and what does it contain?'

'We never shared it, is the answer to your first question. It was hers and hers alone. I wouldn't even know how to get into it.'

'Never mind getting into it. You have it in your possession, that's the main thing. Scotland Yard asked you for it, but you, very wisely and loyally, concluded that it was better in the Office's hands than theirs. We're grateful for that. It's been noted.'

It was a statement, it was a binary question. Tick box A for yes I have it, box B for no I haven't. It was an order and a challenge. And, judging by her crystal stare, it was a threat.

'And disks, obviously,' she added while she waited. 'She was an efficient woman, which makes it all so odd, a lawyer. She's sure to have made copies of whatever was important to her. In the circumstances these disks also constitute a breach of security and we'd like them as well, please.'

'There aren't any disks. Weren't.'

'Of course there were. How can she have run a computer without keeping disks?'

'I looked high and low. There weren't any.'

'How very bizarre.'

'Yes, isn't it?'

'So I think the *best* thing you can do, Justin, on reflection, is bring everything you've got into the Office as *soon* as you've unpacked it, and let us handle it from then on. To spare you the pain and the responsibility. Yes? We can do a deal. Anything that isn't relevant to our concerns belongs to you *exclusively*. We'll print it out, and give it to you, and nobody here will read it or evaluate it or commit it to memory in any way. Shall we send somebody with you now? Would that help? Yes?'

'I'm not sure.'

'Not sure you want a second person? You should be. A sympathetic colleague of your own grade? Someone you can trust entirely? Now are you sure?'

'It was Tessa's, you see. She bought it, she used it.'

'So?'

'So I'm not sure you should be asking me to do that. Give you her property to be plundered just because she's dead.' Feeling sleepy, he closed his eyes a moment, then shook his head to wake himself. 'Anyway, it's not an issue, is it?'

'Why not, pray?'

'Because I haven't got it.' He stood up, taking himself by surprise, but he needed a stretch and some fresh air. 'The Kenyan police probably stole it. They steal most things. Thank you, Alison. You've been very kind.'

Recovering the Gladstone from the head janitor took a little longer than was natural.

'Sorry to be premature,' Justin said while he waited.

'You're not premature at all, sir,' the head janitor retorted, and flushed.

*   *   *

'Justin, my dear fellow!'

Justin had started to give his name to the club porter at the door, but Pellegrin was ahead of him, pounding down the steps to claim him, smiling his decent chap's smile and calling out, 'He's mine, Jimmy, shove his bag in your glory-hole and put him down to me,' before grasping Justin's hand and flinging his other arm round Justin's shoulders in a powerful un-English gesture of friendship and commiseration.

'You're up to this, are you?' he asked confidingly, first making sure no one was within earshot. 'We can take a walk in the park if you'd rather. Or do it another time. Just say.'

'I'm fine, Bernard. Really.'

'The Beast of Landsbury didn't wear you out?'

'Not a bit.'

'I've booked us in the dining room. There's a bar lunch, but it's eat off your crotch and a lot of ex-Office wrinklies moaning about Suez. Need a pee?'

The dining room was a risen catafalque with painted cherubs posturing in a ceiling of blue sky. Pellegrin's chosen place of worship was a corner sheltered by a polished granite pillar and a sad dracaena palm. Round them sat the timeless Whitehall brethren in chemical grey suits and school haircuts. This was my world, Justin explained to her. When I married you, I was still one of them.

'Let's get rid of the hard work first,' Pellegrin proposed masterfully, when a West Indian waiter in a mauve dinner jacket had handed them menus shaped like ping-pong bats. And that was tactful of Pellegrin and typical of his decent chap's image, because by studying menus they were able to settle to each other and avoid eye contact. 'Flight bearable?'

'Very, thank you. They upgraded me.'

'Marvellous, marvellous, *marvellous* girl, Justin,' Pellegrin murmured, over the parapet of his ping-pong bat. 'Enough said.'

'Thank you, Bernard.'

'Great spirit, great guts. Bugger the rest. Meat or fish? – not a Monday – what have you been eating out there?'

Justin had known Bernard Pellegrin in snatches for most of his career. He had followed Bernard in Ottawa and they had briefly coincided in Beirut. In London they had attended a hostage survival course together and shared such gems as how to establish that you are being pursued by a group of armed thugs not afraid to die; how to preserve your dignity when they blindfold you and bind you hand and foot with sticky plaster and sling you into the boot of their Mercedes; and the best way to jump out of an upper-storey window if you can't use the stairs, but presumably have your feet free.

'All journalists are shits,' Pellegrin declared confidently, still from inside his menu. 'Know what I'm going to do one day? Doorstep the buggers. Do what they did to you, but do it back to 'em. Rent a mob, picket the editor of the *Grauniad* and the *Screws of the World* while they're having it away with their floozies. Photograph their kids going to school. Ask their wives what their old men are like in bed. Show the shits what it feels like to be at the receiving end. Did you want to take a machine-gun to the lot of 'em?'

'Not really.'

'Me too. Illiterate bunch of hypocrites. Herring fillet's all right. Smoked eel makes me fart. Sole meunière's good if you like sole. If you don't, have it grilled.' He was writing on a printed pad. It had Sir Bernard P printed in electronic capitals at the top, and the food options listed on the left side, and boxes to tick on the right, and space for the member's signature at the bottom.

'A sole would be fine.'

Pellegrin doesn't listen, Justin remembered. It's what got him his reputation as a negotiator.

'Grilled?'

'Meunière.'

'Landsbury in form?'

'Fighting fit.'

'She tell you she was a Madeira cake?'

'I'm afraid she did.'

'She wants to watch that one. She talk to you about your future?'

'I'm in trauma and on indefinite sick leave.'

'Shrimps do you?'

'I think I'd prefer the avocado, thank you,' Justin said, and watched Pellegrin tick shrimp cocktail twice.

'The Foreign Office formally disapproves of drinking at lunchtime these days, you'll be relieved to hear,' Pellegrin said, surprising Justin with a full-beam smile. Then, in case the first application hadn't taken, a second one. And Justin remembered that the smiles were always the same: the same length, the same duration, the same degree of spontaneous warmth. 'However, you're a compassionate case and it's my painful duty to keep you company. They do a passable sub-Meursault. You good for your half?' His silver propelling pencil ticked the appropriate box. 'You're cleared, by the by. Off the hook. Sprung. Congratulations.' He tore off the chit and weighted it down with the salt cellar to prevent it from blowing away.

'Cleared of what?'

'Murder, what else? You didn't kill Tessa or her driver, you didn't hire contract killers in a den of vice, and you haven't got Bluhm swinging by his balls in your attic. You can leave the courtroom without a stain on your escutcheon. Courtesy of the coppers.' The order form had disappeared from underneath the salt cellar. The waiter must have taken it, but Justin in his out-of-body state had failed to spot the manoeuvre. 'What sort of gardening you get up to out there by the by? Promised Celly

I'd ask you.' Celly short for Céline, Pellegrin's terrifying wife. 'Exotics? Succulents? Not my scene, I'm afraid.'

'Pretty well everything really,' Justin heard himself say. 'The Kenyan climate is extremely benign. I didn't know there *was* a stain on my escutcheon, Bernard. There was a *theory*, I suppose. But it was only a remote hypothesis.'

'Had all *sorts* of theories, poor darlings. Theories *far* above their station, frankly. You must come down to Dorchester some time. Talk to Celly about it. Do a weekend. Play tennis?'

'I'm afraid I don't.'

They *had* all sorts of theories, he was surreptitiously repeating to himself. *Poor darlings*. Pellegrin speaks about Rob and Lesley the way Landsbury spoke about Porter Coleridge. That turd Tom Somebody was about to get Belgrade, Pellegrin was saying, largely because the Secretary of State couldn't stand the sight of his beastly face in London, and who could? Dick Somebody Else was getting his K in the next Honours, then with any luck he'd be kicked upstairs to Treasury – God help the national economy, joke – but of course old Dick's been kissing New Labour arse for the last five years. Otherwise, it was business as usual. The Office continued to fill up with the same red-brick achievers from Croydon with off-colour accents and Fair-Isle pullovers that Justin would remember from his pre-Africa days; in ten years' time there wouldn't be One of Us left. The waiter brought two shrimp cocktails. Justin watched their arrival in slow motion.

'But then they were young, weren't they,' Pellegrin said indulgently, resuming his requiem mode.

'The new entrants? Of course they were.'

'Your little policemen people in Nairobi. Young and hungry, bless 'em. As we all were once.'

'I thought they were rather clever.'

Pellegrin frowned and chewed. '*David* Quayle any relation of yours?'

'My nephew.'

'We signed him up last week. Only twenty-one, but how else

d'you beat the City to the draw these days? Godchild o' mine started up at Barclays last week on forty-five grand a year plus treats. Thick as two planks and still wet behind the ears.'

'Good for David. I didn't know.'

'Extraordinary choice for Gridley to have made, be honest, sending out a woman like that to Africa. Frank's worked diplomats. Knows the scene. Who's going to take a female copper seriously over there? Not Moi's Boys, *that's* for sure.'

'Gridley?' Justin repeated, as the mists in his head cleared. 'That's not Frank *Arthur* Gridley? The fellow who was in charge of diplomatic security?'

'The same, God help us.'

'But he's an absolute ninny. We dealt with him when I was in Protocol Department.' Justin heard his voice rising above the club's approved decibel level, and hastened to bring it down.

'Wood from the neck,' Pellegrin agreed cheerfully.

'So what on earth's he doing investigating Tessa's murder?'

'Limogé to Serious Crime. Specialist in overseas cases. You know what coppers are like,' said Pellegrin, stacking his mouth with shrimps and bread and butter.

'I know what Gridley's like.'

Masticating shrimp, Pellegrin lapsed into High Tory telegramese. 'Two young police officers, one of 'em a woman. T'other thinks he's Robin Hood. High-profile case, eyes of the world on 'em. Start to see their names going up in lights.' He adjusted the napkin at his throat. 'So they cook up *theories*. Nothing like a good *theory* to impress a half-educated superior.' He drank, then hammered his mouth with a corner of his napkin. 'Contract killers – bent African governments – multinational conglomerates – *fabulous* stuff! May even get a part in the movie, if they're lucky.'

'What multinational did they have in mind?' Justin asked, contriving to ignore the disgusting notion of a film about Tessa's death.

Pellegrin caught his eye, measured it a moment, smiled, then smiled again. 'Turn of phrase,' he explained dismissively. 'Not to be taken literally. Those young coppers were looking the wrong way from day one,' he resumed, diverting himself while the waiter refilled their glasses. 'Deplorable, actually. De-fucking-plorable. Not you, Matthew, old chap –' this to the waiter, in a spirit of good fellowship towards ethnic minorities – 'and not a member of this club either, I'm pleased to say.' The waiter fled. 'Tried to pin it on Sandy for five minutes, if you can believe it. Some fatuous theory that he was in love with her, and had 'em both killed out of jealousy. When they couldn't get anywhere with that one, they hit the conspiracy button. Easiest thing in the world. Cherry-pick a few facts, cobble 'em together, listen to a couple of disgruntled alarmists with an axe to grind, throw in a household name or two, you can put together any bloody story you want. What Tessa did, if you don't mind my saying so. Well, *you* know all about that.'

Justin blindly shook his head. I'm not hearing this. I'm back on the plane and it's a dream. 'I'm afraid I don't,' he said.

Pellegrin had very small eyes. Justin hadn't noticed this before. Or perhaps they were a standard size, but had developed the art of dwindling under enemy fire – the enemy, so far as Justin could determine, being anyone who held Pellegrin to what he had just said, or took the conversation into territory not previously charted by him.

'Sole all right? You should have had the meunière. Not so dry.'

His sole was marvellous, Justin said, forbearing to add that meunière was what he had asked for. And the sub-Meursault also marvellous. Marvellous, like *marvellous girl*.

'She didn't show it to you. Her great thesis. *Their* great thesis, if you'll forgive me. That's your story and you're sticking to it. Right?'

'Thesis about *what*? The police asked me the same question. So did Alison Landsbury in a roundabout way. What thesis?' He was acting simple and beginning to believe himself. He was fishing again, but in disguise.

'She didn't show it to you but she showed it to Sandy,' said

Pellegrin, washing the information down with a pull of wine. 'Is that what you want me to believe?'

Justin sat bolt upright. 'She *what?*'

'Absolutely. Secret rendezvous, whole works. Sorry about that. Thought you knew.'

But you're relieved I don't, thought Justin, still staring at Pellegrin in mystification. 'So what did Sandy do with it?' he asked.

'Showed it to Porter. Porter dithered. Porter takes decisions once a year with lots of water. Sandy sent it to me. Co-authored and marked confidential. Not by Sandy. By Tessa and Bluhm. Those aid heroes make me sick, by the way, if you feel like letting off steam. Teddy bears' picnic for international bureaucrats. Diversion. Sorry.'

'So what did *you* do with it? For God's sake, Bernard!'

I'm the deluded widower at the end of my tether. I'm the injured innocent, not quite as innocent as I'm sounding. I'm the indignant husband, cut out of the loop by my wandering wife and her lover. 'Will somebody please *finally* tell me what this is about?' he went on, in the same querulous voice. 'I've been Sandy's reluctant house guest for the better part of an eternity. He never breathed a word to me about a secret rendez-vous with Tessa or Arnold or anybody else. What *thesis?* Thesis about *what?*' Still prodding.

Pellegrin was smiling again. Once. Twice. 'So it's all news to you. Jolly good.'

'Yes. It is. I'm completely fogged.'

'Girl like that, half your age, stepping high, wide and loose, never crossed your mind to ask her what the fuck she's up to.'

The Pellegrin is angry, Justin noted. As Landsbury was. As I am. We're all angry and we're all concealing it.

'No, it didn't. And she wasn't half my age.'

'Never looked in her diary, picked up the telephone extension by-mistake-on-purpose. Never read her mail or peeked in her computer. Zero.'

'Zero to all of it.'

Pellegrin was musing aloud, eyes on Justin. 'So nothing got through to you. Hear no evil, see no evil. Amazing,' he said, barely managing to keep his sarcasm within bounds.

'She was a lawyer, Bernard. She wasn't a child. She was a fully qualified, very smart lawyer. You forget.'

'Do I? Not sure I do.' He put on his reading spectacles in order to work his way to the lower half of his sole. When he had done so, he held up its spine with his knife and fork while he peered round like a helpless invalid for a waiter who could bring him a débris plate. 'Just hope she confined her representations to Sandy Woodrow, that's all. Pestered the main player, we know that.'

'What main player? You mean *you*?'

'Curtiss. Kenny K himself. The man.' A plate appeared and Pellegrin laid the spine on it. 'Surprised she didn't throw herself in front of his bloody racehorses while she was about it. Go sing it to Brussels. Go sing it to the United Nations. Go sing it on TV. Girl like that, mission to save the globe, goes wherever her fancy takes her and to hell with the consequences.'

'That's not true at all,' said Justin, wrestling with astonishment and serious rage.

'Say again?'

'Tessa went to great pains to protect me. And her country.'

'By raking up muck? Blowing it out of all proportion? Importuning hubby's boss? Barging in on overworked company executives with Bluhm on her arm – not my idea of protecting her chap. More like the fast lane to wrecking the poor sod's chances if you ask me. Not that your chances were all that bright by then, if we're honest.' A pull of fizzy water. 'Ah. Got it now. I see what happened.' A double smile. 'You *really* don't know the back story. You're sticking to that.'

'Yes. I am. I'm utterly bewildered. The police ask me, Alison asks me, you ask me – was I really in the dark? Answer, yes I was, and yes I still am.'

Pellegrin was already shaking his head in amused disbelief. 'Old boy. How's this? Listen a mo. I could live with this. So could Alison. They came to you. The two of 'em. Tessa and Arnold. Hand in hand. "Help us, Justin. We've found the smoking gun. Old-established, British-based company is poisoning innocent Kenyans, using 'em as guinea pigs, Christ knows what. Whole villages of corpses out there and here's the proof. Read it." Right?'

'They did nothing of the kind.'

'Not done yet. Nobody's trying to pin anything on you, right? It's open doors round here. Everyone's your chum.'

'So I've noticed.'

'You hear 'em out. Decent chap that you are. You read their eighteen-page Armageddon scenario and you tell 'em they're out of their tiny minds. If they want to foul up Anglo-Kenyan relations for the next twenty years, they've found the ideal formula. Wise chap. If Celly had tried that one with me, I'd have given her a bloody good kick in the arse. And like you, I'd pretend the meeting never happened, which it didn't. Right? We'll forget it as fast as you did. Nothing on your file, nothing in Alison's little black book. Deal?'

'They didn't come to me, Bernard. Nobody pitched me a story, nobody showed me an Armageddon scenario, as you call it. Not Tessa, not Bluhm, not anyone. It's all a total mystery to me.'

'Girl called Ghita Pearson, who the hell's she?'

'A junior member of Chancery. Anglo-Indian. Very bright and locally employed. Mother's a doctor. Why?'

'Apart from that.'

'A friend of Tessa's. And mine.'

'Could she have seen it?'

'The document? I'm sure not.'

'Why?'

'Tessa would have kept it from her.'

'She didn't keep it from Sandy Woodrow.'

'Ghita's too fragile. She's trying to make herself a career with us. Tessa wouldn't have wanted to put her in an untenable position.'

Pellegrin needed more salt, which he distributed by putting a small pile of it in his left palm, taking pinches with his right forefinger and thumb, then brushing his two hands together.

'Anyway. You're off the hook,' he reminded Justin as if this were a consolation prize. 'We won't be standing at the prison gates, shoving *baguettes au fromage* at you through the bars.'

'So you said. I'm glad to hear it.'

'That's the good news. Bad news is – your chum Arnold. Yours and Tessa's.'

'Have they found him?'

Pellegrin shook his head grimly. 'They've rumbled him, but they haven't found him. But they're hoping.'

'Rumbled him for what? What are you talking about?'

'Deep waters, old boy. Very hard to navigate in your state of health. Wish we could be having this conversation in a few weeks' time when you've got your bearings, but we can't. Murder investigations are no respecters of persons unfortunately. They go at their own speed in their own way. Bluhm was your chum, Tessa was your wife. Not much fun for any of us to have to tell you chum killed wife.'

Justin stared at Pellegrin in unfeigned astonishment, but Pellegrin was too busy with his fish to notice. 'But what about the forensic evidence?' he heard himself ask, from some frozen planet. 'The green safari truck? The beer bottles and cigarette ends? The two men who were spotted in Marsabit? What about – I don't know – ThreeBees, all the things the British police were asking me about?'

Pellegrin was smiling the first of his two smiles before Justin had finished speaking. 'Fresh evidence, old boy. Conclusive, I'm afraid.' He popped another piece of roll. 'Coppers have found his clothes. Bluhm's. Buried at the lakeside. Not his safari jacket. He left that in the jeep as a blind. Shirt, trousers, underpants, socks, sneakers. Know what they found in the pocket of the trousers? Car keys. From the jeep. The ones he'd locked the jeep door with. Gives a new meaning to what the Yanks call *closure* these days. Very common thing with your crime of passion, I'm told. You kill somebody, lock the door behind you, lock up your mind. Thing never happened. Memory erased. Classic.'

Distracted by Justin's incredulous expression, Pellegrin paused, then spoke in a voice of conclusion.

'I'm an *Oswald* man, Justin. Lee Harvey Oswald shot John F. Kennedy. Nobody helped him do it. Arnold Bluhm lost his rag and killed Tessa. The driver objected so Bluhm took a swing at him too. Then he chucked his head into the bushes for the jackals. *Basta*. There comes a moment, after all the wanking and fantasising, when we're reduced to accepting the obvious. Sticky toffee pudding? Apple crumble?' He signalled to the waiter for coffee. 'Mind if I give you one quiet word of warning between old friends?'

'Please do.'

'You're on sick leave. You're in hell. But you're old Office, you know the rules and you're still an Africa man. And you're on my watch.' And lest Justin might think this was some kind of romantic definition of his status: 'Plenty of plums out there for a chap who's got himself sorted. Plenty of places I wouldn't be seen dead in. And if you're harbouring so-called confidential information that you shouldn't have – in your head or anywhere else – it belongs to us, not you. Rougher world these days than the one we grew up in. Lot of mean chaps around with everything to go for and a lot to lose. Makes for bad manners.'

As we have learned to our cost, thought Justin from far inside his glass capsule. He rose weightlessly from the table and was surprised to see his own image in a great number of mirrors at the same time. He saw himself from all angles, at all ages of his life. Justin the lost child in big houses, friend of cooks and gardeners. Justin the schoolboy rugby star. Justin the professional bachelor, burying his loneliness in numbers. Justin the Foreign Office white hope and no-hoper, photographed with his friend the dracaena palm. Justin the newly widowed father of his dead and only son.

'You've been very kind, Bernard. Thank you.'

Thank you for the master-class in sophistry, he meant, if he meant anything. Thank you for proposing a film of my wife's murder and riding roughshod over every last sensitivity I had left. Thank you for her eighteen-page Armageddon scenario and her secret rendezvous with Woodrow, and other tantalising additions to my awakening recollection. And thank you for the quiet word of warning, delivered with the glint of steel in your eye. Because when I look closely, I see the same glint in mine.

'You've gone pale,' Pellegrin said accusingly. 'Something wrong, old boy?'

'I'm fine. All the better for seeing you, Bernard.'

'Get some sleep. You're running on empty. And we must do that weekend. Bring a chum. Someone who can play a bit.'

'Arnold Bluhm never hurt a living soul,' Justin said, carefully and clearly, as Pellegrin helped him into his raincoat and gave him back his bag. But whether he said this aloud, or to the thousand voices screaming in his head, he could not be absolutely sure.

CHAPTER TEN

It was the house he hated in his memory whenever he was away from it: big and shaggy and overbearingly parental, number four of a leafy Chelsea backwater, with a front garden that stayed as wild as it wanted, however much Justin pampered it when he had a bit of home leave. And the remains of Tessa's tree-house stuck like a rotting life-raft in the dead oak that she wouldn't let him cut down. And broken balloons of ancient vintage, and shreds of kite harpooned on the dead tree's wiry branches. And a rusted iron gate that, when he shoved it against a slough of rotting leaves, sent the neighbour's wall-eyed tomcat slinking into the undergrowth. And a pair of ill-tempered cherry trees that he supposed he should worry about because they had peach-curl.

It was the house he had dreaded all day long, and all last week while he was serving out his time in the lower ground, and all through his pounding westward walk through the lonely half-dark of a London winter's afternoon, while his mind puzzled its way through the labyrinth of monstrosities in his head, and the Gladstone bag bumped against his leg. It was the house that held the parts of her he had never shared and now he never would.

A keen wind was rattling the awnings of the greengrocer's across the road, sending leaves and late shoppers scurrying along the pavement. But Justin, despite his lightweight suit, had too much inside him to be conscious of the cold. The tiled steps to the front door clanged as he stomped up them. Reaching the top he swung round and took a long stare back, he wasn't sure for what. A dosser lay bundled beneath the NatWest cash machine. An illegally parked man and woman sat arguing in their car. A thin man in a trilby hat and raincoat was leaning into his cellphone. In a civilised country you can never tell. The fan window over the front door was lit from inside. Not wishing to surprise anybody he pressed the bell and heard its familiar rusty sound, like a ship's klaxon, honking on the first floor landing. Who's at home? he wondered, waiting for a footstep. Aziz the Moroccan painter and his boyfriend Raoul. Petronilla, the Nigerian girl in search of God, and her fifty-year-old Guatemalan priest. Tall, chain-smoking Gazon the cadaverous French doctor, who had worked with Arnold in Algeria, and had Arnold's same regretful smile, and Arnold's way of halting in mid-sentence and half closing his eyes in painful memory, and waiting for his head to clear itself of Heaven knew what nightmares before taking up the thread again.

Hearing no call or thump of feet, he turned the key and stepped into the hall, expecting smells of African cooking, the din of reggae over the radio and raucous coffee-chatter from the kitchen.

'Hullo there!' he called. 'It's Justin. Me.'

No answering yell, no surge of music, no kitchen smells or voices. No sounds at all, beyond the shuffle of traffic from the street outside, and the echo of his own voice climbing up the stairwell. All he saw instead was Tessa's head, cut at the neck from a newspaper and backed on cardboard, staring at him from a parade of jam-jars filled with flowers. And amid the jam-jars, a folded sheet of cartridge paper torn, he guessed, from Aziz's drawing book, with handwritten messages of sorrow, love and farewell from Tessa's vanished tenants: *Justin, we didn't feel we could stay*, dated last Monday.

He refolded the paper and replaced it among the jars. He stood to attention, eyes dead ahead as he blinked away his tears. Leaving the Gladstone on the hall floor, he made his way to the kitchen, using the wall to steady himself. He pulled open the fridge. Empty except for one forgotten bottle of prescription medicine, a woman's name on the label, unfamiliar. Annie Somebody. Must be one of Gazon's. He groped his way down the corridor to the dining room and put on the lights.

Her father's hideous pseudo-Tudor dining room. Six scrolled and crested chairs for fellow megalomaniacs to either side of it. An embroidered carver head and tail for the royal couple. *Daddy knew it was terribly ugly but he loved it, so I do too*, she was telling him. *Well, I don't*, he was thinking, *but God forbid I say so*. In their first months together Tessa had talked of nothing but her father and mother, till under Justin's artful guidance she set to work exorcising their ghosts by filling the house with people of her own age, the crazier the merrier: Etonian Trotskyists, drunken Polish prelates and oriental mystics, plus half the freeloaders of the known world. But once she discovered Africa, her aim steadied, and number four became instead a haven for introverted aid workers and activists of every dubious shade. Still scanning the room, Justin's eye settled disapprovingly on a crescent of soot that lay around the marble fireplace, coating the fire-dogs and fender. Jackdaws, he thought. And let his eye continue drifting round the room until once more it settled on the soot. Then let his mind settle on it too. And stay settled while he argued with himself. Or with Tessa, which was much the same.

Which jackdaws?

When jackdaws?

The message in the hall is dated Monday.

Ma Gates comes on Wednesdays – Ma Gates being Mrs Dora Gates, Tessa's old nanny, never anything but Ma.

And if Ma Gates is under the weather, her daughter Pauline comes.

And if Pauline can't make it, there's always her tarty sister Debbie.

And it was unthinkable that any one of these women would ignore such a conspicuous patch of soot.

Therefore the jackdaws launched their attack *after* Wednesday and *before* this evening.

So if the house emptied on the *Monday* – see message – and Ma Gates cleaned on *Wednesday* – why was there a crisp male-sized, heavily profiled footprint, probably a track shoe, in the soot?

A telephone stood on the sideboard, next to an address book. Ma Gates' number was scrawled in red crayon in Tessa's hand on the inside cover. He dialled it and got Pauline, who burst into tears and passed him to her mother.

'I'm very, very sorry, dear,' said Ma Gates, slowly and clearly. 'Sorrier than you or I can say, Mr Justin. Or ever will be able to.'

His interrogation of her began: long and tender as it had to be, with a lot more listening than asking. Yes, Ma Gates had come as usual on the Wednesday, nine till twelve, she'd wanted to . . . It was a chance to be with Miss Tessa all alone . . . She'd cleaned the way she'd always cleaned, nothing skimped or forgotten . . . And she'd had a cry and a pray . . . And if it was all right by him, she'd like to continue coming as before, please, Wednesdays just like when Miss Tessa was alive, it wasn't the money, it was the memory . . .

Soot? Certainly not! There'd been no soot on the dining room floor Wednesday or she'd have seen it for sure, and cleared it up before it got trodden in. London soot's so greasy! With those big fireplaces she *always* had an eye for soot! And no, Mr Justin, the chimney sweep certainly *didn't* have a key.

And did Mr Justin know whether they had found Dr Arnold yet, because of all the gentlemen who ever used the house, Dr Arnold was the one she cared about the most, whatever you read in the papers, they only make it up . . .

'You're very kind, Mrs Gates.'

Switching on the chandelier in the drawing room, he allowed himself a glimpse of the things that were for ever Tessa: the riding rosettes from her childhood; Tessa after her first communion; their wedding portrait on the steps of the tiny church of Sant'Antonio, Elba. But the fireplace was what he was thinking about hardest. The hearth was of slate, the grate a low Victorian affair, brass and steel mixed, with brass claws to hold the fire irons. Hearth and grate were coated in soot. The same soot lay in black lines along the steel shafts of the tongs and poker.

So here's a fine mystery of nature then, he told Tessa: two unrelated colonies of jackdaws elect at the identical moment to hurl soot down two unconnected chimneys. What do we make of that? You a lawyer and me a protected species?

But in the drawing room, no footprint. Whoever searched the dining room fireplace had obligingly left a footprint. Whoever searched the drawing room fireplace – whether the same man or a different one – had not.

Yet why should anyone search a fireplace, let alone two? True, ancient fireplaces traditionally provide hiding-places for love letters, wills, shameful diaries and bags of gold sovereigns. True also, according to legend, that chimneys were inhabited by spirits. True that the wind used old chimneys to tell stories, many of them secret. And a cold wind was blowing this evening, snapping at shutters and rattling locks. But why search *these* fireplaces? *Our* fireplaces? Why number four? Unless of course the chimneys were part of a more general search of the entire house – sideshows, as it were, to the main thrust.

At the half-landing, he paused to study Tessa's medicine chest, an old Italian spice cabinet of no merit screwed into the angle of the stairwell and marked with a green cross hand-stencilled by herself. Not for nothing was she a doctor's daughter. The door of the cabinet was ajar. He poked it open the rest of the way.

Pillaged. Tins of plaster, tipped open, lint and packets of boracic powder strewn about in an angry mess. He was closing the door on it as the landing telephone shrieked beside his head.

It's for you, he told Tessa. I'll have to say you're dead. It's for me, he told her. I'll have to listen to condolences. It's the Madeira Cake asking whether I've got everything I need to keep me safe and quiet in my trauma. It's somebody who had to wait until the line was clear after my five-mile conversation with Ma Gates.

He lifted the receiver and heard a busy woman. Tinny voices echoed behind her, footsteps chimed. A busy woman in a busy place with a stone floor. A humorously spoken, busy cockney woman with a voice like a barrow-girl's.

'Now then! Can I speak to a Mr Justin Quayle, please, if he's at home?' Delivered with ceremony, as if she were about to perform a card trick. 'He's in, darling, I can hear' – aside.

'This is Quayle.'

'Do you want to talk to him yourself, darling?' Darling didn't. 'Only it's Jeffrey's the florists here, Mr Quayle, in the King's Road. We've got a lovely floral arrangement of I-won't-say-whats to be delivered to you personally without fail this evening if you're in, as soon as possible, and I'm not to say who from – right, darling?' It evidently was. 'So how would it be if I send the boy round *now* is the question, Mr Quayle? Two minutes he'll be there, won't you, Kevin? One, if you give him a nice drink.'

Then send him, said Justin distractedly.

*   *   *

He was facing the door to Arnold's room, so named because when Arnold stayed in the house he never failed to leave behind a wistful claim to permanence – a pair of shoes, an electric razor, an alarm clock, a pile of papers on the abysmal failure of medical aid to the Third World. The sight of Arnold's camel-hair cardigan sprawled over the back of his chair nevertheless stopped Justin short, and he was close to calling Arnold's name as he advanced on the desk.

Ransacked.

Drawers prised open, papers and stationery yanked out and slung carelessly back.

The klaxon was honking. He raced downstairs, steadying himself as he reached the front door. Kevin the flower boy was red-cheeked and small, a Dickensian flower boy shiny from the winter cold. The irises and lilies across his arms were as big as he was. A white envelope was tied to the wire that bound the stems. Rummaging through a fistful of Kenyan shillings, Justin found two English pounds, gave them to the boy and closed the door on him. He opened the envelope and took out a white card wrapped in thick paper so that the writing wouldn't show through the envelope. The message was electronically printed.

Justin. Leave your house at seven-thirty tonight. Bring a briefcase stuffed with newspaper. Walk to the Cineflex theatre in the King's Road. Buy a ticket for Screen Two and watch the film till nine o'clock. Leave with your briefcase by the side (western) exit. Look for a parked blue minibus close to the exit. You will recognise the driver. Burn this.

No signature.

He examined the envelope, sniffed it, sniffed the card, smelled nothing, didn't know what he was expecting to smell. He took the card and envelope to the kitchen, set a match to them and, in the best traditions of the Foreign Service security course, put them in the sink to burn. When they had burned, he broke the ash and coaxed the fragments into the disposal unit, which he ran for longer than necessary. He started back up the stairs, two at a time till he reached the top of the house. It was not haste that drove him but determination: *don't think, act.* A locked attic door faced him. He held a key ready. His expression was resolute but apprehensive. He was a desperate man steeling himself for the leap. He flung back the door and strode into the tiny hall. It led to a run of attic rooms set amid jackdaw-infested chimney pots and secret bits of flat roof for growing pot plants and making love. He barged forward, eyes wrinkled into slits to resist the glare of memory. Not an object, picture, chair or corner but Tessa owned it, dwelled in it, spoke from it. Her father's pompous desk, made over to him on her wedding day, stood in its familiar alcove. He threw back the top. What did I tell you? Pillaged. He yanked open her clothes cupboard and saw her winter coats and frocks, torn from their hangers and left to die with their pockets inside out. Honestly, darling, you could have hung them up. *You know perfectly well that I did, and someone pulled them down.* Delving beneath them he unearthed Tessa's old music case, the nearest he could get to a briefcase.

'Let's do this together,' he told her, aloud now.

About to leave, he paused to spy on her through the open bedroom door. She had come out of the bathroom and was standing naked in front of the mirror, head to one side as she combed out her wet hair. One bare foot was turned ballet-style towards him, which was what it always seemed to do when she was naked. One hand was lifted to her head. Watching her, he felt the same inexpressible estrangement from her that he had felt when she was alive. You're too perfect, too young, he told her. I should have left you in the wild. *Bullshit*, she replied sweetly, and he felt much better.

Descending to the ground floor kitchen he found a heap of old copies of the *Kenyan Standard, Africa Confidential, The Spectator* and *Private Eye.* He stuffed them into her music case, returned to the hall, took a last look at her makeshift shrine and the Gladstone. I'm leaving it where they can find it in case they're not satisfied with their work this morning at the Office, he explained to her, and stepped into the freezing dark. The walk to the cinema took him ten minutes. Screen Two was three-quarters empty. He paid no attention to the film. Twice he had to slink to the men's lavatory, music case in hand, to consult his wristwatch unobserved. At five to nine he left by the western exit to find himself in a bitterly cold side street. A parked blue minibus stared at him, and he had an absurd moment of imagining it was the green safari truck from Marsabit. Its headlights winked. An angular figure in a seaman's cap lounged in the driver's seat.

'Back door,' Rob ordered.

Justin walked to the rear of the bus and saw the door already open, and Lesley's arm outstretched to receive the music case. Landing on a wooden seat in pitch blackness, he was in Muthaiga again, on the slatted bench of the Volkswagen van, with Livingstone at the wheel and Woodrow sitting opposite him giving orders.

'We're following you, Justin,' Lesley explained. Her voice in the darkness was urgent, yet mysteriously despondent. It was as if she too had suffered a great loss. 'The surveillance team followed you to the cinema and we're part of it. Now we're covering the side exit in case you come out that way. There's always a possibility that the quarry gets bored and leaves early. You just did. In five minutes, that's what we'll report to mission control. Which way are you heading?'

'East.'

'So you'll hail a cab and go east. We'll report the number of your cab. We won't follow you because you'd recognise us. There's a second surveillance car waiting for you at the front of the cinema and a spare lying up in the King's Road for contingencies. If you decide to walk or take a tube, they'll drop a couple of pedestrians behind you. If you catch a bus, they'll be grateful because there's nothing easier than getting stuck behind a London bus. If you go into a phone box and make a call, they'll listen to it. They have a Home Office warrant and it works wherever you happen to phone from.'

'Why?' Justin asked.

His eyes were growing accustomed to the light. Rob had draped his long body over the back of the driver's seat, making himself part of the conversation. His manner was as abject as Lesley's but more hostile.

'Because you crapped on us,' he said.

Lesley was dragging newspaper out of Tessa's music case and stuffing it into a plastic carrier bag. A wad of large envelopes lay at her feet, perhaps a dozen. She began loading them into the music case.

'I don't understand,' Justin said.

'Well, try,' Rob advised. 'We're under sealed orders, right? We tell Mr Gridley what you do. Someone up there says why you do it, but not to us. We're the help.'

'Who searched my house?'

'In Nairobi or Chelsea?' Rob countered sardonically.

'Chelsea.'

'Not ours to enquire. The team was stood down for four hours while whoever did it did it. That's all we know. Gridley put one uniformed copper on the doorstep in case anyone tried to wander in off the street. If they did, his job was to tell them that our officers were investigating a burglary of the premises, so bugger off. *If* he was a copper at all, *which* I doubt,' Rob added, snapping his mouth shut.

'Rob and me are off the case,' Lesley said. 'Gridley would assign us to traffic duties in the Orkney Islands if he could, except he daren't.'

'We're off everything,' Rob put in. 'We're unpersons. Thanks to you.'

'He wants us where he can see us,' Lesley said.

'Inside the tent, pissing out,' said Rob.

'He's sent two new officers to Nairobi to help and advise the local police in the search for Bluhm and *that's all*,' said Lesley. 'No looking under stones, no deviations. Period.'

'No Marsabit Two, no more grief about dying nigger-women and phantom doctors,' Rob said. 'Gridley's own lovely words. And our replacements aren't allowed to talk to us in case they catch our disease. They're a couple of no-brains with a year to go, same as Gridley.'

'It's a top security situation and you're part of it,' Lesley said, closing the clasp on the music case but hugging it to her lap. 'What part is anybody's guess. Gridley wants your life story. Who you meet, where, who comes to your house, who you phone, what you eat, who with. Every day. You're a material player in a top secret operation is all we're allowed to know. We're to do what we're told and mind our own business.'

'We'd not been back in the Yard ten minutes before he was yelling for all notebooks, tapes and exhibits on his desk *now*,' said Rob. 'So we gave them to him. The original set, complete and uncut. After we'd made copies, naturally.'

'The glorious House of ThreeBees is never to be mentioned again and that's an order,' Lesley said. 'Not their products, their operations or their staff. Nothing's allowed to rock the boat. Amen.'

'What boat?'

'Lots of boats,' Rob cut in. 'Take your pick. Curtiss is untouchable. He's halfway to brokering a bumper British arms deal with the Somalis. The embargo's a nuisance but he's found ways of getting round it. He's front-runner in the race to provide a state-of-the-art East African telecom system using British high-tech.'

'And I'm standing in the way of all that?'

'You're in the way, *period*,' Rob replied venomously. 'If we'd been able to get past you, we'd have had them cold. Now we're on the pavement, back at day one of our careers.'

'They think you know whatever Tessa knew,' Lesley explained. 'It could be bad for your health.'

'They?'

But Rob's anger was not to be contained. 'It was a set-up from day one and you were part of it. The Blue Boys laughed at us, so did the bastards in ThreeBees. Your friend and colleague Mr Woodrow lied to us all ways up. So did you. You were the only chance we had and you kicked us in the teeth.'

'We've got one question for you, Justin,' Lesley came in, scarcely less bitterly. 'You owe us one straight answer. Have you got somewhere to go? A safe place you can sit and read? Abroad is best.'

Justin prevaricated. 'What happens when I go home to Chelsea and put out my bedroom light? Do you people stay outside my house?'

'The team sees you home, it sees you to bed. The watchers grab a few hours' sleep, the listeners stay tuned to your telephone. The watchers return bright and early next morning to get you up. Your best time is between one and four a.m.'

'Then I have somewhere I can go,' Justin said after a moment's thought.

'Fantastic,' said Rob. 'We haven't.'

'If it's abroad, use land and sea,' Lesley said. 'Once you're there, break the chain. Take country buses, local trains. Dress plain, shave every day, don't look at people. Don't hire cars, don't fly anywhere from anywhere, even inland. People say you're rich.'

'I am.'

'Then get yourself a lot of cash. Don't use credit cards or traveller's cheques, don't touch a cellphone. Don't make a collect call or speak your name on the open line or the computers will kick in. Rob here's made you up a passport and a UK press card from the *Telegraph*. He nearly couldn't get your photo till he rang the FO and said we needed one for records. Rob's got friends in places where we're not supposed to have places, right, Rob?' No answer. 'They're not perfect because Rob's friends didn't have the time, did they, Rob? So don't use them coming in and out of England. Is that a deal?'

'Yes,' said Justin.

'You're Peter Paul Atkinson, newspaper reporter. And *never*, whatever you do, carry two passports at the same time.'

'Why are you doing this?' Justin asked.

'What's it to you?' Rob countered furiously from the darkness. 'We had a job to do, that's all. We didn't like losing it. So we've given it to you to fuck up. When they throw us out, maybe you'll let us clean your Rolls-Royce now and then.'

'Maybe we're doing it for Tessa,' Lesley said, dumping the music case in his arms. 'On your way, Justin. You didn't trust us. Maybe you were right. But if you had, we might have got there. Wherever *there* is.' She reached for the door handle. 'Look after yourself. They kill. But you've noticed that.'

He started down the street and heard Rob speaking into his microphone. *Candy is emerging from the cinema. Repeat, Candy is emerging with her handbag.* The minibus door slammed shut behind him. *Closure*, he thought. He walked a distance. Candy is hailing a cab, and she's a boy.

*   *   *

Justin stood at the long sash window of Ham's office, listening to the ten o'clock chimes above the night growl of the city. He was looking down into the street but standing back a little, at a point where it was easy enough to see, but less easy to be seen. A pallid reading light was burning on Ham's desk. Ham reclined in a corner, in a wing chair worn old by generations of unsatisfied clients. Outside, an icy mist had come up from the river, frosting the railings outside St Etheldreda's tiny chapel, scene of Tessa's many unresolved arguments with her Maker. A lighted green noticeboard advised passers-by that the chapel had been restored to the Ancient Faith by the Rosminian Fathers. Confessions, Benedictions and Weddings by Appointment. A trickle of late worshippers passed up and down the crypt steps. None was Tessa. On the floor of the office, heaped onto Ham's plastic tray, lay the former contents of the Gladstone. On the desk lay Tessa's music case and beside it, in files marked with his firm's name, Ham's diligent assembly of the printouts, faxes, photo-copies, notes of phone conversations, postcards and letters that he had accumulated in the course of his correspondence with Tessa over the last year.

'Bit of a snafu, I'm afraid,' he confessed awkwardly. 'Can't find her last lot of e-mails.'

'Can't *find* them?'

'Or anybody else's, for that matter. Computer's got a bug in the works. Bloody thing's gobbled up the mailbox and half the hard drive. Engineer's still working on it. When he gets it back, I'll let you have it.'

They had talked Tessa, then Meg, then cricket, where Ham's

217

large heart was also invested. Justin was not a cricket fan but he did his best to sound enthusiastic. A fly-blown travel poster of Florence lurked in the twilight.

'Do you still have that tame courier service back and forth to Turin every week, Ham?' Justin asked.

'Absolutely, old boy. Been taken over, of course. Who hasn't? Same people, just a bigger cock-up.'

'And you still use those nice leather hatboxes with the firm's name on them that I saw in your safe this morning?'

'Last bloody thing to go if I have anything to do with it.'

Justin squinted downward into the dimly lighted street. They're still there: one large woman in a bulky overcoat and one emaciated man with a curly trilby and bandy legs like a dismounted jockey's, and a skiing jacket with the collar rolled to his nose. They had been staring at St Etheldreda's noticeboard for the last ten minutes, when anything it had to tell them on an ice-cold February night could be committed to memory in ten seconds. Sometimes, in a civilised society, you know after all.

'Tell me, Ham.'

'Anything you like, old boy.'

'Did Tessa have loose cash sitting around in Italy?'

'Pots. Want to see the statements?'

'Not very much. Is it mine now?'

'Always was. Joint accounts, remember? What's mine is his. Tried to talk her out of it. Told me to get lost. Typical.'

'Then your chap in Turin could send me some, couldn't he? To this or that bank. Wherever I was abroad, for instance.'

'No problem.'

'Or to anyone I named, really. As long as they produced their passport.'

'Your lolly, old boy. Do what you want with it. Enjoy it, that's the main thing.'

The dismounted jockey had turned his back to the noticeboard and was affecting to study the stars. The bulky overcoat was looking at her watch. Justin again remembered his tiresome instructor on the security course. *Watchers are actors. The hardest thing for them to do is nothing.*

'There's a chum of mine, Ham. I never talked to you about him. Peter Paul Atkinson. He has my absolute confidence.'

'Lawyer?'

'Of course not. I've got you. He's a journalist with the *Daily Telegraph*. Old friend from my undergraduate days. I want him to have complete power of attorney over my affairs. If you or your people in Turin should ever receive instructions from him, I'd like you to treat them in exactly the same way as if they came from me.'

Ham hawed and rubbed the end of his nose. 'Can't be done just like *that*, old boy. Can't just wave a bloody wand. Have to have his signature and stuff. Formal authorisation from you. Witnessed, probably.'

Justin crossed the room to where Ham was sitting, and gave him the Atkinson passport to look at.

'Maybe you could copy down the details from that,' he suggested.

Ham turned first to the photograph at the back and, without any discernible change in his expression at first, compared it with Justin's features. He took a second look and read the personal details. He flipped slowly through the much-stamped pages.

'Done a good bit of travelling, your chum,' he remarked phlegmatically.

'And will be doing a good deal more, I suspect.'

'I'll need a signature. Can't move without a signature.'

'Give me a moment and you shall have one.'

Ham got up and, handing the passport back to Justin, walked deliberately to his desk. He opened a drawer and extracted a couple of official-looking forms and some blank paper. Justin set the passport flat under the reading lamp and, with Ham peering officiously over his shoulder, made a few practice passes before signing over his affairs to one Peter Paul Atkinson, care of Messrs Hammond Manzini of London and Turin.

'I'll have it notarised,' said Ham. 'By me.'

'There's one more thing, if you don't mind.'

'Christ.'

'I'll need to write to you.'

'Any time, old boy. Delighted to keep in touch.'

'But not here. Not in England at all. And not to your office in Turin either, if you don't mind. I seem to remember you have a bevy of Italian aunts. Might one of them receive mail for you and hang on to it safely till the next time you dropped by?'

'Got one old dragon lives in Milan,' said Ham with a shudder.

'An old dragon in Milan is just what we need. Perhaps you'd give me her address.'

*   *   *

It was midnight in Chelsea. Dressed in a blazer and grey flannels, Justin the dutiful desk officer sat at the hideous dining table under an Arthurian chandelier, writing once more. In fountain pen, on number four stationery. He had torn up several drafts before he was satisfied, but his style and handwriting remained unfamiliar to him.

Dear Alison,

I was grateful for your considerate suggestions at our meeting this morning. The Office has always shown its human face at critical moments, and today was no exception. I have given due thought to what you propose, and spoken at length with Tessa's lawyers. It appears that her affairs have been much neglected in recent months, and my immediate attention is needed. There are matters of domicile and taxation to resolve, not to mention the disposal of properties here and abroad. I have therefore decided that I must address these business matters first, and I suspect I may welcome the task.

I hope therefore that you will bear with me for a week or two before I respond to your proposals. As to sick leave, I do not feel I should trespass unnecessarily upon the Office's goodwill. I have taken no leave

this year, and I believe I am owed five weeks' disembarkation leave
in addition to my normal annual entitlement. I would prefer to claim
what is due to me before asking your indulgence. My renewed thanks.

A hypocritical, dishonest placebo, he decided, with satisfaction. Justin the incurably civil servant fusses about whether it is proper for him to take sick leave while winding up his murdered wife's affairs. He went back to the hall and took another look at the Gladstone lying on the floor beneath the marble-topped side table. One padlock forced and no longer functional. The other padlock missing. The contents replaced at random. You're so *bad*, he thought in contempt. Then he thought: unless you're trying to scare me, in which case you're rather good. He checked his jacket pockets. My passport, genuine, to be used when leaving or entering Britain. Money. No credit cards. With an air of firm purpose, he set to work adjusting the house lights in the pattern that best suggested sleep.

CHAPTER ELEVEN

The mountain stood black against the darkening sky, and the sky was a mess of racing cloud, perverse island winds and February rain. The snake road was strewn with pebbles and red mud from the sodden hillside. Sometimes it became a tunnel of overhanging pine branches and sometimes it was a precipice with a free fall to the steaming Mediterranean a thousand feet below. He would make a turn and for no reason the sea would rise in a wall in front of him, only to fall back into the abyss as he made another. But no matter how many times he turned, the rain came straight at him, and when it struck the windscreen he felt the jeep wince under him like an old horse no longer fit for heavy pulling. And all the time the ancient hill-fort of Monte Capanne watched him, now from high above, now squatting at his right shoulder on some unexpected ridge, drawing him forward, fooling him like a false light.

'Where the hell is it? Somewhere off to the left, I swear,' he complained aloud, partly to himself and partly to Tessa. Reaching a crest, he pulled irritably into the side of the road and put his fingertips to his brow while he took a mental bearing. He was acquiring the exaggerated gestures of solitude. Below him lay the lights of Portoferraio. Ahead of him, across the sea, Piombino twinkled on the mainland. To left and right, a timber track cut a gully into the forest. This is where your murderers lay up in their green safari truck while they waited to kill you, he explained to her in his mind. This is where they smoked their beastly Sportsmans and drank their bottles of Whitecap and waited for you and Arnold to drive by. He had shaved and brushed his hair and put on a clean denim shirt. His face felt hot and there was a pulsing in his temples. He plumped for left. The jeep jogged over an unruly mat of twigs and pine needles. The trees parted, the sky lightened and it was nearly day again. Below him at the foot of a clearing lay a cluster of old farmhouses. *I'll never sell them, I'll never rent them out,* you told me, the first time you brought me here. *I'll give them to people who matter, then later we'll come and die here.*

Parking the jeep, Justin tramped through wet grass towards the nearest cottage. It was neat and low with freshly limed walls and old pink roof tiles. A light burned in the lower windows. He hammered on the door. A sedate plume of woodsmoke, sheltered by the surrounding forest, rose vertically from the chimney into the evening light, only to be swept away as the wind seized it. Ragged black birds wheeled and argued. The door opened and a peasant woman in a garish headscarf let out a cry of pain, lowered her head and whispered something in a language he did not expect to understand. Her head still lowered, body sideways to him, she took his hand in both of hers and pressed it against each cheek in turn, before kissing it devoutly on the thumb.

'Where's Guido?' he asked in Italian as he followed her into the house.

She opened an inner door and showed him. Guido was seated at a long table under a wooden cross, a crooked, breathless old man of twelve, white-faced, bone-thin with haunted eyes. His emaciated hands rested on the table and there was nothing in them, so that it was hard to think what he could have been doing before Justin walked in on him, alone in a low dark room

223

with beams along the ceiling, not reading or playing or looking at anything. With his long head craned to one side and his mouth open, Guido watched Justin enter, then stood up and, using the table to help him, toppled towards Justin and made a crablike lunge to embrace him. But his aim was short and his arms flopped back to his sides as Justin caught him and held him steady.

'He wants to die like his father and the signora,' his mother complained. ' "All the good people are in Heaven," he tells me. "All the bad people stay behind." Am I a bad person, Signor Justin? Are you a bad person? Did the signora bring us from Albania, buy him his treatment in Milan, put us in this house, just so that we should die of grief for her?' Guido hid his hollowed face in his hands. 'First he faints, then he goes to bed and sleeps. He doesn't eat, doesn't take his medicine. Refuses school. This morning as soon as he comes out to wash himself I lock his bedroom door and hide the key.'

'And it's good medicine,' said Justin quietly, his eyes on Guido.

Shaking her head she took herself to the kitchen, clanked saucepans, put on a kettle. Justin led Guido back to the table and sat with him.

'Are you listening to me, Guido?' he asked in Italian.

Guido closed his eyes.

'Everything stays exactly as it was,' Justin said firmly. 'Your school fees, the doctor, the hospital, your medicine, everything that is necessary while you recover your health. The rent, the food, your university fees when you get there. We're going to do everything she planned for you, exactly the way she planned it. We can't do less than she would wish, can we?'

Eyes down, Guido reflected on this before giving a reluctant shake of the head: no, we cannot do less, he conceded.

'Do you still play chess? Can we have a game?'

Another shake, this time a prudish one: it is not respectful of Signora Tessa's memory to play chess.

Justin took Guido's hand and held it. Then gently swung it,

waiting for the glimmer of a smile. 'So what do you do when you're not dying?' he asked in English. 'Did you read the books we sent you? I thought you'd be an expert on Sherlock Holmes by now.'

'Mr Holmes is a great detective,' Guido replied, also in English, but without a smile.

'And what about the computer the signora gave you?' Justin asked, reverting to Italian. 'Tessa said you were a big star. A genius, she told me. You used to e-mail each other passionately. I got quite jealous. Don't tell me you've abandoned your *computer*, Guido!'

The question provoked an outburst from the kitchen. 'Of course he has abandoned it! He has abandoned everything! Four million lira, it cost her! All day long he used to sit at that computer, tap, tap, tap. Tap, tap tap. "You make yourself blind," I tell him, "you get sick from too much concentration." Now nothing. Even the computer must die.'

Still holding Guido's hand, Justin peered into his averted eyes. 'Is that true?' he asked.

It was.

'But that's *awful*, Guido. That's a real waste of talent,' Justin complained, as Guido's smile began to dawn. 'The human race is in serious need of good brains like yours. D'you hear me?'

'Maybe.'

'So do you remember Signora Tessa's computer, the one she taught you on?'

Of course Guido did – and with an air of great superiority, not to say smugness.

'All right, so it's not as good as yours. Yours is a couple of years younger and cleverer. Yes?'

Yes. Very much yes. And the smile widening.

'Well, I'm an idiot, Guido, unlike you, and I can't even work *her* computer with any confidence. And my problem is, Signora Tessa left a stack of messages on it, some of them for me, and I'm frightened to death of losing them. And I think she would like you to be the person who made sure I didn't lose them.

OK? Because she wanted very much to have a son like you. And so did I. So the question is, will you come down to the villa, and help me to read whatever is in her laptop?'

'You got the printer?'

'I have.'

'Disk drive?'

'That too.'

'CD drive? Modem?'

'And the handbook. And the transformers. And the cables, and an adaptor. But I'm still an idiot, and if there's a chance of making a hash of it I will.'

Guido was already standing, but Justin tenderly drew him back to the table.

'Not this evening. Tonight you sleep, and tomorrow morning early, if you're willing, I'll come and fetch you in the villa jeep, but afterwards you must go to school. Yes?'

'Yes.'

'You are too tired, Signor Justin,' Guido's mother murmured, setting coffee before him. 'So much grief is bad for the heart.'

*　　*　　*

He had been on the island for two nights and two days, but if somebody had proved it was a week he would not have been surprised. He had taken the Channel ferry to Boulogne, bought a train ticket for cash, and somewhere along his route a second ticket to a different destination, long before the first ticket was used up. He had shown his passport, to the best of his awareness, only once and cursorily, as he crossed into Italy from Switzerland by way of some precipitous and very beautiful mountain ravine. And it was his own passport. Of that too he was certain. Obedient to Lesley's instructions, he had sent Mr Atkinson's ahead of him via Ham rather than risk being caught with two. But as to which ravine or which train – for that, he would have had to study a map, and make a guess at the town where he had boarded.

For much of the journey Tessa had ridden alongside him, and now and then they had shared a good joke together – usually after some deflating and irrelevant comment of Tessa's, delivered sotto voce. Other times, they had reminisced, shoulder to shoulder, heads back and eyes closed like an old couple, until abruptly she left him again, and the pain of grief overtook him like a cancer he had known all the time was there, and Justin Quayle mourned his dead wife with an intensity that exceeded his worst hours in Gloria's lower ground, or the funeral in Langata, or the visit to the mortuary, or the top floor of number four.

Finding himself standing on the railway station platform in Turin, he had taken a hotel room to clean up, then from a second-hand luggage shop purchased two anonymous canvas suitcases to contain the papers and objects that he had come to regard as her reliquary. And *si*, Signor Justin, the black-suited young lawyer, heir to the Manzini half of the partnership, had assured him – amid protestations of sympathy that were all the more painful for their sincerity – the hatboxes had arrived safely and on schedule, together with orders from Ham to hand over numbers five and six *unopened* to Justin *personally* – and if there was *anything, but anything further at all* that the young man could do, of a legal, or professional or any *other* nature, then it went without saying that loyalty to the Manzini family did not end with the tragic death of the signora, et cetera. Oh, and of course there was the money, he added disdainfully – and counted out fifty thousand US dollars in cash against Justin's signature. After which Justin withdrew to the privacy of an empty conference room where he transferred Tessa's reliquary and Mr Atkinson's passport to their new resting-place in the canvas suitcases and, soon afterwards, took a taxi to Piombino where, by fortuitous timing, he was able to board a garish high-rise hotel, calling itself a ship, bound for Portoferraio on the island of Elba.

Seated as far from the king-sized television set as he could get, the only guest in a gigantic plastic self-service dining room on the sixth deck, with the suitcases either side of him, Justin treated himself indiscriminately to a seafood salad, a salami baguette and half a bottle of really bad red wine. Docking at Portoferraio, he was afflicted by a familiar sense of weightlessness as he fought his way through the unlit bowels of the ship's lorry park while foul-mannered drivers revved their engines or simply drove straight at him, shoving him, and his suitcases, against the bolted iron casing of the hull to the amusement of unemployed porters looking on.

It was dusk and deep winter and bitterly cold as he scrambled shivering and furious onto the quayside, and the few pedestrians moved with unaccustomed haste. Fearful of being recognised or worse still pitied, his hat pulled low over his brow, he dragged his suitcases to the nearest waiting taxi and established to his relief that the driver's face was unfamiliar to him. On the twenty-minute journey the man enquired whether he was German and Justin replied that he was Swedish. The unpremeditated answer served him well, for the man asked no further questions.

The Manzini villa lay low against the island's northern shore. The wind was blowing straight off the sea, rattling palm trees, whipping over stone walls, slapping shutters and roof tiles and making the outbuildings creak like old rope. Alone in the faltering moonlight Justin remained standing where the cab had dropped him, at the entrance to a flagstoned courtyard with its ancient water pump and olive press, waiting for his eyes to grow accustomed to the dark. The villa loomed ahead of him. Two lines of poplar trees, planted by Tessa's grandfather, marked the walk from its front door to the sea's edge. One by one, Justin distinguished retainers' cottages, stone staircases, gateposts and shadowy bits of Roman masonry. Not a light burned anywhere. The estate manager was in Naples, according to Ham, gadding with his fiancée. Housekeeping was entrusted to a pair of itinerant Austrian women who called themselves painters and were camped in a disused chapel on the other side of the estate. The two labourers' cottages, converted by Tessa's mother the *dottoressa*, a title the island preferred to *contessa*, and christened Romeo and Giulietta for the benefit of German tourists, were the responsibility of a letting agency in Frankfurt.

So welcome home, he told Tessa, in case she was a bit slow on the uptake after all the zigzag travelling.

The villa keys were kept on a ledge inside the wooden cladding of the water pump. *First you take off the lid, darling – like so – then you reach your arm in and if you're lucky you hoick them out. Then you unlock the front door to the house and take your bride to the bedroom and make love to her, like so.* But he didn't take her to the bedroom, he knew a better place. Picking up the canvas suitcases once more, he struck out across the courtyard. As he did so the moon obligingly lifted itself clear of the clouds, lighting his way for him and throwing white bars between the poplars. Reaching the furthest corner of the courtyard he passed by way of a narrow alley resembling an ancient Roman backstreet to an olivewood door on which was carved a Napoleonic heraldic bee in honour – thus the family legend – of the great man himself who, treasuring the good conversation and even better wine of Tessa's great-great-grandmother, had appointed himself a frequent guest at the villa during his ten restless months of exile.

Justin selected the largest of the keys and turned it. The door groaned and yielded. *This is where we counted our money,* she is telling him severely, in her rôle of Manzini heiress, bride and tour-guide. *Today the superb Manzini olives are shipped to Piombino to be pressed like any other. But in my mother the* dottoressa's *time this room was still the Holy of Holies. It was where we recorded the oil, jar by jar, before we stored it at a preciously preserved temperature in the* cantina *downstairs. It was here that – you're not listening.*

'That's because you are making love to me.'

You are my husband and I shall make love to you whenever I wish. Pay close attention. In this room the weekly wage was counted into every peasant's hand, and signed for, usually with a cross, in a ledger larger than your English Doomsday Book.

'Tessa, I can't –'

You can't what? Of course you can. You are extremely resourceful. Here also we received our chain gangs of life-prisoners from the house of correction on the other side of the island. Hence the spy-hole in the door. Hence the iron rings in the wall where the prisoners could be fastened while they were waiting to be taken to the olive groves. Are you not proud of me? A descendant of slave-masters?

'Immeasurably.'

Then why are you locking the door? Am I your prisoner?

'Eternally.'

The oil room was low and raftered, the windows set too high for prying eyes, whether money was being counted, or prisoners chained, or two newlyweds were making languorous love on the upright leather sofa that sat primly against the seaward wall. The counting table was flat and square. Two carpenter's work-benches loomed behind it in arched recesses. Justin needed all his strength to drag them over the flagstones and position them as wings either side of it. Above the door ran a line of ancient bottles scavenged from the estate. Fetching them down, he dusted each with his handkerchief before setting them on the table to use as paperweights. Time had stopped. He felt no thirst or hunger, no need of sleep. Placing one suitcase on each workbench he drew out his two most treasured bundles and laid them on the counting table, careful to choose the very centre lest in grief or madness they took it into their heads to hurl themselves over the edge. Cautiously he began undressing the first bundle, layer by layer – her cotton housecoat, her angora cardigan, the one she had worn the day before she left for Lokichoggio, her silk blouse, still with her scent around the neck – until he held the unveiled prize in his hands: one sleek grey box twelve inches by ten with the logo of its Japanese maker blazoned on the lid. Unscathed by days and nights of hellish solitude and travel. From the second bundle, he extracted the accessories. When he had done this, he gingerly transported the whole assembly piece by piece to an old pine desk at the other end of the room.

'Later,' he promised her aloud. 'Patience, woman.'

Breathing more easily, he took a radio alarm clock from his hand luggage and fiddled with it until he had the local wave-length for the BBC World Service. All through his journey he had kept abreast of the fruitless search for Arnold. Setting the alarm to the next hourly bulletin he turned his attention to the uneven heaps of letters, files, press cuttings, printouts and bundles of official-looking papers of the sort that, in another life, had been his refuge from reality. But not tonight, not by any stretch. These papers offered no refuge from anything, whether they were Lesley's police files, Ham's record of Tessa's imperious demands of him, or her own carefully ordered wads of letters, essays, newspaper cuttings, pharmaceutical and medical texts, messages to herself from the noticeboard in her workroom, or her fevered jottings in the hospital, retrieved by Rob and Lesley from their hiding-place in Arnold Bluhm's apartment. The radio had switched itself on. Justin lifted his head and listened. Of the missing Arnold Bluhm, doctor of medicine, suspected killer of British envoy's wife Tessa Quayle, the announcer had once again nothing to say. His devotions over, Justin delved among Tessa's papers until he found the object he had determined to keep beside him throughout his explorations. She had brought it with her from the hospital – *the only thing of Wanza's that they left behind*. She had retrieved it from an unemptied wastebin next to Wanza's abandoned bed. For days and nights after her return, it had stood like an accusing sentinel on her workroom desk: one small cardboard box, red and black, five inches by three, empty. From there it had made its way to the centre drawer, where Justin had found it during his overhasty search of her possessions. Not forgotten, not rejected. But relegated, flattened, shoved aside while she gave herself to more immediate matters. The name Dypraxa printed in a band on all four sides, the leaflet showing indications and contra-indications inside the box. And three jokey little gold bees in arrow formation on the lid. Opening it, restoring it to its status as a box, Justin placed it at the centre of an empty shelf on the wall directly before him. *Kenny K thinks he's Napoleon with his ThreeBees*, she had whispered to him in her fever. *And their sting is fatal, did you know that?* No, darling, I didn't know, go back to sleep.

*   *   *

231

To read.

To travel.

To slow down his head.

To accelerate his wits.

To charge and yet stand still, to be as patient as a saint, and impulsive as a child.

Never in his life had Justin been so eager for knowledge. There was no more time for preparation. He had been preparing night and day ever since her death. He had withheld, but he had prepared. In Gloria's ghastly lower ground, he had prepared. In his interviews with the police, when the withholding had been at moments almost unbearable, still in some sleepless corner of his head, he had prepared. On the interminable flight home, in Alison Landsbury's office, in Pellegrin's club, in Ham's office and at number four, while a hundred other things were going on in his mind, he had prepared. What he needed now was one huge plunge into the heart of her secret world; to recognise each signpost and milestone along her journey; to extinguish his own identity and revive hers; to kill Justin, and bring Tessa back to life.

Where to begin?

Everywhere!

Which path to follow?

All of them!

The civil servant in him was in abeyance. Fired by Tessa's impatience, Justin ceased to be accountable to anyone but her. If she was scattershot, so would he be. Where she was methodical, he would submit to her method. Where she made an intuitive leap, he would take her hand and they would leap together. Was he hungry? If Tessa wasn't, neither was he. Was he tired? If Tessa could sit up half the night in her housecoat, huddled at her desk, then Justin could sit up the whole night, and all next day as well, and the next night too!

Once, prising himself from his labours, he made a raid on the villa's kitchens, returning with salami, olives, crispbread, *reggiano* and bottled water. Another time – was it dusk or daybreak? – he had an impression of grey light – he was in the middle of her hospital diary, logging the attendances of Lorbeer and his acolytes at Wanza's bedside, when he woke to discover himself drifting round the walled garden. It was here, under Tessa's doting eye, that he had planted wedding lupins, wedding roses and, inevitably, wedding freesias for love of her. The weeds came up to his knees, drenching his trousers. A single rose was in bloom. Remembering he had left the oil room door open, he fled back across the flagstoned courtyard, only to find it safely locked and the key inside his jacket pocket.

* * *

Press cutting from the *Financial Times*:

ThreeBees Buzzing

Rumours are flying that whiz-kid playboy Kenneth K. Curtiss of the House of ThreeBees, Third World venturers, is planning a runaway marriage of convenience with Swiss-Canadian pharma-giant Karel Vita Hudson. Will KVH show up at the altar? Can ThreeBees come up with the dowry? Answer yes and yes so long as Kenneth K's typically daring pharma-gamble pays off. In a deal believed unprecedented in the secretive and immensely profitable world of pharmaceuticals, ThreeBees Nairobi will reportedly take up one quarter of the estimated £500 million research and development costs of KVH's innovative anti-TB wonder-drug DYPRAXA in exchange for all-Africa sale and distribution rights and an unnamed piece of the drug's worldwide profits . . .

ThreeBees Nairobi-based spokesperson Vivian Eber is cautiously jubilant: 'This is brilliant, typical, totally Kenny K. It's a humanitarian act, good for the company, good for shareholders, good for Africa. DYPRAXA is as easy to administer as a Smartie. ThreeBees will be at the forefront of the fight against the terrifying worldwide rise in new strains of TB.'

KVH Chairman, Dieter Korn, speaking in Basel last night, was quick to echo Eber's optimism: 'DYPRAXA converts six or eight months of laborious treatment into a twelve-hit swallow. We believe ThreeBees are the right people to be pioneering DYPRAXA in Africa.'

Handwritten note, Tessa to Bluhm, presumably recovered from Arnold's flat:

Arnold heart:
    You didn't believe me when I told you KVH were bad. I've checked. They're bad. Two years ago they were charged with polluting half Florida, where they have a huge 'facility', and got off with a caution. Undisputed evidence presented by plaintiffs showed that KVH had exceeded their permitted quota of toxic effluents by nine hundred per cent, poisoning conservation areas, wetlands, rivers and beaches and probably the milk. KVH performed a similar public service in India, where two hundred children in the region of Madras allegedly died of related causes. The Indian court case will be heard in about fifteen years, or longer if KVH continue to pay off the right people. They're also famous as front-runners in the pharma industry's humanitarian campaign to prolong the life of their patents in the interest of suffering white billionaires. Goodnight, darling. Never again doubt a word I say. I'm immaculate. So are you. T.

Press cutting from the financial pages of the *Guardian*, London:

Happy Bees

The dramatic rise (40 per cent in twelve weeks) in the value of ThreeBees Nairobi reflects growing market confidence in the company's recently acquired all-African franchise in the cheap and innovative cure for multi-resistant TB, Dypraxa. Speaking from his home in Monaco, ThreeBees CEO Kenneth K. Curtiss said: 'What's good for ThreeBees is good for Africa. And what's good for Africa is good for Europe and America and the rest of the world.'

Separate folder marked HIPPO in Tessa's hand containing some forty exchanges, first by letter, then by printed-out e-mail, between Tessa and a woman named Birgit, who works for an independently funded pharma-watch outfit called Hippo based in a small town called Bielefeld in north Germany. The logo at the top of her letter-paper explains that her organisation owes its name to Greek physician Hippocrates, born c. 460 BC, whose oath all doctors swear. The correspondence begins formally but once the e-mails take over it softens. Key players quickly acquire nicknames. KVH becomes Giant, Dypraxa becomes Pill, Lorbeer becomes Goldmaker. Birgit's source on the activities of Karel Vita Hudson becomes 'Our Friend' and Our Friend must be protected at all times, since 'what she is telling us is completely against Swiss law'.

E-mail printout Birgit to Tessa:

. . . for his two doctors Emrich and Kovacs, Goldmaker opened a company on Isle of Man, maybe two companies, because this was still Communist times. Our Friend says L put the companies in his own name so that the women wouldn't get bad trouble with the authorities. Since then there has been bad argument between the women. It is scientific, also personal. Nobody in Giant is allowed to know details. Emrich emigrated to Canada one year ago. Kovacs stays in Europe, mostly Basel. The elephant mobile you sent Carl drives him completely crazy with happiness and now he trumpets like an elephant every morning to tell me he is awake.

E-mail printout Birgit to Tessa:

Here is some more history regarding Pill. Five years ago when Goldmaker was looking for financial backing for the women's molecule not everything went easy for him. He tried to persuade some big German pharmas to sponsor but they are resisting strongly because they don't see big profits. The problem with the poor is always the same: they are not rich enough to buy expensive medicines! Giant came in late and only after big market researches. Also Our Friend says they were very clever in their deal with BBB. This was a masterstroke, to sell off poor Africa and keep the rich world for themselves! The plan is very simple, the timing perfect. It is to test Pill in Africa for two or three years, by which time KVH calculate that TB will have become a BIG PROBLEM in the West. Also in three years BBB will be so compromised financially that Giant will be able to buy them out for pennies! Therefore according to Our Friend, BBB have bought the wrong end of the horse and Giant have the whip. Carl is asleep beside me. Dear Tessa, I hope very much your baby will be as beautiful as Carl. He will be a great fighter like his mother, I am sure! Ciao, B.

Final entry in the Birgit/Tessa file of correspondence:

Our Friend is reporting very secretive activities at Giant regarding BBB and Africa. Maybe you have stirred a wasps' nest? Kovacs will be flown in great secrecy to Nairobi where Goldmaker is waiting to receive her. Everyone speaks bad things about *die schöne* Lara. She is a traitor, a bitch, etc. How does such a boring corporation become suddenly so passionate?! Take care of yourself, Tessa. I think you are a little bit *waghalsig* but it is late and my English does not translate this word so maybe you ask your good kind husband to translate it for you! B.
P.S. Come soon to Bielefeld, Tessa, it is a beautiful and very secret little town that you will love! B.

*   *   *

It is evening. Tessa is heavily pregnant. She is pacing the drawing room of the Nairobi house, now sitting, now standing. Arnold has told her she must not go down to Kibera until she has had the baby. Even sitting at her laptop is a tiresome chore for her. After five minutes of it she must prowl about again. Justin has come home early to keep her company in her travail.

'Who or what is *waghalsig*?' she demands of him, as soon as he opens the front door.

'Who is *what*?'

She pronounces the word with deliberate anglicisation: *wag* like wag the dog, *halsig* like hall-sick. She has to say it twice more before the penny drops.

'Reckless,' Justin replies cautiously. 'Daredevilish. Why?'

'Am *I* waghalsig?'

236

'Never. Impossible.'

'Somebody's just called me it, that's all. Fat lot of dare-devilling I can do in *this* condition.'

'Don't you believe it,' Justin replies devoutly, and they break out laughing simultaneously.

*   *   *

Letter from Messrs Oakey, Oakey & Farmeloe, Solicitors of London, Nairobi and Hong Kong to Ms T. Abbott, Postbox Nairobi:

Dear Ms Abbott,

We act for House of ThreeBees, Nairobi, who have passed to us your several letters addressed personally to Sir Kenneth Curtiss, Chief Executive Officer of that company, and to other directors and officers of the managing board.

We are to advise you that the product to which you refer has passed all requisite clinical trials, many of them conducted to standards far higher than those laid down by national or international regulation. As you rightly point out, the product has been fully tested and registered in Germany, Poland and Russia. At the request of the Kenyan health authorities, that registration has also been independently verified by the World Health Organization, a copy of whose certificate is appended to this letter.

We must therefore advise you that any further representations made by you or your associates in this matter, whether directed at House of ThreeBees or some other quarter, will be interpreted as a malicious and unwarranted slur on this highly prestigious product, and on the good name and high standing in the market place of its distributors House of ThreeBees Nairobi. In such an eventuality, we are under standing instruction to institute legal proceedings with full vigour and without further reference to our clients.

Yours faithfully . . .

*   *   *

'Old chap. A quick word with you, if I may.'

The speaker is Tim Donohue. The old chap is Justin himself, in whose memory the scene is playing. The game of Monopoly has been voted into temporary suspense while the Woodrow sons hurry late to their karate class and Gloria fetches drinkies from the kitchen. Woodrow has taken himself off to the High Commission in a huff. Justin and Tim are therefore seated alone and head to head at the garden table, surrounded by millions of imitation pounds.

'Mind if I tread on holy ground in the interests of the greater good?' Donohue enquires in a low, tight voice that travels no further than it needs to.

'If you must.'

'I must. It's this unseemly feud, old chap. The one your late-lamented was conducting with Kenny K. Bearding him at his farm, poor fellow. Phone calls at unsociable hours. Rude letters left at his club.'

'I don't know what you're talking about.'

'Of course you don't. Not a good subject around the halls just now. Particularly where the coppers are concerned. Sweep it under the carpet, our advice. Not relevant. Ticklish times for all of us. Kenny included.' His voice lifted. 'You're bearing up marvellously. Nothing but boundless admiration for him, right, Gloria?'

'He's completely superhuman, aren't you, Justin, darling?' Gloria confirms as she sets down her tray of gin and tonic.

Our advice, Justin remembers, still staring at the solicitors' letters. Not his. Theirs.

*　　　*　　　*

E-mail printout Tessa to Ham:

Coz. Angel heart. My deep-throat at BBB swears they are in much worse financial doodoo than anyone lets on. She says there are in-house rumours that Kenny K is considering mortgaging his entire

238

non-pharma op to a shady South American syndicate based in Bogota! Question: can he mount a company sell-out without telling his shareholders in advance? I know even less company law than you do, which is saying a lot. Elucidate or else! Love, love, Tess.

But Ham had no time to elucidate, even if he was able to, immediately or otherwise, and neither did Justin. The clatter of an elderly car hauling itself up the drive, followed by a thundering on the door, brought Justin leaping to his feet and peering through the prisoners' spy-hole, straight into the well-nourished features of Father Emilio Dell'Oro, parish priest, arranged in an expression of pitiful concern. Justin opened the door to him.

'But what are you doing, Signor Justin?' the priest cried, in his operatic boom, embracing him. 'Why must I hear it from Mario the taxi driver that the signora's grief-demented husband has locked himself in the villa and is calling himself a Swede? What is a priest for, in the name of Heaven, if he is not the companion of the bereaved, a father to his stricken son?'

Justin mumbled something about needing solitude.

'But you are working!' – peering over Justin's shoulder at the piles of papers strewn about the oil room. 'Even now, in your grief, you are serving your country! No wonder you English commanded a greater empire than Napoleon!'

Justin offered something fatuous about a diplomat's work never being done.

'Like a priest's, my son, like a priest's! For every soul that turns to God, there are a hundred that do not!' He drew closer. 'But *la signora* was a believer, Signor Justin. As her mother the *dottoressa* was, even if they disputed it. With so much love for their fellow men, how could they close their ears to God?'

Somehow Justin shooed the priest away from the doorway to the oil room, sat him in the salon of the freezing villa and, under the flaking frescoes of sexually precocious cherubs, plied him with a glass and then another of Manzini wine while sipping at his own. Somehow he accepted the good Father's assurances that Tessa was safely in the arms of God, and consented without

239

demur to the celebration of a memorial mass to Tessa on her next saint's day and a handsome donation to the church's restoration fund, and another for the conservation of the island's superb hilltop castle, one of the gems of mediaeval Italy, which scholarly surveyors and archaeologists assure us is soon to fall down unless, with God's will, the walls and foundations are secured . . . Escorting the good man to his car, Justin was so keen not to detain him that he passively accepted his benediction before hastening back to Tessa.

She was waiting for him with her arms folded.

I refuse to believe in the existence of a God who permits the suffering of innocent children.

'So why are we getting married in a church?'

To melt His heart, she replied.

*   *   *

PIGBITCH. STOP SUCKING YOUR NIGGERDOCTOR'S COCK! GO BACK TO YOUR RIDICULOUS EUNUCH HUSBAND AND BEHAVE YOURSELF. GET YOUR SHITTY NOSE OUT OF OUR BUSINESS <u>NOW</u>! IF NOT, YOU WILL BE DEAD MEAT AND THAT'S A SOLEMN PROMISE.

The sheet of plain typing paper that he was holding in his trembling hands was not intended to melt anybody's heart. Its message was typed in thick black capitals half an inch high. The signature, unsurprisingly, omitted. The spelling, surprisingly, immaculate. And the impact upon Justin so violent, so accusing, so inflaming, that for a fearful few seconds he lost his temper with her completely.

Why didn't you *tell* me? *Show* me? I was your husband, your protector supposedly, your man, your other bloody half!

I give up. I resign. You receive a death threat, through the letter box. You pick it up. You read it – once. *Ugh!* Then if you're like me, you hold it away from you because it's so vile, so physically repellent that you don't want it coming near your face. But you read it again. And again. Till you're word perfect. Like me.

So then what do you do? Phone me – 'Darling, something simply foul has happened, you've got to come home at once'? Leap in a car? Drive like Jehu to the High Commission, wave the letter at me, march me in to Porter? Do you hell. Not a bit of it. As usual, your pride comes first. You don't *show* me the letter, you don't *tell* me about it, you don't burn it. You keep it secret. You classify it and you file it. Deep in a drawer of your no-go-area desk. You do exactly what you would laugh at me for doing: you file it among your papers and you preserve what in me you would mockingly call a patrician discretion about the matter. How you live with yourself after this – how you live with *me* – is anybody's guess. God knows how you live with the threat, but that's your business. So thanks. Thanks a lot, OK? Thanks for delivering the ultimate in marital apartheid. Bravo. And thanks again.

The rage left him as quickly as it had seized him, to be replaced by a sweating shame and remorse. You couldn't bear it, could you? The idea of actually showing someone that letter. Starting a whole landslide you couldn't control. The stuff about Bluhm, the stuff about me. It was just too much. You were protecting us. All of us. Of course you were. Did you tell Arnold? Of course not. He'd try to talk you out of going on.

* * *

Justin took a mental step back from this benign line of reasoning.

Too sweet. Tessa was tougher than that. And when her dander was up, nastier.

Think lawyer's intellect. Think icy pragmatism. Think very tough young girl, closing in for the kill.

She knew she was getting warm. The death threat confirmed it. You don't issue death threats to people who don't threaten you.

To scream 'Foul!' at this stage would mean handing herself over to the authorities. The British are helpless. They have no powers, no jurisdiction. Our only recourse is to show the letter to the Kenyan authorities.

But Tessa had no faith in the Kenyan authorities. It was her frequently repeated conviction that the tentacles of Moi's empire reached into every corner of Kenyan life. Tessa's faith, like her marital duty, was invested for better or worse in the Brits: witness her secret assignation with Woodrow.

The moment she went to the Kenyan police, she would have to provide a list of her enemies, real and potential. Her pursuit of the great crime would be stopped in its tracks. She would be forced to call off the hunt. She would never do that. The great crime was more important to her than her own life.

Well, it is for me too. Than mine.

*   *   *

As Justin struggles to recover his balance, his eye falls on a hand-addressed envelope which in an earlier life he had extracted in blind haste from the same middle drawer of Tessa's workroom desk in Nairobi in which he had found the empty Dypraxa box. The writing on the envelope is reminiscent, but not yet familiar. The envelope has been torn open. Inside is a single folded page of HM Stationery Office blue. The script is hectic, the text dashed off in haste as well as passion.

My darling Tessa, whom I love beyond all others and always shall,
    This is my only absolute conviction, my one piece of self-knowledge as I write. You were terrible to me today, but not as terrible as I was to you. The wrong person was speaking out of both of us. I desire and worship you beyond bearing. I am ready if you are. Let's both chuck in our ridiculous marriages and bolt to wherever you want, as soon as you want. If it's to the end of the earth, so much the better. I love you, I love you and I love you.

But this time the signature was not omitted. It was written loud and clear in letters of a size to match the death threat: Sandy. My name is Sandy, he was saying, and you can tell the whole damn world.

Date and time also given. Even in the throes of great love, Sandy Woodrow remains a conscientious man.

CHAPTER TWELVE

Justin the deceived husband is struck motionless by the moon-light as he stares rigidly at the sea's silvered horizon and takes long breaths of chill night air. He has the feeling he has inhaled something nauseous and needs to clean out his lungs. *Sandy leads from weakness into strength*, you once told me. *Sandy deceives himself first and the rest of us afterwards . . . Sandy is the coward who needs the protection of grand gestures and grand words because anything less leaves him unprotected . . .*

So if you knew all this, what in God's name did you do to bring this down on yourself? he demanded, of the sea, the sky, the snapping night wind.

Nothing whatever, she replied serenely. *Sandy mistook my flirtations for a promise, exactly as he mistook your good manners for weakness.*

For a moment nonetheless, almost as a luxury, Justin lets his courage fail him, as in his inmost heart he has sometimes let it fail him over Arnold. But his memory is stirring. Something he has read yesterday, last night, the night before. But what? A printout, Tessa to Ham. A long e-mail, a little too intimate for Justin's blood at first reading, so he put it aside in a folder dedicated to enigmas to be resolved when I am strong enough to face them. Returning to the oil room, he exhumes the printout and examines the date.

E-mail printout Tessa to Ham, dated exactly eleven hours after Woodrow, contrary to Service rules regarding the use of official writing paper, declared his passion for a colleague's wife on Her Majesty's Stationery Office blue:

I'm not a girl any more, Ham, and it's time I put away girlish things, but what girl does, even when she's in pig? And now I've landed myself with a five-star mega-creep with the hots for me. Problem is, Arnold and I have struck gold at last, more accurately true excrement of the foulest sort, and we desperately need said creep to speak for us in the corridors of power, which is the only way I can bear to go if I'm Justin's wife and the loyal Brit I aspire to be despite all. Do I hear you say I'm still the same ruthless bitch who likes leading men around on a string even when they're super-creeps? Well, don't say it, Ham. Don't say it even if it's true. Shut up about it. Because I have promises to keep, and so have you, sweetheart. And I need you to stick by me like the dear, sweet pal you are, and tell me I'm a good girl really, because I am. And if you don't, I'll give you the wettest kiss since the day I pushed you into the Rubicon in your sailor suit. Love you, darling. Ciao. Tess. PS. Ghita says I'm a complete whore but she can't pronounce it properly so it comes out hoo-er, like a hoover that's lost its V. Love Tess (hooer).

Defendant innocent as charged, he told her. And I as usual can be duly ashamed of myself.

*   *   *

Mystically calmed, Justin resumed his puzzled journey.

Extract from Rob and Lesley's joint report to Superintendent Frank Gridley, Overseas Crime Division, Scotland Yard, on their third interview with Woodrow, Alexander Henry, Head of Chancery, British High Commission, Nairobi:

Subject forcefully echoes what he claims to be the opinion of Sir Bernard Pellegrin, FO director of affairs for Africa, that further enquiry along the lines urged by Tessa Quayle's memorandum would needlessly jeopardise HMG's relations with the Kenyan Republic and harm UK trade interests . . . Subject refuses on security grounds to divulge the contents of the said memorandum . . . Subject disclaims all knowledge of an innovative drug being presently marketed by House of ThreeBees . . . Subject advises us that any request for a sight of Tessa Quayle's memorandum should be addressed directly to Sir Bernard, assuming that it still exists, which Subject is prepared to doubt. Subject portrays Tessa Quayle as a tiresome and hysterical woman who was mentally unstable in respect of matters related to her aid work. We interpret this as a convenient method of discounting the significance of her memorandum. A request is hereby made that a formal application be sent as soon as practical to the Foreign Office for copies of all papers submitted to Subject by the deceased Tessa Quayle.

Marginal note signed by F. Gridley, Deputy Commissioner: SPOKE SIR B. PELLEGRIN. APPLICATION REFUSED ON GROUNDS OF NATIONAL SECURITY.

Extracts from learned medical journals of varying obscurity extolling, in appropriately oblique terms, the sensational benefits of the innovative drug Dypraxa, its 'absence of mutagenicity' and its 'long half-life in rats'.

Extract from the *Haiti Journal of Health Sciences*, meekly expressing reservations about Dypraxa, signed by a Pakistani doctor who has conducted clinical trials of the drug at a Haitian research hospital. The words 'potential for toxicity' underlined in red by Tessa, spectres of liver failure, internal bleeding, dizziness, damage to the optic nerves.

Extract from the next issue of the same rag in which a string of medical eminences with impressive professorships and initials deliver a withering counterblast, citing three hundred test cases. The same article accuses the poor Pakistani of 'bias' and 'irresponsibility towards his patients' and calls down curses on his head.

(Handwritten note from Tessa: These unbiased opinion-leaders are one and all contracted to KVH by highly paid 'roving commissions' to spot promising biotech research projects worldwide.)

Extract from a book entitled *Clinical Trials* by Stuart Pocock, written out in Tessa's handwriting as her preferred means of committing it to memory. Some passages blazoned in red in contrast to the writer's sober style:

> There is a tendency for students, and indeed many clinicians, to treat the medical literature with undue respect. Major journals such as the *Lancet* and the *New England Journal of Medicine* are presumed to present new medical facts which are not to be disputed. Such a naive faith in the 'clinical gospels' is perhaps encouraged by the dogmatic style that many authors adopt, so that the uncertainties inherent in any research project often receive inadequate emphasis . . .

(Tessa's note: Articles are constantly planted by pharmas, even in the so-called quality rags.)

> As regards talks at scientific meetings and advertising by pharmaceutical companies one needs to be even more sceptical . . . the opportunities for bias are enormous . . .

(Tessa's note: According to Arnold, big pharmas spend zillions buying up scientists and medics to plug their product. Birgit reports that KVH recently donated fifty million dollars to a major US teaching hospital, plus salaries and expenses for three top clinicians and six research assistants. Corruption of university Common Room affiliations is even easier: professorial chairs, biotech labs, research foundations, etc. 'Unbought scientific opinion is increasingly hard to find.' – Arnold.)

More from Stuart Pocock:

. . . there is always the risk that authors are persuaded towards a greater emphasis on positive findings than is really justified.

(Tessa's note: Unlike the rest of the world's press, pharma journals don't like printing bad news.)

. . . Even if they do produce a trial report of their negative findings it is likely to be in an obscure specialist journal rather than in the major general journals . . . consequently this negative rebuttal of the earlier positive report could not be made available to such a wide audience.

. . . Many trials lack essential features of design to achieve an unbiased assessment of therapy.

(Tessa's note: Are geared to prove a point, not question it, i.e. worse than useless.)

Occasionally, authors may deliberately dredge the data to prove a positive . . .

(Tessa's note: Spin it.)

Extract from the London *Sunday Times*, headed 'Drug Firm Put Patients at Risk in Hospital Trials'. Heavily scored and underlined by Tessa and presumably reproduced or faxed to Arnold Bluhm since it bore the superscription: Arnie, have you SEEN this?!

ONE of the world's largest drug companies placed hundreds of patients at risk of potentially fatal infections by failing to disclose crucial safety information to six hospitals at the start of a nationwide drug trial.

Up to 650 people underwent surgery in Britain in the experiment organised by Bayer, the German pharmaceutical giant, despite the company having conducted studies which showed its drug reacted badly with others, seriously impairing its ability to kill bacteria.

This prior research, obtained by *The Sunday Times*, was not revealed at the start of the study to the hospitals involved.

The trial, whose flaw has never been revealed to the patients or their families, resulted in nearly half of those operated on at one test centre in Southampton developing a variety of life-threatening infections.

248

Bayer declined to reveal overall numbers for post-operative infections and fatalities, on the grounds that the data remained confidential.

'The study was approved by the competent regulatory authority and all local ethics committees prior to initiation,' said a spokesman.

Full-colour, full-page advertisement torn from a popular African magazine, captioned: I BELIEVE IN MIRACLES! Centre stage, one pretty young African mother in low white blouse and long skirt, smiling radiantly. Happy baby sits sideways across her lap, one hand to her breast. Happy brothers and sisters cluster round, handsome father towers over all. Everyone including mother is admiring conspicuously healthy child on her lap. Along the bottom of the page, the words THREEBEES BELIEVE IN MIRACLES TOO! Speech bubble issuing from pretty young mother's mouth reads: 'When they told me my baby had TB, I prayed. When my GP told me about Dypraxa, I knew my prayer was heard in Heaven!'

Justin returns to the police file.

Extract from officers' report on their interview with PEARSON, Ghita Janet, locally employed member of Chancery, British High Commission, Nairobi:

We interviewed Subject on three occasions of nine minutes, fifty-four minutes and ninety minutes respectively. At Subject's request our interviews were conducted on neutral ground (the house of a friend) in discreet circumstances. Subject is aged twenty-four, of Anglo-Indian birth, ed. UK convent schools (RC), adopted daughter of professional parents (lawyer and doctor), both strong Catholics. Subject is an honours graduate of Exeter University (English, American and Commonwealth Arts), of obvious intelligence and highly nervous. Our impression of her was that, in addition to being grief-stricken, she was in considerable fear. For instance, Subject made several statements which she then withdrew, e.g.: 'Tessa was murdered to keep her quiet.' E.g.: 'Anybody who takes on the pharmaceutical industry is liable to get her throat cut.' E.g.: 'Some pharmaceutical companies are arms dealers in shining raiment.' Pressed about these statements, she refused to substantiate them and requested they be wiped from the record. She also dismissed the suggestion that BLUHM could have committed the Turkana murders. BLUHM and QUAYLE, she said, were not an 'item' but they were 'the two best people on earth' and those around them 'just had dirty minds'.

Under further questioning, Subject first claimed to be bound by the Official Secrets Act, then by oath of secrecy to the deceased. For our third and final meeting we adopted a more hostile attitude to Subject, pointing out to her that by withholding information she could be shielding Tessa's murderers and impeding the search for BLUHM. We attach edited transcripts at Appendix A and B. Subject has read this transcript but refuses to sign it.

APPENDIX A

Q. Did you at any time assist or accompany Tessa Quayle on field expeditions?

A. At weekends and in my spare time I accompanied Arnold and Tessa on several field trips to Kibera slum and up-country in order to assist at field clinics and witness the administration of medicines. This is the particular remit of Arnold's NGO. Several of the medicines that Arnold examined turned out to be long past their expiry date and had destabilised, though they might work to a certain level. Others were inappropriate to the condition they were supposed to treat. We were also able to confirm a common phenomenon experienced in other parts of Africa, namely that the indications and contra-indications on some packets had been rewritten for the Third World market in order to broaden the use of the medicine far beyond its licensed application in developed countries, e.g. a painkiller used in Europe or US for the relief of extreme cancer cases was being offered as a cure for period pain and minor joint aches. Contra-indications were not given. We also established that even when the African doctors diagnosed correctly, they routinely prescribed the wrong treatment due to lack of adequate instructions.

Q. Was ThreeBees one of the distributors affected?

A. Everyone knows that Africa is the pharmaceutical dustbin of the

world and ThreeBees is one of the main distributors of pharmaceutical products in Africa.

Q. So was ThreeBees affected in this instance?

A. In certain instances ThreeBees was the distributor.

Q. The guilty distributor?

A. All right.

Q. In how many instances? What proportion?

A. *(after much prevarication)* All.

Q. Repeat, please. Are you saying that in every case where you
found fault with a product, ThreeBees was the distributor of that
product?

A. I don't think we should be talking like this while Arnold may be
alive.

APPENDIX B

Q. Was there one particular product that Arnold and Tessa felt particularly strongly about, do you remember?

A. This just can't be right. It can't be.

Q. Ghita. We're trying to understand why Tessa was killed and why
you think that by discussing these things we put Arnold in greater
danger than he's already in.

A. It was everywhere.

Q. *What* was? Why are you crying? Ghita.

A. It was killing people. In the villages. In the slums. Arnold was sure
of it. It was a good drug, he said. With five more years' development
they'd probably get there. You couldn't quarrel with the idea of the
drug. It was short-course, cheap and patient-friendly. But they'd
been too quick. The tests had been selectively designed. They hadn't
covered all the side-effects. They had tested on pregnant rats and
monkeys and rabbits and dogs, and had no problems. When they
got to humans – all right, there were problems, but there always
are. That's the grey area the drug companies exploit. It's at the
mercy of statistics and statistics prove anything you want them to
prove. In Arnold's opinion they had been too intent on getting the
product onto the market ahead of a competitor. There are so many
rules and regulations that you'd think that wasn't possible, but

Arnold said it happened all the time. Things look one way when you're sitting in a plush UN office in Geneva. Quite another when you're on the ground.

Q. Who was the manufacturer?

A. I really don't want to go on with this.

Q. What was the drug called?

A. Why didn't they test it more? It's not the Kenyans' fault. You can't ask, if you're a Third World country. You have to take what you're given.

Q. Was it Dypraxa?

A. *(unintelligible)*

Q. Ghita, calm down please and just tell us. What's the drug called, what's it for and who makes it?

A. Africa's got eighty-five per cent of the world's Aids cases, did you know that? How many of those have access to medication? One per cent! It's not a human problem any more! It's an economic one! The men can't work. The women can't work! It's a heterosexual disease, which is why there are so many orphans! They can't feed their families! Nothing gets done! They just die!

Q. So is this an Aids drug we're talking about?

A. Not while Arnold is alive! . . . It's associated. Where there's tuberculosis, you suspect Aids . . . Not always but usually . . . That's what Arnold said.

Q. Was Wanza suffering from this drug?

A. *(unintelligible)*

Q. Did Wanza die of this drug?

A. Not while Arnold is alive! Yes. Dypraxa. Now get out.

Q. Why were they heading for Leakey's place?

A. I don't know! Get out!

Q. What was behind their trip to Lokichoggio? Apart from women's awareness groups?

A. Nothing! Stop it!

Q. Who's Lorbeer?

A. *(unintelligible)*

That a formal request is made of the High Commission that the witness be offered protection in exchange for a full statement. She should be given assurances that any information she provides regarding the activities of Bluhm and the deceased will not be used in a way that might place Bluhm in jeopardy, assuming he is alive.

RECOMMENDATION REJECTED ON SECURITY GROUNDS.

F. Gridley (Superintendent)

Chin in hand Justin gazed at the wall. Memories of Ghita, the second most beautiful woman in Nairobi. Tessa's self-appointed disciple who dreams only of bringing standards of common decency to a wicked world. *Ghita is me without the bad bits*, Tessa likes to say.

Ghita the last of the innocents, head to head over green tea with very pregnant Tessa, solving the world's problems in the garden in Nairobi while Justin the absurdly happy sceptic and father-to-be in a straw hat clips, weeds and prunes his way through the flower beds, tying and watering and playing the middle-aged English bloody fool.

'Watch your feet, please, Justin,' they would call to him anxiously. They were warning him against the safari ants that marched out of the ground in columns after rain, and could kill a dog or a small child by sheer force of their generalship and numbers. In late pregnancy, Tessa feared that safari ants might mistake his watering for an unseasonable shower.

Ghita permanently shocked by everything and everyone, from Roman Catholics who oppose Third World birth control and demonstratively burn condoms in Nyayo Stadium, to American tobacco companies who spike their cigarettes in order to create child addicts, to Somali warlords who drop cluster bombs on undefended villages and the arms companies that manufacture the cluster bombs.

'Who *are* these people, Tessa?' she would whisper earnestly. 'What is their *mentality*, tell me, please? Is this original sin we are talking about? If you ask me, it is something much worse than that. To original sin belongs in my opinion some notion of innocence. But where is innocence today, Tessa?'

And if Arnold dropped by, which at weekends he frequently did, the conversation would take a more specific turn. Their three heads would draw together, their expressions tighten, and if Justin out of mischief watered too close for their comfort, they would make ostentatious small talk till he had removed himself to a more remote flower bed.

*   *   *

Police officers' report of meeting with representatives of House of ThreeBees, Nairobi:

We had sought an interview with Sir Kenneth Curtiss and had been given to understand he would receive us. On arrival at House of ThreeBees' headquarters, we were told that Sir Kenneth had been summoned to an audience with President Moi after which he was obliged to fly to Basel for policy discussions with Karel Vita Hudson (KVH). It was then suggested to us that we should address any questions we had to House of ThreeBees' pharmaceutical marketing manager, a Ms Y. Rampuri. In the event, Ms Rampuri was attending to family matters and was not available. We were then advised to seek an interview with Sir Kenneth or Ms Rampuri at a later date. When we explained the limitations of our time-frame, we were eventually offered an interview with 'senior staff members' and after an hour's delay were eventually received by a Ms V. Eber and a Mr D. K. Crick, both of customer relations. Also present, a Mr P. R. Oakey who described himself as a 'lawyer for the London end who happened to be visiting Nairobi on other business'.

Ms Vivian Eber is a tall attractive African woman in her late twenties and has a Business Affairs degree from an American university.

Mr Crick, who comes from Belfast, is similarly aged, of impressive physique and speaks with a slight Northern Irish brogue.

Subsequent enquiries indicate that Mr Oakey, the London lawyer, is identical with Percy Ranelagh Oakey, QC, of the London firm of Oakey, Oakey & Farmeloe. Mr Oakey has recently successfully defended several large pharmaceutical companies in class actions for damages and compensation, among them KVH. We were not advised of this at the time.

See Appendix for note on D. K. Crick.

SUMMARY OF MEETING

1. Apologies on behalf of Sir Kenneth K. Curtiss and Ms Y. Rampuri.
2. Expressions of regret by BBB (Crick) regarding death of Tessa Quayle and concern re fate of Dr Arnold Bluhm.

BBB (CRICK): This damn country gets hairier by the day. The Mrs Quayle thing, that's just awful. She was a fine lady who'd earned herself a great reputation around town. How can we help you officers? Any way at all. The chief sends his personal greetings and instructs us to afford you every assistance. He has a great regard for the British police.

OFFICER: We gather Arnold Bluhm and Tessa Quayle made a variety of representations to ThreeBees regarding a new TB cure you're marketing, name of Dypraxa.

BBB (CRICK): Did they though? We must look into that. You see, Ms Eber here is more on the PR side, and I'm sort of on secondment from other duties pending a major restructuring of the company. The chief has a theory that anyone sitting still is wasting money.

OFFICER: The representations resulted in a meeting between Quayle, Bluhm and members of your staff here and we'd like to ask you for a sight of any records that were kept of this meeting, and any other documents relevant to it.

BBB (CRICK): Right, Rob. No problem. We're here to help. Only when you say she made representations to ThreeBees – do you happen to know which branch you have in mind at all? Only there are a hell of a lot of bees in this outfit, believe me!

OFFICER: Mrs Quayle addressed letters, e-mails and phone calls to Sir Kenneth personally, to his private office, to Ms Rampuri and to pretty well everyone on your Nairobi board. She faxed some of her letters and sent hard copies by mail. Others she hand-delivered.

BBB (CRICK): Well, great. That should give us something to go on. And you have copies of that correspondence, presumably?

OFFICER: Not at present.

BBB (CRICK): But you know who attended the meeting on our side, presumably?

OFFICER: We assumed you'd know that.

BBB (CRICK): Oh dear. So what do you have?

OFFICER: Written and verbal testimony by witnesses that such representations were made. Mrs Quayle went so far as to visit Sir Kenneth at his farm last time he was in Nairobi.

BBB (CRICK): Did she though? Well, that's news to me, I must say. Did she have an appointment?

OFFICER: No.

BBB (CRICK): So who invited her?

OFFICER: No one. She just showed up.

BBB (CRICK): Wow. Brave girl. How far did she get?

OFFICER: Not far enough, apparently, because she afterwards attempted to confront Sir Kenneth here at his offices, but was unsuccessful.

BBB (CRICK): Well, I'm damned. Still the chief's a busy bee. A lot of people want a lot of favours from him. Not many of them are lucky.

OFFICER: This wasn't favours.

BBB (CRICK): What was it?

OFFICER: Answers. Our understanding is, Mrs Quayle also presented Sir Kenneth with a bunch of case histories describing the side-effects of the drug on identified patients.

BBB (CRICK): Did she, by Christ? Well, well. I didn't know there were any side-effects. Is she a scientist, a doctor? Was, I should say?

OFFICER: She was a concerned member of the public, a lawyer, and a rights campaigner. And she was deeply involved in aid work.

BBB (CRICK): When you say *presented*, what are we talking here?

OFFICER: Delivered them by hand to this building, personal for Sir Kenneth.

BBB (CRICK): She get a receipt?

OFFICER: *(shows it)*

BBB (CRICK): Ah. Well. Received one package. Question of what's in the package, isn't it? Still, you've got copies, I'm sure. Bunch of case histories. You must have.

OFFICER: We expect to have them any day.

BBB (CRICK): Is that so? Well, we'd be really interested to have a sight of them, right, Viv? I mean Dypraxa's our lead line right now, what the chief calls our flagship. Lot of happy mums and dads and kids out there, feeling a lot better for Dypraxa. So if Tessa had a grouse about it, that's something we'd really need to know and act on. If the chief was here he'd be the first to say that. Just that he's one of those guys who lives in a Gulfstream. I'm surprised he gave her the brush-off, all the same. That's not like him at all. Still, I suppose if you're as busy as he is –

BBB (EBER): We have a set procedure here for customer complaints regarding our pharmaceutical list, you see, Rob. We're only the distributor here. We import, we distribute. Provided the Kenyan government has green-lighted a drug and the medical centres are comfortable with using it, we are just acting as the intermediary, you see. That's pretty much where our responsibility ends. We take advice about storage, naturally, and make sure we are providing the right temperatures and humidity and so forth. But basically the buck stops with the manufacturer and the Kenyan government.

OFFICER: What about clinical trials? Aren't you supposed to be conducting trials?

BBB (CRICK): No trials. I'm afraid you haven't done your homework on that one, Rob. Not if you're talking your structured, fully fledged type, double blind, put it that way.

OFFICER: So what are we talking?

BBB (CRICK): Not once a drug is out there in a given country like Kenya, being distributed, that wouldn't be policy. A drug, once you're distributing it in a country and you've got the local health boys behind you a hundred per cent, is what I call a done thing.

OFFICER: So what trials, tests, experiments *are* you conducting, if any?

BBB (CRICK): Look. Don't do the words with me, all right? If you're talking about adding to a drug's track record, a real good drug like this one, if you're gearing up for distribution in another very major country – right outside the African market – the US of A for instance

– yes, all right, I grant you, in an indirect way we can call what we are doing here trials. In that sense only. The preparatory sense, for the situation ahead of us, which is the day when ThreeBees and KVH jointly enter the new exciting market I'm alluding to. With me?

OFFICER: Not yet. I'm waiting for the word guinea pig.

BBB (CRICK): All I'm saying is, that in the very best way for all parties, every patient is in some degree a test case for the benefit of the greater good. Nobody's talking guinea pigs. Back off.

OFFICER: The greater good being the American market, you mean?

BBB (CRICK): For fuck's sake. All I'm saying is, every result, every time we record a thing, a patient is recorded, those results are carefully stored and monitored at all times in Seattle and Vancouver and Basel for future reference. For the future validation of the product when we're looking to register it elsewhere. So that we're totally fail-safe at all times. Plus we've got the Kenyan health boys behind us at all times.

OFFICER: Doing what? Mopping up the bodies?

P. R. OAKEY, QC: You didn't say that, Rob, I'm sure, and we didn't hear it. Doug has been extremely forthright and generous with his information. Perhaps too generous. Yes, Lesley?

OFFICER: So what do you do with complaints meanwhile? Bin them?

BBB (CRICK): Mainly, Les, what we do, we shoot them straight back at the manufacturer, Messrs Karel Vita Hudson. Then we either reply to the complaining party under KVH's guidance, or KVH may prefer to reply direct. Horses for courses. But that's the shape and size of it, Rob. Anything else we can do for you? Maybe we should pencil in another meeting for when you've got your documentation to hand?

OFFICER: Just a minute, d'you mind? According to our information Tessa Quayle and Dr Arnold Bluhm came here in person last November at your invitation – ThreeBees' invitation – to discuss the effects, positive or negative, of your product Dypraxa. They also presented members of your staff with copies of the case notes they had sent to Sir Kenneth Curtiss personally. Are you saying you have no record of that meeting, not even who attended it from ThreeBees?

BBB (CRICK): Got a date for it, Rob?

OFFICER: We have a diary entry confirming that a meeting was set at ThreeBees' suggestion for 11 a.m. on November 18. The appointment was made through the office of Ms Rampuri, your marketing manager, who we now hear is not available.

BBB (CRICK): News to me, I must say. How about you, Viv?

BBB (EBER): Me too, Doug.

BBB (CRICK): Listen, why don't I look in Yvonne's diary for you?

OFFICER: Good idea. We'll help you.

BBB (CRICK): Hang on, hang on. I'll have to get her OK on it first, obviously. Yvonne's a lot of girl. I wouldn't be going through her diary without her say-so, any more than I would yours, Lesley.

OFFICER: Ring her up. We'll pay.

BBB (CRICK): No way, Rob.

OFFICER: Why not?

BBB (CRICK): You see, Rob, Yvonne and her boyfriend have gone to this mega-wedding in Mombasa. When we said 'attending to family affairs', that was the affair, right? A pretty bloody red-hot one, believe you me. So I would guess Monday would be the absolute earliest we could contact her. I don't know whether you've ever been to a wedding in Mombasa but believe you me –

OFFICER: Let's not worry about the diary. What about the notes they left with her?

BBB (CRICK): You mean these so-called case histories you're talking about?

OFFICER: Among other things.

BBB (CRICK): Well, if it's your actual case histories and that – obviously, Rob – technical discussion of symptoms, indications, dosage – side-effects, Rob – then it's like we said, it's down to your manufacturer every time. We're talking Basel, we're talking Seattle and we're talking Vancouver. I mean, fuck. We would be behaving with *criminal irresponsibility*, wouldn't we, Viv, if we didn't *immediately* turn to the experts for evaluation. That's not just company policy. I'd say that was Holy Writ here at ThreeBees, wouldn't you?

BBB (EBER): Absolutely. No question, Doug. The chief insists. The moment there's a problem, it's get KVH on the helpline.

OFFICER: What are you telling us? This is ridiculous. What happens to paper in this place, for Christ's sake?

BBB (CRICK): I'm telling you that we're hearing you and we'll mount a search and see what we come up with. This isn't the civil service, Rob. Or Scotland Yard. This is Africa. We don't all march on our fucking files, right? We got better ways of spending our fucking time than –

P. R. OAKEY, QC: I think there are two points here. Perhaps three. Can I take them separately? The first is, how certain are you officers that the meeting between Mrs Quayle, Dr Bluhm and representatives of ThreeBees that you're referring to actually took place?

OFFICER: As we already told you, we have documentary evidence in Bluhm's handwriting, from Bluhm's diary, that a meeting was arranged for November 18 through Ms Rampuri's office.

P. R. OAKEY, QC: Arranged is one thing, Lesley. Consummated is quite another. Let's hope Ms Rampuri has a good memory. She conducts an awful lot of meetings, you may be sure. My second point is tone. Insofar as you are able to say, would the alleged representations have been *adversarial* in tone? Might there, for instance, have been a whiff of litigation in the air? *De mortuis* and so on, but from all one hears about Mrs Quayle, she wasn't exactly one to pull her punches, was she? She was also a lawyer, as you say. And Dr Bluhm is by way of being a professional watchdog in the pharmaceutical field, I understand. We're not dealing with nobodies.

OFFICER: What if they were adversarial? If somebody's died of a drug, people have got a right to be adversarial.

P. R. OAKEY, QC: Well, obviously, Rob, if Ms Rampuri smelled a claim in the air, or worse, or the chief did, assuming he did indeed receive the written materials, which is clearly open to question, then their very *first* instinct would be to send them on to the firm's legal department. Which would be another place to look, wouldn't it, Doug?

OFFICER: I thought you were their legal department.

P. R. OAKEY, QC: *(humour)* I'm a last resort, Rob. Not a first resort. I'm far too expensive.

260

BBB (CRICK): We'll get back to you, Rob. It's been our pleasure. Next time let's make it lunch. But don't expect the moon is my advice. It's like I say. We don't spend all day filing paper here. We have a lot of irons in the fire and as the chief likes to say, ThreeBees does business from the hip. That's how this company became what it is today.

OFFICER: We'd like one more moment of your time, please, Mr Crick. We're interested in speaking to a gentleman named Lorbeer, probably Doctor Lorbeer, of German, Swiss or perhaps Dutch origin. I'm afraid we don't have a first name for him but we understand he's been closely involved with the career of Dypraxa here in Africa.

BBB (CRICK): On which side, Lesley?

OFFICER: Does that matter?

BBB (CRICK): Well, it does, rather. If Lorbeer's a doctor, which you seem to think he is, he's more likely to be with the manufacturers than with us. ThreeBees don't run to medics, you see. We're laymen in the market place. Salesmen. So it's try KVH again, I'm afraid, Les.

OFFICER: Look, do you know Lorbeer or not? We're not in Vancouver or Basel or Seattle. We're in Africa. It's your drug, your territory. You import the stuff, you advertise it, distribute it and sell it. We're telling you a Lorbeer has been involved with *your* drug here in Africa. Have you heard of Lorbeer or not?

P. R. OAKEY, QC: I think you've had your answer, haven't you, Rob? Try the manufacturers.

OFFICER: How about a woman called Kovacs, could be Hungarian?

BBB (EBER): A doctor too?

OFFICER: Do you know the *name*? Never mind her title. Has any of you heard the name Kovacs? Female? In the context of marketing this drug?

BBB (CRICK): Try the phone book, I should, Rob.

OFFICER: There's also a Dr Emrich we'd like to talk to —

P. R. OAKEY, QC: Looks as though you've drawn a blank, officers. I'm awfully sorry we can't be more use to you. We've pulled out all the stops for you, but it just doesn't seem to be our day.

Note added one week after this meeting took place:

Despite assurances from ThreeBees that searches were under way, we are informed that no papers, letters, case histories, e-mails or faxes from Tessa Abbott or Quayle or Arnold Bluhm have so far come to light. KVH deny all knowledge of them, so does the ThreeBees' legal department in Nairobi. Our attempts to recontact Eber and Crick have also proved unsuccessful. Crick is 'attending a retraining course in South Africa', Eber has been 'moved to another department'. Replacements have not yet been appointed. Ms Rampuri remains unavailable, 'pending the restructuring of the company'.

RECOMMENDED: That Scotland Yard make direct representations to Sir Kenneth K. Curtiss with a request for a full statement of his company's dealings with the deceased and Dr Bluhm, that he instruct his staff to mount a strenuous search for Ms Rampuri's diary and the missing documents, and that Ms Rampuri be produced immediately for interview.

[Initialled by Superintendent Gridley, but no action ordered or recorded.]

APPENDIX

Crick, Douglas (Doug) James, b. Gibraltar 10 Oct 1970 (ex Criminal Records Office, MOD and Judge Advocate General's Dept.)

Subject is the illegitimate son of Crick, David Angus, Royal Navy (dishonourable discharge). Crick senior served eleven years in UK gaols for multiple offences including two of manslaughter. He now lives lavishly in Marbella, Spain.

Crick, Douglas James (Subject) himself arrived in UK from Gibraltar at age nine in the care of his father (see above) who was arrested on landing. Subject was given into care. While in care Subject came to notice in a succession of juvenile courts for varied offences including drug-peddling, grievous bodily harm, procuring and affray. He was also suspected of complicity in the gang murder of two black youths in Nottingham (1984) but not charged.

In 1989 Subject claimed to be a reformed character and volunteered for police service. He was rejected, but appears to have been retained as a part-time informant.

In 1990 Subject successfully volunteered for service with the British Army, received special forces training and was attached to British Army Intelligence, Northern Ireland on plain clothes assignment with the rank and entitlements of sergeant. Subject served three years in Ireland before being reduced to the rank of private and dishonourably discharged. No other record of his service is available.

Although D. J. Crick (Subject) was presented to us as a public relations officer for House of ThreeBees, he was until recently better known as a leading light in their protection and security branch. He reportedly enjoys the personal confidence of Sir Kenneth K. Curtiss, for whom he has on many occasions acted as personal bodyguard, e.g. on Curtiss's visits to the Gulf, Latin America, Nigeria and Angola, in the last twelve months alone.

*   *   *

Bearding him at his farm, poor fellow, Tim Donohue is saying across the Monopoly board in Gloria's garden. *Phone calls at unsociable hours. Rude letters left at his club. Sweep it under the carpet, our advice.*

They kill, Lesley is saying in the darkness of the van in Chelsea. *But you've noticed that.*

With these memories still echoing in his head, Justin must have fallen asleep at the counting table because he woke to hear a dawn air battle of land birds versus seagulls, that turned out on closer inspection to be not dawn but dusk. And at some point not long after that, he was bereft. He had read everything there was to read and he knew, if he had ever doubted it, that without her laptop he was looking at only a corner of the canvas.

CHAPTER THIRTEEN

Guido was waiting on the cottage doorstep, sporting a black coat that was too long for him and a school satchel that couldn't find anywhere on his shoulders to hang. In one spidery hand he clutched a tin box for his medicines and his sandwiches. It was six in the morning. The first rays of spring sun were gilding the cobwebs on the grass slope. Justin drove the jeep as close to the cottage as he could and Guido's mother watched from a window as Guido, rejecting Justin's hand, swung himself into the passenger seat, arms, knees, satchel, tin box and coat-tails, to crash at his side like a young bird at the end of his first flight.

'How long were you waiting there?' Justin asked, but Guido's only answer was a frown. *Guido is a master of self-diagnosis*, Tessa reminds him, much impressed by her recent visit to the sick kids' hospital in Milan. *If Guido's ill he asks for the nurse. If he's very ill he asks for the Sister. And if he thinks he may be dying he asks for the doctor. And there's not one of them who doesn't come running.*

'I must be at the school gates at five to nine,' Guido told Justin stiffly.

'No problem.' They were speaking English for Guido's pride.

'Too late, I arrive in class out of breath. Too early, I hang around and make myself conspicuous.'

'Understood,' said Justin and, glancing in the mirror, saw that Guido's complexion was waxy white, the way it looked when he needed a blood transfusion. 'And in case you were wondering, we'll be working in the oil room, not the villa,' Justin added reassuringly.

Guido said nothing, but by the time they reached the coast road the colour had returned to his face. Sometimes I can't stand her proximity either, thought Justin.

The chair was too low for Guido and the stool was too high, so Justin went alone to the villa and fetched two cushions. But when he came back Guido was already standing at the pine desk, nonchalantly fingering the components of her laptop – the telephone connections for her modem, transformers for her computer and printer, the adaptor and printer cables and finally her computer itself which he handled with reckless disrespect, first flipping open the lid, then jamming the power socket into the laptop, but not – thank God – or not yet, connecting it to the mains. With the same cavalier confidence Guido shoved aside the modem, the printer and whatever else he didn't need and plonked himself onto the cushions on the chair.

'OK,' he announced.

'OK what?'

'Switch on,' said Guido in English, nodding at the wall socket at his feet. 'Let's go.' And he handed Justin the cable to plug in. His voice, to Justin's oversensitive ear, had acquired an unpleasant mid-Atlantic twang.

'Can anything go wrong?' Justin asked nervously.

'Like what, for instance?'

'Can we wipe it clean or something, by mistake?'

'By switching it on? No way.'

'Why not?'

Guido grandly circumnavigated the screen with his scarecrow hand. 'Everything that's in there she saved. If she don't save it, she don't want it, so it's not in there. Is that reasonable or is that reasonable?'

Justin felt a bar of hostility form at the front of his head, which was what happened to him when people talked computer gobbledygook at him.

'Then all right. If you say so. I'll switch on.' And crouching, gingerly poked the plug into the wall socket. 'Yes?'

'Oh man.'

Reluctantly Justin dropped the switch and stood up in time to see absolutely nothing happen on the screen. His mouth went dry and he felt sick. I'm trespassing. I'm a clumsy idiot. I should have got an expert, not a child. I should have learned to work the bloody thing myself. Then the screen lit up and gave him a procession of smiling, waving African children lined up outside a tin-roofed health clinic, followed by an aerial view of coloured rectangles and ovals scattered over a blue-grey field.

'What's that?'

'The desktop.'

Justin peered over Guido's shoulder and read: *My Briefcase . . . Network Neighborhood . . . Shortcut to Connect*. 'Now what?'

'You want to see files? I show you files. We go to files, you read.'

'I want to see what Tessa saw. Whatever she was working on. I want to follow her footsteps and read whatever's in there. I thought I made that clear.'

In his anxiety he was resenting Guido's presence here. He wanted Tessa for himself again, at the counting table. He wanted her laptop not to exist. Guido directed an arrow to a panel on the lower left side of Tessa's screen.

'What's that thing you're tapping?'

'The mouse pad. These are the last nine files she worked on. You want I show you the others? I show you the others, no problem.'

A panel appeared, headed *Open File, Tessa's Documents*. He tapped again.

'She's got like twenty-five files in this category,' he said.

'Do they have titles?'

Guido leaned to one side, inviting Justin to look for himself:

Pharma	Plague	Trials
pharma-general	plague-history	Russia
pharma-pollution	plague-Kenya	Poland
pharma-in-3rd world	plague-cures	Kenya
pharma-watchdogs	plague-new	Mexico
pharma-bribes	plague-old	Germany
pharma-litigation	plague-charlatans	Known-mortalities
pharma-cash		Wanza
pharma-protest		
pharma-hypocrisy		
pharma-trials		
pharma-fakes		
pharma-cover-ups		

Guido was moving the arrow and tapping again. 'Arnold. Who's this Arnold suddenly?' he demanded.

'A friend of hers.'

'He's got documents too. Jesus, has *he* got documents!'

'How many?'

'Twenty. More.' Another tap. '*Bits and Bobs*. That some kind of British idiom?'

'Yes, it's English. Not American, perhaps, but certainly English,' Justin replied huffily. 'What's that? What are you doing now? You're going too fast.'

'No, I'm not. I'm going slow for you. I'm looking in her briefcase, how many folders she got. Wow. She got a *lot* of folders. Folder one, folder two. Then more folders.' He pressed again. His phoney American was driving Justin mad. Where did he pick it up? He's been seeing too many American films. I shall speak to the headmaster. 'See this? This is her recycle bin. Here's where she puts whatever she's thinking of throwing out.'

'But she didn't, presumably. Throw them out.'

'What's there, she don't throw out. What's not, she did.' Another tap.

'What's AOL?' Justin asked.

'America Online. I.S.P. Internet Service Provider. Whatever she got from AOL and kept, she stored it in this programme, same as her old e-mails. New messages, you've got to go on-line to get them. You want to *send* messages, you've got to go on-line to send them. No on-line, no new messages in or out.'

'I know that. It's obvious.'

'You want I go on-line?'

'Not yet. I want to see what's in there already.'

'All of it?'

'Yes.'

'Then you've got like days of reading. Weeks, maybe. All you do, you point the mouse and you click. You want to sit where I'm sitting?'

'You're absolutely sure nothing can go wrong?' Justin insisted, lowering himself into the chair while Guido stood himself behind him.

'What she saved is saved. It's like I said. Why else would she save it for?'

'And I can't lose it?'

'Holy smoke, man! Not unless you click on delete. Even if you click on delete, it's going to ask you, Justin, are you sure you want to delete? If you're not sure, you say no. You press no. Press no means, *No. I'm not sure*. Click. That's all there is. Go for it.'

Justin is cautiously tapping his way through Tessa's labyrinth while Guido the tutor stands patronisingly at his side, incanting commands in his mid-Atlantic cyber-voice. When a procedure is new to Justin or confuses him, he calls a break, takes a sheet of paper and writes out the moves to Guido's imperious dictation. New landscapes of information are unfolding before his eyes. Go here, go there, now go back to here. It's all too vast, you ranged too wide, I'll never catch you up, he tells her. If I read for a year, how will I ever know I've found what you were looking for?

* * *

Handouts from the World Health Organization.

Records of obscure medical conferences held in Geneva, Amsterdam and Heidelberg under the aegis of yet another unheard-of outpost of the United Nations' sprawling medical empire.

Company prospectuses extolling unpronounceable pharmaceutical products and their life-enhancing virtues.

Notes to herself. Memos. A shocking quotation from *Time* magazine, framed with exclamation marks, raised in bold capitals and visible across the room to those who have eyes and do not avert them. A terrifying generality to galvanise her search for the particular:

IN 93 CLINICAL TRIALS RESEARCHERS ENCOUNTERED 691 ADVERSE REACTIONS BUT REPORTED ONLY 39 TO THE NATIONAL INSTITUTES OF HEALTH.

A whole folder devoted to PW. Who in God's name is PW when she's at home? Despair. Take me back to the paper I understand. But when he clicks on *Bits and Bobs*, there is PW again, staring him in the face. And after one more click, all is clear: PW is short for PharmaWatch, a self-styled cyber-underground notionally based in Kansas with 'a mission to expose the excesses and malpractices of the pharmaceutical industry', not to mention 'the inhumanity of self-styled humanitarians who are ripping off the poorest nations'.

Reports of so-called Off-Broadway conferences among demonstrators planning to converge on Seattle or Washington DC to make their feelings known to the World Bank and the International Monetary Fund.

High talk of 'The Great American Corporate Hydra', and the 'Monster Capital'. A frivolous article from Heaven knows where entitled 'Anarchism is Back in Style'.

He clicks again to find the word *Humanity* under attack. Humanity is Tessa's H-word, he discovers. Whenever she hears it, she confides to Bluhm in a chatty e-mail, she reaches for her revolver.

Every time I hear a pharma justifying its actions on the grounds of Humanity, Altruism, Duty to Mankind, I want to vomit, and that's not because I'm pregnant. It's because I'm reading at the same time how the US pharma-giants are trying to extend the life of their patents so that they can preserve their monopoly and charge what they damn well like and use the State Dept. to frighten the Third World out of manufacturing their own generic products at a fraction of the price of the branded version. All right, they've made a cosmetic gesture on Aids drugs. But what about –

*   *   *

I know all that, he thinks, and clicks back to the desktop, thence to *Arnold's Documents*.

'What's this?' he asks sharply, lifting his hands from the keyboard as if to disclaim responsibility. For the first time in their relationship, Tessa is demanding a password of him before she will let him in. Her command is finite: PASSWORD, PASSWORD, like a brothel sign winking on and off.

'Shit,' says Guido.

'Did she have a password when she taught you how to work this thing?' Justin demands, ignoring this scatological outburst.

Guido puts one hand across his mouth, leans forward and with his other hand types five characters. 'Me,' he says proudly.

Five asterisks appear, otherwise nothing.

'What are you doing?' Justin demands.

'Typing my name. Guido.'

'Why?'

'That was the password,' he says, dropping into voluble Italian in his nervousness. 'The I isn't an I. It's a one. The O's a nought. Tessa was crazy about that stuff. In a password, you had to have at least one numeral. She insisted.'

'Why am I looking at stars?'

'Because they don't want you to see Guido! Otherwise you could look over my shoulder and read the password! It didn't work! Guido is not her password!' He buries his face in his hands.

'So what we can do is guess,' Justin suggests, trying to calm him.

'Guess how? Guess what? How many guesses do they give you? Like three!'

'You mean, if we guess wrong we don't get there,' Justin says, valiantly trying to make light of the problem. 'Hey. You. Come out of there.'

'Damn right we don't!'

'All right, then. Let's think. What other numerals are made from letters?'

'Three could be E back to front. Five could be S. There's half a dozen of them. More. It's awful –' still from inside his hands.

'And what happens exactly when we run out of chances?'

'It locks up and won't try any more. What do you think?'

'Ever?'

'Ever!'

Justin hears the lie in his voice and smiles.

'And you think three shots is all we get?'

'Look, I'm not a lexicon, OK? I'm not a handbook. What I don't know, I don't say. It could be three. It could be ten. I've got to go to school. Maybe you should call the helpline.'

'Think. After Guido, what's her favourite thing?'

Guido's face at last emerges from his hands. 'You. Who do you think? Justin!'

'She wouldn't do that.'

'Why not?'

'Because it's her kingdom, not mine.'

'You're just guessing! You're ridiculous. Try Justin. I'm right, I know I am!'

'Look. *After* Justin, what's her *next* favourite thing?'

'I wasn't married to her. OK? You were!'

Justin thinks *Arnold*, then *Wanza*. He tries *Ghita*, entering the I as a 1. Nothing happens. He emits a nervous scoffing sound that says this childish game is beneath him, but this is because his mind is stretching in all directions and he doesn't know which to follow. He thinks of *Garth* her dead father, and *Garth* her dead son, and rules them both out on aesthetic and emotional grounds. He thinks of *Tessa* but she is not an egomaniac. He thinks *ARNO1D* and *ARN0LD* and *ARN01D* but Tessa would not be so crass as to block Arnold's file with a password saying Arnold. He flirts with *Maria*, which was her mother's name, then with *Mustafa*, then *Hammond*, but none presses itself upon him as a code name or password. He looks down into her grave and watches the yellow freesias on the lid of her coffin disappear under the red soil. He sees Mustafa standing in the Woodrows' kitchen, clutching his basket. He sees himself in his straw hat tending them in the garden in Nairobi and again here in Elba. He enters the word *freesia*, typing the I as 1. Seven asterisks appear but nothing happens. He enters the same word again, typing the S as 5.

'Will it still have me?' he asks softly.

'I'm twelve years old, Justin! Twelve!' He relents a little. 'You got maybe *one more* try. Then it's curtains. I resign, OK? It's her laptop. Yours. Leave me out of this.'

He enters *freesia* a third time, leaving the S as 5 but turning the 1 back to an I, and finds himself staring at an unfinished polemical essay. With the aid of his yellow freesias he has invaded the file called *Arnold* and met a tract on human rights. Guido is dancing round the room.

'We got it! I told you! We're fantastic! *She*'s fantastic!'

*   *   *

Why are Africa's Gays Forced to Stay in the Closet?

Hear the comfortable words of that great arbiter of public decency, President Daniel Arap Moi:

'Words like lesbianism and homosexuality do not exist in African languages.' – Moi, 1995.

'Homosexuality is against African norms and religions and even in religion it is considered a great sin.' – Moi, 1998.

Unsurprisingly, Kenya's Criminal Code obediently agrees with

Moi one hundred per cent. Sections 162–165 lay down a term of FIVE TO FOURTEEN YEARS' IMPRISONMENT for 'Carnal Knowledge Against the Order of Nature'. The law goes further:

– Kenyan law defines any sexual relations between men as a CRIMINAL ACT.
– It hasn't even heard of sexual relations between women.

What is the SOCIAL CONSEQUENCE of this antediluvian attitude?
– gay men marry or carry on affairs with women in order to conceal their sexuality.
– they live in misery and so do their wives.
– no sex education is offered to gay men, even in the midst of Kenya's long-denied Aids epidemic.
– sections of Kenyan society are forced to live in a state of deceit. Doctors, lawyers, businessmen, priests and even politicians go in terror of blackmail and arrest.
– a self-perpetuating cycle of corruption and oppression is created, dragging our society still deeper into the mire.

Here the article stops. Why?

And why in Heaven's name do you file an incomplete polemical piece about gay rights under *Arnold* and lock it away with a password?

Justin wakes to Guido's presence at his shoulder. He has returned from his peregrinations and is leaning forward, peering at the screen in puzzlement.

'It's time I drove you to school,' Justin says.

'We don't need to go yet! We've got another ten minutes! Who's Arnold? Is he gay? What do gay guys *do*? My mom goes crazy if I ask her.'

'We're leaving now. We could get stuck behind a tractor.'

'Look. Let me open her mailbox. OK? Somebody could have written to her. Maybe Arnold did. Don't you want to see in her mailbox? Maybe she sent *you* a message you haven't read. So I open the mailbox? Yes?'

Justin gently puts his hand on Guido's shoulder. 'You'll be fine. Nobody's going to laugh at you. Everybody stays away from school now and then. That doesn't make you an invalid. It makes you normal. We'll look in her mailbox when you come back.'

*　　*　　*

The drive to Guido's school and back took Justin a long hour, and in that time he permitted himself no flights of fancy or premature speculation. When he regained the oil room he headed not for the laptop but for the pile of papers given him by Lesley in the van outside the cinema. Moving with greater confidence than he had brought to the laptop, he sorted his way to a photocopy of a clumsily handwritten letter on lined paper that had caught his eye during one of his first skirmishing raids. It was undated. It had 'come to notice', according to the attached minute initialled by Rob, between the pages of a medical encyclopaedia that the two officers had found lying on the kitchen floor of Bluhm's apartment, slung there by frustrated burglars. The writing paper faded and old. The envelope addressed to the PO Box of Bluhm's NGO. Postmark the old Arab slaving island of Lamu.

> *My own dear darling Arni,*
> *I don't never forget our love or your embraces and goodness to me your dear friend. What a luck and bliss for me that you honeur our beautiful island for your holiday! I got to say thank you but it is to god I thank for your generos love and gifts and now the knoledge that will come to me in my studies thanks to you, plus motorbike. For you my darling man I work day and night, always glad in my heart to know that my darling is with me every step, holding and loving me.*

And the signature? Justin, like Rob before him, struggled to decipher it. The style of the letter, as Rob's minute pointed out, suggested an Arabic hand, the writing being long and low with

274

well-completed roundels. The signature, done with a flourish, appeared to possess a consonant at either end and a vowel between: Pip? Pet? Pat? Dot? It was useless to guess. For all anyone could tell, it was actually an Arabic signature.

But was the writer a woman or a man? Would an uneducated Arab woman from Lamu really write so boldly? Would she ride a motorbike?

Crossing the room to the pine desk Justin placed himself in front of the laptop but, instead of calling up *Arnold* again, sat staring at the blank screen.

*　　*　　*

'So who does *Arnold* love, actually?' he is asking her, with feigned casualness, as they lie side by side on the bed one hot Sunday evening in Nairobi. Arnold and Tessa have returned the same morning from their first field trip together. Tessa has declared it one of the experiences of her life.

'Arnold loves the whole human race,' she replies languidly. 'Bar none.'

'Does he sleep with the whole human race?'

'He may. I haven't asked him. Do you want me to?'

'No. I don't think so. I thought I might ask him myself.'

'That won't be necessary.'

'Sure?'

'Certain sure.'

And kisses him. And kisses him again. Till she kisses him back to life.

'And don't ever ask me that question again,' she tells him, as an afterthought, as she lies with her face in the angle of his shoulder, and her limbs sprawled across his. 'Let's just say Arnold lost his heart in Mombasa.' And she draws herself into him, head down and shoulders rigid.

*　　*　　*

In Mombasa?

Or in Lamu, a hundred and fifty miles up the coast?

Returning to the counting table, Justin selected this time Lesley's background report on 'BLUHM, Arnold Moise, MD, missing victim or suspect'. No scandal, no marriage, no known companion, no common-law wife recorded. In Algiers, Subject had lived in a hostel for young doctors of both sexes, occupying single accommodation. No Significant Other recorded with his NGO. Subject's next of kin given as his adoptive Belgian half-sister, resident in Bruges. Arnold had never claimed travel or living expenses for a companion, and never required anything other than bachelor accommodation. Subject's trashed apartment in Nairobi was described by Lesley as 'monkish with a strong air of abstinence'. Subject lived there alone and had no servant. 'In his private life, Subject appears to do without creature comforts, including hot water.'

* * *

'The entire Muthaiga Club has convinced itself that our baby was put there by Arnold,' Justin is informing Tessa, perfectly amiably, as they eat their fish in an Indian restaurant on the edge of town. She is four months pregnant and though their conversation might not suggest it, Justin is more besotted with her than ever.

'Who's the entire Muthaiga Club?' she demands.

'Elena the Greek, I suspect. Conveyed to Gloria, conveyed to Woodrow,' he goes on cheerfully. 'What I'm supposed to do about it I don't quite know. Drive you up there and make love to you on the billiards table might be a solution, if you're game.'

'Then it's double jeopardy, isn't it?' she says thoughtfully. 'And double prejudice.'

'Double? Why?'

She breaks off, lowers her eyes, and gently shakes her head. 'They're a prejudiced bunch of bastards – leave it at that.'

* * *

And at the time, he had done as she commanded. But no longer.

Why *double*? he asked himself, still staring at the screen.

Single jeopardy means Arnold's adultery. But double? *Double* is for what? For his race? Arnold is discriminated against for his supposed adultery and his race? Ergo a double discrimination?

Maybe.

Unless.

Unless the cold-eyed lawyer in her is speaking again: the same lawyer who decided to ignore a death threat rather than imperil her quest for justice.

Unless the *first* perceived prejudice was not directed against a black man who was supposedly sleeping with a married white woman, but against homosexuals at large, *of whom Bluhm* – though his detractors didn't know it – *was one*.

In such a case the cold-eyed, hot-hearted lawyer's reasoning would work this way:

Jeopardy the first: Arnold is homosexual but local prejudice does not allow him to admit it. If he admitted it, he would be unable to continue his relief work since Moi detests NGOs as much as he hates homosexuals, and at the very least he would have Arnold flung out of the country.

Jeopardy the second: Arnold is forced to live in a state of deceit (see unfinished press article by ?). Instead of declaring his sexuality, he is driven to adopt the pose of playboy, thus attracting the criticism reserved for trans-racial adulterers.

Ergo: a double jeopardy.

And why, finally, does Tessa once more not confide this secret to her beloved husband, instead of leaving him with dishonourable suspicions that he will not, must not, cannot admit to, even to himself? he demanded of the screen.

He remembered the name of the Indian restaurant she was so fond of. Haandi.

*   *   *

The tides of jealousy that Justin had for so long held at bay suddenly broke banks and engulfed him. But it was jealousy of a new kind: jealousy that Tessa and Arnold had kept even this secret from him, together with all the others that they shared; that they had deliberately excluded him from their precious circle of two, leaving him to peer after them like a distraught voyeur, never knowing, for all her assurances, that there was nothing to see and never would be; that as Ghita had wanted to explain to Rob and Lesley before she shied away, no spark would ever fly; that the only relationship between them was precisely the brother-and-sister friendship of the sort Justin had described to Ham without, in his deepest heart, totally believing himself.

A perfect man, Tessa had called Bluhm once. Even Justin the sceptic had never thought of him in any other way. A man to touch the homoerotic nerve in all of us, he had once remarked to her in his innocence. Beautiful and soft-spoken. Courteous to friends and strangers. Beautiful from his husky voice to his rounded iron-grey beard, to his long-lidded, plump African eyes that never strayed from you while he spoke or listened. Beautiful in the rare but timely gestures that punctuated his lucid, beautifully delivered, intelligent opinions. Beautiful from his sculpted knuckles to his feather-light, graceful body, trim and lithe as a dancer's and as disciplined in its withholding. Never brash, never unknowing, never cruel, although at every party and conference he encountered Western people so ignorant that Justin felt embarrassed for him. Even the old ones at the Muthaiga said it: that fellow Bluhm, my God, they didn't make blacks like him in our day, no wonder Justin's child-bride has fallen for him.

So why in the name of all that's holy didn't you put me out of my misery? he demanded furiously of her, or the screen.

Because I trusted you and expected the same trust in return.

If you trusted me why didn't you tell me?

Because I do not betray the confidence of friends and I require you to respect that fact and admire me for it. Enormously and all the time.

Because I am a lawyer and where secrets are concerned – as she used to say – *compared with me, the grave is a chatterbox.*

CHAPTER FOURTEEN

And tuberculosis is mega-bucks: ask Karel Vita Hudson. Any day now the richest nations will be facing a tubercular pandemic, and Dypraxa will become the multibillion-dollar earner that all good shareholders dream of. The White Plague, the Great Stalker, the Great Imitator, the Captain of Death is no longer confining himself to the wretched of the earth. He is doing what he did a hundred years ago. He is hovering like a filthy cloud of pollution *over the West's own horizon*, even if it is still their poor who are his victims.

 – One third of the world's population infected with the bacillus,

Tessa is telling her computer, highlighting and underlining as she goes.

 – In the United States incidence has increased by twenty per cent in seven years . . .
 – One untreated sufferer transmits the disease on average to between ten and fifteen people a year . . .
 – Health authorities in New York City have given themselves

powers to incarcerate TB victims who do not willingly submit to
isolation . . .
- Thirty per cent of all known TB cases are now drug-resistant . . .

The White Plague is not born in us, Justin reads. It is forced
upon us by foul breath, foul living conditions, foul hygiene, foul
water and foul administrative neglect.

Rich countries hate it because it is a slur on their good housekeeping, poor countries because in many of them it is synonymous with Aids. Some countries refuse to admit they have it at
all, preferring to live in denial rather than confess the mark of
shame.

And in Kenya, as in other African countries, the incidence
of tuberculosis has increased fourfold since the onset of the HIV
virus.

A chatty e-mail from Arnold lists the practical difficulties of
treating the disease in the field:

- Diagnosis demanding and prolonged. Patients must bring
  sputum samples on consecutive days.
- Lab work essential but microscopes often bust or stolen.
- No dye available to detect bacilli. Dye sold, drunk, run out, not
  replaced.
- Treatment takes eight months. Patients who feel better after a
  month abandon treatment or sell pills. Disease then returns in
  drug-resistant form.
- TB pills are traded on African black markets as cures for
  STD (sexually transmitted diseases). The World Health
  Organization insists that a patient taking a tablet should be
  watched while he or she swallows it. Result: a black market pill
  is sold 'wet' or 'dry' according to whether it's been in someone's
  mouth . . .

A bald postscript continues:

TB kills more mothers than any other disease. In Africa, women always pay the price. Wanza was a guinea pig, and became a victim.

As whole villages of Wanzas were guinea pigs.

*　　*　　*

Extracts from a page four article in the *International Herald Tribune*:

'West Warned it, too, is Vulnerable to Drug-Resistant Strains of TB' by Donald G. McNeil Jr., *New York Times* Service,

some passages highlighted by Tessa.

AMSTERDAM – Deadly strains of drug-resistant tuberculosis are increasing not just in poor countries but in wealthy Western ones, according to a report from the World Health Organization and other anti-TB groups.

'It's a message: Watch out, guys, this is serious,' said Dr Marcos Espinal, the lead author of the report. 'It's a potential major crisis in the future' . . .

But the most powerful weapon that the international medical community has for raising money is the specter that the unchecked explosion of cases in the Third World will let divergent strains merge into something incurable and highly contagious that will attack the West.

Footnote by Tessa, written in a mysteriously restrained hand, as if she is deliberately holding herself back from sensation:

'Arnold says: Russian immigrants to US, particularly those coming straight from the camps, carry all sorts of multi-resistant strains of TB – actually in a higher proportion to Kenya, where multi-resistant is NOT synonymous with HIV positive. A friend of his is treating very bad cases in Brooklyn's Bay Ridge area, and numbers are already frightening, he says. Incidence throughout US, amid crowded urban minority groups, said to be constantly increasing.'

Or, put into the language that stock exchanges the world over understand: if the TB market performs as forecast, billions and billions of dollars are waiting to be earned, and the boy to earn them is Dypraxa – always provided, of course, that the preliminary canter over the course in Africa has not thrown up any disturbing side-effects.

It is this thought that prompts Justin to return, as a matter of urgency, to the Uhuru Hospital in Nairobi. Hastening to the counting table, he again rummages in the police files and unearths six photocopied pages covered in Tessa's fever-driven scrawl as she struggles to record Wanza's case history in the language of a child.

Wanza is a single mother.

She can't read or write.

I met her in her village and again in Kibera slum. She got pregnant by her uncle who raped her and then claimed she had seduced him. This is her first pregnancy. Wanza left the village in order not to be raped again by her uncle, and also by another man who was molesting her.

Wanza says many people in her village were sick with bad coughs. Many of the men had Aids, women too. Two pregnant women had recently died. Like Wanza, they had been visiting a medical centre five miles away. Wanza did not want to use the same medical centre any more. She was afraid their pills were bad. This shows that Wanza is intelligent since most native women have a blind faith in doctors, though they respect injections above pills.

In Kibera, a white man and a white woman came to see her. They wore white coats so she assumed they were doctors. They knew which village she had come from. They gave her some pills, the same pills she is taking in hospital.

Wanza says the man's name was Law-bear. I get her to say it many times. Lor-bear? Lor-beer? Lohrbear? The white woman who came with him did not speak her name but examined Wanza and took samples of her blood, urine and sputum.

They came to see her in Kibera twice more. They were not interested in other people in her hut. They told her she would be having her baby in the hospital because she was sick. Wanza was uneasy about this. Many pregnant women in Kibera are sick but they did not have their babies in hospital.

Lawbear said there would be no charges, all of the charges would be paid on her behalf. She did not ask who by. She says the man and woman were very worried. She did not like them to be so worried. She made a joke of this but they did not laugh.

Next day a car came for her. She was close to full term. It was the first time she had ridden in a car. Two days later Kioko her brother arrived at the hospital to be with her. He had heard she was in the hospital. Kioko can read and write and is very intelligent. Brother and sister love each other very much. Wanza is fifteen years old.

Kioko says that when another pregnant woman in the village was dying, the same white couple came to see her and took samples from her just as they had done with Wanza. While they were visiting the village they heard that Wanza had run away to Kibera. Kioko says they were very curious about her and asked him how to find her and wrote his instructions in a notebook. That is how the white couple found Wanza in Kibera slum and had her confined in the Uhuru for observation. Wanza is an African guinea pig, one of many who have not survived Dypraxa.

*   *   *

Tessa is talking to him across the breakfast table. She is seven months pregnant. Mustafa is standing where he always insists on standing, just inside the kitchen but listening at the partly opened door so that he knows exactly when to make more toast, pour more tea. Mornings are a happy time. So are evenings. But it is in the morning that conversation flows most easily.

'Justin.'

'Tessa.'

'Ready?'

'All attention.'

'If I yelled *Lorbeer* at you – pow, just like that – what would you say to me?'

'Laurel.'

'More.'

'Laurel. Crown. Caesar. Emperor. Athlete. Victor.'

284

'More.'

'Crowned with – bay – bay leaves – laurel berry – rest on one's laurels – bloody laurels, victory won by violent war – why aren't you laughing?'

'So German?' she insists.

'German. Noun. Masculine.'

'Spell it.'

He did.

'Could it be Dutch?'

'I should think so. Nearly. Not the same but close, probably. Have you taken up crosswords or something?'

'Not any more,' she replies thoughtfully. And that, as quite often with Tessa the lawyer, is that. *Compared with me, the grave is a chatterbox.*

*   *   *

No J, no G, no A, her notes continue. She means: Justin, Ghita and Arnold are none of them present. She is alone in the ward with Wanza.

> *15.23 Enter beef-faced white man and tall Slav-looking woman in*
> *white coats, Slav's open at the neck. Three other males in*
> *attendance. All wear white coats. Stolen Napoleonic bees on pockets.*
> *They go to Wanza's bedside, gawp at her.*
> *Self: Who are you? What are you doing to her? Are you doctors?*
> *They ignore me, stare at Wanza, listen to her breathing, check heart,*
> *pulse, temp, eyes, call 'Wanza'. No response.*
> *Self: Are you Lorbeer? Who are you all? What are your names?*
> *Slav woman: It is no concern of yours.*
> <u>*Exeunt.*</u>
>
> *Slav woman one tough bitch. Dyed black hair, long legs, wiggles hips,*
> *can't help it.*

Like a guilty man caught in a felonious act, Justin swiftly slides Tessa's notes beneath the nearest pile of paper, springs to his feet and turns in horrified disbelief towards the oil room door. Somebody is beating on it very hard. He can see it trembling to the rhythm of the blows, and hear above the din the hectoring, horribly familiar, ten-acre voice of an Englishman of the imperious class.

'Justin! Come out, dear boy! Don't hide! We know you're there! Two dear friends bring gifts and comfort!'

Frozen, Justin remains incapable of response.

'You're skulking, dear boy! You're doing a Garbo! There's no need! It's us! Beth and Adrian! Your friends!'

Justin grabs the keys from the sideboard and, like a man facing execution, steps blindly into the sunlight, to be faced by Beth and Adrian Tupper, the Greatest Writing Duo of their Age, the world-famous Tuppers of Tuscany.

'*Beth. Adrian.* How lovely,' he declares, slamming the door behind him.

Adrian seizes him by the shoulders and drops his voice dramatically. 'Dear boy. Justin. Whom the gods love. Mmh? Mmh? Manliness. Only thing,' he intones, all on one confiding note of commiseration. 'You're alone. Don't tell me. *Terribly* alone.' Submitting to his embraces, Justin sees his two tiny, deep-set eyes searching greedily past his shoulder.

'Oh Justin, we really did love her so,' Beth mews, stretching her tiny mouth into a pitiful downward curve, then straightening it up again to kiss him.

'Where's your man Luigi?' Adrian demands.

'In Naples. With his fiancée. They're getting married. In June,' Justin adds uselessly.

'Should be here supporting you. World today, dear boy. No loyalty. No servant classes.'

'The big one is for darling Tessa in memory, and the little one's for poor Garth, to be beside her,' Beth explains in a tinny little voice that has somehow lost its echo. 'I thought we'd plant them in remembrance, didn't I, Adrian?'

In the courtyard stands their pick-up, its back ostentatiously laden with rustic logs for the benefit of Adrian's readers, who are invited to believe he cuts them for himself. Tied across them lie two young peach trees with plastic bags round their roots.

'Beth has these marvellous vibes,' Tupper booms confidingly. 'Wavelength, dear boy. Tuned in all the time, aren't you, darling? "We must take him trees," she said. Knows, you see. Knows.'

'We could plant them now, then they'd be done, wouldn't they?' says Beth.

'After lunch,' says Adrian firmly.

And one simple peasants' picnic – Beth's care package, as she calls it, consisting of a loaf of bread, olives and a trout each from our smokery, darling, just the three of us, over a bottle of your nice Manzini wine.

Courteous unto death, Justin leads them to the villa.

*   *   *

'Can't mourn for ever, dear boy. Jews don't. Seven days is all they get. After that, they're back on their feet, rarin' to go. Their *law*, you see, darling,' Adrian explains, addressing his wife as if she were an imbecile.

They are sitting in the salon under the cherubs, eating trout off their laps in order to satisfy Beth's vision of a picnic.

'All written down for them. What to do, who does it, how long for. After that, get on with the job. Justin should do the same. No good *mooching*, Justin. You must never mooch in life. Too negative.'

'Oh, I'm not mooching,' Justin objects, cursing himself for opening a second bottle of wine.

'What *are* you doing then?' Tupper demands as his small round eyes drill into Justin.

'Well, Tessa left a lot of unfinished business, you see,' Justin explains lamely. 'Well – there's her estate, obviously. And the charitable trust she had set up. Plus odds and ends.'

'Got a computer?'

You saw it! thought Justin, secretly aghast. You can't have done! I was too quick for you, I know I was!

'Most important invention since the printing press, dear boy.

Isn't it, Beth? No secretary, no wife, nothing. What do you use? We resisted it to begin with, didn't you, Beth? Mistake.'

'We didn't realise,' Beth explains, taking a very big pull of wine for such a small woman.

'Oh, I just grabbed whatever they have here,' Justin replies, recovering his balance. 'Tessa's lawyers shoved a bunch of disks at me. I commandeered the estate machine and ploughed through them as best I could.'

'So you've finished. Time to go home. Don't dither. Go. Your country needs you.'

'Well, not *quite* finished, actually, Adrian. I've still got a few days to go.'

'Foreign Office know you're here?'

'Probably,' said Justin. How does Adrian do this to me? Rob me of my defences? Pry into the private places in my life where he has absolutely no business, and I stand by and let him?

A moratorium, during which, to his immense relief, Justin is subjected to an extraordinarily boring account of how the Greatest Writing Couple in the World was converted against all natural inclination to the Net – a dress rehearsal, no doubt, for another riveting chapter of Tuscan Tales, and another free machine from the manufacturers.

'You're running away, dear boy,' Adrian warns severely as the two men untie the peach trees from the truck and cart them to the *cantina* for Justin to plant later. 'Something called duty. Old-fashioned word these days. Longer you put it off, harder it'll be. Go home. They'll welcome you with open arms.'

'Why can't we plant them now?' Beth asks.

'Too emotional, darling. Let him do it on his own. God bless you, dear boy. Wavelength. Most important thing in the world.'

So what were you? Justin demanded of Tupper as he stared after their departing pick-up: a fluke or a conspiracy? Did you jump or were you pushed? Did the smell of blood bring you – or did Pellegrin? At various stages of Tupper's over-publicised life, he had graced the BBC and a vile British newspaper. But he had also worked in the large back rooms of secret Whitehall.

Justin remembered Tessa at her naughtiest. 'What do you think Adrian *does* with all the intelligence he doesn't put into his books?'

*   *   *

He returned to Wanza, only to discover that Tessa's six-page diary of her ward-companion's illness petered to an unsatisfying end. Lorbeer and his team visit the ward three more times. Arnold twice challenges them, but Tessa does not hear what is said. It is not Lorbeer but the sexy Slav woman who physically examines Wanza, while Lorbeer and his acolytes look uselessly on. What happens after that happens at night while Tessa is asleep. Tessa wakes, screams and yells but no nurses come. They are too frightened. Only with the greatest difficulty does Tessa find them and force them to admit that Wanza is dead and her baby has gone back to her village.

Replacing the pages among the police papers, Justin once more addressed the computer. He felt bilious. He had drunk too much wine. His trout, which must have escaped the smoker at half-time, sat like rubber in his belly. He dabbed at a few keys, thought of going back to the villa and drinking a litre of mineral water. Suddenly he was staring at the screen in horrified disbelief. He stared away, shook his head to clear it, resumed his staring. He buried his face in his hands to wipe away the fuzziness. But when he looked again the message was still there.

THIS PROGRAM HAS PERFORMED AN
ILLEGAL OPERATION.
YOU MAY LOSE ANY UNSAVED DATA IN
ALL WINDOWS THAT ARE RUNNING.

And below the death sentence, a row of boxes set out like coffins for a mass funeral: click the one you would most like to be buried in. He hung his hands at his sides, rolled his head around, then with his heels cautiously backed his chair away from the computer.

'Damn you, Tupper!' he whispered. 'Damn you, damn you, damn you.' But he meant: damn me.

It's something I did, or didn't. I should have put the wretched brute to sleep.

Guido. Get me Guido.

He looked at his watch. School ends in twenty minutes but Guido has refused to be picked up. He prefers to take the school bus like all other normal boys, thank you, and he'll ask the driver to hoot when he drops him at the gates – at which point, Justin is graciously permitted to fetch him in the jeep. There was nothing for it but to wait. If he made a dash to beat the bus, chances were he would reach the school too late and have to dash back. Leaving the computer to sulk he returned to the counting table in an attempt to restore his spirits with the hard paper he so vastly preferred to the screen.

PANA Wire Service (09/24/97)
In 1995, sub-Saharan Africa had the highest number of new tuberculosis cases of any global region, as well as a high rate of TB and HIV co-infection, according to the World Health Organization . . .

I knew that already, thank you.

Tropical Mega-Cities will be Hells on Earth
As illegal logging, water and land pollution and unbridled oil extraction destroy the Third World's ecosystem, more and more Third World rural communities are forced to migrate to cities in search of work and survival. Experts predict the rise of tens and perhaps hundreds of tropical mega-cities attracting vast new slum populations of lowest-paid labour, and producing unprecedented rates of killer diseases such as tuberculosis . . .

He heard the honking of a distant bus.

*   *   *

'So you screwed up,' Guido said with satisfaction, when Justin led him to the scene of the disaster. 'Did you go into her mail-box?' He was already tapping the keys.

'Of course not. I wouldn't know how to. What are you doing?'

'Did you add any material and forget to save it?'

'Absolutely no. Neither, nor. I wouldn't.'

'Then it's nothing. You didn't lose any,' said Guido serenely in his computer interglot, and with a few more gentle taps, nursed the machine back to health. 'Can we go on-line now? *Please?*' he begged.

'Why should we?'

'To get her mail, for Chrissakes! There's hundreds of people out there sent her e-mails every day and you won't read them. What about the people who want to send *you* their love and sympathy? Don't you want to *know* what they said? There's e-mails from me in there she never answered! Maybe she never read them!'

Guido was on the verge of tears. Taking him gently by the shoulders, Justin sat him on the stool before the keyboard.

'Tell me what the risk is,' he suggested. 'Give me the worst case.'

'We risk nothing. Everything's saved. There isn't a worst case. We're doing the absolutely simplest things with this computer. If we crash, it's like before. I'll save any new e-mails. Tessa saved everything else. Trust me.'

Guido attaches the laptop to its modem and offers Justin one end of a length of flex. 'Pull out the telephone line and plug this in. Then we're all hooked up.'

Justin does as he is told. Guido taps and waits. Justin is looking over his shoulder. Hieroglyphics, a window, more hieroglyphics. A pause for prayer and contemplation, followed by a full-screen message switching off and on like an illuminated sign, and an exclamation of disgust from Guido.

Hazardous Zone!!
THIS IS A HEALTH WARNING.
DO NOT PROCEED BEYOND THIS POINT.
CLINICAL TRIALS HAVE ALREADY INDICATED
THAT FURTHER RESEARCH CAN ATTRACT
FATAL SIDE-EFFECTS. FOR YOUR SAFETY
AND COMFORT YOUR HARD DISK HAS BEEN
CLEANSED OF TOXIC MATTER.

For a deluded few seconds Justin has no serious concerns. He would have liked, in better circumstances, to sit down at the counting table and pen an angry letter to the manufacturers objecting to their hyperbolic style. On the other hand, Guido has just demonstrated that their bark is worse than their bite. So he is about to exclaim something like, 'Oh it's *them* again, they really are the limit,' when he sees that Guido's head has sunk into his neck as if he has been hit by a bully, and his upturned fingers have bunched like dead spiders either side of the laptop, and his face, what Justin can see of it, has returned to its pre-transfusion pallor.

'Is it bad?' Justin asks softly.

Flinging himself eagerly forward like an air pilot in crisis, Guido clicks through his emergency procedures. In vain apparently, for he flings himself upright again, slaps a palm to his forehead, closes his eyes and lets out a frightful groan.

'Just tell me what's happening,' Justin pleads. 'Nothing is this serious, Guido. Tell me.' And when Guido still does not reply, 'You've switched off. Right?'

Transfixed, Guido nods.

'And now you're unplugging the modem.'

Another nod. The same transfixion.

'Why do you do this?'

'I'm rebooting.'

'What does that mean?'

'We wait one minute.'

'Why?'

'Maybe two.'

'What will that do?'

'Give it time to forget. Settle it down. This is *not* natural, Justin. This is real bad.' He has reverted to computer-American. 'This isn't a bunch of socially inadequate young males having some fun. Very sick people have done this to you, believe me.'

'To me or to Tessa?'

Guido shakes his head. 'It's like somebody hates you.' He switches the computer on again, lifts himself on his stool, draws a long breath like a sigh in reverse. And Justin to his delight sees the familiar line of happy black kids waving at him from the screen.

'You've done it,' he exclaims. 'You're a genius, Guido!'

But even as he says this the kids are replaced by a jaunty little hourglass impaled by a white, diagonal arrow. Then they too disappear, leaving only a blue-black infinity.

'They killed it,' Guido whispers.

'How?'

'They put a bug on you. They told the bug to wipe the hard disk clean and they left you a message telling you what they'd done.'

'Then it's not your fault,' says Justin earnestly.

'Did she download?'

'Whatever she printed out, I've read.'

'I'm not talking printing! Did she make disks?'

'We can't find them. We think she may have taken them up north.'

'What's up north? Why didn't she e-mail them up north? Why does she have to carry disks up north? I don't read it. I don't *get* it.'

Justin is remembering Ham and thinking of Guido. Ham's computer had a virus too.

'You said she e-mailed you a lot,' he says.

'Like once a week. Twice. If she forgot one week, twice the next.' He is speaking Italian. He is a child again, as lost as the day when Tessa found him.

'Have you looked at your e-mail since she was killed?'

Guido shakes his head in vigorous denial. It was too much for him. He couldn't.

'So maybe we could go back to your house, and you could see what's there. Would you mind? I'm not interfering?'

Driving up the hill and into the darkening trees, Justin thought of nothing and nobody but Guido. Guido was a wounded friend and Justin's one aim was to take him safely home to his mother, and restore his calm and make sure that from here on Guido was going to stop moping, and get on with being a healthy, arrogant little genius of twelve instead of a cripple whose life had ended with Tessa's death. And if, as he suspected, *they* – whoever they were – had done to Guido's computer what they had done to Ham's and Tessa's, then Guido must be consoled and, so far as it was possible, have his mind set at rest. That was Justin's sole priority, excluding all other aims and emotions, because to entertain them meant anarchy. It meant deflecting himself from the path of rational enquiry and confusing the quest for vengeance with the quest for Tessa.

He parked and with a sense of last things put his hand under Guido's arm. And Guido, somewhat to Justin's surprise, did not shake himself free. His mother had made a stew with fresh-baked bread that she was proud of, so on Justin's insistence they ate it first, the two of them, and praised it while she kept guard over them. Then Guido fetched his computer from his bedroom and for a while they didn't go on-line, but sat shoulder to shoulder, the two of them, reading Tessa's bulletins about the sleepy lions she had seen on her travels, and the TERRIBLY playful elephants that would have sat on her jeep and squashed it if she had given them half a chance and the really DISDAINFUL giraffes who are NEVER happy unless somebody is admiring their elegant necks.

'You want a disk of all her e-mails?' Guido asked, sensing correctly that Justin had seen as much of this as he could take.

'That would be very kind,' said Justin very politely. 'Then I want you to make copies of your work so that I can read it at my leisure and write to you: essays, your homework and all the things you would have wanted Tessa to see.'

The disks duly made, Guido replaced the telephone flex with the flex attached to the modem, and they watched a fine herd of Thomson's gazelles in full gallop before the screen went dark. But when Guido tried to click back to the desktop he was forced to declare in a husky voice that the hard disk had been wiped clean just like Tessa's, but without that crazy message about clinical trials and toxicity.

'And she didn't send you anything to keep for her,' Justin asked, sounding to himself like a customs officer.

Guido shook his head.

'Nothing that you were to pass on to anyone – she didn't use you as a post office or anything like that?'

More shakes of the head.

'So what material have you lost that is important to you?'

'Only her last messages,' Guido whispered.

'Well, that makes two of us.' Or three if you include Ham, he was thinking. 'So if *I* can handle it, you can. Because I was married to her. OK? Perhaps there was some bug in *her* machine that infected *your* machine. Is that possible? She picked something up and passed it on to you by mistake. Yes? I don't know what I'm talking about, do I? I'm guessing. What I'm really telling you is, we'll never know. So we might just as well say "tough luck" and get on with our lives. Both of us. Yes? And you'll order whatever you need to get yourself set up again. Yes? I'll tell the office in Milan that's what you're going to do.'

Reasonably confident that Guido was restored, Justin took his leave; which was to say he drove down the hill again to the villa, and parked the jeep in the courtyard where he had found it, and from the oil room carried her laptop to the seashore. He had been told on various training courses, and he was willing to believe, that there were clever people who could retrieve the text from computers supposedly wiped clean. But such people were on the official side of life to which he no longer belonged. It crossed his mind to contact Rob and Lesley somehow and prevail on them to assist him, but he was reluctant to embarrass them. And besides, if he was honest, there was something contaminated about Tessa's computer, something obscene that he would like to be rid of in a physical sense.

By the light of a half-hidden moon, therefore, he walked the length of a rickety jetty, passing on his way an ancient and rather hysterical notice declaring that whoever ventured further did so at their peril. Having reached the jetty's end, he then consigned her raped laptop to the deep before returning to the oil room to write his heart out until dawn.

*   *   *

Dear Ham,

Here's the first of what I hope will be a long line of letters to your kind aunt. I don't want to appear maudlin but if I go under a bus I would like you please to hand all the documents personally to the most bloody-minded, unclubbable member of your profession, pay him the earth and start the ball rolling. That way we'll both be doing Tessa a good turn.

As ever,
Justin

CHAPTER FIFTEEN

Until late into the evening, when the whisky finally got the better of him, Sandy Woodrow had remained loyally at his post in the High Commission, shaping, redrafting and honing his forthcoming performance at tomorrow's Chancery meeting; passing it upwards into the hierarchy of his official mind, then downwards into that other mind that, like an erratic counterweight, dragged him without warning through a bedlam of accusing ghosts, forcing him to shout louder than they did: you do not exist, you are a series of random episodes; you are not related in any way to Porter Coleridge's abrupt departure for London with wife and child, on the questionable grounds that they had decided on the spur of the moment to take some home leave and find Rosie a special school.

And sometimes his thoughts had gone off on their own entirely, to be discovered addressing such subversive matters as divorce by mutual consent, and whether Ghita Pearson or that new girl called Tara Something in Commercial Section would make an appropriate life partner and, if so, which of them the boys would prefer. Or whether after all he was better off living this lone-wolf existence, dreaming of connection, finding none, watching the dream slip further and further from his reach. Driving home with locked doors and closed windows, however, he was able once more to see himself as the loyal family bread-winner and husband – all right, still discreetly open to sugges-tions, and what man wasn't? – but ultimately the same decent, stalwart, level-headed soldier's son that Gloria had fallen head-over-heels in love with all those years ago. As he entered his house, he was therefore surprised, not to say hurt, to discover that Gloria had not by some act of telepathy divined his good intentions and waited up for him, but left him instead to forage for food in the refrigerator. After all, dammit, *I am acting High Commissioner.* I'm entitled to a *little* respect, even in my own house.

'Anything on the news?' he called up to her pathetically, eating his cold beef in unstately solitude.

The dining room ceiling, which was one plank of concrete thin, was also the floor to their bedroom.

'Don't you get news at the shop?' Gloria bawled back.

'We don't sit there listening to the radio all day, if that's what you mean,' Woodrow replied, rather suggesting that Gloria did. And again waited, his fork poised halfway to his lips.

'They've killed two more white farmers in Zimbabwe, if that's news,' Gloria announced, after an apparent breakdown in trans-mission.

'Don't I know it! We've had the Pellegrin on our backs the whole damn day. Why can't we persuade Moi to put the brakes on Mugabe? if you please. For the same reason we can't per-suade Moi to put the brakes on Moi, is the answer to *that* one.' He waited for a 'Poor you, darling,' but all he got was cryptic silence.

'Nothing else?' he asked. 'On the news. Nothing else?'

'What should there be?'

Hell's come over the bloody woman? he marvelled sulkily, pouring himself another glass of claret. Never used to be like this. Ever since her widowed lover-boy took himself back to England, she's been moping round the house like a sick cow.

Won't drink with me, won't eat with me, won't look me in the eye. Won't do the other thing either, not that it was ever high on her list. Hardly bothers with her make-up, amazingly.

All the same, he was pleased she had heard no news. At least he knew something she didn't for once. Not often London manages to sit on a red-hot story without some idiot in Information Department bubbling it to the media ahead of the agreed deadline. If they could just hold their water till tomorrow morning he'd get a clear run, which was what he'd asked Pellegrin for.

'It's a morale issue, Bernard,' he'd warned him, in his best military tone. 'Couple of people here are going to take it rather badly. I'd like to be the one to break it to them. Particularly with Porter away.'

Always good to remind them who was in charge too. Circumspect but unflappable, that's what they look for in their high flyers. Not to make an issue of it, naturally; much better to let London notice for themselves how smoothly things are handled when Porter isn't around to agonise over every comma.

Very trying, this will-they-won't-they stand-off, if he was honest. Probably what's getting her down. There's the High Commissioner's Residence a hundred yards up the road, staffed and ready to go, Daimler in the garage, but no flag flying. There's Porter Coleridge, our absentee High Commissioner. And there's little me here doing Coleridge's job for him, rather better than Coleridge has been doing it, waiting night and day to hear whether, having stepped into his shoes, I can wear them not as his stand-in but as his official, formal, fully accredited successor, with trappings to match – to wit, the Residence, the Daimler, the private office, Mildren, another thirty-five thousand pounds' worth of allowances and several notches nearer to a knighthood.

But there was a major snag. The Office was traditionally reluctant to promote a man *en poste*. They preferred to bring him home, pack him off somewhere new. There'd been exceptions, of course, but not many . . .

His thoughts drifted back to Gloria. *Lady Woodrow*: that'll sort her out. Restless, that's what she is. Not to say idle. I should have given her a couple more kids to keep her busy. Well, she won't be idle if she's installed in the Residence, *that's* for sure. One free night a week, if she's lucky. Quarrelsome too. Flaming row with Juma last week about some totally trivial thing like tarting up the lower ground. And on Monday, though he never dreamed he'd live to see the day, she'd engineered some kind of bust-up with the Archbitch Elena, *casus belli* unknown.

'Isn't it about time we had the Els to dinner, darling?' he'd suggested chivalrously. 'We haven't pushed the boat out for the Els for months.'

'If you want them, ask them,' Gloria had advised icily, so he hadn't.

But he felt the loss. Gloria without a woman friend was an engine without cogs. The fact – the *extraordinary* fact – that she'd formed some kind of armed truce with doe-eyed Ghita Pearson consoled him not at all. Only a couple of months ago Gloria was dismissing Ghita as neither one thing nor the other. 'I can't be doing with English-educated Brahmin's daughters who talk like us and dress like dervishes,' she'd told Elena in Woodrow's hearing. 'And that Quayle girl is exerting a bad influence on her.' Well, now the Quayle girl was dead and Elena had been sent to Coventry. And Ghita who dressed like a dervish had been signed up to take Gloria on a conducted tour of Kibera slum with the advertised intention of finding her voluntary work with one of the aid agencies. And this, moreover, at the very time when Ghita's own behaviour was causing Woodrow serious concern.

First there had been her display at the funeral. Well, there was no rule book on how to behave at funerals, it was true. Nevertheless, Woodrow considered her performance self-indulgent. Then there was what he would call a period of aggressive mourning, during which she wandered round Chancery like a zombie, refusing point blank to make eye-contact with him, whereas in the past he had regarded her as – well, a candidate, let's say. Then last Friday, without giving the smallest explanation, she'd asked for the day off, although, as a brand-new member of Chancery – and the most junior – she had not yet technically earned her entitlement. Yet out of the goodness of his heart he had said, 'Well, fine, Ghita, all right, I suppose so, but don't wear him out' – nothing abusive, just an innocent joke between an older married man and a pretty young girl. But if looks could kill, he'd have been dead at her feet.

And what had she done with the time he'd given her – without so much as a by-your-leave? Flown up to Lake bloody Turkana in a chartered plane with a dozen other female members of the self-constituted Tessa Quayle supporters' club, and laid a wreath, and banged drums and sung hymns, at the spot where Tessa and Noah had been murdered! The first that Woodrow knew of this was breakfast on the Monday when he opened his *Nairobi Standard* and saw her photograph, posed centre stage between two enormous African women he vaguely remembered from the funeral.

'Well, *Ghita Pearson*, get *you*, I must say,' he had snorted, shoving the paper across the table at Gloria. 'I mean, for God's sake, it's time to bury the dead, not dig them up every ten minutes. I always thought she was carrying a torch for Justin.'

'If we hadn't had the Italian Ambassador I'd have flown up there with them,' Gloria replied, in a voice dripping with reproach.

The bedroom light was out. Gloria was pretending to be asleep.

*   *   *

'So shall we all sit down, please, ladies and gents?'

A power drill was whining from the floor above. Woodrow despatched Mildren to silence it while he ostentatiously busied himself with papers on his desk. The whining stopped. Taking his time, Woodrow looked up again to find everybody gathered before him, including a breathless Mildren. Exceptionally, Tim

Donohue and his assistant Sheila had been asked to put in an appearance. With no High Commissioner's meetings to rally the full complement of diplomatic staff, Woodrow was insisting on a full turnout. Hence also the Defence and Service Attachés and Barney Long from Commercial Section. And poor Sally Aitken, complete with stammer and blushes, on secondment from the Min of Ag and Fish. Ghita, he noticed, was in her usual corner where, since Tessa's death, she had done her best to make herself invisible. To his irritation she still sported the black silk scarf round her neck that recalled the soiled bandage around Tessa's. Were her oblique glances flirtatious or disdainful? With Eurasian beauties, how did you tell?

'Bit of a sad story, I'm afraid, guys,' he began breezily. 'Barney, would you mind getting the door, as we say in America? Don't bring it to me, just locking it will do.'

Laughter – but of the apprehensive sort.

He went straight into it, exactly as he had planned. Bull-by-the-horns stuff – we're all professionals – necessary surgery. But also something tacitly courageous in your acting High Commissioner's bearing as he first scans his notes, then taps the blunt end of his pencil on them and braces his shoulders before addressing the parade.

'There are two things I have to tell you this morning. The first is embargoed till you hear it on the news, British or Kenyan, whoever breaks it first. At twelve hundred hours today the Kenyan police will issue a warrant for the arrest of Dr Arnold Bluhm for the wilful murder of Tessa Quayle and the driver Noah. The Kenyans have been in touch with the Belgian government and Bluhm's employers will be informed in advance. We're ahead of the game because of the involvement of Scotland Yard, who will be passing their file to Interpol.'

Scarcely a chair creaks after the explosion. No protest, no gasp of astonishment. Just Ghita's enigmatic eyes fixed on him at last, admiring or hating him.

'I know this'll be a hell of a shock to you all, particularly those of you who knew Arnold and liked him. If you want to tip off your partners, you have my permission to do so at your discretion.' Quick flash of Gloria, who until Tessa's death had dismissed Bluhm as a jumped-up gigolo but was now mysteriously concerned for his well-being. 'I can't pretend I'm delighted myself,' Woodrow confessed, becoming the tight-lipped master of understatement. 'There'll be the usual facile press explanations of motive, of course. The Tessa–Bluhm relationship will be raked over ad infinitum. And if they ever catch him, there'll be a noisy trial. So from the point of view of this Mission the news could hardly be worse. I've no information at this stage regarding the strength of the evidence. I'm told it's cast iron, but they would say that, wouldn't they?' The same hint of grit inside the humour. 'Questions?'

None apparently. The news seemed to have taken the wind out of everybody's sails. Even Mildren, who had had it since last night, could find nothing better to do than scratch an itch on the tip of his nose.

'My second piece of news is not unrelated to the first, but it's a damn sight more delicate. Partners will *not* be informed without my prior consent. Junior staff will be *selectively* informed where necessary, on a strictly controlled basis. By myself or by the High Commissioner as and when he returns. Not by you, please. Am I clear so far?'

He was. There were nods of expectation this time, not just cow-like stares. All eyes were on him and Ghita's had never left him. *My God, suppose she's fallen for me: how will I ever get out of it?* He followed the thought through. *Of course! That's why she's making up to Gloria! First it was Justin she was after, now it's me! She's a couple-cruiser, never safe unless she's got the wife aboard as well!* He squared himself and resumed his manly newscast.

'I am extremely sorry to have to tell you that our erstwhile colleague Justin Quayle has gone walkabout. You probably know he refused all reception facilities when he arrived in London, saying he'd prefer to paddle his own canoe, et cetera. He *did* manage a meeting with Personnel on his arrival, he *did* manage a luncheon appointment with the Pellegrin the same

303

day. Both describe him as overwrought, sullen and hostile, poor chap. He was offered sanctuary and counselling and declined them. Meanwhile he's jumped ship.'

Now it was Donohue that Woodrow was discreetly favouring, no longer Ghita. Woodrow's gaze, by careful design, was fixed on neither one of them, of course. Ostensibly it oscillated between the middle air and the notes on his desk. But in reality he was focusing on Donohue and persuading himself with increasing conviction that once again Donohue and his scrawny Sheila had received prior warning of Justin's defection.

'On the same day that he arrived in Britain – the same night, more accurately – Justin sent a somewhat disingenuous letter to the Head of Personnel advising her that he was taking leave to sort out his wife's affairs. He used the ordinary mail, which in effect gave him three days to get clear. By the time Personnel moved to put a restraining hand on him – for his own good, I may add – he'd disappeared from everybody's screens. Signs are, he went to considerable lengths to conceal his movements. He's been traced to Elba, where Tessa had estates, but by the time the Office got on the scent he'd moved on. Where to, God knows, but there are suspicions. He'd made no formal leave application, of course, and the Office, for its part, was in the throes of deciding how it could best help him back on his feet – find him a slot where he could nurse his wounds for a year or two.' A shrug to suggest there wasn't a lot of gratitude in the world. 'Well, whatever he's doing, he's doing it alone. And he's certainly not doing it for us.'

He glanced grimly at his audience, then went back to his notes.

'There's a security aspect to this that I obviously can't share with you, so the Office is doubly exercised about where he's going to pop up next and how. They're also decently worried for him, as I'm sure we all are. Having shown a lot of bearing and self-control while he was here, he seems to have gone to pieces from the strain.' He was coming to the hard part but they were steeled for it. 'We have various readings from the experts, none of them, from our point of view, pleasant.'

The general's son soldiers gallantly on.

'One likelihood, according to the clever people who read entrails in these cases, is that Justin is in denial – that's to say, he refuses to accept that his wife is dead and he's gone looking for her. It's very painful, but we're talking of the logic of a temporarily deranged mind. Or we hope it's temporary. Another theory, equally likely or unlikely, says he's on a vengeance trip, looking for Bluhm. It seems that the Pellegrin, with the best of intentions, let slip that Bluhm was under suspicion for Tessa's murder. Maybe Justin took the ball and ran. Sad. Very sad indeed.'

For a moment, in his ever-fluctuating vision of himself, Woodrow became the embodiment of this sadness. He was the decent face of a caring British civil service. He was the Roman adjudicator, slow to judge, slower to condemn. He was your man of the world, not afraid of hard decisions but determined to let his best instincts rule. Emboldened by the excellence of his performance, he felt free to improvise.

'It seems that people in Justin's condition very often have agendas they themselves may not be aware of. They're on automatic pilot, waiting for an excuse to do what they're unconsciously planning to do anyway. A bit like suicides. Somebody says something in jest and – and bang, they've triggered it.'

Was he talking too much? Too little? Was he straying from the point? Ghita was scowling at him like an angry sibyl, and there was something at the back of Donohue's shaggy yellowed eyes that Woodrow couldn't read. Contempt? Anger? Or just that permanent air of having a different purpose, of coming from a different place and going back to it?

'But the most likely theory of what's in Justin's head at the moment, I'm afraid – the one that best fits the known facts, and is favoured, I must tell you, by the Office shrinks – is that Justin has hit the conspiracy trail, which could be very serious indeed. If you can't deal with the reality, then dream up a conspiracy. If you can't accept that your mother died of cancer, then blame the doctor who was attending her. And the surgeons. And the anaesthetists. And the nurses. Who were all in league with each other, of course. And collectively *conspired* to do away with her. And that seems to be exactly what Justin's saying to himself about Tessa. Tessa wasn't just raped and murdered. Tessa was the victim of an international intrigue. She didn't die because she was young and attractive and desperately unlucky, but because *They* wanted her dead. Who *They* are – I'm afraid that one's up to you. It can be your neighbourhood greengrocer, or the Salvation Army lady who rang your doorbell and flogged you a copy of their magazine. They're all in it. They all conspired to kill Tessa.'

A patter of embarrassed laughter. Had he over-spoken or were they coming to him? Harden up. You're getting too broad.

'Or in Justin's case it can be Moi's Boys, and Big Business, and the Foreign Office and us here in this room. We're all enemies. All conspirators. And Justin's the only person who knows it, which is another element of his paranoia. The victim, in Justin's eyes, is not Tessa but himself. Who your enemies are, if you're in Justin's shoes, depends who you last listened to, what books and newspapers you've read recently, the movies you've seen and where you are in your bio-day. Incidentally, we're told Justin's drinking a lot, which I don't think was the case when he was here. The Pellegrin says lunch for two at his club cost him a month's pay.'

Another trickle of nervous laughter, shared by pretty well everyone except Ghita. He skated on, admiring his own foot-work, cutting figures in the ice, spinning, gliding. This is the part of me you hated most, he is telling Tessa breathlessly as he pirouettes and comes back to her. *This is the voice that ruined England*, you told me playfully as we danced. *This is the voice that sank a thousand ships, and they were all ours*. Very funny. Well, listen to the voice now, girl. Listen to the artful dismantling of your late husband's reputation, courtesy of the Pellegrin and my five mind-warping years in the Foreign Office's ever-truthful Infor-mation Department.

A wave of nausea seized him as for a moment he hated every unfeeling surface of his own paradoxical nature. It was the nausea that could have him scurrying out of the room on the pretext of an urgent phone call or a natural need, just to get away from himself; or send him stumbling to this very desk, to pull open the drawer and grab a page of Her Majesty's Stationery Office blue, and fill the void in himself with declarations of adoration and promises of recklessness. Who did this to me? he wondered while he talked. Who made me what I am? England? My father? My schools? My pathetic, terrified mother? Or seventeen years of lying for my country? *'We reach an age, Sandy,'* you were kind enough to inform me, *'where our childhood is no longer an excuse. The problem in your case is, that age is going to be about ninety-five.'*

He rode on. He was being brilliant again.

'What precise conspiracy Justin has dreamed up – and where *we* come into it, we in the High Commission – whether we're in league with the Freemasons, or the Jesuits, or the Ku Klux Klan, or the World Bank – I'm afraid I can't enlighten you. What I *can* tell you is, he's out there. He's already made some serious insinuations, he's still very plausible, *very* personable – when wasn't he? – and it's perfectly possible that tomorrow or in three months' time he'll head this way.' He hardened again. 'In which case, you all – collectively and individually – are under instruction, please – this is not a request, I'm afraid, Ghita, it's a straight order – whatever your personal feelings towards Justin may be – and believe me, I'm no different, he's a sweet, kind, generous chap, we all know that – whatever time of night or day it is – to inform *me*. Or Porter when he's back. Or –' a glance at him – 'Mike Mildren.' He had nearly said Mildred. 'Or if it's night-time the High Commission's duty officer *immediately*. Before the press or the police or anybody else gets to him – tell *us*.'

Ghita's eyes, covertly observed, seemed darker and more languorous than ever, Donohue's sicklier. Scruffy Sheila's were as hard as diamonds and as unblinking. 'For ease of reference –

and for security reasons – London has given Justin the code name of *Dutchman*. As in Flying Dutchman. If by any chance – it's a long shot, but we're speaking of a deeply disturbed man with unlimited money at his disposal – if by any chance he crosses your path – directly, indirectly, hearsay, whatever – or has done so already – then for his sake as well as ours, pick up the phone, wherever you are, and say, "It's about the Dutchman, the Dutchman is doing this or that, I've got a letter from the Dutchman, he's just phoned or faxed or e-mailed me, he's sitting here in front of me in my armchair." Are we all completely clear on that one? Questions. Yes, Barney?'

'You said "serious insinuations". Who to? Insinuating what?'

It was the dangerous area. Woodrow had discussed it at length with Pellegrin on Porter Coleridge's encrypted telephone. 'There seems to be very little pattern to it. He's obsessed with pharmaceutical stuff. As far as we can fathom, he's convinced himself that the manufacturers of a particular drug – and the *inventors* – were responsible for Tessa's murder.'

'He thinks she didn't get her throat cut? He saw her body!' Barney again, disgusted.

'I'm afraid the drug dates back to her unhappy spell in the hospital here. It killed her child. That was the first shot fired by the conspirators. Tessa complained to the manufacturers, so the manufacturers killed her too.'

'Is he dangerous?' Donohue's Sheila is asking the question, presumably to demonstrate to all present that she possesses no superior knowledge.

'He *could* be dangerous. That's the wisdom from London. His primary target is the pharmaceutical company that manufactured the poison. After that, it's the scientists who designed it. Then there'll be the people who administered it, which means in this case the company here in Nairobi that imports it, which in turn means House of ThreeBees, so we may have to warn them.' From Donohue, not a flicker. 'And do let me repeat that we are dealing with a seemingly rational and composed British diplomat. Don't expect some loony with ash in his hair and yellow cross-garters, frothing at the mouth. Outwardly, he's the chap we all remember and love. Smooth, well dressed, good-looking and *frightfully* polite. Until he starts screaming at you about the world-class conspiracy that killed his child and his wife.' A break. A personal note – God, what wells the man has! 'It's tragic. It's worse than tragic. I think all of us who were close to him must feel that. But that's precisely why I have to beat the drum. *No sentiment*, please. If the Dutchman comes your way, we have to know immediately. Right, guys? Thanks. Other business while we're all here? Yes, Ghita.'

*   *   *

If Woodrow was having a hard time deciphering Ghita's emotions, he was for once closer than he imagined to her state of mind. She was getting to her feet while everyone else, including Woodrow, was sitting. That much she knew. And she was getting up in order to be seen. But mostly she was getting up because she had never in her life listened to such a pack of wicked lies, and because her impulse was quite literally not to take them sitting down. So here she was standing: in protest, in outrage, in preparation for branding Woodrow a liar to his face; and because in her short, bewildering life till now she had never met better people than Tessa, Arnold and Justin.

That much Ghita was aware of. But when she peered across the room – over the stern heads of the Defence Attaché and the Commercial Attaché and Mildren the High Commissioner's private secretary, all turned towards her – straight into the truthless, insinuating eyes of Sandy Woodrow, she knew she must find a different way.

Tessa's way. Not out of cowardice, but out of tactic.

To call Woodrow a liar to his face was to win one minute of doubtful glory, followed by certain dismissal. And what could she prove? Nothing. His lies were not fabrications. They were a brilliantly devised distorting lens that turned facts into monsters, yet left them looking like facts.

'Yes, Ghita dear.'

He had his head back and his eyebrows up and his mouth half open like a choirmaster's, as if he were about to sing along with her. She looked quickly away from him. That old man Donohue's face is all downward lines, she thought. Sister Marie at the convent had a dog like him. A bloodhound's cheeks are called flews, Justin told me. I played badminton with Sheila last night and she's watching me too. To her astonishment, Ghita heard herself addressing the meeting.

'Well, it may be not a good time for me to be suggesting this, Sandy. Perhaps I should leave it over for a few days,' she began. 'With so much going on.'

'Leave *what* over? Don't tease us, Ghita.'

'Only we've had this enquiry through the World Food Programme, Sandy. They are agitating most vigorously for us to send a representative from EADEC to attend the next focus group on Customer Self-Sustainment.'

It was a lie. A working, effective, acceptable lie. By some miracle of deceit she had dug a standing request from her memory, and revamped it to sound like a pressing invitation. If Woodrow should ask to see the file, she would not have the least idea what to do. But he didn't.

'Customer *what*, Ghita?' Woodrow enquired, amid mild, cathartic laughter.

'It is what is also called Aid Parturition, Sandy,' Ghita replied severely, dredging another piece of jargon from the circular. 'How does a community that has received substantial food aid and medicare learn to sustain itself once the agencies withdraw? That is the issue here. What precautions must be taken by the donors to make sure that adequate logistical provisions remain in place and no undue deprivation results? Great store is set by these discussions.'

'Well, that sounds reasonable enough. How long does the jamboree last?'

'Three full days, Sandy. Tuesday, Wednesday and Thursday with a possible overrun. But our problem is, Sandy, we don't have an EADEC representative now that Justin's gone.'

'So you wondered whether *you* might go in his place,' Woodrow cried, with a knowing laugh for the wiles of pretty women. 'Where's it being held, Ghita? Up in Sin City?' His pet name for the United Nations complex.

'Lokichoggio, actually, Sandy,' said Ghita.

*　　*　　*

Dear Ghita,

I had no chance to tell you how much Tessa loved you and valued the times the two of you spent together. But you know that anyway. Thank you for all the things you gave her.

I have a request of you but it is only a request and you should please not let it trouble you unless the spirit takes you. If ever, in the course of your travels, you happen to be in Lokichoggio, please get in touch with a Sudanese woman called Sarah who was Tessa's friend. She speaks English and was some kind of house servant to an English family during the British mandate. Perhaps she may shed some light on what really took Tessa and Arnold up to Loki. It's only a feeling, but it seems to me in retrospect that they went up there with a greater sense of excitement than was justified by the prospect of a gender awareness course for Sudanese women! If so, Sarah may know of it.

Tessa hardly slept the night before she left, and she was, even for Tessa, exceptionally demonstrative when we said goodbye to each other – what Ovid calls 'goodbye for the last time', though I assume neither of us knew it. Here's an address in Italy for you to write to if you should have occasion. But please don't put yourself out. Thank you again.

Fondly,
Justin

Not Dutchman. Justin.

CHAPTER SIXTEEN

Justin arrived in the little town of Bielefeld near Hanover after two unsettling days of trains. As Atkinson he checked into a modest hotel opposite the railway station, made a reconnaissance of the town and ate an undistinguished meal. Come darkness, he delivered his letter. This is what spies do all the time, he thought, as he advanced on the unlit corner house. This is the watchfulness they learn from their cradles. This is how they cross a dark street, scan doorways, turn a corner: are you waiting for me? Have I seen you somewhere before? But no sooner had he posted the letter than his common sense was taking him to task: forget the spies, idiot, you could have sent the damn thing round by taxi. And now by daylight, as he advanced on the corner house a second time, he was punishing himself with different fears: are they watching it? Did they see me last night? Do they plan to arrest me as I arrive? Has someone phoned the *Telegraph* and discovered that I don't exist?

On the train journey he had slept little, and last night in the hotel not at all. He travelled with no bulky papers any more, no canvas suitcases, laptops or attachments. Whatever needed to be preserved had gone to Ham's draconian aunt in Milan.

What didn't, lay two fathoms deep on a Mediterranean sea bed. Freed of his burden, he moved with a symbolic lightness. Sharper lines defined his features. A stronger light burned behind his eyes. And Justin felt this of himself. He was gratified that Tessa's mission was henceforth his own.

The corner house was a turreted German castle on five floors. The ground floor was daubed in jungle stripes which by daylight revealed themselves as parrot-green and orange. Last night under the sodium lighting they had resembled flames of sickly black and white. From an upper floor a mural of brave children of all races grinned at him, recalling the waving children of Tessa's laptop. They were replicated live in a window on the ground floor, seated in a ring round a harassed woman teacher. A hand-made display in the window next to them asked how chocolate grew, and offered curling photographs of cocoa beans.

Feigning disinterest, Justin first walked past the building, then turned abruptly left and sauntered up the pavement, pausing to study the nameplates of fringe medics and psychologists. *In a civilised country you can never tell.* A police car rolled by, tyres crackling in the rain. Its occupants, one a woman, eyed him without expression. Across the street two old men in black rain-coats and black Homburg hats seemed to be waiting for a funeral. The window behind them was curtained. Three women on push-bikes glided towards him down the hill. Graffiti on the walls proclaimed the Palestinian cause. He returned to the painted castle and stood before the front door. A green hippo was painted on it. A smaller green hippo marked the doorbell. An ornate bay window like a ship's prow peered down on him. He had stood here last night to post his letter. Who peered down on me then? The harassed teacher in the window gestured to him to use the other door but it was closed and barred. He gestured his contrition in return.

'They should have left it open,' she hissed at him, unappeased, when she had slid the bolts and hauled back the door.

Justin again apologised and trod delicately between the children, wishing them 'grüss Dich' and 'guten Tag', but his alertness put limits on his once-infinite courtesy. He climbed a staircase past bicycles and a perambulator, and entered a hall that to his wary eye seemed to have been reduced to life's necessities: a water fountain, a photocopier, bare shelves, piles of reference books and cardboard boxes stacked in piles on the floor. Through an open doorway he saw a young woman in horn-rimmed spectacles and a rollneck sitting before a screen.

'I'm Atkinson,' he told her in English. 'Peter Atkinson. I have an appointment with Birgit from Hippo.'

'Why didn't you telephone?'

'I got into town late last night. I thought a note was best. Can she see me?'

'I don't know. Ask her.'

He followed her down a short corridor to a pair of double doors. She pushed one open.

'Your *journalist*'s here,' she announced in German, as if journalist were synonymous with illicit lover, and strode back to her quarters.

Birgit was small and springy with pink cheeks and blond hair and the stance of a cheerful pugilist. Her smile was quick and compelling. Her room was as sparse as the hall, with the same vague air of self-deprival.

'We have our conference at ten,' she explained a little breathlessly as she grasped his hand. She was speaking the English of her e-mails. He let her. Mr Atkinson did not need to make himself conspicuous by speaking German.

'You like tea?'

'Thanks. I'm fine.'

She pulled two chairs to a low table and sat in one. 'If it's about the burglary, we have really nothing to say,' she warned him.

'What burglary?'

'It is not important. A few things were taken. Maybe we had too many possessions. Now we don't.'

'When was this?'

She shrugged. 'Long ago. Last week.'

Justin pulled a notebook from his pocket and, Lesley-style, opened it on his knee. 'It's about the work you do here,' he said. 'My paper is planning a series of articles on drug companies and the Third World. We're calling it Merchants of Medicine. How the Third World countries have no consumer power. How big diseases are in one place, big profits in another.' He had prepared himself to sound like a journalist but wasn't sure he was succeeding. ' "The poor can't pay, so they die. How much longer can this go on? We seem to have the means, but not the will." That kind of thing.'

To his surprise she was smiling broadly. 'You want me to give you the answer to these simple questions before ten o'clock?'

'If you could just tell me what Hippo does, exactly – who finances you – what your remit is, as it were,' he said severely.

She was talking, and he was writing in the notebook on his knee. She was giving him what he supposed was her party piece and he was pretending his hardest to listen while he wrote. He was thinking that this woman had been Tessa's friend and ally without meeting her, and that if they had met, both would have congratulated themselves on their choice. He was thinking that there can be a lot of reasons for a burglary and one of them is to provide cover to anyone installing the devices that produce what the Foreign Office is pleased to call Special Product, for mature eyes only. He was remembering his security training again, and the group visit to a macabre laboratory in a basement behind Carlton Gardens where students could admire for themselves the newest cute places for planting sub-miniature listening devices. Gone the flowerpots, lamp stands, ceiling roses, mouldings and picture frames, enter pretty well anything you could think of from the stapler on Birgit's desk to her Sherpa jacket hanging from the door.

He had written what he wanted to write and she had apparently said what she wanted to say, because she was standing up and peering into a stack of pamphlets on a bookshelf, looking for some background reading she could give him as a prelude to getting him out of her office in time for her ten o'clock conference. While she hunted she talked distractedly about the German Federal Drug Agency and declared it to be a paper tiger. And the World Health Organization gets its money from America, she added with disdain – which means it favours big corporations, reveres profit and doesn't like radical decisions.

'Go to any WHO assembly – what do you see?' she asked rhetorically, handing him a bunch of pamphlets. 'Lobbyists. PR people from the big pharmas. Dozens of them. From one big pharma, maybe three or four. "Come to lunch. Come to our weekend get-together. Have you read this wonderful paper by Professor So-and-So?" And the Third World is not sophisticated. They have no money, they are not experienced. With diplomatic language and manoeuvring, the lobbyists can get behind them easy.'

She had stopped speaking and was frowning at him. Justin was holding up his open notebook for her to read. He was holding it close to his face so that she could see his expression while she read his message; and his expression, he hoped, was quelling and reassuring at the same time. In support of it he had extended the forefinger of his free left hand by way of warning.

I AM TESSA QUAYLE'S HUSBAND AND I DO NOT TRUST THESE WALLS. CAN YOU MEET ME THIS EVENING AT FIVE-THIRTY IN FRONT OF THE OLD FORT?

She read the message, she looked past his raised finger at his eyes and kept looking at them while he filled the silence with the first thing that came into his head.

'So are you saying that what we need is some kind of independent world body that has the power to override these companies?' he demanded, with unintentional aggression. 'Cut down their influence?'

'Yes,' she replied, perfectly calmly. 'I think that would be an excellent idea.'

He walked past the woman in the rollneck and gave her the kind of cheery wave he thought appropriate to a journalist. 'All done,' he assured her. 'Just off. Thank you for your cooperation' – so there's no need to telephone the police and tell them you have an impostor on the premises.

He tiptoed through the classroom and tried once more to woo a smile from the harassed teacher. 'For the last time,' he promised her. But the only people who smiled were the kids.

In the street the two old men in raincoats and black hats were still waiting for the funeral. At the kerbside two stern young women sat in an Audi saloon, studying a map. He returned to his hotel and on a whim enquired at the desk whether he had mail. No mail. Reaching his room, he tore the offending page from his notebook, then the page beneath it because the imprint had come through. He burned them in the handbasin and put on the extractor to get rid of the smoke. He lay on his bed wondering what spies did to kill time. He dozed and was woken by his phone. He lifted the receiver and remembered to say, 'Atkinson.' It was the housekeeper, 'checking', she said. Excuse her, please. *Checking what*, for God's sake? But spies don't ask those questions aloud. They don't make themselves conspicuous. Spies lie on white beds in grey towns and wait.

*   *   *

Bielefeld's old fort stood on a high green mound overlooking cloud-laden hills. Car parks, picnic benches and municipal gardens were laid out among the ivy-covered ramparts. In warmer months it was a favoured spot for the townspeople to perambulate down tree-lined avenues, admire the regiments of flowers and eat beery lunches in the Huntsman's Restaurant. But in the grey months the place had the air of a deserted playground in the clouds, which was how it looked to Justin this evening as he paid off his taxi and, early by twenty minutes, made what he hoped was a casual reconnaissance of his chosen rendezvous. The empty car parks, sculpted into the battlements, were pitted with rainwater. From sodden lawns, rusted signs warned him to control his dog. On a bench beneath the battlements, two veterans in scarves and overcoats sat bolt upright, observing him. Were they the same two old men who had worn black Homburg hats this morning while they waited for the funeral? Why do they stare at me like this? Am I Jewish? Am I a Pole? How long before your Germany becomes just another boring European country?

One road only led to the fort and he strolled along it, keeping at the crown in order to avoid the trenches of fallen leaves. When she arrives I'll wait till she parks before I speak to her, he decided. Cars too have ears. But Birgit's car had no ears because it was a bicycle. At first sight she resembled some kind of ghostly horsewoman, urging her reluctant steed over the brow of the hill while her plastic cape filled behind her. Her fluorescent harness resembled a Crusader's cross. Slowly the apparition became flesh, and she was neither a winged seraph nor a breathless messenger from the battle, but a young mother in a cape riding a bicycle. And from the cape protruded not one head but two, the second belonging to her jolly blond son, strapped into a child's pillion-seat behind her – and measuring, to Justin's inexpert eye, about eighteen months on the Richter scale.

And the sight of them both was so entirely pleasant to him, and so incongruous, and appealing, that for the first time since Tessa's death he broke out in real, rich, unrestrained laughter.

'But at such short notice, how should I get a babysitter?' Birgit demanded, offended by his mirth.

'You shouldn't, you shouldn't! It doesn't matter, it's wonderful. What's his name?'

'Carl. What's yours?'

Carl sends his love . . . The elephant mobile you sent Carl drives him completely crazy . . . I hope very much your baby will be as beautiful as Carl.

He showed her his Quayle passport. She examined it, name, age, photograph, shooting frank looks at him between.

'You told her she was *waghalsig*,' he said, and watched her frown become a smile as she hauled off her cape and wound it up and gave him the bike to hold so that she could unbuckle

318

Carl from his seat. And having released Carl and set him on the road, she unstrapped a saddlebag and turned her back to Justin so that he could load up the backpack she was wearing: Carl's bottle, a packet of *Knäckebrot*, spare nappies and two ham and cheese baguettes wrapped in greaseproof paper.

'You have eaten today, Justin?'

'Not much.'

'So. We can eat. Then we shall not be so nervous. *Carlchen, du machst das bitte nicht.* We can walk. Carl will walk for ever.'

Nervous? Who's nervous? Affecting to undertake a study of the menacing rain clouds, Justin swung himself slowly round on his heel, head in air. They were still there, two old sentries sitting to attention.

*   *   *

'I don't know how much stuff actually went missing,' Justin complained, when he had told her the story of Tessa's laptop. 'I had the impression there was a lot more correspondence between the two of you that she hadn't printed out.'

'You did not read about Emrich?'

'That she had emigrated to Canada. But she was still working for KVH.'

'You do not know what her position is now – her problem?'

'She quarrelled with Kovacs.'

'Kovacs is nothing. Emrich has quarrelled with KVH.'

'What on earth about?'

'Dypraxa. She believes she has identified certain very negative side-effects. KVH believes she has not.'

'What have they done about it?' asked Justin.

'So far they have only destroyed her reputation and her career.'

'That's all.'

'That's all.'

They walked without speaking for a while, with Carl stalking out ahead of them, diving for decaying horse chestnuts and having to be restrained before he put them in his mouth. Evening fog had formed a sea across the rolling hills, making islands of their rounded tops.

'When did this happen?'

'It is happening still. She has been dismissed by KVH and dismissed again by the Regents of Dawes University in Saskatchewan and the governing body of the Dawes University Hospital. She tried to publish an article in a medical journal concerning her conclusions regarding Dypraxa but her contract with KVH had a confidentiality clause, therefore they suited her and suited the magazine and no copies were allowed.'

'Sued. Not suited. Sued.'

'It's the same.'

'And you told Tessa about this? She must have been thrilled.'

'Sure. I told her.'

'When?'

Birgit shrugged. 'Maybe three weeks ago. Maybe two. Our correspondence has also disappeared.'

'You mean they crashed your computer?'

'It was stolen. In our burglary. I had not downloaded her letters and I had not printed them. So.'

So, Justin agreed silently. 'Any idea who took it?'

'Nobody took it. With corporations it is always nobody. The big boss calls in the sub-boss, the sub-boss calls in his lieutenant, the lieutenant speaks to the chef of corporate security who speaks to the sub-chef who speaks to his friends who speak to their friends. And so it is done. Not by the boss or the sub-boss or the lieutenant or the sub-chef. Not by the corporation. Not by anybody at all, actually. But still it is done. There are no papers, no cheques, no contracts. Nobody knows anything. Nobody was there. But it is done.'

'What about the police?'

'Oh, our police are *most* industrious. If we have lost a computer, tell the insurance company and buy a new one, don't come bothering the police. Did you meet Wanza?'

'Only in hospital. She was already very ill. Did Tessa write to you about Wanza?'

'That she was poisoned. That Lorbeer and Kovacs had come to visit her in the hospital and that Wanza's baby survived, but Wanza did not. That the drug killed her. Maybe a combination killed her. Maybe she was too thin, not enough body fat to handle the drug. Maybe if they had given her less, she would have lived. Maybe KVH will fix the pharmacokinetics before they sell it in America.'

'She said that? Tessa did?'

'Sure. "Wanza was just another guinea pig. I loved her, they killed her. Tessa."'

Justin was already protesting. For Heaven's sake, Birgit, what about Emrich? If Emrich, as one of the discoverers of the drug, has declared it unsafe, then surely –

Birgit cut him short. 'Emrich exaggerates. Ask Kovacs. Ask KVH. The contribution of Lara Emrich to the discovery of the Dypraxa molecule was completely minimal. Kovacs was the genius, Emrich was her laboratory assistant, Lorbeer was their Svengali. Naturally because Emrich was also the lover of Lorbeer, her importance has been made bigger than the reality.'

'Where's Lorbeer now?'

'It is not known. Emrich doesn't know, KVH doesn't know – says it doesn't – for the last five months he has been completely invisible. Maybe they killed him also.'

'Where's Kovacs?'

'She is travelling. She is travelling so much that KVH can never tell us where she is or where she will be. Last week she was in Haiti, maybe, three weeks ago she was in Buenos Aires or Timbuktu. But where she will be tomorrow or next week is a mystery. Her home address is naturally confidential, her telephone also.'

Carl was hungry. One minute he was placidly trailing a piece of twig through a puddle, the next he was yelling blue murder for food. They sat on a bench while Birgit fed him from the bottle.

'If you were not here he would feed himself,' she said proudly. 'He would walk along like a little drunkard with the bottle in his mouth. But now he has an uncle to watch him, so he requires your attention.' Something in what she said reminded her of Justin's grief. 'I am so sorry, Justin,' she murmured. 'How can I say it?' But so swiftly and softly that for once it was not necessary for him to say 'thank you' or 'yes, it's terrible' or 'you're very kind' or any other of the meaningless phrases he had learned to mouth when people felt obliged to say the unsayable.

*   *   *

They were walking again and Birgit was reliving the burglary.

'I arrived at the office in the morning – my colleague Roland is at a conference in Rio – it is otherwise a normal day. The doors are locked, I must unlock them as usual. At first I notice nothing. That is the point. What burglar locks doors behind him when he leaves? The police asked us this question also. But our doors were locked without question. The place is not tidy, but that is normal. In Hippo we clean our own rooms. We cannot afford to pay a cleaner and sometimes we are too busy or too lazy to clean for ourselves.'

Three women on push-bikes rode solemnly by, circled the car park and returned, passing them on their way down the hill. Justin remembered the three women cyclists of this morning.

'I go to check the telephone. We have an answering machine at Hippo. A normal hundred-mark affair, but a hundred marks nevertheless, and nobody has taken it. We have correspondents all over the world, so we must have an answering machine. The tape is missing. Oh shit, I think, who took the stupid tape? I go to the other office to look for a new tape. The computer is missing. Oh shit, I think, who is the idiot who has moved the computer and where did they put it? It's a big computer on two storeys but to move it is not impossible, it has wheels. We have a new girl, a trainee lawyer, a great girl actually but new. "Beate, darling," I say, "where the hell is our computer?" Then we start to look. Computer. Tapes. Disks. Papers. Files. Missing and the doors locked. They take nothing else of value. Not the money in the money box, not the coffee machine or the radio or the television or the empty tape recorder. They are not drug addicts. They are not professional thieves. And to the police they are not criminals. Why should criminals lock doors? Maybe you know why.'

'To tell us,' Justin replied after a long pause.

'Please? To tell us what? I don't understand.'

'They locked the doors on Tessa too.'

'Explain, please. What doors?'

'Of the jeep. When they killed her. They locked the jeep doors so that the hyenas wouldn't take away the bodies.'

'Why?'

'They were telling us to be afraid. That's the message they put on Tessa's laptop. To her or to me. "Be warned. Don't go on with what you're doing." They sent her a death threat too. I only found out about it a few days ago. She never told me.'

'Then she was brave,' said Birgit.

She remembered the baguettes. They sat on another bench and ate them while Carl munched a rusk and sang, and the two old sentries marched sightlessly past them down the hill.

'Was there a pattern to what they took? Or was it wholesale?'

'It was wholesale, but there was also a pattern. Roland says there was no pattern, but Roland is relaxed. He is always relaxed. He is like an athlete whose heart beats at half the normal speed so that he can run faster than anyone else. But only when he wishes. When it is useful to go fast he goes fast. When nothing can be done he stays in bed.'

'What was the pattern?' he asked.

She has Tessa's frown, he noticed. It is the frown of professional discretion. As with Tessa, he made no effort to break through her silence.

'How did you translate *waghalsig*?' she demanded at length.

'Reckless, I think. Daredevilish, perhaps. Why?'

'Then I too was *waghalsig*,' said Birgit.

Carl wanted to be carried, which she said was unheard of. Justin could safely insist on shouldering the burden. There was business while she unbuckled her backpack and extended the straps for him and – only when she was satisfied with the fit – lifted Carl into it and exhorted him to be well behaved with his new uncle.

'I was worse than *waghalsig*. I was a full idiot.' She bit her lip, hating herself for what she had to tell. 'We had a letter brought to us. Last week. Thursday. It came by courier from Nairobi. Not a letter, a document. Seventy pages. About Dypraxa. Its history and its aspects and its side-effects. Positive and negative, but mostly negative in view of the fatalities and side-effects. It was not signed. It was in all scientific respects objective, but in other respects a little bit crazy. Addressed to Hippo, not to anyone by name. Just Hippo. To the Lords and Ladies of Hippo.'

'In English?'

'English but not written by an Englishman, I think. Typed, so we do not know the handwriting. It contained many references to God. You are religious?'

'No.'

'But Lorbeer is religious.'

*   *   *

The drizzle had turned to occasional fat spots of rain. Birgit was sitting on a bench. They had come upon a scaffold of children's swings fitted with crossbars across the seats to keep them safe. Carl needed to be lifted into one and pushed. He was fighting sleep. A catlike softness had descended over him. His eyes were half closed and he was smiling while Justin pushed him with obsessive caution. A white Mercedes with Hamburg registration plates came slowly up the hill, passed them, made a circle in the flooded car park and came slowly back. One male driver, one male passenger beside him. Justin remembered the two women in the parked Audi this morning as he stepped into the street. The Mercedes drove back down the hill.

'Tessa said you speak all languages,' Birgit said.

'That doesn't mean I have anything to say in them. Why were you *waghalsig*?'

'You will please call it stupid.'

'Why were you stupid?'

'I was stupid because when the courier delivered the document from Nairobi, I was excited and I telephoned to Lara Emrich in Saskatchewan and I told her, "Lara darling, listen, we have received a long, anonymous, very mystical, very crazy, very authentic history of Dypraxa, no address, no date, from somebody who I think is Markus Lorbeer. It tells about the fatalities of the drug combination and it will greatly help your case." I was so happy because the document is actually called after her name. It is titled "Doctor Lara Emrich is right". "It is crazy," I told her, "but it is fierce like a political statement. Also very polemical, very religious, and very destructive of Lorbeer." "Then it is by Lorbeer," she says. "Markus is whipping himself. It is normal."'

'Have you met Emrich? Do you know her?'

'As I knew Tessa. By e-mail. So we are e-friends. In the paper it said Lorbeer was six years in Russia, two years under old Communism, four years under the new chaos. I tell this to Lara who knows it already. According to the paper, Lorbeer was the agent for certain Western pharmas, lobbying Russian health officials, selling them Western drugs, I tell her. According to the paper, in six years he had dealings with eight different health ministers. The paper provides a saying regarding this period and I am about to tell it to Lara when she interrupts me and tells me what the saying is, exactly as it stands in the document. "The Russian health ministers arrived in a Lada and left in a Mercedes." It is a favourite joke of Lorbeer's, she tells me. This confirms for both of us that Lorbeer is the writer of the document. It is his masochistic confession. Also from Lara I learn that Lorbeer's father was a German Lutheran, very Calvinistic,

325

very strict which accounts for his son's morbid religious conceptions and his desire to confess. Do you know medicine? Chemistry? A little biology perhaps?'

'My education was a little too expensive for that, I'm afraid.'

'Lorbeer claims in his confession that while acting for KVH he obtained the validation of Dypraxa by means of flattery and bribery. He describes buying health officials, fast-tracking clinical trials, purchasing drug registrations and import licences and feeding every bureaucratic hand in the food chain. In Moscow, a validation by top medical opinion-leaders could be bought for twenty-five thousand dollars. So he writes. The problem is that when you bribe one you must also bribe those you do not select, otherwise they will denigrate the molecule out of envy or resentment. In Poland it was not so different, but less expensive. In Germany, influence was more subtle but not *very* subtle. Lorbeer writes of a famous occasion when he chartered a jumbo jet for KVH and flew eighty eminent German physicians to Thailand for an educational trip.' She was smiling as she related this. 'Their education was provided on the journey out, in the form of films and lectures, also Beluga caviar and extremely ancient brandies and whiskies. Everything must be of the finest quality, he writes, because the good doctors of Germany have been spoiled early. Champagne is no longer interesting to them. In Thailand, the physicians were free to do as they wished, but recreation was provided for those who wanted it, also attractive partners. Lorbeer personally organised a helicopter to drop orchids on a certain beach where the physicians and their partners were relaxing. On the flight home, no further education was needed. The physicians were educated out. All they had to remember was how to write their prescriptions and learned articles.'

But although she was laughing she was uneasy with this story, and needed to correct its impact.

'This does not signify that Dypraxa is a bad drug, Justin. Dypraxa is a very good drug that has not completed its trials. Not all doctors can be seduced, not all pharmaceutical companies are careless and greedy.'

She paused, aware that she was speaking too much, but Justin made no attempt to deflect her.

'The modern pharmaceutical industry is only sixty-five years old. It has good men and women, it has achieved human and social miracles, but its collective conscience is not developed. Lorbeer writes that the pharmas turned their backs on God. He has many biblical references I do not understand. Perhaps that is because I do not understand God.'

Carl had gone to sleep on the swing, so Justin lifted him out and, with his hand on his hot back, walked him softly up and down the tarmac.

'You were telling me how you telephoned Lara Emrich,' Justin reminded her.

'Yes, but I distracted myself deliberately because I am embarrassed that I was stupid. Are you comfortable or shall I take him?'

'I'm fine.'

The white Mercedes had stopped at the bottom of the hill. The two men were still sitting inside it.

'In Hippo we have assumed for years that our telephones are listened to, we have a certain pride about this. From time to time our mail is censored. We send ourselves letters and watch them come to us late and in a different condition. We have often fantasised about planting misleading information on the *Organy*.'

'The what?'

'It is Lara's word. It is a Russian word from Soviet times. It means the organs of state.'

'I shall adopt it immediately.'

'So maybe the *Organy* listened to us laughing and rejoicing on the telephone when I promised Lara I would send her a copy of the document to Canada immediately. Lara said unfortunately she does not possess a fax machine because she has spent her money on lawyers and is not permitted to enter the hospital precincts. If she had possessed a fax machine, maybe there would be no problem today. She would have a copy of

Lorbeer's confession, even if we did not. Everything would be saved. Maybe. Everything is maybe. Nothing has a proof.'

'What about e-mail?'

'She has no e-mail any more. Her computer had a cardiac arrest on the day after she attempted to publish her article, and it has not recovered.'

She sat pink and stoical in her vexation.

'And therefore?' Justin prompted her.

'Therefore we have no document. They stole it when they stole the computer and the files and the tapes. I telephoned to Lara in the evening, five o'clock German time. Our conversation finished at maybe five-forty. She was emotional, very happy. I also. "Wait till Kovacs hears about this," she kept saying. So we talked a long time and laughed and I did not think to make a copy of Lorbeer's confession until tomorrow. I put the document in our safe and locked it. It's not an enormous safe but it is considerable. The burglars had a key. As they locked our doors when they left, so they locked our safe after they had stolen our document. When one considers these things they are obvious. Until then they do not exist. What does a giant do when he wants a key? He tells his little people to find out what safe we have, then he phones the giant who made the safe and asks him to have his little people make a key. In the world of giants, this is normal.'

The white Mercedes hadn't moved. Perhaps that too was normal.

*   *   *

They have found a tin shelter. Rows of folded deckchairs stand chained like prisoners to either side of them. The rain rattles and pings on the tin roof and runs in rivulets at their feet. Carl has returned to his mother. He lies sleeping on her breast with his head tucked into her shoulder. She has unfolded a parasol and is holding it over him. Justin sits apart from them on the bench, hands linked between his knees in prayer and his head bowed over his hands. This is what I resented about Garth's death, he remembers. Garth deprived me of my further education.

'Lorbeer was writing a *roman*,' she says.

'Novel.'

'*Roman* is a novel?'

'Yes.'

'Then this novel has the happy end at the beginning. Once upon a time there are two beautiful young woman doctors called Emrich and Kovacs. They are interns at Leipzig University in East Germany. The university has a big hospital. They are researching under the guidance of wise professors and they dream one day they will make a great discovery that will save the world. Nobody speaks of the god Profit, unless it is profit to mankind. At Leipzig hospital there are arriving many returning Russian Germans from Siberia and they have TB. In the Soviet prison camps the prevalence of TB was very high. All the patients are poor, all are sick and without defences, most have multi-resistant strains, many are dying. They will sign anything, they will try anything, they will not make trouble. So it is natural that the two young doctors have been isolating bacteria and experimenting with embryonic remedies for TB. They have tested with animals, maybe they tested also with medical students and other interns. Medical students have no money. They will be doctors one day, they are interested in the process. And in charge of their researches we have an *Oberarzt* –'

'Senior doctor.'

'The team is led by an *Oberarzt* who is enthusiastic for the experiments. All the team wants his admiration so all take part in the experiments. Nobody is evil, nobody is criminal. They are young dreamers, they have a sexy subject to analyse and the patients are desperate. Why not?'

'Why not?' Justin murmurs.

'And Kovacs has a boyfriend. Kovacs has always a boyfriend. Many boyfriends. This boyfriend is a Pole, a good fellow. Married, but never mind. And he has a laboratory. A small, efficient, intelligent laboratory in Gdansk. For love of Kovacs, the Pole tells her she can come and play in his laboratory whenever she has free time. She can bring whom she wants, so she brings her beautiful friend and colleague Emrich. Kovacs and Emrich research, Kovacs and the Pole make love, everyone is happy, nobody talks about the god Profit. These young people are looking only for honour and glory and maybe a bit promotion. And their studies produce positive results. Patients still die but they were dying anyway. And some live who would have died. Kovacs and Emrich are proud. They write articles for medical magazines. Their professor writes articles supporting them. Other professors support the professor, everyone is happy, everyone congratulates his neighbour, there are no enemies, or not yet.'

Carl shuffles on her shoulder. She pats his back and blows softly on his ear. He smiles and goes back to sleep.

'Emrich also has a lover. She has a husband whose name is Emrich but he is not satisfactory, this is Eastern Europe, everyone has been married to everyone. Her lover's name is Markus Lorbeer. He has a South African birth certificate, a German father and a Dutch mother and he is living in Moscow as a pharma agent, self-employed, but also as – as an entrepreneur who identifies interesting possibilities in the field of biotechnology and exploits them.'

'Talent spotter.'

'He is older than Lara by maybe fifteen years, he has swum in all the oceans, as we say, he is a dreamer as she is. He loves science, but never became a scientist. He loves medicine but is not a doctor. He loves God and the whole world, but he also loves hard currency and the god Profit. So he writes: "The young Lorbeer is a believer, he worships the Christian God, he worships women, but he worships also very much the god Profit." That is his downfall. He believes in God but ignores Him. Personally I reject this attitude but never mind. For a humanist, God is an excuse for not being humanistic. We shall be humanistic in the afterlife, meanwhile we make Profit. Never mind. "Lorbeer took God's gift of wisdom" – I guess he means by this the molecule – "and sold it to the Devil." I guess he means KVH. Then he writes that when Tessa came to see him in the desert, he told her the full extent of his sin.'

Justin sits up sharply.

'He *says* that? He told *Tessa*? When? In the hospital? Where did she come to see him? What *desert*? What on earth is he saying?'

'Like I told you, the document is a little crazy. He calls her the Abbott. "When the Abbott came to visit Lorbeer in the desert, Lorbeer wept." Maybe it is a dream, a fable. Lorbeer has become a penitent in the desert now. He is Elijah or Christ, I don't know. It's disgusting actually. "The Abbott called Lorbeer to account before God. Therefore at this meeting in the desert, Lorbeer explained to the Abbott the inmost nature of his sins." This is what he writes. His sins were evidently many. I don't remember them all. There was the sin of self-delusion and the sin of false argument. Then comes the sin of pride, I think. Followed by the sin of cowardice. For this he does not excuse himself at all, which makes me happy actually. But probably he is happy too. Lara says he is only happy when he is confessing or making love.'

'He wrote all this in English?'

She nodded. 'One paragraph he wrote like the English Bible, the next paragraph he was giving extremely technical data about the deliberately specious design of the clinical trials, the disputes between Kovacs and Emrich and the problems of Dypraxa when combined with other drugs. Only a very informed person could know such details. This Lorbeer I greatly prefer to the Lorbeer of Heaven and Hell, I will admit to you.'

'Abbott with a small A?'

'Large. "The Abbott recorded everything I told her." But there was another sin. He killed her.'

Waiting, Justin fixed his gaze on the recumbent Carl.

'Maybe not directly, he is ambiguous. "Lorbeer killed her with his treachery. He committed the sin of Judas, therefore he cut her throat with his bare hands and nailed Bluhm to the tree." When I was reading out these words to Lara, I asked her: "Lara. Is Markus saying that he killed Tessa Quayle?"'

'How did she reply?'

'Markus could not kill his worst enemy. That is his agony, she says. To be a bad man with a good conscience. She is Russian, very depressed.'

'But if he killed Tessa, he's not a good man, is he?'

'Lara swears it would be impossible. Lara has many letters from him. She can only love hopelessly. She has heard many confessions from him, but not this one, naturally. Markus is very proud of his sins, she says. But he is vain and exaggerates them. He is complicated, maybe a bit psychotic, which is why she loves him.'

'But she doesn't know where he is?'

'No.'

Justin's straight, unseeing stare had fixed on the deceptive twilight. '*Judas* didn't kill anyone,' he objected. 'Judas betrayed.'

'But the effect was the same. Judas killed with his treachery.'

Another long contemplation of the twilight. 'There's a missing character. If Lorbeer betrayed Tessa, who did he betray her to?'

'It was not clear. Maybe the Forces of Darkness. I have only what is in my memory.'

'The Forces of Darkness?'

'In the letter he talked of the Forces of Darkness. I hate this terminology. Does he mean KVH? Maybe he knows other forces.'

'Did the document mention Arnold?'

'The Abbott had a guide. In the document he is the Saint. The Saint had called out to Lorbeer in the hospital and told him the drug Dypraxa was an instrument of death. The Saint was more cautious than the Abbott because he is a doctor, and more tolerant because he has experience of human wickedness. But the greatest truth is with Emrich. Of this Lorbeer is certain. Emrich knows everything, therefore she is not allowed to speak.

332

The Forces of Darkness are determined to repress the truth. That is why the Abbott had to be killed and the Saint crucified.'

'*Crucified?* Arnold?'

'In Lorbeer's fable the Forces of Darkness dragged Bluhm away and nailed him to a tree.'

They fell silent, both in some way ashamed.

'Lara says also that Lorbeer drinks like a Russian,' she added, in some kind of mitigation, but Justin was not to be deflected.

'He writes from the desert but he uses a courier service out of Nairobi,' he objected.

'The address was typed, the waybill was written by hand, the package was despatched from the Norfolk Hotel, Nairobi. The sender's name was difficult to read but I think it was McKenzie. Is that Scottish? If the package could not be delivered it should not be returned to Kenya. It should be destroyed.'

'The waybill had a number, presumably.'

'The waybill was attached to the envelope. When I put the document in the safe for the night I first put it back in the envelope. Naturally the envelope has also disappeared.'

'Get back to the courier service. They'll have a copy.'

'The courier service has no record of the package. Not in Nairobi, not in Hanover.'

'How do I find her?'

'Lara?'

The rain clattered on the tin roof and the orange lights of the city swelled and dwindled in the mist while Birgit tore a sheet of paper from her diary and wrote out a long telephone number.

'She has a house but not for much longer. Otherwise you must enquire at the university, but you must take care because they hate her.'

'Was Lorbeer sleeping with Kovacs as well as Emrich?'

'For Lorbeer it would not be unusual. But I believe the quarrel between the women was not about sex but about the molecule.' She paused, following his gaze. He was staring into the distance, but there was nothing to see but the far hilltops poking through the mist. 'Tessa wrote often that she loved you,' she said quietly to his averted face. 'Not directly, that was not necessary. She said you were a man of honour and when it was necessary you would be honourable.'

She was preparing to leave. He passed her the backpack and between them they strapped Carl into his baby-pillion and fixed the plastic cape so that his sleepy head popped through the hole. She stood squat before him.

'So then,' she said. 'You walk?'

'I walk.'

She pulled an envelope from inside her jacket.

'This is all I remember of Lorbeer's novel. I wrote it down for you. My handwriting is very bad but you will decipher it.'

'You're very kind.' He stuffed the envelope inside his raincoat.

'So have good walking then,' she said.

She was going to shake his hand but changed her mind and kissed him on the mouth: one stern, deliberate, necessarily clumsy kiss of affection and farewell while she held the bicycle steady. Then Justin held the bicycle while she buckled her shell-helmet under her chin before swinging into the saddle and pedalling away down the hill.

*   *   *

I walk.

He walked, keeping to the centre of the road, one eye for the darkening rhododendron bushes either side of him. Sodium lights burned every fifty metres. He scanned the black patches between. The night air smelled of apples. He reached the bottom of the hill and approached the parked Mercedes, passing ten yards from its bonnet. No light inside the car. Two men were sitting in the front, but to judge by their motionless silhouettes they were not the same two who had driven up the hill and down again. He kept walking and the car overtook him. He ignored it, but in his imagination the men were not ignoring him. The Mercedes reached a crossroads and turned left. Justin turned right, heading for the glow of the town. A taxi passed and the driver called out to him.

'Thank you, thank you,' he called back expansively, 'but I prefer to walk.'

There was no answering call. He was on a pavement now, keeping to the outer edge. He made another crossing and entered a brightly lit side street. Dead-eyed young men and women crouched in doorways. Men in leather jackets stood on corners, elbows lifted, talking into cellphones. He made two more crossings and saw his hotel ahead of him.

The lobby was in the usual inescapable evening turmoil. A Japanese delegation was checking in, cameras were flashing, porters piling costly luggage into the only lift. Taking his place in the queue he pulled off his raincoat and slung it over his arm, favouring Birgit's envelope in the inside pocket. The lift descended, he stood back to let the women get in first. He rode to the third floor and was the only one to get out. The vile corridor with its sallow strip-lighting reminded him of the Uhuru Hospital. Television sets blared from every room. His own room was three-eleven and the door key was a piece of flat plastic with a black arrow printed on it. The din of competing television sets was infuriating him and he had a good mind to complain to somebody. How can I write to Ham with this din going on? He stepped into his room, laid his raincoat over a chair and saw that his own television set was the culprit. The chambermaids must have turned it on while they made up the room, and not bothered to turn it off when they left. He advanced on the set. It was showing the kind of programme he particularly detested. A half-dressed singer was howling at full volume into a microphone to the delight of an ecstatic juvenile audience while illuminated snow wandered down the screen.

And that was the last thing Justin saw as the lights went out: snowflakes of light falling down his screen. A blackness descended over him, and he felt himself being punched and suffocated at the same time. Human arms clamped his own arms to his sides, a ball of coarse cloth was stuffed into his mouth. His legs were seized in a rugger tackle and crumpled under him and he decided he was having a heart attack. His theory was confirmed when a second blow crushed his stomach and knocked the last of the wind out of him, because when he tried to yell nothing happened, he had no voice or breath and the ball of cloth was gagging him.

He felt knees on his chest. Something was being tightened round his neck, he thought a noose, and he assumed he was going to be hanged. He had a clear vision of Bluhm nailed to a tree. He smelled male body lotion and had a memory of Woodrow's body odour and he remembered sniffing Woodrow's love letter to see if it smelled of the same stuff. For a rare moment there was no Tessa in his memory. He was lying on the floor on his left side and whatever had crushed his stomach crushed his groin with another awful blow. He was hooded but nobody had hanged him yet, and he was still lying on his side. The gag was making him vomit, but he couldn't get the vomit out of his mouth so it was going down his throat. Hands rolled him onto his back and his arms were stretched out, knuckles in the carpet, palms upwards. They're going to crucify me like Arnold. But they weren't crucifying him, or not yet; they were holding his hands down and twisting them at the same time, and the pain was worse than he thought pain could be: in his arms, his chest and all over his legs and groin. Please, he thought. Not my right hand or how will I ever write to Ham? And they must have heard his prayer because the pain ceased and he heard a male voice, north German, maybe Berlin and quite cultured. It was giving an order to turn the swine back on his side and tie his hands behind him, and the order was being obeyed.

'Mr Quayle. Do you hear me?'

The same voice but now in English. Justin didn't answer. But this was not a lack of civility, it was because he had managed to spew out his cloth gag at last and was vomiting again and the vomit was creeping round his neck inside the hood. The sound of the television set faded.

'That's enough, Mr Quayle. You stop now, OK? Or you get what your wife got. You hear me? You want some more punishment, Mr Quayle?'

With the second Quayle came another horrendous kick in the groin.

'Maybe you gone deaf a bit. We leave you a little note, OK? On your bed. When you wake up, you read this little note and you remember. Then you go back to England, hear me? You don't ask no more bad questions. You go home, you be a good boy. Next time we kill you like Bluhm. That's a very long process. You hear me?'

Another kick to the groin rammed the lesson home. He heard the door close.

*   *   *

He lay alone, in his own darkness and his own vomit, on his left side with his knees drawn to his chin and his hands tied back to back behind him and the inside of his skull on fire from the electric pains that were tearing through his body. He lay in a black agony taking a rollcall of his shattered troops – feet, shins, knees, groin, belly, heart, hands – and confirmed that they were all present, if not correct. He stirred in his bonds and had a sensation of rolling into burning charcoal. He lay still again and a terrible pleasure began to wake in him, spreading in a victorious glow of self-knowledge. *They did this to me but I have remained who I am. I am tempered. I am able. Inside myself there's an untouched man. If they came back now, and did everything to me again, they would never reach the untouched man. I've passed the exam I've been shirking all my life. I'm a graduate of pain.*

Then either the pain eased or nature came to his aid, because he dozed, keeping his mouth tight shut and breathing with his nose through the stinking, sodden black night of his hood. The television set was still on, he could hear it. And if his sense of orientation hadn't gone astray he was looking at it. But the hood must be double-lined because he couldn't see so much as a flicker of it, and when, at huge cost to his hands, he rolled onto his back, he saw no hint of ceiling lights above him, although they had been lit as he wandered into the room, and he had no memory of hearing them switched off as his torturers departed. He rolled onto his side and panicked for a while, waiting for the strong part of himself to fight its way back to the top again. Work it out, man. Use your stupid head, it's the only thing they left intact. *Why* did they leave it intact? Because they wanted no scandal. Which is to say, whoever sent them wanted no scandal. 'Next time we kill you like Bluhm' – but not this time, however much they might have wished it. So I scream. Is that what I do? I roll around on the floor, kick furniture about, kick the party walls, kick the television set and generally go on behaving like a maniac until somebody decides that we are not two passionate lovers lost in the outer reaches of sado-masochism, but one bound and beaten Englishman with his head in a bag?

The trained diplomat painstakingly sketched out the consequences of such a discovery. The hotel calls the police. The police take a statement from me and call the local British Consulate, in this case Hanover, if we still have one there. Enter the Duty Consul, furious to be called away from his dinner to inspect yet another bloody Distressed British Subject, and his knee-jerk response is to check my passport – which passport scarcely matters. If it's Atkinson's, we have a problem because it's forged. One phone call to London establishes. If it's Quayle's, we have a different problem, but the likely upshot will be much the same: the first plane back to London without the option, an unwholesome Welcome Home Committee waiting to receive me at the airport.

His legs were not bound. Until now he had been reluctant to separate them. He did so, and his groin and belly caught fire and his thighs and shins followed quickly afterwards. But he could definitely separate his legs, and he could tap his feet together again and hear his heels click. Emboldened by this discovery, he took the extreme step, rolled onto his stomach and let out an involuntary scream. Then he bit his lips together so that he didn't scream again.

But he stayed doggedly face down. Patiently, careful not to disturb his neighbours in the bedrooms either side, he began working on his bonds.

CHAPTER SEVENTEEN

The plane was an elderly twin-engined Beechcraft on UN charter with a rawhide fifty-year-old captain from Johannesburg and a burly African co-pilot with side whiskers, and one white cardboard lunch box on each of its nine torn seats. The airport was Wilson, next to Tessa's grave, and as the plane sweated and waited on the runway Ghita strained to catch sight of her burial mound through the window and wondered how much longer she would have to wait for her headstone. But all she saw was silver-backed grass and a red-robed tribesman with a staff standing on one leg over his goats, and a herd of gazelles twitching and grazing under blue-black cloud stacks. She had wedged her travel bag under her seat but the bag was too big and she had to splay her churchy shoes to make space for it. It was terribly hot in the plane and the captain had already warned the passengers that there could be no air-conditioning until the plane took off. In the zip compartment she had stowed her briefing notes and her credentials as the British High Commission's delegate from EADEC. In the main compartment, her pyjamas and a change of clothes. I'm doing this for Justin.

I'm following in Tessa's footsteps. I have no need to feel ashamed of my inexperience or duplicity.

The back of the fuselage was stuffed with sacks of precious *miraa*, a permitted, mildly narcotic plant adored by northern tribesmen. Its woody scent was gradually filling the plane. In front of her sat four case-hardened aid workers, two men, two women. Maybe the *miraa* was theirs. She envied their gritty, carefree air, their threadbare clothes and unwashed dedication. And realised with a pinch of self-reproach that they were her age. She wished she could break the habits of learned humility, of drawing her heels together whenever she shook hands with her betters, a practice instilled in her by nuns. She peeked inside her box and identified two plantain sandwiches, an apple, a bar of chocolate and a box of passion-fruit juice. She had barely slept and she was famished, but her sense of decorum forbade her to eat a sandwich before take-off. Last night her phone had rung non-stop from the moment she returned to her flat as her friends one by one vented their outrage and disbelief at the news that Arnold was a wanted man. Her position in the High Commission required her to play the elder stateswoman to them all. At midnight, though she was dead tired, she attempted to take a step from which she could not retreat; one that, if it had succeeded, would have rescued her from the no-man's land where she had been hiding like a recluse for the last three weeks. She had delved in the old brass pot where she kept odds and ends and extracted from it a slip of paper she had secreted there. This is where you ring us, Ghita, if you decide you want to talk to us again. If we're not there, leave a message and one of us will always get back to you within the hour, I promise. An aggressive male African voice answered her and she hoped she had the wrong number.

'I'd like to speak to Rob or Lesley, please.'

'What's your name?'

'I want to speak to Rob or Lesley. Is either of them there?'

'Who are you? Give me your name and state your business immediately.'

'I'd like to speak to Rob or Lesley, please.'

As the phone was slammed down on her she accepted without drama that she was, as she had suspected, alone. Henceforth no Tessa, no Arnold, no wise Lesley from Scotland Yard could spare her the responsibility for her actions. Her parents, though she adored them, were not a solution. Her father the lawyer would listen to her testimony and declare that on the one hand this, but then again on the other hand that, and ask her what objective proof she had for these very serious allegations. Her mother the doctor would say you're overheating, darling, come home and have a bit of R and R. With this thought uppermost in her bleary head she had opened up her laptop, which she did not doubt would also be cram-full of cries of pain and indignation about Arnold. But no sooner had she gone on-line than the screen popped and dwindled to nothing. She went through her procedures – in vain. She phoned a couple of friends only to establish that their machines were unaffected.

'Wow, Ghita, maybe you've picked up one of these crazy viruses from the Philippines or wherever those cyber-freaks hang out!' one of her friends had cried enviously, as if Ghita had been singled out for special attention.

Maybe she had, she agreed, and slept badly from worrying about the e-mails she had lost, the ping-pong chats she'd had with Tessa that she had never printed out because she preferred rereading them on screen, they were more vivid that way, more Tessa.

The Beechcraft had still not taken off so Ghita, as was her habit, gave herself over to the larger questions of life, while studiously avoiding the largest of them all, which was what am I doing here and why? A couple of years ago in England – in my Era Before Tessa, as she secretly called it – she had agonised about the injuries, real and imagined, that she endured every day for being Anglo-Indian. She saw herself as an unsavable hybrid, half black girl in search of God, half white woman superior to lesser breeds without the law. Waking and sleeping, she had demanded to know where she belonged in a white man's world, and how and where she should invest her ambitions and her humanity, and whether she should continue to study dance and music at the London college she was attending after Exeter, or, in the image of her adoptive parents, follow her other star and enter one of the professions.

Which explains how one morning she found herself, almost on an impulse, sitting an examination for Her Majesty's Foreign Service which, unsurprisingly since she had never given a thought to politics, she duly failed, but with the advice that she should reapply in two years' time. And somehow the very decision to sit the exam, though unsuccessful, released the reasoning behind it, which was that she was more at ease with herself joining the System than staying apart from it and achieving little beyond the partial gratification of her artistic impulses.

And it was at this point, visiting her parents in Tanzania, that she decided, again on impulse, to apply for local employment by the British High Commission, and to look for advancement once she was accepted. And if she had not done this she would never have met Tessa. She would never, as she thought of it now, have put herself in the firing line where she was determined to remain, fighting for the things she was determined to be loyal to – even if, boiled down, they made pretty simplistic reading: truth, tolerance, justice, a sense of life's beauty and a near-violent rejection of their opposites – but, above all, an inherited belief, derived from both her parents and entrenched by Tessa, that the System itself must be forced to reflect these virtues, or it had no business to exist. Which brought her back to the largest question of them all. She had loved Tessa, she had loved Bluhm, she loved Justin still and, if she was truthful, a little more than was proper or comfortable or whatever the word was. And the fact that she was working for the System did not oblige her to accept the System's lies, as she had heard them only yesterday from Woodrow's mouth. On the contrary, it obliged her to reject them, and put the System back where it belonged, which was on the side of truth. Which explained to Ghita's total satisfaction what she was doing here and why. 'Better to be inside the System and fighting it,' her father – an iconoclast in other ways – would say, 'than outside the System, howling at it.'

And Tessa, which was the wonderful thing, had said exactly the same.

The Beechcraft shook itself like an old dog and lurched forward, bumping laboriously into the air. Through her tiny window Ghita saw all Africa spread itself below her: slum cities, herds of running zebra, the flower farms of Lake Naivasha, the Aberdares, Mount Kenya faintly painted on the far horizon. And joining them like a sea, the endless tracts of misted brown bush scribbled over with pocks of green. The plane entered rain cloud, a brown dusk filled the cabin. Scorching sunlight replaced it, and was accompanied by an almighty explosion from somewhere out to Ghita's left. Without warning the plane rolled on its side. Lunch boxes, rucksacks and Ghita's travel bag skeltered across the gangway to a chorus of alarm bells and sirens and a flashing of red lights. Nobody spoke except for one old African man, who let out a peal of laughter and bellowed, 'We love you, Lord, and don't you go forgettin' that,' to the relief and nervous merriment of the other passengers. The plane had still not righted itself. The engine note dropped to a murmur. The African co-pilot with side whiskers had found a handbook and was consulting a checklist while Ghita tried to read it over his shoulder. The rawhide captain turned in his seat to address his craven passengers. His sloped, leathern mouth matched the angle of the plane's wings.

'As you may have noticed, ladies and gentlemen, one engine has cracked up,' he said drily. 'Which means we're going to have to go back to Wilson and pick up another of these things.'

And I'm not afraid, Ghita noted, pleased with herself. Until Tessa died, things like this happened to other people. Now they're happening to me, and I can handle them.

Four hours later, she was standing on the tarmac at Lokichoggio.

*   *   *

'You Ghita?' an Australian girl yelled over the roar of engines and other people's shouted greetings. 'I'm Judith. Hi!'

She was tall and red-cheeked and happy and wore a man's curly brown trilby and a T-shirt proclaiming the United Tea Services of Ceylon. They embraced, spontaneous friends in a wild roaring place. White UN cargo planes were taking off and landing, white lorries shunted and thundered and the sun was a furnace and the heat of it leaped up at her from the runway and the fumes of aircraft fuel shimmered in her eyes and dazzled her. With Judith to guide her, she squeezed herself into the back of a jeep amid sacks of mail to sit beside a sweating Chinese man in a dog collar and a black suit. Jeeps hurtled past them in the opposite direction, pursued by a convoy of white lorries headed for the cargo planes.

'She was a real nice lady!' Judith shouted from the passenger seat in front of her. 'Very dedicated!' She was evidently talking about Tessa. 'Why would anybody want to arrest Arnold? They're just plain stupid! Arnold wouldn't squash a fly. You're booked three nights, right? Only we got a bunch of nutritionists coming in from Uganda!'

Judith is here to feed the living not the dead, thought Ghita as the jeep clattered through a gateway and joined a strip of hard road. They drove past a camp-followers' shanty town of bars, stalls and a facetious notice saying Piccadilly This Way. Tranquil brown hills rose ahead of them. Ghita said she'd love to walk up there. Judith said if she did she'd never come back.

'Animals?'

'People.'

They approached the camp. On a patch of red dust beside the main gates, children were playing basketball with a white food bag nailed to a wooden post. Judith led Ghita to reception to collect her pass. Signing the book, Ghita leafed casually back, only to have it fall open at the page she was pretending not to look for:

Tessa Abbott, PO Box, Nairobi, Tukul 28.

A. Bluhm, Médecins de l'Univers, Tukul 29.

And the same date.

'The press boys had a ball,' Judith was saying enthusiastically. 'Reuben charged them fifty US a shot, cash. Eight hundred bucks total, that's eight hundred sets of drawing books and colouring crayons. Reuben reckons that'll produce two Dinka van Goghs, two Dinka Rembrandts and one Dinka Andy Warhol.'

Reuben the legendary camp organiser, Ghita remembered. Congolese. Friend of Arnold's.

They were walking down a wide avenue of tulip trees, their fiery red trumpets brilliant against overhead cables and white-painted *tukuls* with thatched roofs. A lank Englishman like a prep-school master rode sedately past them on an old-fashioned policeman's push-bike. Seeing Judith he rang his bell and gave her a lovely wave.

'Showers and honey-boxes across the road from you, first session tomorrow eight a.m. sharp, meet in the doorway to hut thirty-two,' Judith announced, as she showed Ghita to her quarters. 'Mosquito spray beside your bed, use the net if you're wise. Care to mosey down to the club around sunset for a beer before dinner?'

Ghita would.

'Well, look out for yourself. Some of the boys are pretty hungry when they come back from the field.'

Ghita tried to sound casual. 'Oh by the by, there's a woman called Sarah,' she said. 'She was some kind of a friend of Tessa's. I wondered whether she was around so that I could say hullo to her.'

She unpacked her things and, armed with her sponge-bag and towel, set out bravely across the avenue. Rain had fallen, damping the din from the airfield. The dangerous hills had turned black and olive. The air smelled of gasoline and spices. She showered, returned to her *tukul* and sat herself before her work notes at a rickety table where, sweating helplessly, she lost herself in the intricacies of Aid Self-Sufficiency.

*　　*　　*

Loki's clubhouse was a spreading tree with a long thatched roof under it, a drinks bar with a mural of jungle fauna and a video projector that threw fuzzy images of a long-dead soccer match onto a plastered wall while the sound system belted out African dance music. Shrieks of delighted recognition pierced the evening air as aid workers from distant places rediscovered each other in different languages, embraced, touched faces and walked arm in arm. This should be my spiritual home, she thought wistfully. These are my rainbow people. Their classless-ness, their racelessness, their zeal, their youth are mine. Sign up for Loki and tune in to saintliness! Bum around in aeroplanes, enjoy a romantic self-image and the adrenalin of danger! Get your sex out of a tap and a nomadic life that keeps you clear of entanglements! No dreary office work and always a bit of grass to smoke along the way! Glory and boys when I come out of the field, money and more boys waiting for me on my R and R! Who needs more?

I do.

I need to understand why this mess was necessary in the first place. And why it's necessary now. I need to have the courage to say after Tessa at her most vituperative: 'Loki sucks. It has no more right to exist than the Berlin Wall. It's a monument to the failure of diplomacy. What the hell's the point of running a Rolls-Royce ambulance service when our politicians do noth-ing to prevent the accidents?'

Night fell in a second. Yellow strip-lights replaced the sun, the birds stopped chattering, then resumed their conversations at a more acceptable level. She was seated at a long table and Judith was sitting three down from her with her arm round an anthropologist from Stockholm, and Ghita was thinking that she hadn't felt like this since she was a new girl at convent school, except that at convent school you didn't drink beer or have half a dozen personable young men of all the world's nations at your table, and half a dozen pairs of male eyes assessing your sexual weight and availability. She was listen-ing to tales of places she had never heard of, and exploits so hair-raising she was convinced she would never qualify to share them, and she was doing her best to appear knowledgeable and only distantly impressed. The spokesman of the moment was a surefire Yankee from New Jersey whose name was Hank the Hawk. According to Judith, he was a one-time boxer and loan-shark who had embraced aid work as an alternative to a life of crime. He was holding forth about the warring factions of the Nile area: how the SPLE had temporarily kissed the asses of the SPLM; how the SSIM were beating the shit out of another set of letters, butchering their menfolk, stealing their women and cattle and generally making their contribution to the couple of million dead already notched up by Sudan's brainless civil wars. And Ghita was sipping her beer and doing her best to smile along with Hank the Hawk because his monologue seemed to be addressed exclusively at her as the newcomer and his next conquest. She was therefore grateful when a plump African woman of indeterminate age wearing shorts and sneakers and a London costermonger's peaked cap appeared out of the dark-ness, clapped her on the shoulder and yelled, 'I'm Sudan Sarah, honey, so you got to be Ghita. Nobody told me you were so pretty. Come and have a cup of tea, dear.' And without further ceremony marched her through a maze of offices to a *tukul* like a beach hut on stilts, with a single bed, a refrigerator and a bookcase filled with matching volumes of classical English litera-ture from Chaucer to James Joyce.

And outside, a tiny verandah with two chairs for sitting under the stars and fighting off the bugs once the kettle boils.

*   *   *

'I hear they're going to arrest Arnold now,' Sudan Sarah said comfortably when they had duly lamented Tessa's death. 'Well, they should do that. If you've set your mind on hiding the truth, then the first thing you've got to do is give people a different truth to keep them quiet. Otherwise they'll start to wonder whether the *real* truth isn't out there hidden somewhere, and that will *never* do.'

A schoolmistress, Ghita decided. Or a governess. Used to spreading out her thoughts and repeating them to inattentive children.

'And after the murder comes the cover-up,' Sarah continued in the same benign cadences. 'And we should never forget that a good cover-up is a lot harder to achieve than a bad murder. A crime, you can maybe always get away with a crime. But a cover-up is going to land you in gaol every time.' She was indicating the problem with her big hands. 'You cover *this* bit up, then out pops *another* bit. So you cover *that* bit up. Then you turn round and that first bit's showing again. And you turn round again and there's a third bit, just sticking its toe out of the sand over there, sure as Cain ever killed Abel. So what should I be telling you, dear? I'm getting a feeling we're not talking about the things you wish to talk about.'

Ghita began cunningly. Justin, she said, was trying to piece together a picture of Tessa's final days. He would like to be assured that her last visit to Loki had been happy and productive. In what way exactly had Tessa contributed to the gender awareness seminar, could Sarah say? Had Tessa delivered a paper perhaps, drawing on her legal knowledge or her experiences with women in Kenya? Was there a particular episode or happy moment that Sarah recalled and Justin would like to hear about?

Sarah heard her out contentedly, eyes twinkling under the brim of her costermonger's hat while she pecked at her tea and flapped a big loose hand at the mosquitoes, never ceasing to smile at passers-by or call to them – 'Hi there, Jeannie sweet, you bad girl! What you doing with that layabout Santo? You going write to Justin all about this, dear?'

The question unsettled Ghita. Was it good or bad that she should be proposing to write to Justin? Was there innuendo in *all*? In the High Commission Justin was an unperson. Was he one here as well?

'Well, I'm sure Justin would *like* me to write to him,' she conceded awkwardly. 'But I'll only do that if I can tell him things that will put his mind to rest, if that's possible. I mean I wouldn't tell him anything that was going to *hurt* him,' she protested, .losing her direction. 'I mean Justin knows that Tessa and Arnold were *travelling* together. The whole world knows by now. Whatever was between them, he's reconciled to *that.*'

'Oh, there was nothing between those two, darling, believe me,' Sarah said with an easy laugh. 'That was all newspaper talk. There was just no way. I know that for a fact. Hi, Abby, how you doing, darling? That's my sister Abby. She's had more than many. She's been married almost four times.'

The significance of both statements, if there was any, passed Ghita by. She was too busy shoring up what sounded increasingly like a silly lie. 'Justin wants to fill in the blanks,' she struggled on bravely. 'Get the details shipshape in his mind. So that he can piece together everything she did and thought about in her last few days. I mean, obviously – if you told me something that was going to be, well, painful to him – I wouldn't dream of passing it on. Obviously.'

'Shipshape,' Sarah repeated, and shook her head again, smiling to herself. 'That's why I always loved the English language. Shipshape is a right word for that good lady. Now what do *you* think they did when they were up here, darling? Spooning around like honeymooners? That wasn't their way at all.'

'Attending the gender workshop, obviously. Did you attend it yourself? You were probably running it or something grand. I never asked you what you do here. I should know. I'm sorry.'

'Don't apologise, darling. You're not sorry. You're just a little bit at sea. Not quite *shipshape* yet.' She laughed. 'Yes, well, now I remember. I *did* attend that workshop. Maybe I led it too. We take it in turns. It was a good group, I remember that. Two bright tribeswomen from Dhiak, a medical widow woman from Aweil, a bit pompous but receptive despite her pomposity, and a couple of paralegals from I don't know. That was a good team, I'll say that straight. But what those women will do when they get home again to Sudan, that you can never tell. You can scratch your head and you can wonder as much as you will.'

'Maybe Tessa related to the paralegals,' Ghita put in hopefully.

'Maybe she did, dear. But a lot of those women never rode in an aeroplane before. A lot of them get sick and scared, so we're obliged to cheer them up before they'll talk and listen, which is what they're brought here to do. Some of them get so afraid they never talk to anyone at all, just want to go home to their indignities. Never get into this business if you're afraid of failure, darling, I tell people. Count your successes is Sudan Sarah's advice and don't even think about the occasions when you failed. D'you still want to ask me about that workshop?'

Ghita's confusion increased. 'Well, did she shine at it? Did she enjoy it?'

'Now I don't know about that, darling, do I?'

'There must be *something* you remember that she did or said. Nobody forgets Tessa for long.' She sounded rude to herself, and didn't mean to. 'Or Arnold.'

'Well, I won't say she *did* contribute to that discussion, dear, because she didn't. Tessa did not contribute to that discussion. I can say that with certainty.'

'Did Arnold?'

'No.'

'Not even read a paper or anything?'

'Nothing at all, darling. Neither of them.'

'You mean they just sat there, silent? Both of them? It's not like Tessa to keep quiet. Nor Arnold for that matter. How long did the course last?'

'Five days. But Tessa and Arnold didn't stay in Loki five days. Not many people do. Everyone who comes here likes to feel they're going somewhere else. Tessa and Arnold were no different from the rest.' She paused and examined Ghita, as if measuring her suitability for something. 'Do you know what I'm saying, darling?'

'No. I'm afraid I don't.'

'Maybe it's what I'm not saying that you know.'

'I don't know that either.'

'Well, what the hell are you up to then?'

'I'm trying to find out what they did. Arnold and Tessa. In their last few days. Justin wrote and asked me to particularly.'

'You got his letter with you then, by any chance, dear?'

Ghita produced it with a trembling hand from a new shoulder bag she'd bought for the trip. Sarah took it into the *tukul* to read it by the overhead light bulb, then stood by herself before returning to the verandah and sitting herself down in her chair with an air of considerable moral confusion.

'You going to tell me something, dear?'

'If I can.'

'Did Tessa tell you with her own sweet mouth that she and Arnold were coming up to Loki for a gender workshop?'

'It's what they told all of us.'

'And you believed her?'

'Yes, I did. All of us did. Justin did. We still do.'

'And Tessa was a close friend of yours? Like a sister, as I heard. But all the same she never even *told* you she had some other reason to come up here? Or that the gender workshop was a straight pretext, an excuse, same as Self-Sustainment is a pretext for *you*, I expect?'

'At the beginning of our friendship, Tessa told me things. Then she became worried for me. She thought she'd told me too much. It wasn't fair to burden me. I'm a temporary employee, locally employed. She knew I was thinking of applying for a permanent post. Sitting the exams again.'

'You still thinking along those lines, dear?'

'Yes, I am. But that doesn't mean I can't be told the truth.'

Sarah took a sip of her tea, tugged at the brim of her cap

and sat herself comfortably in her chair. 'You going to stay here three nights is my understanding.'

'Yes. Back to Nairobi on Thursday.'

'That's nice. That's very nice. And you will have a good conference. Judith is a gifted practical woman who takes no shit from anybody. A little sharp with the slower-witted ones, but never deliberately unkind. And tomorrow evening, I shall introduce you to my good friend Captain McKenzie. You never heard of him?'

'No.'

'Tessa or Arnold never mentioned a Captain McKenzie in your hearing?'

'No.'

'Well, the captain is a pilot here with us at Loki. He flew down to Nairobi today so I guess you and he crossed each other in the air. He had some supplies to pick up and a little business to attend to. You will like Captain McKenzie very much. He is a nice-mannered man with more heart to him than most people have body, and that's a fact. Very little takes place in these parts that escapes the notice of Captain McKenzie, and very little escapes his lips either. The captain has fought in many unpleasant wars but now he is a devoted man of peace, which is why he's here in Loki feeding my starving people.'

'Did he know Tessa well?' Ghita asked fearfully.

'Captain McKenzie knew Tessa and he thought she was a fine lady, and that was that. Captain McKenzie would no more presume on a married lady than – well, than Arnold would. But Captain McKenzie knew Arnold better than he knew Tessa. And he thinks the police in Nairobi are all mad to be going after Arnold like that, and he's proposing to tell them so while he's there. I would say that is one of the pivotal reasons for his making the journey to Nairobi at this time. And they won't like what he is going to tell them because, believe me, Captain McKenzie speaks his mind without let or hindrance.'

'Was Captain McKenzie here in Loki when Tessa and Arnold came up for the workshop?'

'Captain McKenzie was here. And he saw a lot more of Tessa than I did, dear, by a long chalk.' She broke off for a while and sat smiling at the stars, and it seemed to Ghita that she was trying to reach a decision in her mind – such as whether to speak out or keep her secrets to herself, questions that Ghita had been asking herself these last three weeks.

'Now, dear,' Sarah went on finally. 'I've been listening to you. And I've been watching you and thinking about you and worrying about you. And I came to the conclusion that you're a girl with a brain in your head, and you're also a good, decent human being with a well-developed sense of responsibility, which I value. But if you're not that person and I have misread you, between us we could get Captain McKenzie into a whole heap of trouble. This is dangerous knowledge I'm about to acquaint you with and there's no way, once you have it, to get it back in the bottle. So I suggest you tell me now whether I am over-judging you or whether I have read you accurately. Because people who talk out of turn, they never reform. That's something else I've learned. They can swear on the Bible one day and the next day they're at it just like before, talking out of turn again. The Bible didn't make a whit of difference to them.'

'I understand,' said Ghita.

'Now are you going to advise me that I have misinterpreted what I have seen and heard and thought of you? Or shall I tell you what I have in my mind and you bear that heavy burden of responsibility for ever after?'

'I'd like you to trust me, please.'

'That's what I thought you'd say, so listen to me. I'll say it quietly, so bring your ear a little closer to me.' Sudan Sarah gave a tug to the brim of her hat so that Ghita could get alongside her. 'There. And maybe the geckos will favour us with some loud burping, I hope. Tessa never came to that workshop, nor Arnold neither. As soon as they were able, Tessa and Arnold got into the back of my friend Captain McKenzie's jeep and drove quietly and sedately out to the airstrip with their heads down. And Captain McKenzie, as soon as *he* was able, he put them in his Buffalo aeroplane and flew them up north without benefit of passports or visas or any of the normal formalities imposed by South Sudanese rebels who can't stop fighting one another and haven't got the spirit or intelligence to unite themselves against those bad Arabs in the north who seem to think Allah forgives everything even if his Prophet doesn't.'

Ghita thought Sarah had finished and was about to speak, but she had only begun.

'A further complication is that Mr Moi, who couldn't manage a flea-circus with the assistance of his entire Cabinet, even if there was money in it for him, has taken it into his head that he's got to have the managing of Loki airstrip, as you will have noticed. Mr Moi has a very limited affection for NGOs but a great appetite for airport taxes. And Dr Arnold was very particular that Mr Moi and his people did not take cognisance of their journey to wherever they wished to go.'

'So where *did* they go?' Ghita whispered, but Sarah rolled straight on.

'Now I never asked where that place was, because what I don't know I can't end up saying in my sleep. Not that there's anyone to hear me these days, I'm too old. But Captain McKenzie knows, that stands to reason. Captain McKenzie brought them back early next day from wherever he took them to, discreetly, the way he took them out the day before. And Dr Arnold, he says to me, "Sarah," he says, "we never went anywhere except here to Loki. We were attending your gender workshop twenty-four hours a day. Tessa and I are grateful to you for continuing to remember that important fact." But Tessa's dead now, and she's not likely to be grateful to Sudan Sarah or anybody else any more. And Dr Arnold, if I know anything, he's worse than dead. Because that Moi has his people everywhere, and they kill and steal to their hearts' content, and that means a lot of killing. And when they take a man prisoner with the intention of extracting certain truths from him, they abandon all compassion, and that's a fact you'd do well to remember on your own account, my darling, because you are treading in very deep waters. Which is why I've decided it is essential that you get into conversation with Captain McKenzie, who knows things I'd rather not. Because Justin, who's a good man from all that I hear, he needs to have all the information that's available on the subject of his dead wife and Dr Arnold. Now is that the right way for me to be thinking, or is there a better way?'

'It's the right way,' Ghita said.

Sarah drained her tea and set down the cup. 'Very well then. So you go and eat and get your strength up and I'll stay here for a little while, dear, because this place is talk, talk, talk, as you will already have appreciated. And don't touch the goat curry, darling, however much you like goat. Because that young Somali chef, who is a gifted boy and will one day become a fine lawyer, has a blind spot where goat curry is concerned.'

*   *   *

Ghita never knew how she got through the first day of the focus group on Self-Sustainment, but by the time the bell sounded for five o'clock – though the bell was only in her head – she had the satisfaction of knowing that she had not made a fool of herself, had spoken neither too much nor too little, had listened with humility to the opinions of older and more knowledgeable participants, and had taken copious notes for yet another unread EADEC report.

'Glad you came?' Judith asked her, cheerfully grabbing her arm as the meeting broke up. 'See you down the club, then.'

'This is for you, darling,' said Sarah, emerging from a staff hut to hand her a brown envelope. 'Enjoy your evening.'

'You too.'

Sarah's handwriting came straight out of a school copybook.

Ghita dear. Captain McKenzie occupies Entebbe tukul which is number fourteen on the airstrip side. Take a hand-torch with you for when the generators are switched off. He will be happy to receive you at nine o'clock after your dinner. He is a gentleman so you need have no fear. Please give him this note so that I can be sure it has been sensibly disposed of. Take very good care of yourself now and remember your responsibilities as regards discretion.

Sarah

*   *   *

The names of the *tukuls* read to Ghita like regimental battle honours in the village church close to her convent school in England. The front door to Entebbe was ajar, but the mosquito door inside it was wedged tight. A blue-shaded hurricane lamp burned and Captain McKenzie sat in front of it, so that as Ghita approached the *tukul* she saw only his silhouette, bowed over his desk while he wrote like a monk. And because first impressions counted greatly with her, she stood a moment observing his craggy look and extreme stillness, anticipating an unbending military nature. She was about to tap on the door frame but Captain McKenzie had either heard or seen her or guessed her, because he sprang to his feet and made two athletic strides to the mosquito door and pulled it back for her.

'Ghita, I'm Rick McKenzie. You're bang on time. Got a note for me?'

New Zealand, she thought, and knew she'd got it right. Sometimes she forgot her knowledge of English names and accents, but this was not one of the times. New Zealand and on closer inspection nearer to fifty than thirty, but she could only guess this from the hairline cracks on the gaunt cheeks and the silver tips to the trim black hair. She handed him Sarah's note and watched while he turned his back on her and held the note to the blue lamp. By the brighter glow she saw a sparse, clean room with an ironing board and polished brown shoes and a soldier's bed made the way she was taught to make her bed at convent school, with hospital corners and the sheet folded over the blanket at the top, then folded back on itself to make an equilateral triangle.

'Why don't you sit yourself over there?' he asked, indicating a kitchen chair. As she moved towards it, the blue lamp moved behind her, to settle on the floor at the centre of the doorway to the *tukul*. 'That way nobody gets to see in,' he explained. 'We've got full-time *tukul*-watchers here. Take a Coke?' He handed it to her at arm's length. 'Sarah says you're a trustworthy person, Ghita. That's good enough for me. Tessa and Arnold didn't trust anyone except each other in this. And me because they had to. That's the way I like to work too. You came up on a Self-Sustainment jag, I hear.' It was a question.

'The Self-Sustainment focus group was a pretext. Justin wrote to me asking me to find out what Tessa and Arnold were doing in Loki in the days before she died. He didn't believe the story of the gender workshop.'

'He's damn right. Got his letter?'

My identity paper, she thought. My proof of good faith as Justin's messenger. She passed it to him and watched while he stood up, pulled on a pair of austere steel-framed spectacles and stepped obliquely into the arc of the blue lamp, keeping himself out of the eyeline of the door.

He handed the letter back. 'So listen up,' he said.

But first he turned on his radio, anxious to establish what he pedantically termed *the level of acceptable sound*.

*   *   *

Ghita lay on her bed, under a single sheet. The night was no cooler than the day. Through the netting that surrounded her she could watch the red glow of the mosquito coil. She had drawn the curtains but they were very thin. Footsteps and voices kept passing her window and every time they passed she had an urge to leap out of bed and shout 'Hi!' Her thoughts turned to Gloria, who a week ago, to her confusion, had invited her to a game of tennis at the club.

'Tell me, dear,' Gloria had asked her, having trounced her six games to two in each of three sets. They were walking arm in arm towards the clubhouse. 'Did Tessa have some kind of crush on Sandy, or was it the other way round?'

At which Ghita, despite her addiction to the altar of truth, lied straight and fairly into Gloria's face without even blushing. 'I am quite sure there was nothing of the kind on *either* side,' she said primly. 'Whatever makes you think that, Gloria?'

'Nothing, darling. Nothing at all. Just the way he looked during the funeral, I suppose.'

And after Gloria, she went back to Captain McKenzie.

'There's this crazy Boer who runs a food station five miles west of a little town called Mayan,' he was saying, keeping his voice just below Pavarotti's. 'Bit of a God-thumper.'

CHAPTER EIGHTEEN

His face had darkened, its lines deepened. The white light of
the huge Saskatchewan sky could not penetrate its shadows.
The little town was a lost city, three hours' rail ride out of
Winnipeg in the middle of a thousand-mile snowfield, and Justin
walked in it determinedly, avoiding the gaze of rare passers-by.
The constant wind from the Yukon or the high Arctic that all
year round whipped across the flat prairie, icing the snow, bend-
ing the wheat, buffeting street signs and overhead wires, raised
no points of colour on his hollowed cheeks. The freezing cold
– twenty and more below zero – only spurred his aching body
forward. In Winnipeg before he took the train here, he had bought
a quilted jacket, a fur cap and gloves. The fury in him was a
thorn. A rectangle of plain typing paper nestled in his wallet:
GO HOME NOW AND KEEP QUIET OR YOU JOIN YOUR WIFE.

*　　　*　　　*

But it was his wife who had got him here. She had worked his
hands free, untied his hood. She had raised him to his knees at
the bedside and by stages helped him to the bathroom. Cheered

on by her, he had hauled himself to a standing stoop with the aid of the bathtub, had turned on the shower tap and hosed down his face and shirt front and the collar of his jacket, because he knew – she warned him – that if he undressed he would not be able to dress himself again. His shirt front was filthy, his jacket was smeared with vomit but he managed to mop them fairly clean. He wanted to go back to sleep but she wouldn't let him. He tried to brush his hair but his arms wouldn't go that high. He had a twenty-four-hour stubble but it must stay there. Standing made his head swim and he was lucky to reach the bed before he toppled over. But it was on her advice that, lying in a seductive half-swoon, he refused to pick up the telephone to the concierge or invoke the medical skills of Dr Birgit. Trust nobody, Tessa told him, so he didn't. He waited till his world had righted itself, then stood up again and reeled across the room, grateful for its miserable size.

He had laid his raincoat over a chair. It was still there. To his surprise so was Birgit's envelope. He opened the wardrobe. The wall-safe was built into the back of it, its door closed. He tapped out the date of his wedding day, almost fainting from the pain each time he prodded. The door popped open to reveal Peter Atkinson's passport slumbering peacefully inside. His hands battered but seemingly unbroken, he coaxed the passport out and fed it into his inside jacket pocket. He fought his way into his raincoat and contrived to button it at the neck, then at the waist. Determined to travel light, he possessed only a shoulder bag. His money was still inside it. He collected his shaving things from the bathroom and his shirts and underclothes from the chest of drawers and dropped them into it. He placed Birgit's envelope on top of them and closed the zip. He eased the strap over his shoulder and yelped like a dog at the pain. His watch said five in the morning and it seemed to be working. He lurched into the corridor and rolled himself along the wall to the lift. In the ground floor lobby two women in Turkish costume were operating an industrial-sized vacuum cleaner. An elderly night porter dozed behind the reception desk. Somehow Justin gave his room number and asked for his bill. Somehow he got a hand into his hip pocket, detached the notes from their wad and added a fat tip 'belatedly for Christmas'.

'Mind if I grab one of these?' he asked in a voice he didn't recognise. He was indicating a cluster of doorman's umbrellas that were jammed into a ceramic pot beside the door.

'Many as you like,' the old porter said.

The umbrella had a stout ash handle that came up to his hip. With its aid he crossed the empty square to the railway station. Reaching the steps that led up to the concourse he paused for a rest and was puzzled to find the porter at his side. He had thought it was Tessa.

'Can you make it?' the old man asked solicitously.

'Yes.'

'Shall I get your ticket?'

Justin turned and offered the old man his pocket. 'Zurich,' he said. 'Single.'

'First class?'

'Absolutely.'

*   *   *

Switzerland was a childhood dream. Forty years ago his parents had taken him on a walking holiday in the Engadine and they had stayed in a grand hotel on a spit of forest between two lakes. Nothing had changed. Not the polished parquet or the stained glass or the stern-faced châtelaine who showed him to his room. Reclining on the daybed on his balcony, Justin watched the same lakes glistening in the evening sun, and the same fisherman huddled in his rowing boat in the mist. The days passed uncounted, punctuated by visits to the spa and the death knell of the dinner gong summoning him to solitary meals among whispery old couples. In a side street of old chalets, a pallid doctor and his woman assistant dressed his bruises. 'A car smash,' Justin explained. The doctor frowned through his spectacles. His young assistant laughed.

By night his interior world reclaimed him, as it had every night since Tessa's death. Toiling at the marquetry desk in the window bay, doggedly writing to Ham with his bruised right hand, following the travails of Markus Lorbeer as retold by Birgit, then gingerly resuming his labour of love to Ham, Justin was conscious of a dawning sense of his own completion. If Lorbeer the penitent was in the desert, purging his guilt with a diet of locusts and wild honey, Justin too was alone with his destiny. But he was resolved. And in some dark sense purified. He had never supposed that his search would have a good end. It had never occurred to him that there could be one. To take up Tessa's mission – to shoulder her banner and put on her courage – was purpose enough for him. She had witnessed a monstrous injustice and gone out to fight it. Too late, he too had witnessed it. Her fight was his.

But when he remembered the eternal night of the black hood and smelled his own vomit, when he surveyed the systematic bruising of his body, the oval imprints of yellow and blue that ran like coloured musical notes across his trunk and back and thighs, he experienced a different kind of kinship. I'm one of you. I no longer tend the roses while you murmur over your green tea. You needn't lower your voices as I approach. I'm with you at the table, saying *yes*.

On the seventh day Justin paid his bill and, almost without telling himself what he was doing, took a post-bus and a train to Basel, to that fabled valley of the upper Rhine where pharma-giants have their castles. And there, from a frescoed palace, he posted a fat envelope to Ham's old dragon in Milan.

Then Justin walked. Painfully, but walked. First up a cobbled hill to the mediaeval city with its bell towers, merchant houses, statues to free thinkers and martyrs of oppression. And when he had duly reminded himself of this inheritance, as it seemed to him, he retraced his steps to the river's edge, and from a children's playground gazed upward in near-disbelief at the ever-spreading concrete kingdom of the pharma-billionaires, at their faceless barracks ranged shoulder to shoulder against the individual enemy. Orange cranes fussed restlessly above them. White chimneys like muted minarets, some chequered at the tip, some striped or dazzle-painted as a warning to aircraft, poured their invisible gases into a brown sky. And at their feet lay whole railways, marshalling yards, lorry parks and wharfs, each protected by its very own Berlin Wall capped with razor wire and daubed with graffiti.

Drawn forward by a force he had ceased to define, Justin crossed the bridge and, as in a dream, wandered a dismal wasteland of rundown housing estates, secondhand clothes shops and hollow-eyed immigrant labourers on bicycles. And gradually, by some accident of magnetic attraction, he found himself standing in what at first appeared to be a pleasant tree-lined avenue at the far end of which stood an ecologically-friendly gateway so densely overgrown with creeper that at first you barely spotted the oak doors inside, with their polished brass bell to press, and their brass letter box for mail. It was only when Justin looked up, and further up, and then right up into the sky above his head, that he woke to the immensity of a triptych of white tower-blocks linked by flying corridors. The stonework was hospital clean, the windows were of coppered glass. And from somewhere behind each monstrous block rose a white chimney, sharp as a pencil jammed into the sky. And from each chimney the letters KVH, done in gold and mounted vertically down its length, winked at him like old friends.

How long he remained there, alone, trapped like some insect at the triptych's base, he had no notion then or later. Sometimes it seemed to him that the building's wings were closing in to crush him. Sometimes they were toppling down on him. His knees gave way and he discovered he was sitting on a bench, on some bit of beaten ground where cautious women walked their dogs. He noticed a faint but pervasive smell and was for a moment returned to the mortuary in Nairobi. How long do I have to live here, he wondered, before I stop noticing the smell? Evening must have fallen because the coppered windows lightened. He made out moving silhouettes and winking pinpoints of computer blue. Why do I sit here? he asked her as he went on watching. What am I thinking of, except you?

She was sitting beside him, but for once she had no answer ready. I am thinking about your courage, he replied for her. I am thinking, it was you and Arnold against all this, while dear old Justin worried about keeping his flower beds sandy enough to grow your yellow freesias. I am thinking I don't believe in me any more, and all I stood for. That there was a time when, like the people in this building, your Justin took pride in submitting himself to the harsher judgments of a collective will – which he happened to call *Country*, or the *Doctrine of the Reasonable Man* or, with some misgiving, the *Higher Cause*. There was a time when I believed it was expedient that one man – or woman – should die for the benefit of many. I called it sacrifice, or duty, or necessity. There was a time when I could stand outside the Foreign Office at night and stare up at its lighted windows and think: good evening, it's me your humble servant, Justin. I'm a piece of the great wise engine, and proud of it. I serve, therefore I feel. Whereas all I feel now is: it was you against the whole pack of them and, unsurprisingly, they won.

*   *   *

From Main Street of the little town Justin turned left and northwest onto Dawes Boulevard, taking the full blast of the prairie wind on his darkened face as he continued his wary examination of his surroundings. His three years as Economic Attaché in Ottawa had not been wasted. Though he had never been here in his life, everything he saw was familiar to him. Snow from Hallowe'en to Easter, he remembered. Plant after the first moon in June and harvest before the first hard frost in September. It would be several weeks yet before scared crocuses started appearing in the tufts of dead grass and on the bald prairie. Across the road from him stood the synagogue, feisty and functional, built by settlers dumped at the railroad station with their bad memories, cardboard suitcases and promises of free land.

A hundred yards on rose the Ukrainian Church and along from it the Roman Catholics, the Presbyterians, Jehovah's Witnesses and Baptists. Their car parks were got up like electrified horse-pens so that the engines of the faithful could be warmed while their owners prayed. A line of Montesquieu drifted through his head: there have never been so many civil wars as in the Kingdom of Christ.

Behind the houses of God stood the houses of Mammon, the industrial sector of the town. Beef prices must be through the floor, he reckoned. Why else would he be looking at Guy Poitier's spanking-new Delectable Porkmeat factory? And grain was faring no better by the looks of things – or what was a Sunflower Seed Pressing Company doing in the middle of a wheatfield? And that cluster of timid folk standing around the old tenements down in the station square, they must be Sioux or Cree. The towpath turned a bend and led him north through a short tunnel. He emerged in a different country of boathouses and mansions with river frontage. This is where the rich Anglos mow their lawns and wash their cars and varnish their boats and fume about the Yids, the Ukies and those darned Indians on welfare, he decided. And up there on the hill, or as near to a hill as you get round here, stood his goal, the pride of the town, the jewel of Eastern Saskatchewan, its academic Camelot, the Dawes University, an organised medley of mediaeval sandstone, colonial red brick and glass domes. Reaching a fork in the towpath, Justin scaled the short rise and by way of a nineteen-twenties Ponte Vecchio arrived at a crenellated gatehouse surmounted with a gilded coat of arms. Through its archway he was able to admire the immaculate mediaeval campus and its bronze founder, George Eamon Dawes Junior himself, mine-owner, railroad baron, lecher, land-thief, Indian-shooter and local saint resplendent on a granite plinth.

He kept walking. He had studied the handbook. The road widened and became a parade ground. The wind threw up grainy dust from the tarmac. On the far side of it stood an ivy-clad pavilion and, enfolding it, three purpose-built blocks of steel and concrete. Long neon-lit windows sliced them into layers. A signboard in green and gold – Mrs Dawes' favourite colours, thus the handbook – proclaimed in French and English the University Hospital for Clinical Research. A lesser sign said Outpatients. Justin followed it and came to a row of swing doors overhung by a curly concrete canopy and watched over by two bulky women in green topcoats. He wished them good evening and received a jolly greeting in return. Face frozen, his beaten body throbbing from the walk, hot snakes running up his thighs and back, he stole a last surreptitious glance behind him and strode up the steps.

The lobby was high and marbled and funereal. A large, awful portrait of George Eamon Dawes Junior in hunting gear reminded him of the entrance hall of the Foreign Office. A reception desk, staffed by silver-haired men and women in green tunics, ran along one wall. In a moment they're going to call me 'Mr Quayle, sir' and tell me Tessa was a fine, fine lady. He sauntered down a miniature shopping mall. The Dawes Saskatchewan bank. A post office. A Dawes news stand. McDonald's, Pizza Paradise, a Starbuck's coffee shop, a Dawes boutique selling lingerie, maternity wear and bedjackets. He reached a convergence of corridors filled with the clank and squeak of trolleys, the growl of elevators, the tinny echo of quick heels and the peep of telephones. Apprehensive visitors stood and sat about. Staff in green gowns hurried out of one doorway and back through another. None wore golden bees on his pocket.

A large noticeboard hung beside a door marked Doctors Only. With his hands linked behind his back in a manner to denote authority, Justin examined the notices. Babysitters, boats and cars, wanted and on offer. Rooms to rent. The Dawes Glee Club, the Dawes Bible Study Class, the Dawes Ethics Society, the Dawes Scottish Reel & Eightsome Group. An anaesthetist is looking for a good brown dog of medium height not less than three years old, 'must be an ace hiker'. Dawes Loan Schemes, Dawes Deferred Payment Study Schemes. A service in the Dawes Memorial Chapel to give thanks for the life of Doctor

Maria Kowalski – does anyone know what sort of music she used to like, if any? Rosters for Doctors on Call, Doctors on Vacation, Doctors on Duty. And a jolly poster announcing that this week's free pizzas for medical students arrive with compliments of Karel Vita Hudson of Vancouver – *and why not come to our KVH Sunday Brunch and Film Show at the Haybarn Disco too? Just fill in the Please Invite Me form available with your pizza and get a free ticket to a lifetime's experience!*

But of Dr Lara Emrich, until recently the leading light of the Dawes academic staff, expert on multi- and non-resistant strains of tuberculosis, sometime KVH-sponsored Dawes research professor and co-discoverer of the wonder-drug Dypraxa, there was not a word. She wasn't going on vacation, she wasn't on call. Her name wasn't included in the glossy internal telephone directory hanging by a tasselled green cord at the noticeboard's side. She was not in search of a male brown dog of middle height. The one reference to her, perhaps, was a handwritten postcard, relegated to the bottom of the noticeboard and almost out of sight, regretting that 'on the Dean's orders' the scheduled meeting of Saskatchewan Doctors for Integrity would not be taking place on Dawes University premises. A new venue would be announced a.s.a.p.

*   *   *

His body screaming blue murder from cold and exertion, Justin relents sufficiently to take a cab back to his characterless motel. He has been clever this time. Borrowing a leaf from Lesley's book he has sent his letter by way of a florist, together with a generous bunch of lover's roses.

> I am an English journalist and a friend of Birgit at Hippo. I am investigating the death of Tessa Quayle. Please could you telephone me at the Saskatchewan Man.Motel, room eighteen, after seven this evening. I suggest you use a public callbox a good distance from your home.
> Peter Atkinson

Tell her who I am later, he had reasoned. Don't scare her. Pick the time and place. Wiser. His cover was wearing thin but it was the only cover he had. He had been Atkinson at his German hotel and Atkinson when they beat him up. But they had addressed him as Mr Quayle. As Atkinson nonetheless he had flown from Zurich to Toronto, gone to earth in a brick boarding house close to the railway station and, with a surreal sense of detachment, learned from his little radio of the world-wide manhunt for Dr Arnold Bluhm, wanted in connection with the murder of Tessa Quayle. *I'm an Oswald man, Justin . . . Arnold Bluhm lost his rag and killed Tessa . . .* And it was as nobody at all that he had boarded the train to Winnipeg, waited a day, then boarded another to this little town. All the same he wasn't fooling himself. At best, he had a few days' march on them. But in a civilised country you could never tell.

*   *   *

'Peter?'

Justin woke abruptly and glanced at his watch. Nine at night. He had set a pen and notebook beside the telephone.

'This is Peter.'

'I am *Lara*.' It was a complaint.

'Hullo, Lara. Where can we meet?'

A sigh. A forlorn, terminally tired sigh to match the forlorn Slav voice. 'It is not possible.'

'Why not?'

'There is a car outside my house. Sometimes they put a van. They watch and listen all the time. To meet discreetly is not possible.'

'Where are you now?'

'In a telephone kiosk.' She made it sound as if she would never get out of it alive.

'Is anybody watching you now?'

'Nobody is visible. But it is night. Thank you for the roses.'

'I can meet you wherever suits you. At a friend's house. Out in the country somewhere, if you prefer.'

'You have a car?'

'No.'

'Why not?' It was a rebuke and a challenge.

'I don't have the right documents with me.'

'Who are you?'

'I told you. A friend of Birgit's. A British journalist. We can talk more about that when we meet.'

She had rung off. His stomach was turning and he needed the lavatory, but the bathroom contained no telephone extension. He waited till he could wait no longer and scurried to the bathroom. With his trousers round his ankles he heard the phone ringing. It rang three times but by the time he had hobbled to it, it was dead. Head in hands he sat on the edge of the bed. I'm no bloody good at this. What would the spies do? What would crafty old Donohue do? With an Ibsen heroine on the line, the same as I'm doing now and probably worse. He checked his watch again, fearing he had lost his sense of time. He took it off and set it beside his pen and notepad. Fifteen minutes. Twenty. Thirty. What the hell's happened to her? He put his watch back on, losing his temper while he tried to get the damned strap home.

'Peter?'

'Where can we meet? Anywhere you say.'

'Birgit says you are her husband.'

Oh God. Oh earth stand still. Oh Jesus.

'Birgit said that on the *telephone*?'

'She did not mention names. "He is her husband." That is all. She was discreet. Why did you not tell me you are her husband? Then I would not think you were a provocation.'

'I was going to tell you when we met.'

'I will telephone to my friend. You should not send me roses. It is exaggerated.'

'What friend? Lara, be careful what you say to her. My name's Peter Atkinson. I'm a journalist. Are you still in the phone box?'

'Yes.'

'The same one?'

'I am not observed. In winter they observe only from cars. They are lazy. No car is visible.'

'Have you got enough coins?'

'I have a card.'

'Use coins. Don't use a card. Did you use a card when you called Birgit?'

'It is not important.'

It was half past ten before she called again. 'My friend is assisting at an operation,' she explained without apology. 'The operation is complicated. I have another friend. She is willing. If you are afraid, take a taxi to Eaton's and walk the remaining distance.'

'I'm not afraid. I'm prudent.'

For God's sake, he thought, writing down the address. We haven't met, I've sent her two dozen exaggerated roses and we're having a lover's tiff.

*   *   *

There were two ways to leave his motel: by the front door and one step down to the car park, or by the back door to the corridor that led, by a warren of other corridors, to reception. Switching out the lights in his room, Justin peered through the window at the car park. Under a full moon each parked car wore a silver halo of frost. Of the twenty-odd in the car park, only one was occupied. A woman sat in the driving seat. Her front passenger was a man. They were arguing. About roses? Or about the god Profit? The woman gesticulated, the man shook his head. The man got out and barked a final word at her, a curse, slammed the door, got into another car and drove away. The woman remained where she was. She lifted her hands in despair and drove them onto the top of the steering wheel, knuckles upward. She bowed her head into her hands and wept, shoulders heaving. Overcoming an absurd desire to comfort her, Justin hastened to the reception desk and ordered a cab.

*   *   *

The house was one of a terrace of new white townhouses built in a Victorian street. Each house was set at an angle, like a line of ships' prows nosing their way into an old harbour. Each had a basement with its own stairway, and a front door set above street level, and stone steps leading up to it, and iron railings, and brass horseshoes for door knockers that didn't knock. Watched by a fat grey cat that had made itself at home between the curtains and the window of number seven, Justin climbed the steps of number six and pressed the bell. He was carrying everything he possessed: one travel bag, money and, despite Lesley's injunction not to do so, both his passports. He had paid the motel in advance. If he returned to it, he would do so of his own free will and not because he needed to. It was ten o'clock of a frosted, freezing, ice-clear night. Cars were parked nose to tail along the kerb, pavements empty. The door was opened by a tall woman in silhouette.

'You are Peter,' she told him accusingly.

'Are you Lara?'

'Naturally.'

She closed the door after him.

'Were you followed here?' he asked her.

'It is possible. Were you?'

They faced each other under the light. Birgit was right: Lara Emrich was beautiful. Beautiful in the haughty intelligence of her stare. In its chill, scientific detachment that, already at first scenting, caused him inwardly to recoil. In the way she shoved her greying hair aside with the back of her wrist; then, with her elbow still raised and her wrist at her brow, continued critically to survey him with an arrogant yet inconsolable stare. She wore black. Black slacks, a long black smock, no make-up. The voice, heard close, even gloomier than on the telephone.

'I am very sorry for you,' she said. 'It is terrible. You are sad.'

'Thank you.'

'She was murdered by Dypraxa.'

'So I believe. Indirectly, but yes.'

'Many people have been murdered by Dypraxa.'

'But not all of them were betrayed by Markus Lorbeer.'

From upstairs came a roar of televised applause.

'Amy is my friend,' she said, as if friendship were an affliction. 'Today she is a registrar at Dawes Hospital. But unfortunately she signed a petition favouring my reinstatement and is a founding member of Saskatchewan Doctors for Integrity. Therefore they will be looking for an excuse to fire her.'

He was going to ask her whether Amy knew him as Quayle or Atkinson when a strong-voiced woman bawled down at them and a pair of furry slippers appeared on the top stair.

'Bring him on up here, Lara. Man needs a drink.'

Amy was middle-aged and fat, one of those serious women who have decided to play themselves as comedy. She wore a crimson silk kimono and pirate's earrings. Her slippers had glass eyes. But her own eyes were ringed with shadow, and there were pain-lines at the corners of her mouth.

'Men who killed your wife should be hanged,' she said. 'Scotch, Bourbon or wine? This is Ralph.'

It was a large attic room, lined in pine and roof-high. At the far end stood a bar. A huge television set was playing ice hockey. Ralph was a wispy-haired old man in a dressing gown. He sat in an imitation leather armchair with a matching stool to put his slippered feet on. Hearing his name, he flapped a liver-spotted hand in the air but kept his eyes on the game.

'Welcome to Saskatchewan. Grab yourself a drink,' he called, in a mid-European accent.

'Who's winning?' Justin asked, to be friendly.

'Canucks.'

'Ralph's a lawyer,' Amy said. 'Aren't you, honey?'

'Not much of anything now. Damned Parkinson's dragging me into the grave. That academic body behaved like a bunch of horses' arses. That what you came about?'

'Pretty much.'

'Stifle free speech, interpose yourself between doctor and patient, it's time educated men and women had some balls to speak out for truth instead of cringing in the shit-house like a bunch of craven cowards.'

'It is indeed,' said Justin politely, accepting a glass of white wine from Amy.

'Karel Vita's the piper, Dawes dances to their tune. Twenty-five million dollars start-up money they give for a new biotech building, fifty more promised. That's not peanuts, even for a shower of rich no-brains like Karel Vita. And if everybody keeps their nose clean, plenty more to come. How the hell d'you resist pressure like that?'

'You *try*,' Amy said. 'If you don't try, you're fucked.'

'Fucked if you try, fucked if you don't. Speak out, they take away your salary, fire you and run you out of town. Free speech comes mighty costly in this town, Mr Quayle – more than most of us can afford. What's your other name?'

'Justin.'

'This is a one-crop city, Justin, when it comes to free speech. Everything's fine and dandy, long as some crazy Russian bitch doesn't take it into her head to publish harebrained articles in the medical press badmouthing a clever little pill she's invented that happens to be worth a couple of billion a year to the House of Karel Vita, whom Allah preserve. Where you planning to put them, Amy?'

'In the den.'

'Mind you switch the phones over so's they don't get disturbed. Amy's the technical one round here, Justin. I'm the old fart. Anything you want, have Lara fix it for you. Knows the house better than we do, which is a waste, seeing as we're gonna be thrown out of it in a couple of months.'

He went back to his victorious Canucks.

*   *   *

She no longer sees him, though she has put on heavy spectacles that should have been a man's. The Russian in her has brought a 'perhaps' bag and it lies mouth-open at her feet, stuffed with

374

papers that she knows by heart: lawyers' letters threatening her, faculty letters dismissing her, a copy of her unpublishable article, and finally her own lawyer's letters, but not too many of them because, as she explains, she has no money and besides, her lawyer is more comfortable defending the rights of the Sioux than doing battle with the limitless legal resources of Messrs Karel Vita Hudson of Vancouver. They sit like chess players without a board, square to each other, knees almost touching. A memory of oriental postings tells Justin not to point his feet at her, so he sits askew, at some discomfort to his battered body. For a while now she has talked into the shadows past his shoulder and he has barely interrupted her. Her self-absorption is absolute, her voice by turn despondent and didactic. She lives only with the monstrosity of her case and its hopeless insolubility. Everything is a reference to it. Sometimes – quite often, he suspects – she forgets him entirely. Or he is something else for her – a hesitant faculty meeting, a timid convocation of university colleagues, a vacillating professor, an inadequate lawyer. It is only when he speaks Lorbeer's name that she wakes to him and frowns – then offers some mystical generality that is a palpable evasion: Markus is too romantic, he is so weak, all men do bad things, women also. And no, she does not know where to find him:

'He is hiding somewhere. He is erratic, each morning a different direction,' she explains with unrelenting melancholy.

'If he says the desert, is it a real desert?'

'It will be a place of great inconvenience. That also is typical.'

To plead her cause she has absorbed phrases that he would not have credited her with: 'I will fast-forward here . . . KVH are taking no prisoners.' She even speaks of 'my patients on death row'. And when she presses a lawyer's letter on him, she quotes from it while he reads it, lest he miss the most offensive parts:

You are again reminded that under the confidentiality clause in your contract you are expressly forbidden to impart this *mis*information to

375

your patients ... You are formally warned against any further dissemination, verbally or by any other means, of these inaccurate and malicious opinions based on the false interpretation of data obtained while you were under contract to Messrs Karel Vita Hudson ...

This is followed by the superbly arrogant non sequitur that 'our clients deny absolutely that at any time did they attempt in any way to suppress or influence legitimate scientific debate ...'

'But why did you *sign* the wretched contract in the first place?' Justin cuts in roughly.

Pleased by his animus she gives a mirthless laugh. 'Because I *trusted* them. I was a *fool.*'

'You're anything but a fool, Lara! You're a highly intelligent woman, for God's sake,' Justin exclaims.

Insulted, she lapses into a brooding silence.

*   *   *

The first couple of years after Karel Vita acquired the Emrich–Kovacs molecule through the agency of Markus Lorbeer, she tells him, were a golden age. Initial short-term tests were excellent, the statistics made them better, the Emrich–Kovacs partnership was the talk of the scientific community. KVH provided dedicated research laboratories, a team of technicians, clinical trials all over the Third World, first-class travel, glamorous hotels, respect and money galore.

'For frivolous Kovacs, it was her dream come true. She will drive Rolls-Royces, she will win Nobel prizes, she will be famous and rich, she will have many, many lovers. And for serious Lara, the clinical trials will be scientific, they will be responsible. They will test the drug in a wide range of ethnic and social communities that are vulnerable to the disease. Many lives will be improved, others will be saved. That will be very satisfactory.'

'And for Lorbeer?'

An irritable glance, a grimace of disapproval.

'Markus wishes to be a rich saint. He is for Rolls-Royces, also for saved lives.'

'For God and Profit, then,' Justin suggests lightly, but her only response is another scowl.

'After two years I was making an unfortunate discovery. The KVH trials were bullshit. They had not been scientifically written. They were designed only to get the drug onto the market as soon as possible. Certain side-effects were deliberately excluded. If side-effects were identified, the trial was immediately rewritten so that they did not reappear.'

'What *were* the side-effects?'

Her lecture room voice again, mordant and arrogant. 'At the time of the unscientific trials, few side-effects were observed. This was due also to the excessive enthusiasm of Kovacs and Lorbeer, and the determination of clinics and medical centres in Third World countries to make the trials look good. Also the trials were being favourably reported in important medical journals by distinguished opinion-leaders who did not declare their profitable connections with KVH. In reality such articles were written in Vancouver or Basel and only signed by the distinguished opinion-leaders. It was remarked that the drug did not suit an insignificant proportion of women of childbearing age. Some had blurred vision. There were some deaths, but an unscientific manipulation of dates ensured that they were not included in the period under review.'

'Did nobody complain?'

The question angers her. 'Who shall complain? Third World doctors and medical workers who are making money from the trials? The distributor who is making money from marketing the drug and does not wish to lose the profits from the whole range of KVH drugs – maybe lose their entire business?'

'How about the patients?'

Her opinion of him has reached rock bottom. 'Most of the patients are in undemocratic countries with very corrupt systems. Theoretically they gave their informed consent to the treatment. That is to say, their signatures are on the consent forms even if they cannot read what they have signed. They are not allowed by law to be paid, but they are generously recompensed for their travel and loss of earnings and they have free food, which they like very much. Also they are afraid.'

'Of the pharmas?'

'Of everybody. If they complain they are threatened. They are told their children will receive no more medicines from America and their men will go to prison.'

'But *you* complained.'

'No. I did not complain. I protested. Vigorously. When I discovered that Dypraxa was being promoted as a safe drug and not as a drug on trial, I gave a lecture at a scientific meeting of the university at which I described accurately the unethical position of KVH. This was not popular. Dypraxa is a good drug. That is not the issue. The issue is threefold.' Three slender fingers have already gone up. 'Issue one: the side-effects are being deliberately concealed in the interest of profit. Issue two: the world's poorest communities are used as guinea pigs by the world's richest. Issue three: legitimate scientific debate of these issues is stifled by corporate intimidation.'

The fingers are withdrawn while with her other hand she delves in her bag and unearths a glossy blue leaflet with the banner headline GOOD NEWS FROM KVH.

DYPRAXA is a highly effective, safe, economic substitute for the hitherto accepted treatments of tuberculosis. It has proved itself to be of outstanding advantage to emerging nations.

She takes back the leaflet and replaces it with a much-thumbed solicitor's letter. One paragraph is highlighted.

The study of Dypraxa was designed and implemented in an entirely ethical manner over a number of years with the informed consent of all patients. KVH does not distinguish in its trials between rich and poor countries. It is solely concerned to select conditions appropriate to the project in hand. KVH are rightly praised for their high quality of care.

'Where is Kovacs in this?'

'Kovacs is totally on the side of the corporation. She is without integrity. It is with the assistance of Kovacs that much of the clinical data is distorted or suppressed.'

'And Lorbeer?'

'Markus is divided. This is normal to him. In his self-perception he has become chief of all Africa for Dypraxa. But he is also frightened and ashamed. Therefore he confesses.'

'Employed by ThreeBees or KVH?'

'If it is Markus, maybe both. He is complicated.'

'So how on earth does KVH come to set you up at Dawes?'

'Because I was a fool,' Lara repeats proudly, putting to rest his earlier assertion to the contrary. 'Why would I accept to sign unless I was a fool? KVH were very polite, very charming, very understanding, very clever. I was in Basel when two young men came from Vancouver to see me. I was flattered. Like you, they sent me roses. I told them the trials were shit. They agreed. I told them they should not be selling Dypraxa as a safe drug. They agreed. I told them that many side-effects had never been properly assessed. They admired me for my courage. One of them was a Russian from Novgorod. "Come to lunch, Lara. Let's talk this thing through." Then they told me they would like to bring me to Dawes to design my own trial of Dypraxa. They were reasonable, unlike their superiors. They accepted that we had not made enough correct tests. Now at Dawes we would make them. It was my drug. I was proud of it, they also. The university was proud. We made a harmonious arrangement. Dawes would welcome me, KVH would pay for me. Dawes is ideally located for such trials. We have native Indians from the reservations who are susceptible to old tuberculosis. We have multi-resistant cases from the hippy community in Vancouver. For Dypraxa, this is a perfect combination. It was on the basis of this arrangement that I signed the contract and accepted the confidentiality clause. I was a fool,' she repeated, with the sniff that says 'case proven'.

'And KVH has offices in Vancouver.'

'*Big* offices. Their third biggest facility in the world after Basel and Seattle. So they could watch me. Which was the object. To put a muzzle on me and to control me. I signed the stupid contract and went to work with a good heart. Last year I completed my study. It was extremely negative. I felt it necessary to inform my patients of my opinion concerning the potential side-effects of Dypraxa. As a doctor, I have a sacred duty. I also concluded that the world medical community must be informed by means of publication in an important journal. Such journals do not like to print negative opinions. I knew this. I knew also that the journal would invite three distinguished scientists to comment on my findings. What the journal did not know was that the distinguished scientists had just signed rich contracts with KVH Seattle to research biotechnical cures for other diseases. They immediately informed Seattle of my intentions, who informed Basel and Vancouver.'

She hands him a folded sheet of white paper. He opens it and has a chilling sense of recognition.

COMMUNIST WHORE. GET YOUR SHITCOVERED HANDS OFF OUR UNIVERSITY. GO BACK TO YOUR BOLSHEVIK PIGSTY. STOP POISONING DECENT PEOPLE'S LIVES WITH YOUR CORRUPT THEORIES.

Large electronic capitals. No spelling mistakes. The familiar use of compounds. Join the club, he thinks.

'It is arranged that Dawes University will participate in the worldwide profits of Dypraxa,' she continues, carelessly snatching the letter back from him. 'Staff who are loyal to the hospital will receive preferential shares. Those who are not loyal receive such anonymous letters. It is more important to be loyal to the hospital than loyal to the patients. It is most important to be loyal to KVH.'

'Halliday wrote it,' Amy says, sweeping into the room with a tray of coffee and biscuits. 'Halliday's the pre-eminent bull-dyke of the Dawes medical mafia. Everybody in the faculty has to kiss her ass or die. Except me and Lara and a couple of other idiots.'

'How d'you know she wrote it?' Justin asks.

'DNA-d the cow. Picked the stamp off the envelope, DNA-d her spit. She likes to work out in the hospital gym. Me and Lara stole a hair from her pink Bambi hairbrush and made the match.'

'Did anyone confront her?'

'Sure. The whole board. Cow confessed. Excess of zeal in execution of her duties, which consist solely of protecting the university's best interests. Humbly apologised, pleaded emotional stress, which is her word for salivating sexual envy. Case dismissed, cow congratulated. Meanwhile they trashed Lara. I'm next.'

'Emrich is a Communist,' Lara explains, relishing the irony. 'She is Russian, she grew up in Petersburg when it was Leningrad, she attended Soviet colleges, therefore she is a Communist and anti-corporate. It is convenient.'

'Emrich didn't invent Dypraxa either, did you, honey?' Amy reminds her.

'It was Kovacs,' Lara agrees bitterly. 'Kovacs was the complete genius. I was her promiscuous laboratory assistant. Lorbeer was my lover, therefore he claimed the glory for me.'

'Which is why they're not paying you any more money, OK, honey?'

'No. It is a different reason. I have broken the confidentiality clause, therefore I have broken my contract. It is logical.'

'Lara's a prostitute too, aren't you, honey? Screwed the pretty boys they sent her from Vancouver, except she didn't. Nobody at Dawes fucks. And we're all Christians except the Jews.'

'Since the drug is killing patients I would wish very much that I had not invented it,' says Lara softly, choosing not to hear Amy's parting sally.

'When did you last see Lorbeer?' Justin asks when they are alone again.

*   *   *

381

Her tone still guarded, but softer.

'He was in Africa,' she said.

'When?'

'One year ago.'

'Less than a year,' Justin corrected her. 'My wife spoke to him in the Uhuru Hospital six months ago. His apologia, or whatever he calls it, was sent from Nairobi several days ago. Where is he now?'

Being corrected was not what Lara Emrich liked. 'You asked me when I last saw him,' she retorted, bridling. 'It was one year ago. In Africa.'

'Where in Africa?'

'In Kenya. He sent for me. The accumulation of evidence had become unbearable to him. "Lara, I need you. It is essential and very urgent. Tell nobody. I will pay. Come." I was affected by his appeal. I told Dawes my mother was ill and flew to Nairobi. I arrived on a Friday. Markus met me at Nairobi airport. Already in the car he asked me: "Lara, is it possible that our drug is increasing pressure on the brain, crushing the optic nerve?" I reminded him that anything was possible since basic scientific data had not been assembled, although we were attempting to remedy this. He drove me to a village and showed me a woman who could not stand up. Her headaches were terrible. She was dying. He drove me to another village where a woman could not focus her eyes. When she went out of her hut the world went dark. He related other cases to me. The health workers were reluctant to speak frankly to us. They too were afraid. ThreeBees punishes all criticism, Markus says. He also was afraid. Afraid of ThreeBees, afraid of KVH, afraid for the sick women, afraid of God. "What shall I do, Lara, what shall I do?" He has spoken to Kovacs, who is in Basel. She says he is a fool to panic. These are not the side-effects of Dypraxa, she says, they are the effects of a bad combination with another drug. This is typical Kovacs, who has married a rich Serbian crook and spends more time at the opera than in the laboratory.'

'So what should he do?'

'I told him what was the truth. What he is observing in Africa is what I am observing in the Dawes Hospital in Saskatchewan. "Markus, these are the same side-effects that I am documenting in my report to Vancouver, based on objective clinical trials of six hundred cases." Still he cries to me, "What must I do, Lara, what must I do?" "Markus," I tell him. "You must be courageous, you must do unilaterally what the corporations refuse to do collectively, you must withdraw the drug from the market until it has been exhaustively tested." He wept. It was our last night together as lovers. I also wept.'

*   *   *

Some savage instinct now took hold of Justin, a root resentment he could not define. Did he grudge this woman her survival? Did he resent it that she had slept with Tessa's self-confessed betrayer and even now spoke tenderly about him? Was he offended that she could sit before him, beautiful and alive and self-obsessed, while Tessa lay dead beside their son? Was he insulted that Lara displayed so little concern for Tessa, and so much for herself?

'Did Lorbeer ever mention Tessa to you?'

'Not at the time of my visit.'

'So when?'

'He wrote to me that there was a woman, the wife of a British official, who was putting pressure on ThreeBees regarding Dypraxa, writing letters and making unwelcome visits. This woman was supported by a doctor from one of the aid agencies. He did not mention the doctor's name.'

'When did he write this?'

'On my birthday. Markus remembers always my birthday. He congratulated me on my birthday and told me of a British woman and her lover the African doctor.'

'Did he suggest what should be done with them?'

'He feared for her. He said she was beautiful and very tragic. I think he was attracted to her.'

Justin was assailed by the extraordinary notion that Lara was jealous of Tessa.

'And the doctor?'

'Markus admires all doctors.'

'Where did he write from?'

'Cape Town. He was examining the ThreeBees operation in South Africa, privately making comparisons with his experiences in Kenya. He was respectful of your wife. Courage does not come easily to Markus. It must be learned.'

'Did he say where he'd met her?'

'At the hospital in Nairobi. She had challenged him. He was embarrassed.'

'Why?'

'He was obliged to ignore her. Markus believes that if he ignores somebody he will make them unhappy, specially if they are a woman.'

'Nevertheless he managed to betray her.'

'Markus is not always practical. He is an artist. If he says he betrayed her, that can also be figurative.'

'Did you reply to his letter?'

'Always.'

'Where to?'

'It was a box number in Nairobi.'

'Did he mention a woman called Wanza? She shared a ward with my wife in the Uhuru Hospital. She died of Dypraxa.'

'The case is not known to me.'

'I'm not surprised. All traces of her were removed.'

'It is predictable. Markus told me of such things.'

'When Lorbeer visited my wife's ward, he was accompanied by Kovacs. What was Kovacs doing in Nairobi?'

'Markus wanted me to come to Nairobi a second time but my relationship with KVH and the hospital was by this time bad. They had heard about my earlier visit and were already threatening to have me expelled from the university because I lied about my mother. Therefore Markus telephoned to Kovacs in Basel and persuaded her to come to Nairobi as my substitute and observe the situation with him. He was hoping she would spare him the difficult decision and herself advise ThreeBees to withdraw the drug. KVH in Basel was at first reluctant to allow Kovacs to go to Nairobi, then they consented on condition that the visit remained a secret.'

'Even from ThreeBees?'

'From ThreeBees that would not have been possible. ThreeBees were too close to the situation and Markus was advising them. Kovacs visited Nairobi for four days in great secrecy, then returned to her Serbian crook in Basel for more opera.'

'Did she file a report?'

'It was a contemptible report. I was educated as a scientist. This was not science. This was polemic.'

'Lara.'

'What is it?' She was staring combatively at him.

'Birgit read you Lorbeer's letter over the telephone. His apologia. His confession. His whatever he calls it.'

'So?'

'What did it mean to you – the letter?'

'That Markus cannot be redeemed.'

'From what?'

'He is a weak man who looks for strength in the wrong places. Unfortunately it is the weak who destroy the strong. Maybe he did something very bad. Sometimes he is too much in love with his own sins.'

'If you had to find him, where would you look for him?'

'I do not have to find him.' He waited. 'I have only a postbox number in Nairobi.'

'May I have it?'

Her depression had reached new depths. 'I will write it for you.' She wrote on a pad, tore off the sheet and gave it him. 'If I was looking for him, I would look among those that he has injured,' she said.

'In the desert.'

'Maybe it is figurative.' The aggressive edge had left her voice, as it had left Justin's. 'Markus is a child,' she explained simply. 'He acts from impulse and reacts to the consequences.' She actually smiled, and her smile too was beautiful. 'Often he is very surprised.'

'Who provides the impulse?'

'Once it was me.'

He stood up too quickly, meaning to fold the papers she had given him into his pocket. His head swam, he felt nauseous. He thrust a hand to the wall to steady himself, only to discover that the professional doctor had taken his arm.

'What's the matter?' she said sharply, and kept holding him while she sat him down again.

'I just get giddy now and then.'

'Why? You have high blood pressure? You should not wear a tie. Undo your collar. You are ridiculous.'

She was holding her hand across his brow. He felt weak as an invalid and desperately tired. She left him and returned with a glass of water. He drank some, handed her the glass. Her gestures were assured but tender. He felt her gaze on him.

'You have a fever,' she said accusingly.

'Maybe.'

'Not maybe. You have a fever. I will drive you to your hotel.'

It was the moment that the tiresome instructor had warned him against on his security course, the moment when you are too bored, too lazy or simply too tired to care; when all you can think of is getting back to your lousy motel, going to sleep and, in the morning when your head has cleared, making up a fat parcel for Ham's long-suffering aunt in Milan containing everything that Dr Lara Emrich has told you, including a copy of her unpublished paper on the harmful side-effects of the drug Dypraxa, such as blurred vision, bleeding, blindness and death, also a note of Markus Lorbeer's postbox number in Nairobi, and another describing what you intend should be your next move, in case you are impeded from taking it by forces outside your control. It is a moment of conscious, culpable, wilful lapse, when the presence of a beautiful woman, another pariah like himself, standing at his shoulder and feeling his pulse with her kind fingers can be no excuse for failing to observe the basic principles of operational security.

'You shouldn't be seen with me,' he objects lamely. 'They know I'm around. I'll only make things worse for you.'

'There *is* no worse,' she retorts. 'My negative situation is complete.'

'Where's your car?'

'It is five minutes. Can you walk?'

It is a moment also when Justin in his state of physical exhaustion gratefully reverts to the excuses of good manners and ancient chivalry that were bred in him from his Etonian cradle. A single woman should be accompanied to her coach at night, should not be exposed to vagabonds, footpads and highwaymen. He stands. She puts a hand under his elbow and keeps it there as they tiptoe together across the drawing room to the stairs.

' 'Night, children,' Amy calls, through a closed door. 'Have fun now.'

'You've been very kind,' Justin replies.

CHAPTER NINETEEN

Descending Amy's staircase to the front door, Lara goes ahead of Justin, carrying her Russian bag in one hand and holding the banister with the other while she watches him over her shoulder. In the hall she unhooks his coat for him and helps him into it. She puts on her own coat and an Anna Karenina fur hat and makes to shoulder his travel bag, but Etonian chivalry forbids this, so she watches him with her brown, unblinking gaze, Tessa's gaze without the scamp in it, while he adjusts the strap over his own shoulder and, as a tight-lipped Englishman, suppresses any sign of pain. Sir Justin holds open the door for her and whispers his surprise as the ice-cold air slices viciously into him, ignoring his quilted coat and fur boots. On the pavement Dr Lara takes his left forearm in her left hand and reaches her right arm across his back to steady him but this time not even the case-hardened Etonian can suppress an exclamation of pain as the chorus of nerves in his back bursts into song. She says nothing, but their eyes meet naturally as he swings his head defensively away from the direction of the pain. Her gaze under the Anna Karenina fur hat is alarmingly reminiscent of other eyes. The hand that is no longer across his back has joined the hand that enfolds his left forearm. She has slowed her pace to match his. Hip to hip, they are performing a stately march along the icy pavement when she stops dead and, still clutching his arm, stares across the road.

'What is it?'

'It is nothing. It is predictable.'

They are in the town square. A small grey car of indeterminate make stands alone beneath an orange lamp. It is very dirty despite the frost. It has a wire coat-hanger for a radio aerial. Stared at this way, it has something ominous and unprotected about it. It is a car waiting to explode.

'Is it yours?' Justin asks.

'Yes. But it is no good.'

The great spy belatedly observes what Lara has already spotted. The front offside tyre is flat.

'Don't worry. We'll change the wheel,' Justin says boldly, forgetting for a ludicrous moment the ferocious cold, his bruised body, the late hour and any last considerations of operational security.

'It will not be sufficient,' she replies with appropriate gloom.

'Of course it will. We'll turn the engine on. You can sit in the car and keep warm. You've got a spare wheel and a jack, haven't you?'

But by now they have reached the far pavement and he has seen what she has anticipated: the nearside tyre is also flat. Seized by a need for action, he attempts to break free of her but she clings onto him and he understands that it is not the cold that is causing her to shiver.

'Does this happen a lot?' he asks.

'Frequently.'

'Do you call a garage?'

'At night they will not come. I find a taxi home. In the morning when I return, I have a parking ticket. Maybe also a ticket regarding the unsafe condition of the car. Sometimes they are towing it away and I must collect it from an inconvenient location. Sometimes there is no taxi but tonight we are fortunate.'

He follows her gaze and sees to his surprise a taxi parked in a far corner of the square with its interior lights burning and its engine running and one figure huddled at the wheel. Still holding his arm, she urges him forward. He goes along with her for a few yards, then stops, his internal alarm bells sounding.

'Do cabs normally sit around town as late as this?'

'It is not important.'

'Yes, it is, actually. Very.'

Releasing himself from her gaze he becomes aware of a second cab pulling up behind the first. Lara sees it too.

'You are being ridiculous. Look. Now we have two cabs. We can take one each. Maybe we take only one. Then I shall first accompany you to your hotel. We shall see. It is unimportant.'

And forgetting his condition, or simply losing patience with him, she tugs again at his arm, with the result that he stumbles and breaks free of her and stands in front of her, blocking her way.

'No,' he says.

No meaning, I refuse. Meaning, I have seen the unlogic of this situation. If I was rash before, I shall not be rash now, and nor will you. The coincidences are too many. We are in the empty square of a godforsaken town in the middle of the tundra on a freezing March night when even the town's one horse is asleep. Your car has been deliberately disabled. One taxi stands conveniently available, a second has now joined it. Who else are the taxis waiting for but us? Is it not reasonable to assume that the people who disabled your car are the same people who would like us to ride in theirs?

But Lara is not accessible to this scientific argument. Waving her arm at the nearer driver, she is striding forward to claim him. Justin grabs her by the other arm, stops her in mid-stride and hauls her back. The action infuriates her as much as it hurts him. She has had enough of being pushed around.

'Leave me alone. Get away from me! Give that back!'

He has seized her Russian bag. The first cab is pulling out from the kerb. The second is pulling out behind it. Speculatively? In support? In a civilised country you can never tell.

'Get back to the car,' he orders her.

'What car? It is useless. You are mad.'

She is pulling at her Russian bag but he is rummaging in it, shoving aside her papers, tissues and whatever else obstructs his search. 'Give me the car keys, Lara, *please*!'

He has found her purse inside the bag and opened it. He has the keys in his hand – a whole bunch of them, enough to get into Fort Knox. Why the hell does a single woman in disgrace need so many keys? He is sidling towards her car, sorting through her keys, shouting 'Which is it? Which is it?', drawing her with him, keeping the shopping bag away from her, dragging her into the lamplight where she can pick out the car key for him – which she does, vituperatively, vindictively, holding it up to him and jeering at him.

'Now you have the key to a car with flat tyres! Do you feel better now? Do you feel a big man?'

Is this how she talked to Lorbeer?

The cabs are edging round the square towards them, nose to tail. Their posture is inquisitive, not yet aggressive. But there is stealth to them. There is evil purpose, Justin is convinced: an air of menace and premeditation.

'Is it central locking?' he is yelling. 'Does the key open all the doors at once?'

She doesn't know or she's too furious to answer. He is on one knee, her shopping bag wedged under his arm, trying to get the key into the passenger door. He is rubbing away the ice with his fingertips and his skin is sticking to the metalwork and his muscles are howling as loud as the voices in his head. She is tugging at the Russian shopping bag and yelling at him. The car door opens and he seizes hold of her.

'Lara. For the love of Heaven. Will you *please* be so kind as to shut up and get *into* the car *now*!'

The use of courteous emphasis is well judged. She stares at him in disbelief. He has her bag in his hand. He hurls it into the car. She darts after it like a dog after a ball, lands on the passenger seat as he slams the door. Justin steps back into the road and heads round the car. As he does so the second cab overtakes the first and accelerates at him, sending him leaping for the kerb. The cab's front wing snaps vainly at his flying coat as it passes him. Lara pushes open the driver's door from inside. Both cabs come to a halt in the middle of the road forty yards behind them. Justin turns the key in the ignition. The windscreen wipers are thick with frost but the rear window is fairly clear. The engine coughs like an old donkey. At this time of night? it is saying. In *this* temperature? *Me?* He turns the key again.

'Have you got petrol in this thing?'

In the driving mirror he makes out two men climbing out of each cab. The second pair must have been hiding in the back below the window-line. One man carries a baseball bat, another an object that Justin concludes successively to be a bottle, a hand grenade or a life-preserver. All four men are walking deliberately towards the car. By God's will the engine catches. Justin revs and releases the handbrake. But the car is automatic and Justin for the life of him can't remember how automatic cars work. So having put the car into drive he restrains it with the footbrake until sanity prevails. The car finally lurches forward, shaking and protesting. The steering wheel is as stiff as iron in his grasp. In the mirror, the men break into a trot. Justin cautiously accelerates, the front wheels shriek and bump but somehow the car is going along despite itself, it is actually gathering speed to the alarm of their pursuers who no longer trot but run. They are dressed for the occasion, Justin notices, in bulky tracksuits and soft boots. One wears a sailor's woollen hat with a bobble on it, and he's the one with the baseball bat. The rest wear fur hats. Justin glances at Lara. She has one hand to her face, the fingers crammed between her teeth. Her other hand clutches the console in front of her. Her eyes have closed and she is whispering, perhaps praying, a thing that Justin finds puzzling since until now he has regarded her as godless, in contrast to her lover Lorbeer. They are leaving the little square and bumping and farting down a poorly lit street of terraced cottages fallen on hard times.

'Where's the brightest part of town? The most public?' he asks her.

Lara shakes her head.

'Where's the station?'

'It is too far. I have no money.'

She seems to think they are going to escape together. Smoke or steam is rising from the bonnet and a frightful smell of burning rubber reminds him of student riots in Nairobi, but he continues to accelerate while in the mirror he watches the men running and he muses again on what fools they are and how badly they do these things, it must be their training. And how a better-commanded team would never have left the cars behind. And how the best thing they could do if they had any sense would be turn round *now* – or maybe just two of them turn round – and run like hell back to their cars, but they show no sign of doing this, perhaps because they are coming closer and everything depends on who gives up first, this car or those men. A sign in French and English warns him of an approaching crossroads. As a Sunday philologist, he finds himself comparing the two languages.

'Where's the hospital?' he asks her.

She takes her fingers out of her mouth. 'Doctor Lara Emrich is not permitted to enter the precincts of the hospital,' she intones.

He laughs for her, determined to buck her up. 'Oh well, we can't go there then, can we? Not if it's forbidden. Come on. Where is it?'

'To the left.'

'How far?'

'In normal conditions it will be very little time.'

'How little?'

'Five minutes. If there is no traffic, less.'

There is no traffic, but there is steam or smoke belching out of the bonnet, the road surface is icy cobble, the speedometer is reading an optimistic fifteen miles an hour at most, the men in the mirror show no sign of tiring, there is no sound except

393

for the lumpy whine of spinning wheel-rims like a thousand fingernails scraping on blackboards. Suddenly to Justin's amazement the road ahead becomes a frosted parade ground. He sees the crenellated gatehouse and the Dawes heraldic crest garishly floodlit ahead of him, and to his left the ivy-covered pavilion and its three satellite blocks of steel and glass looming like icebergs above it. He drags the steering wheel to the left and increases his pressure on the accelerator, to no avail. The speedometer registers nought miles an hour, but that's ridiculous because they are still moving, if only just.

'Who do you know?' he shouts at her.

She must have been asking herself the same question. 'Phil.'

'Who's Phil?'

'A Russian. An ambulance driver. Now he is too old.'

She reaches into the back of the car for her bag, takes out a packet of cigarettes – not Sportsmans – lights one and hands it to him, but he ignores it.

'The men have gone,' she says, keeping the cigarette for herself.

Like a faithful mount that has run its last, the car dies under them. The front axle collapses, acrid black smoke oozes from the bonnet, a frightful grinding from beneath them announces that the car has found its final resting-place at the centre of the parade ground. Watched by a pair of drug-eyed Cree in kapok coats, Justin and Lara clamber out of the car.

*   *   *

Phil's business premises consisted of a white wooden box beside an ambulance park. It contained a stool, a telephone, a rotating red light, a coffee-stained electric heater and a calendar that was permanently opened at December, a month when a lightly dressed female Santa Claus offers her naked backside to grateful male carol singers. Phil sat on the stool, talking into the telephone, wearing a leather cap with ear-flaps. His face was leather too, cracked and lined and polished, then dusted over with silver stubble. When he heard Lara's voice speaking Russian he did what old prisoners do: kept his head still and his hooded eyes looking straight ahead of him while he waited to have it proved to him that he was being addressed. Only when he was sure did he face her, and become what Russian men of his age become in the presence of beautiful younger women: a little mystical, a little shy, a little abrupt. Phil and Lara spoke for what seemed to Justin an unnecessary eternity, she in the doorway with Justin lurking like an unacknowledged lover in her shadow, and Phil from his stool, his gnarled hands knotted on his lap. They asked – as Justin supposed – after each other's families, and how Uncle this or Cousin that was doing, until finally Lara stood back to let the old man push past her, which he did by holding her quite gratuitously by the waist before trotting down the ramp of an underground car park.

'Does he know you're banned?' Justin asked.

'It is not important.'

'Where's he gone?'

No answer but none was needed. A shiny new ambulance was pulling up beside them, and Phil in his leather cap was at the wheel.

* * *

Her house was new and rich, part of a luxury lakeside development built to accommodate the favourite sons and daughters of Messrs Karel Vita Hudson of Basel, Vancouver and Seattle. She poured him a whisky and for herself a vodka, she showed him the jacuzzi, and demonstrated the sound system and the eye-level multi-functional super-microwave oven and, with the same wry detachment, indicated the point along her fence where the *Organy* parked when they came to watch over her, which happened most days a week, she said, usually from around eight in the morning, depending on the weather, until nightfall unless there was an important hockey match in which case they left earlier. She showed him the absurd night sky in her bedroom, the cupola of white plaster that was pierced with tiny lights to imitate the stars, and the dimmer that turned them up or down to the whim of the occupants of the great round bed beneath it. And there was a moment that they both watched come and go when it seemed possible they might themselves become the occupants – two outlaws from the System consoling one another, and what could be more reasonable than that? But Tessa's shadow came between them and the moment passed without either of them commenting on it. Justin commented on the icons instead. She had half a dozen of them: Andrew, Paul and Simon Peter and John and the Virgin Mother herself, with tin haloes and their attenuated hands at prayer or held up to bestow a blessing or signify the Trinity.

'I suppose Markus gave you those,' he said, acting confused by this renewed display of unlikely religiosity.

She put on her gloomiest scowl.

'It is a totally scientific position. If God exists, He will be grateful. If not, it is irrelevant.' And blushed when he laughed, then laughed too.

The spare bedroom was in the basement. With its barred window looking into the garden it reminded him of Gloria's lower ground. He slept till five, wrote to Ham's aunt for an hour, dressed and crept upstairs intending to leave a note for Lara and take his chances of a lift into town. She was sitting in the window bay smoking a cigarette and wearing the clothes she had worn last night. The ashtray beside her was full.

'You may take a bus to the train station from the top of the road,' she said. 'It will leave in one hour.'

She made him coffee and he drank it at a table in the kitchen. Neither of them seemed disposed to discuss the night's events.

'Probably just a bunch of crazy muggers,' he said once, but she remained sunk in her own meditations.

Another time he asked her about her plans. 'How much longer have you got this place for?'

A few days, she replied distractedly. Maybe a week.

'What will you do?'

It would depend, she replied. It was not important. She would not starve.

'Go now,' she said suddenly. 'It is better that you wait at the bus stop.'

As he left she stood with her back to him and her head tipped tensely forward, as if she were listening to a suspicious sound.

'You will be merciful with Lorbeer,' she announced.

But whether this was a prediction or a command, he couldn't tell.

CHAPTER TWENTY

'What the fuck does your man Quayle think he's playing at, Tim?' Curtiss demanded, swinging his huge body round on one heel to challenge Donohue down the echoing room. It was big enough for a good-sized chapel, with teak poles for rafters, and doors with prison hinges and tribal shields on the log-cabin walls.

'He's not our man, Kenny. He never was,' Donohue replied stoically. 'He's straight Foreign Office.'

'Straight? What's straight about him? He's the most devious sod I ever heard of. Why doesn't he come to me if he's worried about my drug? The door's wide open. I'm not a monster, am I? What does he want? Money?'

'No, Kenny. I don't think so. I don't think money's what's on his mind.'

That voice of his, thought Donohue, while he waited to learn why he had been sent for. I'll never get rid of it. Bullying and wheedling. Lying and self-pitying. But bullying its favourite mode by far. Rinsed but never laundered. The shadow of his Durham backstreet still peeping through, to the despair of all those elocution tutors who came and left at night.

'What's bugging him then, Tim? You know him. I don't.'

'His wife, Kenny. She had an accident. Remember?'

Curtiss swung back to the great picture window and lifted his hands, palms upmost, appealing to the African dusk for reason. Beyond the bulletproof glass lay darkening lawns, at the end of them a lake. Lights twinkled on the hillsides. A few early stars penetrated the deep-blue evening mist.

'So his wife gets hers,' Curtiss reasoned, in the same plaintive tone. 'A bunch of bad boys went wild on her. Her piece of the black stuff did her over, what do I know? The way she was carrying on, she was asking for it. This is Turkana we're talking about, not fucking Surrey. But I'm sorry, yes? Very, very sorry.'

But not perhaps as sorry as you ought to be, thought Donohue.

Curtiss had houses from Monaco to Mexico and Donohue hated all of them. He hated their stink of iodine and their cowed servants and vibrating wooden floors. He hated their mirrored bars and odourless flowers that eyed you like the bored hookers Curtiss kept around him. In his mind Donohue lumped them together with the Rolls-Royces, the Gulfstream and the motor yacht as a single tasteless gin palace straddled over half a dozen countries. But most of all he hated this fortified farm stuck on the shores of Lake Naivasha with its razor-wire fences and security guards and zebra-skin cushions and red-tiled floors and leopard-skin rugs and antelope sofas and pink-lit mirrored booze-cabinet and satellite television set and satellite telephone, and motion sensors and panic buttons and hand-held radios – because it was to this house, to this room and to this antelope sofa that he had been summoned cap in hand at Curtiss's whim for the last five years, to receive whatever scraps the great Sir Kenny K in his erratic magnanimity had seen fit to toss into the eager jaws of British Intelligence. And it was to this place that he had been summoned again tonight, for reasons he had yet to learn, just as he was uncorking a bottle of South African white before sitting down to a bit of lake salmon with his beloved wife Maud.

Here's how we see it, Tim, old boy, for better or worse,

ran a tense, eyes-only signal, written in the vaguely Wodehousian style of his regional director in London.

On the visible front you should maintain friendly contact to match the public face you have established over the last five years. Golf, the odd drink, the odd lunch, etc., sooner you than me. On the covert side you should continue to act natural and look busy since the alternatives – severance, subject's consequent outrage, etc. – are too ghastly to contemplate in the present crisis. For your personal information, all hell has broken out on both sides of the river here, and the situation changes from day to day but always for the worse.

Roger

'Why did you come by car then, anyway?' Curtiss demanded in an aggrieved tone, as he continued to gaze out over his African acres. 'You could have had the Beechcraft if you'd asked for it. Doug Crick had a pilot standing by for you. Are you trying to make me feel bad or something?'

'You know me, chief.' Sometimes, out of passive aggression, Donohue called him chief, a title reserved in eternity for the head of his own Service. 'I'm a car driver. Open the car windows, blow the dust out. Nothing I like more.'

'On these fucking roads? You're out of your mind. I told the Man. Yesterday. I lie. Sunday. "What's the very first fucking thing a punter sees when he arrives at Kenyatta and gets on his safari bus?" I asked him. "It's not the fucking lions and giraffes. It's *your* roads, Mr President. It's your crumbling, horrible roads." The Man sees what he wants, that's his trouble. Plus he flies wherever he can. "It's the same with your trains," I told him. "Use your fucking prisoners," I said, "you've got enough of them. Put your prisoners to work on the tracks and give your trains a chance." "Talk to Jomo," he says. "Which Jomo's that?" I say. "Jomo my new transport minister," he says. "Since when?" I say. "Since just now," he says. Fuck him.'

'Fuck him indeed,' said Donohue devoutly, and smiled the way he often smiled when there was nothing to smile about: with his long, drooping head tipped goatishly to one side and back a notch, his yellowed eyes twinkling, and missing nothing while he stroked the fangs of his moustache.

An unprecedented silence filled the great room. The African servants had walked back to their villages. The Israeli bodyguards, those who weren't policing the grounds, were in the gatehouse watching a kung fu movie. Donohue had been treated to a couple of quick garrottings while he waited to be allowed to pass. The private secretaries and the Somali valet had been ordered to the staff compound on the other side of the farm. For the first time in living history, not a single telephone was ringing in a Curtiss household. A month ago Donohue would have had to fight to get a word in, and threaten to remove himself unless Curtiss gave him a few clear minutes one to one. Tonight he would have welcomed the chirrup of the house telephone or the squawk of the satcom that stood scowling on its trolley beside the enormous desk.

With his wrestler's back still turned to Donohue, Curtiss had adopted what for him was a ruminative pose. He was wearing what he always wore in Africa: white shirt with double cuffs and gold ThreeBees links, navy-blue trousers, lacquered shoes with cockscombs at the sides and a gold watch thin as a penny round his great hairy wrist. But it was the black crocodile belt that held Donohue's attention. With other fat men of his acquaintance, the belt ran low at the front and the gut hung over it. But with Curtiss the belt stayed dead level like a perfect line drawn across the centre of an egg, giving him the appearance of an enormous Humpty Dumpty. His mane of dyed black hair was swept back Slav-style from his wide forehead and duck's-arsed at the nape. He was smoking a cigar and frowning each time he drew on it. When the cigar bored him, he would leave it smouldering on whatever priceless piece of furniture came to hand. When he wanted it, he would accuse the staff of stealing it.

'You know what the bastard's up to now, I suppose,' he demanded.

'Moi?'

'Quayle.'

'I don't think I do. Should I?'

'Don't they tell you? Or don't they care?'

'Perhaps they don't know, Kenny. All I've been told is, he's taking up his wife's cause – whatever that was – that he's out of touch with his employers, and he's flying solo. We know his wife owned a place in Italy and there's a theory that's where he may have gone to earth.'

'What about fucking Germany?' Curtiss interrupted.

'What about fucking Germany?' Donohue asked, mimicking a style of speech he detested.

'He was in Germany. Last week. Poking around a bunch of long-haired liberal do-gooders who've got their knives into KVH. If it hadn't been for me being soft, he'd be off the voters' list by now. But your boys back in London don't know that, do they? They're not bothered. They've got better things to do with their time. *I'm talking to you, Donohue!*'

Curtiss had swung round to face him. His huge upper body had dropped into a crouch, his crimson jaws were struck forward. He had one hand thrust into a pocket of his tent-like trousers. With the other he clutched the cigar, lighted end leading, affecting to hammer it like a red-hot tent-peg into Donohue's head.

'I'm afraid you're ahead of me, Kenny,' Donohue replied equably. 'Is my Office tracking Quayle? you ask. I haven't an earthly. Are precious national secrets at risk? I doubt it. Is our valued source Sir Kenneth Curtiss in need of protection? We never promised to protect you commercially, Kenny. I don't think there's an institution in the world that would do that, if I may say so, financial or other. And survive.'

'*Fuck you!*' Curtiss had flattened both vast hands on the great refectory table and was steering himself along it like a gorilla as he headed in Donohue's direction. But Donohue smiled his fanged smile and sat his ground. 'I can bury your fucking Service single-handed if I want, d'you know that?' Curtiss screamed.

'My dear chap, I never doubted it.'

'I buy lunch for the boys who pay you your money. I give them binges on my fucking boat. Girls. Caviar. Bubbly. They get offices from me election time. Cars, cash, secretaries with good tits. I do business with companies that make ten times what your shop spends in a year. If I told them what I know, you'd be history. So *fuck* you, Donohue.'

'You too, Curtiss, you too,' Donohue murmured wearily, like a man who has heard it all before, which he had.

All the same, inside his operational skull he was wondering very hard what on earth these histrionics were leading up to. Curtiss had thrown tantrums before, God knows. Donohue could no longer count the times he had sat here waiting for a storm to blow over or – if the insults became too vile to ignore – staged a tactical retreat from the room until Kenny decided it was time to call him back and apologise, sometimes with the assistance of a crocodile tear or two. But tonight Donohue had the feeling of sitting in a booby-trapped house. He remembered the clinging look Doug Crick gave him at the gate, the extra deference in his 'Oh good *evening*, Mr Donohue, sir, I'll tell the chief *immediately*.' He was listening with increasing unease to the deathly stillness each time Curtiss's manic outbursts echoed to nothing.

In the picture window two slow-marching Israelis in shorts passed by, leading rebellious guard dogs. Huge yellow fever trees dotted the lawn. Colobus monkeys skipped between them, driving the dogs crazy. The grass was lush and perfect, watered by the lake.

'Your mob's paying him!' Curtiss accused Donohue suddenly, striking out a hand and dropping his voice for effect. 'Quayle's *your* man! Right? Acting on *your* orders so that you can screw me. Right?'

Donohue offered a knowing smile. 'Dead right, Kenny,' he

said placatingly. 'Completely wrong-headed and cuckoo but otherwise bang on the nail.'

'Why are you doing this to me? I've a right to know! I'm *Sir* fucking *Kenneth* Curtiss! I have subscribed – last year alone – half a fucking *million* quid to party funds. I have provided *you* – British *fucking* Intelligence – with nuggets of pure gold. I have performed, *voluntarily*, certain services for you of a very, *very* tricky sort – I have –'

'Kenny,' Donohue interrupted quietly. 'Shut up. Not in front of the servants, OK? Now listen to me. Why should we have the slightest interest in encouraging Justin Quayle to shaft you? Why should my Service – stretched to its limits and under heavy fire in Whitehall as usual – why should we want to shoot ourselves in the foot by sabotaging a valuable asset like Kenny K?'

'Because you've sabotaged every other fucking thing in my life, that's why! Because you've had the City banks call me in! Ten thousand British jobs are at risk, but who gives a fuck when we're putting the boot into Kenny K? Because you've warned your political friends to wash their hands of me before I go down the tube. Haven't you? Haven't you? I said *haven't you?*'

Donohue was busily separating the information from the question. *The City banks have called him in? Does London know? And if they do, why in God's name didn't Roger warn me?*

'I'm sorry to hear that, Kenny. When did the banks do that?'

'What the fuck does it matter when? Today. This afternoon. By phone and fax. The phone to tell me, the fax in case I forgot, hard copy to follow in case I didn't read the fucking fax.'

Then London *does* know, thought Donohue. But if they know, why did they leave me dangling? Resolve later. 'Did the banks offer any reason for their decision, Kenny?' he asked solicitously.

'Their grave ethical concern about certain trade practices is uppermost in their minds. *What* fucking practices? What fucking ethics? Their idea of ethics is a small county east of London. Loss of market confidence is also said to be a worry. Who the fuck caused that then? They did! Unsettling rumours is another. Screw them. I've been there before.'

'And your political friends – who are washing their hands of you – the ones we didn't warn?'

'Phone call from a flunky at Number Ten with a potato up his arse. Speaking on behalf of, et cetera. They're eternally grateful et cetera, but in the present climate of having to be holier than the Pope they're sending back my very generous contributions to party funds, and where should they send them, please, because the sooner my money is off their fucking books the happier they'll be and can we all pretend it never happened? Know where he is now? Where he was two nights ago, getting his end off?'

It took Donohue a blink and a shake to realise that Curtiss was talking not about the incumbent of 10 Downing Street any more, but Justin Quayle.

'Canada. Fucking Saskatchewan,' Curtiss snorted, in reply to his own question. 'Freezing his arse off, I hope.'

'Doing what?' Donohue asked, mystified not so much by the notion of Justin in Canada but by the ease with which Curtiss was able to follow him there.

'Some university. There's a woman there. A fucking scientist. She's taken it into her head to go round telling everybody the drug's a killer in violation of her contract. Quayle shacked up with her. A month after his wife's death.' His voice rose, threatening another storm-force gale. 'He's got a phoney passport, for fuck's sake! Who gave it to him? *You* did. He pays cash. Who sends it to him? *You buggers do*. He slips through their net like a fucking eel every time. Who taught him to do that? You lot!'

'No, Kenny. We didn't. None of it.' *Their* net, he thought. Not yours.

Curtiss was pumping himself up for another scream. Now it came. 'Then *what*, if you'd be so kind as to inform me, is Mr Porter fucking Coleridge doing, lodging inaccurate and defamatory information with the Cabinet Office regarding *my* company and *my* drug, what the *fuck* is he doing threatening to go to fucking *Fleet Street* if he isn't promised a full impartial enquiry by our lords and masters in the Brussels loony-bin? And why the *fuck* do the wankers in *your shop* let him do it – or more like it, *encourage* the bastard?'

And how did you get to know about that? Donohue was marvelling silently. How in Heaven's name did even a man as resourceful and duplicitous as Curtiss manage to get his hairy paws on a piece of top-secret encrypted information just eight hours after it had been sent personally to Donohue over the Service link? And having asked himself this question Donohue, craftsman of his trade, set about obtaining the answer to it. He smiled his jolly smile, but a really pleased one this time, reflecting his honest pleasure that a few things in this world are still decently done among friends.

'Of course,' he said. 'Old Bernard Pellegrin tipped you the wink. Brave of him. And timely. I just hope I'd have done the same. I've always had a soft spot for Bernard.'

His smiling eyes fixed on Curtiss's flushed features, Donohue watched as they first hesitated, then formed themselves into an expression of contempt.

'*That* limp-wristed faggot? I wouldn't trust him to pee his poodle in the park. I've been keeping a top job warm for his retirement, and the bugger hasn't lifted a finger to protect me. Want some?' Curtiss demanded, shoving a brandy decanter at him.

'Can't, old boy. Leech's orders.'

'I told you. Go to my doctor. Doug gave you his address. He's only down in Cape Town. We'll fly you there. Take the Gulfstream.'

'Bit late to change horses, thanks, Kenny.'

'It *never* is,' Curtiss retorted.

So it's Pellegrin, thought Donohue, confirming an old suspicion as he watched Curtiss pour himself another lethal dose from the decanter. Some things about you are predictable after all, and one of them is, you never learned to lie.

* * *

Five years ago, impelled by a desire to do something useful, the childless Donohues had driven up-country to stay with a poor African farmer who in his spare time was setting up a network of kids' football teams. The problem was money: money for a truck to drive the kids to matches, money for team uniforms and other precious symbols of dignity. Maud had recently come into a small inheritance, Donohue a life policy. By the time they returned to Nairobi they had pledged the whole lot in instalments over the next five years and Donohue had never been so happy. His only regret, looking back, was that he had spent so little of his life on kids' football, and so much of it on spies. The same thought for some reason flitted through his head as he watched Curtiss lower his vast bulk into a teak armchair, nodding and winking like a kind granddad. Here comes the fabled charm that leaves me cold, Donohue told himself.

'I popped down to Harare a couple of days ago,' Curtiss confided artfully, clapping his hands on his knees and leaning forward for greater confidence. 'That stupid peacock Mugabe's appointed himself a new Minister of National Projects. Quite a promising lad, I must say. Did you read about him at all, Tim?'

'Yes, indeed.'

'Young bloke. You'd like him. He's helping us with a little scheme we've got going up there. Very fond of a nice backhander, he is. Mustard, in fact. I thought you might value that piece of information. It's worked for us in the past all right, hasn't it? A bloke who'll take a backhander from Kenny K is not averse to taking one from Her Maj. Right?'

'Right. Thanks. Good idea. I'll pass it up the line.'

More nods and winks accompanied by a grateful pull of cognac. 'Know that new skyscraper I built off the Uhuru Highway?'

'And very fine it is, Kenny.'

'I sold it to a Russian last week. A mafia boss he is, Doug tells me. A big one, too, apparently, not a tiddler like some of the fellows we've got here. Word is, he's cutting himself a very big drug deal with the Koreans.' He sat back and surveyed

Donohue with the deep concern of a close friend. 'Here. Tim. What's the matter with you? You look faint.'

'I'm fine. It's the way I go sometimes.'

'It's the chemotherapy, that is. I told you to go to my doctor and you wouldn't. How's Maud?'

'Maud's fine, thanks.'

'Take the yacht. Give yourselves a break, just the two of you. Talk to Doug.'

'Thanks again, Kenny, but it might be stretching cover a bit, mightn't it?'

Another mood-swing threatened them as Kenny breathed a long sigh and let his great arms flop to his sides. No man could take it harder that his generosity had been rejected. 'You're not joining the hands-off-Kenny brigade, are you, Tim? You're not cold-shouldering me like those banking boys?'

'Of course not.'

'Well, don't. You'll only get hurt. This Russian I was telling you about. Listen. Know what he's got tucked away for a rainy day? Which he showed Doug?'

'I'm all ears, Kenny.'

'I built a basement for that skyscraper. Not a lot do that here, but I decided I'd give it a basement for a car park. Cost me an arm and a leg, but that's how I am. Four hundred spaces for two hundred apartments. And this Russian, whose name I'm going to give you, he's got a big white lorry in every fucking car space, with UN painted on the lid. Never been driven, he tells Doug. Fell off a freighter on their way to Somalia. Wants to flog them.' He flung up his arms, amazed by his own anecdote. 'What the fuck's that about then? The Russian mafia flogging UN lorries! To *me*. Know what he wanted Doug to do?'

'Tell me.'

'Import them. From Nairobi to Nairobi. He'll respray them for us, and all we've got to do is square the customs boys and put the lorries through our books a few at a time. If that's not organised crime, what is? A Russian crook ripping off the UN, here in Nairobi in broad daylight, that's anarchy. And I disapprove of anarchy. So you can have that item of intelligence. Gratis and for fuck all. With Kenny K's compliments. Tell them it's a freebie. On me.'

'They'll be over the moon.'

'I want him stopped, Tim. In his tracks. Now.'

'Coleridge or Quayle?'

'Both of them. I want Coleridge stopped, I want the Quayle woman's stupid report *lost –*'

My God, he knows about that too, thought Donohue. 'I thought Pellegrin had already lost it for you,' he complained, with the kind of frown that older men put on when their memory is failing them.

'You keep Bernard out of this! He's no friend of mine and never will be. And I want you to tell your Mister Quayle that if he goes on coming at me, there's fuck all I can do to help him because he's taking on the *world*, not me! Got it? They'd have done him in Germany if I hadn't gone down on my hands and knees for him! Hear me?'

'I hear you, Kenny. I'll pass it up the line. That's all I can promise.'

With bearish agility Curtiss sprang from his chair and rolled away down the room.

'I'm a patriot,' he shouted. 'Confirm that, Donohue! I'm a fucking patriot!'

'Of course you are, Kenny.'

'Say it again. I am a patriot!'

'You're a patriot. You're John Bull. Winston Churchill. What do you want me to say?'

'Give me one example of *me* being patriotic. One of dozens. The best example you can think of. *Now.*'

Where the hell is this leading? Donohue gave one all the same. 'How about the Sierra Leone job we did last year?'

'Tell me about it. Go on. *Tell me!*'

'A client of ours wanted guns and ammunition on a no-name basis.'

'So?'

'So we bought the guns −'

'I bought the fucking guns!'

'You bought the guns with our money, we provided you with a phoney end-user certificate saying they were destined for Singapore −'

'You've forgotten the fucking ship!'

'ThreeBees chartered a forty-thousand-ton freighter and loaded up the guns. The ship got itself lost in the fog −'

'Pretended to, you mean!'

'− and had to put in to a small harbour near Freetown, where our client and his team were standing by ready to unload the guns.'

'And I didn't *have* to do it for you, did I? I could have chickened. I could have said, "Wrong address, try next door." But I did it. I did it for love of my fucking country. Because I'm a patriot!' The voice dropped, to become conspiratorial. 'All right. Listen. Here's what you do − what the Service does.' He was pacing the long room as he gave his orders in low, staccato sentences. 'Your Service − not the Foreign Office, they're a bunch of cissies − your Service, in person, you go to the banks. And you *identify*, in each bank − I'll mark your card for you − *a real Englishman*. Or woman. Are you listening, because you're going to be passing this on to them when you get home tonight.' He had put on his visionary's voice. High tones, a bit of quaver, the people's millionaire.

'I'm listening,' Donohue assured him.

'Good. And you call them together. These good Englishmen and true. Or women. To a nice panelled room in the City somewhere. You boys will know the places. And you say to them in your formal capacity as the British Secret Service, you say to them: "Gentlemen. Ladies. Lay off Kenny K. We're not telling you why. All we're saying is, lay off in the name of the Queen. Kenny K has done great work for his country but we can't tell you what it is, and there's more to come. You're to give him three months' ride on his credits and you'll be striking a blow for your country, same as Kenny K is." And they'll do it. If one says yes, they'll all say yes, because they're sheep. And the other banks will follow suit, because they're sheep too.'

Donohue had never supposed he could feel sorry for Curtiss. But if he ever had, this might have been the moment.

'I'll ask them, Kenny. The trouble is, we haven't got that kind of power. If we had, they'd have to disband us.'

But the effect of these words was more drastic than anything he could have feared. Curtiss was roaring and his roars were echoing in the rafters. He had flung up his white-sleeved arms in priestlike oblation above his head. The room was drumming to the thunder of his tyrant's voice.

'You're history, Donohue. You think *countries* run the fucking world! Go back to fucking Sunday school. It's "God save our multinational" they're singing these days. And here's another thing you can tell your friends Mr Coleridge and Mr Quayle and whoever else you're lining up against me. *Kenny K loves Africa* –' a sweep of the whole upper body took in the picture window and the lake bathed in silken moonlight – 'it's in his fucking blood! And Kenny K loves his *drug*! And Kenny K was put on earth to get his drug to every African man, woman and child who needs it! And that's what he's going to do, so fuck the lot of you! And if somebody sets himself up to stand in the way of science, he's only got himself to blame. Because I can't stop those boys, not any more, and nor can you. Because that drug has been tried and tested all ways up by the best brains money can buy bar none. And not *one* of them –' the voice soaring to a crescendo of hysterical menace – 'not *one* of them has found a fucking word to say against it or will. *Ever!* Now fuck off.'

As Donohue did as he was bidden, a furtive cacophony of haste broke out around him. Shadows sidled into the corridors, dogs barked and a chorus of telephones began their chant.

*   *   *

411

Stepping into the fresh air, Donohue paused to let the night smells and sounds of Africa wash him clean. He was, as ever, unarmed. A ragged veil of cloud had spread itself across the stars. In the glare of the security lights the acacia trees were paper yellow. He heard nightjars and the braying of a zebra. He peered slowly round, forcing his gaze to rest longest on the darkest places. The house stood on a high terrace and behind it lay the lake and before it a tarmac sweep which by moonlight resembled a deep crater. His car stood at the centre of it. From habit he had parked it clear of the surrounding undergrowth. Unsure whether he had glimpsed a moving shadow he remained motionless. He was thinking, oddly enough, of Justin. He was thinking that if Curtiss was right, and Justin had in quick succession been in Italy, Germany and Canada, travelling on a false passport, then this was a Justin he didn't know, but had in recent weeks come to suspect might exist: Justin the loner, taking nobody's orders but his own; Justin impassioned and on the warpath, determined to uncover what, in an earlier life, he might have helped to cover up. And if that was who Justin was these days, and that was the task he had set himself, then where better to start looking than here, at the lakeside residence of Sir Kenneth Curtiss, importer and distributor of '*my drug*'?

Donohue took a half-pace towards his car and, hearing a sound close to him, stopped in mid-stride and laid his foot oh-so-softly on the tarmac. What are we playing, Justin? Grandmother's Footsteps? Or are you just another colobus monkey? A tread this time, a palpable footstep behind him. Man or beast? Donohue raised his right elbow in defence and, suppressing a desire to whisper Justin's name, swung round to see Doug Crick standing four feet from him in the moonlight, his hands hanging demonstratively free at his sides. He was a big fellow, as tall as Donohue but half his age, with a wide pale face and fair hair and an appealing if effeminate smile.

'Hullo, Doug,' Donohue said. 'Keeping well?'

'Very, sir, thank you and I hope I can say the same for you.'

'Something I can do for you?'

They were both speaking very quietly.

'Yes, sir. You can drive to the main road, turn towards Nairobi, drive as far as the turn-off to Hell's Gate National Park which closed an hour ago. It's a dirt road, no lights. I'll meet you there in ten minutes.'

Donohue drove down a ride of black grevillea trees to the gatehouse and let the guard shine a torch in his face, then in his car, in case he had stolen the leopard-skin rugs. The kung fu had given way to badly focused pornography. He turned slowly onto the main road, watching for animals and pedestrians. Hooded natives crouched and lay along the verges. Lone walkers with long sticks lifted a slow hand at him or leaped mockingly into his headlights. He kept driving until he saw a smart sign indicating the national park. He stopped, switched off his lights and waited. A car pulled up behind him. He unlocked his passenger door and opened it a foot, making the courtesy light go on. There was no cloud and no moon. Through the windscreen, the stars were double-bright. Donohue made out Taurus and Gemini; and after Gemini, Cancer. Crick slipped onto the passenger seat and slammed the door after him, leaving them in pitch darkness.

'The chief's desperate, sir. I haven't seen him like this – well, ever,' said Crick.

'I don't suppose you have, Doug.'

'He's going a bit screwy, frankly.'

'Overwrought, I expect,' said Donohue sympathetically.

'I've been sitting in the communications room all day, putting the calls through to him. The London banks, Basel, then it's the banks again, then it's finance companies he's never heard of, offering him monthly credit at forty per cent compound, then it's what he calls his rat-pack, the political ones. You can't help listening, can you?'

A mother with a child on her arm was scraping timidly on the windscreen with her emaciated hand. Donohue lowered his window and handed her a twenty-shilling note.

'He's mortgaged his houses in Paris, Rome and London, and there's to be a charge on his house in Sutton Place, New York. He's trying to find a buyer for his stupid football team, though you'd have to be deaf and dumb to want them. He's asked his special friend in Crédit Suisse for twenty-five million US today, pay you back thirty million Monday. Plus KVH are after him for payment on his marketing deals. And if he hasn't got cash they'll stretch a point and take over his company.'

A dazed family trio was gathering at the window, refugees from somewhere, going nowhere.

'Want me to sort them out, sir?' Crick asked, reaching for the door handle.

'You'll do no such thing,' Donohue ordered sharply. He started the engine and edged slowly along the road while Crick kept talking.

'He screams at them is all he does. It's pathetic, frankly. KVH don't want his money. They want his business, which is what we all knew, but he didn't. I don't know where the shock waves will end, do I?'

'I'm sorry to hear that, Doug. I'd always thought of you and Kenny as hand in glove.'

'Me too, sir. It's taken a lot to bring me to this point, I'll confess. It's not like me to be two-faced, is it?'

A bunch of ostracised male gazelles had come to the roadside to watch them pass.

'What do you want, Doug?' Donohue asked.

'I was wondering whether there was informal work available, sir. Anyone you'd like visited or kept an eye on. Any special documents you needed.' Donohue waited, unimpressed. 'Plus I've got this friend. From the Ireland days. Lives in Harare, which wouldn't be my cup of tea.'

'What about him?'

'He was approached, wasn't he? He's a freelance.'

'Approached to do what?'

'Certain European people who were friends of friends of his approached him. Offering him mega-bucks to pacify a white woman and her black boyfriend up Turkana way. Like by yesterday. Leave tonight, we've got a car waiting.'

Donohue pulled onto the verge and again stopped the car. 'Date?' he asked.

'Two days before Tessa Quayle was killed.'

'Did he take the contract?'

'Of course not, sir.'

'Why not?'

'He's not the sort. He won't touch women, for one thing. He's done Rwanda, he's done Congo. He'll never touch another woman.'

'So what did he do?'

'He advised them to speak to certain people he knew who weren't so particular.'

'Such as who?'

'He's not saying, Mr Donohue. And if he was, I wouldn't let him tell me. There are some things that are too dangerous to know.'

'Not a lot on offer then, is there?'

'Well, he *is* prepared to talk the wider parameters, if you know what I mean.'

'I don't. I buy names, dates and places. Retail. Cash in a bag. No parameters.'

'I think what he's really talking about, sir, if you cut away the fancy language is: would you like to buy what happened to Dr Bluhm, including map references? Only being by way of a writer, he's written an account of the events in Turkana as they affected the doctor, based on what his friends told him. For your eyes only, assuming the price is right.'

Another group of night migrants had assembled round the car, led by an old man in a lady's broad-brimmed hat with a bow on it.

'Sounds crap to me,' said Donohue.

'I don't think it's crap, sir. I think it's the real McCoy. I know it is.'

A chill passed over Donohue. *Know?* he wondered. Know

how? Or is your friend from Ireland days a cipher for Doug Crick?

'Where is it? This account he's written.'

'It's to hand, sir. I'll put it that way.'

'I'll be at the pool bar of the Serena Hotel tomorrow at midday for twenty minutes.'

'He's looking at fifty Ks, Mr Donohue.'

'I'll tell you what he's looking at when I've seen it.'

Donohue drove for an hour, swerving between craters, slowing down for very little. A jackal scurried through his headlights, bound for the game park. A group of women from a local flower farm hailed a lift from him, but for once he didn't stop. Even passing his own house he refused to slow down, but headed directly for the High Commission. The lake salmon would have to keep until tomorrow.

CHAPTER TWENTY-ONE

'Sandy Woodrow,' Gloria announced with playful severity, standing arms akimbo before him in her new fluffy dressing gown, 'it's jolly well time you showed the flag.'

She had risen early and brushed out her hair by the time he had shaved. She had packed the boys off to school with the driver, then cooked him bacon and eggs which he wasn't allowed, but once in a while a girl's allowed to spoil her man. She was mimicking the school prefect in herself, using her head girl voice, though none of this was yet apparent to her husband, who was ploughing his way as usual through a heap of Nairobi newspapers.

'Flag goes back up on Monday, dear,' Woodrow replied distractedly, masticating bacon. 'Mildred's been on to Protocol Department. Tessa's been half-masted longer than a prince of the blood.'

'I'm not talking about that flag, *silly*,' said Gloria, removing the newspapers from his reach and setting them prettily on a side table beneath her watercolours. 'Are you sitting comfortably? So listen. I'm talking about throwing an absolutely bumper party to cheer us all up, you included. It's *time*, Sandy. It really is. It's time we all said to each other, "Right. Done that. Been there. Dreadfully sorry. But life has to go on." Tessa would feel exactly the same. Vital question, darling. What's the inside story? When are the Porters coming back?' *The Porters* like *the Sandys* and *the Elenas*, which is how we talk about people when we're being cosy.

Woodrow transferred a square of egg to his fried bread. ' "Mr and Mrs Porter Coleridge are taking an extended period of home leave while they settle their daughter Rosie into school," ' he intoned, quoting an imaginary spokesman. 'Inside story, outside story, only story there is.'

But a story that, despite his seeming ease, exercised Woodrow considerably. What the hell was Coleridge up to? Why this radio silence? All right, he was on home leave. Good luck to him. But Heads of Mission on home leave have telephones and e-mails and addresses. They get withdrawal symptoms, phone their number twos and private secretaries on the flimsiest excuse, wanting to know about their servants, gardens, dogs and how's the old place ticking over without me? And they get huffy when it's suggested to them that the old place ticks over rather better when they're not in it. But from Coleridge, ever since his abrupt departure, not a dicky-bird. And if Woodrow called London with the professed aim of bouncing a few innocent questions off him – and quite incidentally to pump him about his aims and dreams – he was met by one blank wall after another. Coleridge was 'doing a stint at Cabinet Office', said a neophyte in Africa Department. He was 'attending a ministerial working party', said a satrap in the permanent under-secretary's department.

And Bernard Pellegrin, when Woodrow finally reached him from the digital phone on Coleridge's desk, was as airy as the rest of them. 'One of those Personnel cock-ups,' he explained vaguely. 'PM wants a briefing so the Secretary of State has to have one, so they all want one. Everyone wants a bit of Africa. What's new?'

'But is Porter coming back here or not, Bernard? I mean this is *very* unsettling. For all of us.'

418

'I'd be the last to know, old boy.' Slight pause. 'You alone?'
'Yes.'

'That little shit Mildred hasn't got her ear to the keyhole?'

Woodrow glanced at the closed door to the ante-room and lowered his voice. 'No.'

'Remember that thick bit o' paper you sent me not so long ago? – Twenty pages-odd – woman author?'

Woodrow's stomach lurched. Anti-listening devices might be safe against outsiders, but are they safe against *us*?

'What about it?'

'My view is – best scenario would be – solve everything – it never arrived. Lost in the mails. That play?'

'You're talking about your end, Bernard. I can't speak for your end. If you didn't receive it, that's your business. But I sent it to you. That's all I know.'

'Suppose you *didn't* send it, old boy. Suppose none of it happened. Never written, never sent? Would that be viable your end?' The voice absolutely at ease with itself.

'No. It's impossible. Not at all viable, Bernard.'

'Why not?' Interested, but not the smallest degree perturbed.

'I sent it to you by bag. It was listed. Personal for you. Inventoried. The Queen's Messengers signed for it. I told –' he was going to say 'Scotland Yard' but changed his mind in time – 'I told the people who came out here about it. I had to. They'd already got the background by the time they spoke to me.' His fear made him angry. 'I *told* you I'd told them! I *warned* you, actually! Bernard, is something unravelling? You're making me a bit jumpy, actually. I'd rather understood from you that the whole thing had been laid peacefully to rest.'

'Nothing to it, old boy. Calm down. These things pop up now and then. Bit of toothpaste slips out of the tube, you put it back. People say it can't be done. Happens every day. Wife well?'

'Gloria's fine.'
'Kiddywinks?'
'Fine.'

'Give our love.'

'So I've decided it's to be a really *super* dance,' Gloria was saying enthusiastically.

'Oh, right, splendid,' said Woodrow and, giving himself time to recover the thread of their conversation, helped himself to the pills she made him swallow every morning: three oat-bran tablets, one cod-liver oil and half an aspirin.

'I know you hate dancing but that's not your fault, it's your mother's,' Gloria went on sweetly. 'I shan't be letting Elena interfere, not after the rather tacky little do she gave recently. I shall just keep her informed.'

'Oh. Right. You two have kissed and made up, have you? Don't think I knew that. Congratulations.'

Gloria bit her lip. Memories of Elena's dance had momentarily cast her down. 'I do have *friends*, Sandy, you know,' she said, a little pitifully. 'I rather need them, to be frank. It gets quite lonely waiting all day for you to come back. Friends laugh, they chat, they do each other favours. And sometimes they fall out. But then they get together again. That's what friends do. I just wish *you* had someone like that. Well, don't I?'

'But I've got you, darling,' Woodrow said gallantly as he embraced her goodbye.

*　　*　　*

Gloria went to work with all the drive and efficiency she had put into Tessa's funeral. She formed a working committee of fellow wives and members of the staff too junior to refuse her. First among them was Ghita, a choice that mattered greatly to her since Ghita had been the unwitting cause of the rift between Elena and herself and the ghastly scene that had followed it. The memory would haunt her all her days.

Elena had given her dance, and it had been, to a point, one had to say, well, a success. And Sandy, it was well known, was a great believer in couples splitting up at parties and *working the room*, as he called it. Parties, he liked to say, were where he did his best diplomacy. And so they should be. He was charming. So for most of the evening Gloria and Sandy hadn't seen much of one another, except for the odd woo-hoo across the room and the odd wave on the dance floor. Which was perfectly normal, though Gloria could have wished for just *one* dance, even if it had to be a foxtrot so that Sandy could get the rhythm. And beyond that Gloria had had very little to say about the evening, except that she really thought Elena could cover up a *bit* more at her age, instead of having her bust springing out all over, as we used to say, and she wished the Brazilian Ambassador had not insisted on putting his hand on her bottom for the samba, but Sandy says that's what Latins do.

So it came as a total bolt from the blue when, on the morning *after* the dance – at which Gloria had noticed nothing untoward, be it repeated, and she did consider herself *rather* observant – over a post-mortem coffee at the Muthaiga, Elena had *let slip* – completely casually, as if it were just another bit of perfectly ordinary gossip rather than a *total* bombshell, wrecking her complete life – that Sandy had *come on so heavily with Ghita Pearson* – Elena's very words – that Ghita had pleaded a headache and gone home early, which Elena considered tedious of her, because if everyone did that, one might just as well not bother to give a party at all.

Gloria was at first speechless. Then she refused point blank to believe a word of it. What did Elena mean, *come on*, exactly? Come on *how*, El? Be specific, please. I think I'm rather upset. No, it's perfectly all right, just go on, please. Now you've said it, let's have it all.

Feeling her up, for openers, Elena retorted with deliberate coarseness, incensed by what she perceived as Gloria's prudishness. Groping her tits. Pressing his nasty up against her crotch. What do you expect a man to do when he's got the hots for somebody, woman? You must be the only girl in town *not* to know that Sandy is the biggest pussy-hound in the business. Look at the way he padded round Tessa all those months with his tongue hanging out, even when she was eight months pregnant!

The mention of Tessa did it. Gloria had long accepted that Sandy had had a harmless *thing* about Tessa, though of course he was far too upright to let his feelings get out of hand. Rather to her shame, she had quizzed Ghita on the subject and drawn a satisfying blank. Now Elena had not only reopened the wound: she had poured vinegar into it. Incredulous, mystified, humiliated and plain bloody angry, Gloria stormed home, dismissed the staff, settled the boys at their homework, locked the drinks cupboard and waited darkly for Sandy to return. Which he finally did around eight o'clock, pleading pressure of work as usual but, so far as she could tell in her fraught state, sober. Not wishing to be earwigged by the boys, she grabbed him by the arm and frogmarched him down the servants' staircase to the lower ground.

'What the hell's the matter with you?' he complained. 'I need a Scotch.'

'*You* are the matter, Sandy,' Gloria retorted fearsomely. 'I want no circumlocutions, please. No diplomatic sweet-talk, thank you. No courtesies of any kind. We're both grown-ups. Did you, or did you not, have an affair with Tessa Quayle? I warn you, Sandy. I know you very well. I shall know *immediately* if you're lying.'

'No,' said Woodrow simply. 'I didn't. Any more questions?'

'Were you in love with her?'

'No.'

Stoical under fire like his father. Not budging an eyebrow. The Sandy she loved best, if she was honest. The kind of man you know where you are with. I'll never talk to Elena again.

'Did you make up to Ghita Pearson while you were dancing with her at Elena's party, or not?'

'No.'

'Elena says you did.'

'Then Elena's talking bilge. What's new?'

'She says Ghita left early in tears because you pawed her.'

'Then I assume Elena is pissed off because I didn't paw Elena.'

Gloria had not expected such straight, unequivocal, almost

reckless denials. She could have done without 'pissed off', and she'd just stopped Philip's pocket money for saying it, but Sandy might be right all the same. 'Did you *stroke* Ghita – feel her up – did you press yourself against her – tell me!' she shouted, and gave way to a burst of tears.

'No,' Woodrow replied again, and made a step towards her, but she brushed him aside.

'Don't touch me! Leave me alone! Did you *want* to have an affair with her?'

'With Ghita or Tessa?'

'Either of them! Both of them! What does it matter?'

'Shall we take Tessa first?'

'Do what you want!'

'If you mean by "affair", go to bed with her, I'm sure the idea occurred to me, as it would to most men of heterosexual appetite. Ghita I find less appealing, but youth has its attractions, so let's throw her in too. How about the Jimmy Carter formula? "I committed adultery in my heart." There. I've confessed. Want a divorce or can I have my Scotch?'

By which time she was doubled up, weeping helplessly with shame and self-loathing, and begging Sandy to forgive her because it had become horribly obvious to her what she had been doing. She had been accusing him of all the things she had been accusing herself of ever since Justin slipped into the night with his suitcases. She had been working out her guilt on him. Mortified, she hugged herself and blurted, 'I'm so *sorry*, Sandy,' and 'Oh Sandy, please,' and 'Sandy, forgive me, I'm so awful,' as she struggled to release herself from his grasp. But Sandy by now had an arm round her shoulders and was helping her up the stairs like the good doctor he should have been. And when they reached the drawing room she gave him the key to the drinks cupboard and he poured a stiff one for both of them.

Nonetheless the healing process took its time. Suspicions so monstrous are not laid to rest in a day, particularly when they echo other suspicions that have been laid to rest in the past. Gloria thought back a distance, then another distance. Her memory, which had a way of going off on its own, insisted on retrieving incidents that at the time she had dismissed. After all, Sandy was an attractive man. Of course women would make up to him. He was the most distinguished-looking person in the room. And a little innocent flirtation never did anyone any harm. But then memory kicked in again, and she wondered. Women from previous postings came to mind – tennis partners, babysitters, young wives with promotable husbands. She found herself reliving picnic parties, swimming parties, even – an involuntary shudder – a rather drunken *nude* swimming party in the French Ambassador's pool in Amman, when nobody *really* looked, and we all ran shrieking for our towels, but all the same . . .

It took Gloria several days to forgive Elena, and in a way, of course, she never would. But then Elena was so *unhappy*, she reflected, with her generous side. How could she not be, married to that dreadful little Greek, and trying to make up for him with one seedy affair after another?

*   *   *

Otherwise, the only thing that slightly bothered Gloria was *what* precisely they ought to be celebrating. Obviously it had to be a Day – like Independence Day or May Day. Obviously it had to be soon, or the Porters would come back, which was not what Gloria wanted at all. She wanted Sandy in the limelight. Commonwealth Day was looming but it was too far away. With a little doctoring, they could have an *early* Commonwealth Day that got in ahead of everybody else's. That would show initiative. She would have preferred *British* Commonwealth Day, but everything has to be cut down to size these days, it's the age we live in. She would have preferred St George's Day, and let's slay the bloody dragon for good! Or Dunkirk Day and let's fight them on the beaches! Or Waterloo Day or Trafalgar Day or Agincourt Day, all resounding British victories – but unfortunately they were victories over the French who, as Elena acidly pointed out, had the best cooks in town. But since none of these days fitted, Commonwealth Day it had to be.

Gloria decided it was now time to embark on her master plan, for which she needed the blessing of the Private Office. Mike Mildren was a man in flux. Having had a rather unwholesome New Zealand girl sharing his flat for the last six months, he had overnight exchanged her for a good-looking Italian boy who reputedly spent his day lounging by the pool at the Norfolk Hotel. Choosing just after lunch when Mildren was said to be at his most receptive, she telephoned him from the Muthaiga Club, using all her wiles and promising herself not to call him Mildred by mistake.

'Mike, it's Gloria here. How *are* you? Have you got a minute? Two even?'

Which was nice and modest of her because after all she was the acting High Commissioner's wife, even if she wasn't Veronica Coleridge. Yes, Mildred had a minute.

'Well, Mike, as you may have heard, I and a bunch of stalwarts are planning a *rather* large pre-Commonwealth Day knees-up. A sort of curtain-raiser for everybody else's do. Sandy's spoken to you about it, obviously. Hasn't he?'

'Not yet, Gloria, but no doubt he will.'

Sandy being useless as usual. Forgetting everything about her as soon as he walks out of the front door. And when he comes home, drinking himself to sleep.

'Well, anyway, what we're looking at, Mike,' she bowled on, 'is a *big* marquee. As big as we can find, frankly, with a kitchen at the side. We're going to have a slap-up *hot* buffet, and a live, really good local band. Not a disco like Elena's, and not cold salmon either. Sandy's offering up a hefty chunk of his precious allowances, and the Service attachés are digging into *their* piggy-banks, which is a start, shall we say. Still with me?'

'Indeed I am, Gloria.'

Pompous little boy. Too many of his master's airs and graces. Sandy will knock him into shape, once he gets the chance.

'So two questions, really, Mike. Both a bit delicate, but never mind, I'll plunge in. *One.* With Porter AWOL, if I dare say it, and no financial input from H.E.'s *frais*, as it were, is there, well, a slush fund available, or might Porter be persuaded to chip in from afar, as it were?'

'Two?'

He really *is* insufferable.

'Two, Mike, is *where?* Given the size of the event – and the *vast* marquee – and its importance to the British community at this *rather* difficult time, and the *cachet* we want to attach to it, if that's what you do with a cachet – well, we were thinking – I was – not Sandy, he's too busy, obviously – that the best place to have a five-star knees-up for Commonwealth Day just might be – provided everybody agreed, of course – the High Commissioner's lawn. Mike?' She had the eerie feeling that he had dived underwater and swum away.

'Still listening, Gloria.'

'Well, wouldn't it? For parking and everything. I mean nobody need go inside the *house*, obviously. It's Porter's. Well, except for pit-stops, obviously. We can't put Portaloos in H.E.'s garden, can we?' She was getting hung up over Porter and Portaloos, but forged on. 'I mean everything's there *waiting*, isn't it? Servants, cars, security, and so on?' She hastily corrected herself. 'I mean waiting for Porter and Veronica, obviously. Not waiting for *us*. Sandy and I are just holding the fort till they come back. It's not a takeover or anything. Mike, are you still there? I feel I'm talking to myself.'

She was. The rebuff came the same evening in the form of a typed, hand-delivered note of which Mildred must have kept a copy. She didn't see him deliver it. All she saw was an open car driving away with Mildred in the passenger seat and his pool-boy at the wheel. Department was emphatic, he wrote pompously. The High Commissioner's Residence and its lawns were a no-go area for functions of all kinds. There was to be no 'de facto annexation of High Commissioner status', he ended cruelly. A formal Foreign Office letter to this effect was on its way.

Woodrow was furious. He had never let fly at her like this before. 'Serves you bloody well right for asking,' he raged, stomping up and down the drawing room. 'Do you really suppose I'll land Porter's job by going and camping on his bloody lawn?'

'I was only *prodding* them a bit,' she protested pathetically, as he ranted on. 'It's perfectly *natural* to want you to be Sir Sandy one day. It isn't the borrowed glory I'm after. I just want you to be happy.'

But her afterthought was typically resilient. 'Then we'll jolly well have to do it better here,' she vowed, staring mistily into the garden.

*   *   *

The great Commonwealth Day bash had begun.

All the frantic preparations had paid off, the guests had arrived, music was playing, drink flowing, couples were chatting, the jacarandas in the front garden were in bloom, life was really rather super at last. The wrong marquee had been replaced with the right one, paper napkins with linen, plastic knives and forks with plate, vile puce bunting with royal blue and gold. A generator that brayed like a sick mule had been replaced with one that bubbled like a hot saucepan. The sweep in front of the house no longer looked like a building site and some brilliant last-minute whipping-in by Sandy on the telephone had procured some jolly good Africans, including two or three from Moi's retinue. Sooner than rely on untried waiters – just look at what had happened at Elena's! – or rather hadn't happened! – Gloria had mustered staff from other diplomatic households. One such recruit was Mustafa, Tessa's spearman, as she used to call him, who had been too grief-stricken, by all accounts, to find another job. But Gloria had sent Juma off in pursuit of him, and here he finally was, flitting among the tables on the other side of the dance floor, a bit down in the mouth, bless him, but obviously pleased to have been thought of, which was the important thing. The Blue Boys miraculously had arrived on time to direct parking, and the problem as usual would be to keep them away from the drink, but Gloria had read them the riot act and all one could do was hope. And the band was marvellous, really *jungle*, and a good strong beat for Sandy to dance to if he had to. And didn't he look simply splendid in the new dinner jacket Gloria had bought him as a 'sorry' present? What a parade horse he was going to make one day! And the hot buffet, what she had tasted of it – well, good enough. Not sensational, you didn't expect that in Nairobi, there was a limit to what you could buy even if you could afford it. But *streets* better than Elena's, not that Gloria felt in the least competitive. And darling Ghita in her gold sari, divine.

*   *   *

Woodrow too has every reason to congratulate himself. Watching the couples gyrate to music he detests, sipping methodically at his fourth whisky, he is the storm-tossed mariner who has made it back to harbour against all odds. *No*, Gloria, I never made a pass at her – or at any other her. *No* to all of it. *No*, I will not provide you with the means to destroy me. Not you, not the Archbitch Elena, and not Ghita, the scheming little puritan. I'm a status quo man, as Tessa rightly observed.

Out of the corner of his eye Woodrow spots Ghita, matching bodies with some gorgeous African she has probably never seen in her life until tonight. Beauty like yours is a sin, he tells her in his mind. It was a sin with Tessa, it is with you. How can any woman inhabit a body like yours and not share the desires of the man she inflames? Yet when I point this out to you – just the odd confiding touch, nothing gross – your eyes blaze and you hiss at me in a stage whisper to get my hands off you. Then you flounce home in a huff, closely observed by the Archbitch Elena . . . His reverie was disturbed by a pallid, balding man, who looked as though he had lost his way, accompanied by a six-foot Amazon in bangs.

'Why, Ambassador, how awfully good of you to come!' Name forgotten but with this bloody music going no one's counting. He bawled at Gloria to join him – 'Darling, meet the new Swiss Ambassador who arrived a week ago. Very sweetly called to pay his compliments to Porter! Poor chap got me instead! Wife will be joining you in a couple of weeks' time, isn't that right, Ambassador? So he's on the loose tonight, ha ha! Lovely to see you here! Forgive me if I do the rounds! *Ciao!*'

The bandleader was singing, if that was how you described his caterwaul. Clutching his microphone in one fist and fondling its tip with the other. Rotating his hips in copulative ecstasy.

'Darling, aren't you the teeniest bit turned on?' Gloria whispered as she whirled past him in the arms of the Indian Ambassador. 'I am!'

A tray of drinks went by. Woodrow deftly put his empty glass on it and helped himself to a full one. Gloria was being led back to the dance floor by the jovial, shamelessly corrupt Morrison M'Gumbo, known also as Minister for Lunch. Woodrow cast round gloomily for somebody with a decent enough body to dance with. It was this *non*-dancing that got his goat. This mincing about, parading your parts. It made him feel like the clumsiest, most useless lover a woman ever had to put up with. It evoked all the *do-this-don't-do-thats* and the *for-God's-sake-Woodrows* that had rung in his ears since the age of five.

'I said, I've been running away from myself all my life!' he was bellowing into the puzzled face of his dancing partner, a busty Danish aid worker called Fitt or Flitt. 'Always known what I was running away *from*, but never had the least idea where I was heading. How about you? *I said, how about you?*' She laughed and shook her head. 'You think I'm mad or drunk, don't you?' he shouted. She nodded. 'Well, you're wrong. I'm both!' Chum of Arnold Bluhm's, he remembered. Jesus, what a saga. When on earth will *that* show end? But he must have pondered this loud enough for her to hear him above the awful din because he saw her eyes go down and heard her say, 'Maybe never,' with the kind of piety good Catholics reserve for the Pope. Alone again, Woodrow headed upstream towards tables of deafened refugees, huddled together in shell-shocked groups. *Time I ate something.* He untied his bow tie and let it hang loose.

'Definition of a gentleman, my daddy used to say,' he explained to an uncomprehending black Venus. 'Chap who ties his own bow tie!'

Ghita had staked a territorial claim at one corner of the dance floor and was twisting pelvises with two jolly African girls from the British Council. Other girls were joining them in a witches' circle and the entire band was standing at the edge of the rostrum, singing yeh, yeh, *yeh* at them. The girls were slapping each other's palms, then turning round and tipping their bottoms at each other and Christ alone knew what the neighbours were saying up and down the road because Gloria hadn't invited all of them, or the tent would have been knee-deep in gunrunners and dope dealers – a joke Woodrow must have shared with a brace of very big chaps in native rig because they dissolved into hoots of laughter and retold the whole thing to their womenfolk who cracked up too.

Ghita. What the hell's she up to now? It's the Chancery meeting all over again. Every time I look at her she looks away. Every time I look away, she looks at me. It's the damnedest thing I ever saw. And once again Woodrow must have externalised his thoughts because a bore called Meadower from the Muthaiga Club immediately agreed with him, saying that if young people were determined to dance like that, why didn't they just fuck on the dance floor and be done with it? Which as it happened accorded perfectly with Woodrow's opinion, a point he was bellowing into Meadower's ear as he came face to face with Mustafa the black angel, standing square in front of him as if he were trying to stop him passing, except that Woodrow wasn't proposing to go anywhere. Woodrow noticed that Mustafa wasn't carrying anything, which struck him as impertinent. *If Gloria out of the goodness of her heart has hired the poor dear man to fetch and carry, why the hell isn't he fetching and carrying? Why's he standing here like my bad conscience,* empty-handed except for a folded bit of paper in one hand, mouthing unintelligible words at me like a goldfish?

'Chap says he's got a message for you,' Meadower was shouting.

'*What?*'

'Very personal, very urgent message. Some beautiful girl fallen base-over-bum in love with you.'

'Mustafa said that?'

'What?'

'I said, *did Mustafa say that?*'

'Aren't you going to find out who she is? Probably your wife!' roared Meadower, dissolving in hysterics.

Or Ghita, thought Woodrow, with an absurd leap of hope.

He took half a step away and Mustafa kept alongside him, turning his shoulder into him so that from Meadower's eyeline they resembled two men hunched together lighting their cigarettes in the wind. Woodrow held out his hand and Mustafa reverently laid the note onto his palm. Plain A4 paper, folded small.

'Thank you, Mustafa,' Woodrow yelled, meaning bugger off.

But Mustafa stood firm, commanding Woodrow with his eyes to read it. All right, damn you, stay where you are. You can't read English anyway. Can't speak it either. He unfolded the paper. Electronic type. No signature.

Dear Sir,
    I have in my possession a copy of the letter that you wrote to Mrs Tessa Quayle inviting her to elope with you. Mustafa will bring you to me. Please tell nobody and come at once, or I shall be forced to dispose of it elsewhere.

No signature.

*   *   *

With one burst of the riot police's water cannon, it seemed to Woodrow, he had been drenched cold sober. A man on his way to the scaffold thinks of a multitude of things at once and Woodrow, for all that he had a skinful of his own tax-free whisky inside him, was no exception. He suspected that the transaction between Mustafa and himself had not escaped Gloria's attention and he was right: she would never again take her eyes off him at a party. So he threw her a reassuring wave across the room, mouthed something to suggest 'no problem' and set himself submissively in Mustafa's wake. As he did so, he caught Ghita's gaze full beam for the first time this evening and found it calculating.

Meanwhile, he was speculating hard about the identity of his blackmailer and associating him with the presence of the Blue Boys. His argument went as follows. The Blue Boys had at some point searched the Quayles' house and discovered what Woodrow himself had failed to find. One of their number had kept the letter in his pocket until he saw an opportunity to exploit it. That opportunity had now arisen.

A second possibility occurred to him pretty well simultaneously, which was that Rob or Lesley or both, having been removed from a high-profile murder case against their will, had decided to cash in. But why here and now, for Christ's sake? Somewhere in this mix he also included Tim Donohue, but that was because Woodrow regarded him as an active if senile non-believer. Only this evening, seated with his beady wife Maud in the darkest corner of the tent, Donohue had, in Woodrow's opinion, maintained a malign and untrusting presence.

Meanwhile Woodrow was taking intimate note of the physical things around him, rather in the way he might look for emergency doors when an aeroplane hits turbulence: the inadequately driven tent-pegs and slack guy-ropes – my God, the smallest breeze could blow the whole thing over! – the mud-caked coconut matting along the tented corridor – somebody could slip on that and sue me! – the unguarded open doorway to the lower ground – bloody burglars could have emptied the whole house and we'd never have been the wiser.

Skirting the edges of the kitchen, he was disconcerted by the number of unauthorised camp-followers who had converged on his house in the hope of a few leftovers from the buffet, and were sitting around like Rembrandt groups in the glow of a hurricane lamp. Must be a dozen of them, more, he reckoned indignantly. Plus about twenty children camping on the floor. Well, six, anyway. He was equally incensed by the sight of the Blue Boys themselves, sodden with sleep and drink at the kitchen table, their jackets and pistols draped over the backs of their chairs. Their condition, however, persuaded him that they were unlikely to be the authors of the letter that he was still clutching, folded, in his hand.

Leaving the kitchen by the back stairs, Mustafa led the way by hand-torch up to the hall, and so to the front door. Philip and Harry! Woodrow remembered in sudden terror. God in Heaven, if they should see me now. But what would they see? Their father in a dinner jacket with his black tie loose around his neck. Why should they suppose it was loosened for the hangman? Besides – he remembered now – Gloria had farmed the boys out to friends for the night. She had seen enough diplomatic children at dances and couldn't be doing with any of it for Philip and Harry.

Mustafa was holding the front door open, waving his torch at the drive. Woodrow stepped outside. It was pitch dark. For romantic effect, Gloria had had the outside lights switched off, relying on rows of candles in sandbags which had for the most part mysteriously gone out. Talk to Philip, who had recently taken up domestic sabotage as a pastime. It was a fine night but Woodrow wasn't in a mood to study stars. Mustafa was skimming towards the gate like a will-o'-the-wisp, beckoning him forward with his torch. The Baluhya gateman opened the gates while his extended family observed Woodrow with their usual intense interest. Cars were parked on both sides of the road, their minders dozing on the verge or murmuring to each other over little flames. Mercedes with drivers, Mercedes with minders, Mercedes with Alsatian dogs in them, and the usual crowd of tribespeople with nothing to do but watch life pass them by. The din from the band was as bloody awful out here as it was in the marquee. Woodrow wouldn't be surprised if he got a couple of formal complaints tomorrow. Those Belgian shippers in number twelve will slap a writ on you the moment your dog farts in their air space.

Mustafa had stopped at Ghita's car. Woodrow knew it well. Had watched it often from the safety of his office window, usually with a glass in his hand. It was a tiny Japanese thing, so small and low that when she wriggled into it, he could imagine her putting on her swimsuit. But why are we stopping here? his gaze was demanding of Mustafa. What's Ghita's car got to do with me being blackmailed? He began to work out what he was worth in terms of ready cash. Would they want hundreds? Thousands? Tens of thousands? He'd have to borrow from Gloria, but what could he dream up for an excuse? Well, it was only money. Ghita's car was parked as far from a street lamp as possible. The lamps were out with the power cut, but you never knew when they might come on. He worked out that he had around eighty pounds in Kenyan shillings on him. How much silence would *that* buy? He began thinking in terms of negotiation. What sanctions did he have as the purchaser? What guarantee would there be that the fellow didn't come back in six months or six years? Get on to Pellegrin, he thought, in a burst of gallows humour: ask old Bernard to get the toothpaste back in the tube.

Unless.

Drowning, Woodrow reached for the craziest straw of them all.

Ghita!

Ghita stole the letter! Or, more likely, Tessa gave it to her for safekeeping! Ghita sent Mustafa to haul me out of the party, and she's about to punish me for what happened at Elena's. *And look, there she is!* In the driver's seat, waiting for me! She slipped round the back of the house and she's sitting in the car, my subordinate, waiting to blackmail me!

His spirits soared, if only for a second. If it's Ghita, we can do business. I can outgun her any time. Maybe more than business. Her desire to hurt me is only the reverse side of different, more constructive desires.

But it wasn't Ghita. Whoever the figure was or wasn't, it was unmistakably male. Ghita's driver, then? Her regular boyfriend, come to take her home after the dance so that nobody else gets her? The passenger door stood open. Under Mustafa's impassive gaze, Woodrow lowered himself into the car. Not like wriggling into his swimsuit, not for Woodrow. More like getting into a bumper car with Philip at the fair. Mustafa closed the door after him. The car rocked, the man in the driver's seat made no movement. He was dressed the way some urban Africans dress, Saint Moritz-style in defiance of the heat, in a dark quilted anorak and woollen skullcap low over the brow. Was the fellow black or white? Woodrow breathed in, but caught no sweet scent of Africa.

'Nice music, Sandy,' Justin said quietly, reaching out an arm to start the engine.

CHAPTER TWENTY-TWO

Woodrow sat at a carved desk of rainforest teak priced at five thousand US dollars. He was hunched sideways, one elbow on a silver-framed blotter which cost less. The glow of a single candle glistened on his sweated, sullen face. From the ceiling above him mirrored stalactites reflected the same candle flame to infinity. Justin stood across the room from him in the darkness, leaning against the door, much as Woodrow had leaned against Justin's door on the day he brought him the news of Tessa's death. His hands were squeezed behind his back. Presumably he wanted no trouble from them. Woodrow was studying the shadows thrown onto the walls by the candlelight. He could make out elephants, giraffes, gazelles, rhinos rampant and rhinos couchant. The shadows on the wall opposite were all birds. Roosting birds, water birds with long necks, birds of prey with smaller birds in their talons, giant singing birds perched on tree trunks with musical boxes inside them, price on application. The house was in a wooded side street. Nobody drove past it. Nobody tapped on the window to find out why a half-drunk white man in a dinner jacket with his tie untied was talking to a candle in Mr Ahmad Khan's African & Oriental Art

Emporium, on a leafy hillside five minutes' drive from Muthaiga at half past midnight.

'Khan a friend of yours?' Woodrow asked.

No answer.

'Where did you get the key from then? Friend of Ghita's, is he?'

No answer.

'Friend of the family, probably. Ghita's, I mean.' He took a silk handkerchief from the top pocket of his dinner jacket and surreptitiously wiped a couple of tears from his cheeks. He had no sooner done so than a fresh crop appeared, so he had to wipe them away too. 'What do I tell them when I get back? If I ever do?'

'You'll think of something.'

'I usually do,' Woodrow admitted into his handkerchief.

'I'm sure you do,' said Justin.

Frightened, Woodrow swung his head round to look at him, but Justin was still standing against the door, his hands safely wedged behind his back.

'Who told you to suppress it, Sandy?' Justin asked.

'Pellegrin, who d'you think? "Burn it, Sandy. Burn all copies." Order from the throne. I'd only kept one. So I burned it. Didn't take long.' He sniffed, resisting the urge to weep again. 'Good boy, you see. Security conscious. Didn't trust the janitors. Took it down to the boiler room with my own fair hands. Bunged it in the furnace. Well trained. Go to the top of the class.'

'Did Porter know you'd done that?'

'Sort of. Half. Didn't like it. Doesn't care for Bernard. Open warfare between them. Open by Office standards, anyway. Porter has a running joke about it. *Pellegrin and bear it.* Seemed funny enough at the time.'

It seemed funny enough now, apparently, for he attempted a harsh laugh which only ended in more tears.

'Did Pellegrin say *why* you had to suppress it – burn it? Burn all copies?'

'Christ,' Woodrow whispered.

Long silence in which Woodrow appeared to hypnotise himself with the candle.

'What's the matter?' Justin asked.

'Your voice, old boy, that's all. It's grown up.' Woodrow passed his hand across his mouth, then studied his fingertips for traces. 'You were supposed to have reached your ceiling.'

Justin asked the question again, rephrasing it as one might for a foreigner or child. 'Did you think to ask Pellegrin *why* the document had to be destroyed?'

'Two-pronged, according to Bernard. British interests at stake, for openers. Got to protect our own.'

'Did you believe him?' Justin asked, and again had to wait while Woodrow stemmed another wave of tears.

'I *believed* about ThreeBees. 'Course I did. Spearhead of British enterprise in Africa. Jewel in the crown. Curtiss the darling of African leaders, doling out bribes left, right and centre, chap's a major national asset. Plus he's in bed with half the British Cabinet, which doesn't do him any harm.'

'What was the other prong?'

'KVH. The boys in Basel had been putting out mating signals about opening some vast chemical plant in South Wales. Second one in Cornwall in three years' time. A third in Northern Ireland. Bringing wealth and prosperity to our depressed areas. But if we jumped the gun on Dypraxa, they wouldn't.'

'Jumped the gun?'

'The drug was still at the trial stage. Still is, theoretically. If it poisons a few people who were going to die anyway, what's the big deal? Drug wasn't licensed in the UK so it wasn't an issue, was it?' His truculence had returned. He was appealing to a fellow professional. 'I mean, Christ, Justin. Drugs have got to be tried on *somebody*, haven't they? I mean, who do you choose, for Christ's sake? Harvard Business School?' Puzzled not to have Justin's endorsement of his neat debating point, he ventured another. 'I mean, Jesus. Foreign Office isn't in the business of passing judgment on the safety of non-indigenous drugs, is it? Supposed to be greasing the wheels of British industry, not going round telling everybody that a British company in Africa is poisoning its customers. You know the game. We're not paid to be bleeding hearts. We're not killing people who wouldn't otherwise die. I mean, Christ, look at the death rate in this place. Not that anybody's counting.'

Justin took a moment to dwell on these fine arguments. 'But you *were* a bleeding heart, Sandy,' he objected finally. 'You loved her. Remember? How could you chuck her report into the furnace when you loved her?' His voice seemed unable to prevent itself from gathering power. 'How could you lie to her when she trusted you?'

'Bernard said she had to be stopped,' Woodrow muttered, after another sliding glance into the shadows to confirm that Justin was still safely at his post before the door.

'Oh, she was stopped all right!'

'For Christ's sake, Quayle,' Woodrow whispered. 'Not like that. Different people entirely. Not my world. Not yours.'

Justin must have alarmed himself with his outburst, for when he spoke again it was in the civilised tone of a disappointed colleague.

'How could you *stop* her, as you call it, when you adored her so, Sandy? The way you wrote to her, she was your salvation from *all this* –' He must have forgotten where he was for a moment, for the widespread gesture of his arms embraced not the dismal trappings of Woodrow's imprisonment, but herd upon herd of carved animals, dressed by the right in the darkness of their glass shelves. 'She was your escape from everything, your path to happiness and freedom, or so you told her. Why didn't you support her cause?'

'I'm sorry,' Woodrow whispered, and lowered his eyes as Justin chose a different question.

'So what were you burning, exactly? Why was the document such a threat to you and Bernard Pellegrin?'

'It was an ultimatum.'

'Who to?'

'The British government.'

'*Tessa* was presenting an ultimatum to the British government? *Our* government?'

'To act or else. She felt bound to us. To you. By loyalty. She was a British diplomatic wife and she was determined to do things the British diplomatic way. "The easy way is, bypass the System and go public. The hard way is make the System work. I prefer the hard way." She said that. She clung to a pathetic notion that the Brits had more *integrity* – *virtue* in government – than any other nation. Something her father drummed into her, apparently. She said Bluhm had agreed the Brits could handle it, provided they played fair. If the Brits had such a big stake in it, let them take the word to ThreeBees and KVH. Nothing confrontational. Nothing dire. Just persuade them to withdraw the drug from the market until it was ready. And if they didn't –'

'Did she set a time limit?'

'She accepted that it would be different from zone to zone. South America, Middle East, Russia, India. But her first concern was Africa. She wanted evidence within three months that the drug was being disappeared. After that the shit would hit the fan. Not her words, but nearly.'

'And that's what you sent to London?'

'Yes.'

'What did London do?'

'Pellegrin did it.'

'Did what?'

'Said it was a load of naive bullshit. Said he was buggered if Foreign Office policy was going to be dictated to him by some born-again British wife and her black lover. Then he flew to Basel. Had lunch with the KVH boys. Asked them whether they might consider hoisting a temporary red flag. They replied to the effect that the flag wasn't red enough and there was no soft way to withdraw a drug. Shareholders wouldn't countenance it. Not that the shareholders were being asked, but if they were asked, they wouldn't. Ergo, nor would the board. Drugs aren't cookbook recipes. Can't just fish one bit out, an atom or whatever, add another bit, try again. Only thing you can do is fiddle the dosage, reformulate, not redesign. Want to change it, you've got to go back to square one, they told him, and nobody does that at this stage. Then they rattled their sabres about curtailing their investment in Britain, adding to the Queen's jobless.'

'What about ThreeBees?'

'That was a different lunch. Caviar and Krug on Kenny K's Gulfstream. Bernard and Kenny agreed there'd be mayhem in Africa if the story got out that ThreeBees were poisoning people. Only thing to do, stonewall while KVH's scientists put the polish on the formula and fine-tune the dose. Bernard's only got a couple of years to go. Fancies his chances on the ThreeBees board. On the KVH board too, if they'll have him. Why settle for one directorship when two will do?'

'What was the evidence KVH disputed?'

The question appeared to send a shiver of pain through Woodrow's entire body. He lifted himself upward, seized his head with both hands and rubbed his scalp vigorously with his fingertips. He flopped forward, his head still in his hands, and whispered, 'Jesus.'

'Try water,' Justin suggested, and led him along the corridor to a handbasin, and stood over him, much as he had stood over him in the mortuary when he was vomiting. Woodrow held his hands under the tap and sluiced water into his face.

'The evidence was bloody massive,' Woodrow muttered, back in his chair. 'Bluhm and Tessa had gone from village to clinic, talking to patients, parents, relatives. Curtiss had got wind of them and launched a cover-up. Had his man Crick organise it. But Tessa and Bluhm kept a log of the cover-up too. Went back and looked for the people they'd spoken to. Couldn't find them. Put it all in their report, how ThreeBees wasn't just poisoning people but destroying the evidence afterwards. "This witness has since vanished. This witness has since been charged with criminal acts. This village has been cleared of its inhabitants." Made a bloody good job of it. You should be proud of her.'

'Did the woman Wanza feature in the report?'

'Oh, the woman Wanza was a star. But they put the muzzle on that brother of hers all right.'

'How?'

'Arrested him. Extracted a voluntary confession. He came up before the beak last week. Ten years for mugging a white tourist in Tsavo National Park. The white tourist never gave evidence, but a lot of very frightened Africans saw the boy do it so it was all right. The judge threw in hard labour and twenty strokes of the cane for good measure.'

Justin closed his eyes. He saw the crumpled face of Kioko squatting on the floor beside his sister. He felt Kioko's crumpled hand as it thrust into his own at Tessa's graveside.

'And you still didn't feel any need – when you first read that report – and knew more or less it was true, I suppose – to say anything to the Kenyans?' he suggested.

The truculence again. 'For God's sake, Quayle. When did *you* ever put on your best suit, trolley round to the Blue Boys' headquarters, and accuse them of mounting an orchestrated cover-up and taking Kenny K's shilling for their trouble? That's no way to make friends and influence people in sunny Nairobi.'

Justin took a step away from the door, checked himself and resumed his self-imposed distance. 'There was clinical evidence too, presumably.'

'There was what?'

'I am asking you about the clinical evidence contained in the memorandum written by Arnold Bluhm and Tessa Quayle and destroyed at Bernard Pellegrin's request by *you!* A copy of which was nonetheless submitted by Bernard Pellegrin to KVH who trashed it over lunch!'

The echo of this blast resounded in the glass shelves. Woodrow waited for it to subside.

'The clinical evidence was Bluhm's department. It was in the annexe. She'd put it in a separate annexe. Took a leaf from your book. You're an annexe man. Were once. So was she.'

'Clinical evidence saying what?'

'Case histories. Thirty-seven of them. Chapter and verse.

Names, addresses, treatment, place and date of burial. Same symptoms every time. Sleepiness, blindness, bleeding, liver collapse, bingo.'

'Bingo meaning death?'

'In a way. Put like that. I suppose so. Yes.'

'And KVH disputed this evidence?'

'Unscientific, inductive, biased, tendentious ... emotionalised. That was one I hadn't heard before. Emotionalised. Means you care too much to be trusted, I suppose. I'm the other way round. De-emotionalised. Un-emotionalised. Emotioned out. Less you feel, louder you yell. Bigger the vacuum you've got to fill. Not you. Me.'

'Who's Lorbeer?'

'Her bête noire.'

'Why?'

'Driving force behind the drug. Its champion. Talked KVH into developing it, took the gospel to ThreeBees. Mega-shit, in her book.'

'Does she say Lorbeer betrayed her?'

'Why should she? We all betrayed her.' He was weeping uncontrollably. 'How about you, sitting on your arse and growing flowers while she was out there being a saint?'

'Where's Lorbeer now?'

'Not the faintest. Nobody has. Saw which way the wind was blowing and did a duck-dive. ThreeBees looked for him for a while, then got bored. Tessa and Bluhm took up the hunt. Get Lorbeer for chief witness. Find Lorbeer.'

'Emrich?'

'One of the drug's inventors. She came out here once. Tried to blow the whistle on KVH. They headed her off at the pass.'

'Kovacs?'

'Third member of the gang. Wholly owned asset of KVH. Tart, apparently. Never met her. I saw Lorbeer once, I think. Big fat Boer. Bubbly eyed. Red hair.'

He leaped round in terror. Justin was standing at his shoulder. He had laid a piece of paper on the blotter and was offering

Woodrow a ballpoint pen, the cap towards him, the way polite people pass things to each other.

'It's a travel authorisation,' Justin explained. 'One of yours.' He read the text aloud for Woodrow's benefit. ' "Traveller is a British subject acting under the auspices of the UK High Commission Nairobi." Sign it.'

Woodrow squinted at it, holding it to the candle. 'Peter Paul Atkinson. Who the hell's he?'

'What the form says. A British journalist. Writes for the *Telegraph*. If anyone calls the High Commission to check on him, he's a bona fide journalist in good standing. Will you remember that?'

'What the hell's he want to go to Loki for? Arsehole of the world. Ghita went up there. Supposed to have a photo on it, isn't it?'

'It will have.' Woodrow signed it, Justin folded it, put it in his pocket and returned stiffly to the door. A row of Taiwanese cuckoo clocks announced that it was one o'clock in the morning.

*   *   *

Mustafa was waiting at the kerbside with his torch as Justin drew up in Ghita's little car. He must have been listening for its engine. Woodrow, unaware that he had been returned to his own house, sat staring through the windscreen with his hands clasped on his lap while Justin leaned across him and spoke to Mustafa through the open passenger window. He spoke English, laced with the few words of kitchen kiSwahili that he knew.

'Mr Woodrow is not well, Mustafa. You brought him into the fresh air to be sick. He should go to his bedroom, please, and lie down until Mrs Woodrow can look after him. Kindly tell Miss Ghita that I'm about to leave.'

Woodrow started to climb out, then turned to Justin. 'You won't be bubbling this stuff to Gloria, old boy, will you? Nothing to be gained, now you've heard it all. She hasn't got our sophistication, you see. Old colleagues and so on. Will you?'

Like a man moving a bundle of something that disgusted him though he was trying not to show it, Mustafa plucked Woodrow from the car and escorted him to his front door. Justin had put on his woollen hat and anorak again. Beams of coloured spotlight were escaping from the marquee. The band was playing relentless rap. Still seated in the car Justin glanced to his left and thought he saw the shadow of a tall man standing in front of the rhododendron bushes at the kerbside, but when he looked closely, it was gone. He kept staring nonetheless, first at the bushes, then at the parked cars to either side of them. Hearing a footfall, he turned to see a figure hastening towards him, and it was Ghita with a shawl across her shoulders, dancing shoes in one hand and a pocket torch in the other. She slipped into the passenger seat as Justin started the car.

'They're wondering where he is,' she said.

'Was Donohue in there?'

'I don't think so. I'm not sure. I didn't see him.'

She started to ask him something and decided better not.

He was driving slowly, peering into parked cars, glancing repeatedly at his wing mirrors. He passed his own house but gave it hardly a look. A yellow dog rushed at the car, snapping at its wheels. He swerved, keeping his eyes on the mirrors while he softly rebuked it. Craters came at them like black lakes in the headlights. Ghita peered out of the rear window. The road was pitch dark.

'Keep your eyes front,' he commanded her. 'I'm in danger of losing the way. Give me some lefts and rights.'

He was driving faster now, swinging between craters, bouncing over tar bumps, veering to the centre of the road whenever he distrusted the sides. Ghita was murmuring: left here, left again, big pothole coming up. Abruptly he slowed down and a car overtook them, followed by a second.

'See anyone you recognise?' he asked.

'No.'

They entered a tree-lined avenue. A battered sign reading HELP VOLUNTEER barred their way. A line of emaciated boys with poles and a wheelbarrow with no wheel were gathered behind it.

'Are they always here?'

'Day and night,' said Ghita. 'They take the stones from one hole and put them in another. In this way their job is never done.'

He pumped the footbrake. The car rolled to a halt just before the sign. The boys clustered round the car, slapping their palms on the roof. Justin lowered his window as a flashlight lit up the inside of the car, followed by the quick-eyed, smiling head of their spokesman. He was sixteen at most.

'Good evening, Bwana,' he cried in a tone of high ceremony. 'I am Mr Simba.'

'Good evening, Mr Simba,' said Justin.

'You wish to contribute to this fine road we're making, man?'

Justin passed a hundred-shilling note through the window. The boy danced triumphantly away, waving it above his head while the others clapped.

'What's the usual tariff?' Justin asked Ghita as he drove on.

'About a tenth of that.'

Another car overtook them and Justin again peered intently at its occupants, but seemed not to see whatever he was looking for. They entered the town centre. Shop lights, cafés, teeming pavements. Matutu buses racing by with music blasting. Out to their left, a smash of metal was followed by the blaring of horns and screams. Ghita was directing him again: right here, through these gates *now*. Justin drove up a ramp and into the crumbling forecourt of a square three-storey building. By the perimeter lights he read the words COME UNTO JESUS *NOW*! daubed on the slab wall.

'Is this a church?'

'It was a Seventh Day Adventist dental clinic,' Ghita replied. 'Now it is converted into flats.'

The car park was a piece of low ground surrounded by razor

wire and if she had been alone she would never have driven into it, but he was already heading down the slipway with his hand out for the key. He parked and she watched him while he stared back up the slipway, listening.

'Who are you expecting?' she whispered.

He led her past grinning groups of kids to the entrance and up the steps to the lobby. A handwritten notice said LIFT SERVICE SUSPENDED. They crossed to a grey staircase lit by low-watt bulbs. Justin climbed beside her until they arrived at the top floor which was in darkness. Producing his own pocket torch, Justin lit the way. Asian music and smells of oriental food issued from closed doors. Handing her his torch, Justin returned to the stairwell while she unchained her iron grille and turned the three locks. As she stepped into the flat, she heard her phone ringing. She looked round for Justin, to find him standing beside her.

'Ghita, my dear, *hullo*,' cried a charming male voice she couldn't immediately place. 'How radiant you looked tonight. Tim Donohue here. Wondered whether I might pop up a minute, have a cup of coffee with the two of you underneath the stars.'

*   *   *

Ghita's flat was small, three rooms only, and all looking at the same run-down warehouse and the same bustling street with broken neon signs and honking cars and intrepid beggars who stood in their path until the last moment. A barred window gave onto an outside iron staircase that was supposed to be a fire-escape, though for reasons of self-preservation the tenants had sawn off the bottom flight. But the upper flights were still intact, and on warm evenings Ghita could climb up to the roof and settle herself against the wooden cladding of the water tank, and study for the Foreign Service examination that she was determined to sit next year, and listen to the clatter of her fellow Asians up and down the building, and share their music and

447

their arguments and their children, and almost convince herself she was among her own people.

And if this illusion vanished as soon as she drove through the gates of the High Commission and put on her other skin, the rooftop with its cats and chicken coops and washing and aerials remained one of the few places where she felt at ease – which was why perhaps she was not unduly surprised when Donohue proposed that they enjoy their coffee underneath the stars. How he knew she had a rooftop was a mystery to her, since he had never, so far as she knew, set foot in her apartment. But he knew. With Justin warily looking on, Donohue stepped over the threshold and, holding a finger to his lips, threaded his angular body through the window and onto the platform of the iron staircase, then beckoned them to follow him. Justin went next and by the time Ghita joined them with the coffee tray, Donohue was perched on a packing case, knees level with his ears. But Justin could settle nowhere. One minute he was posed like an embattled sentinel against the neon strips across the street, the next squatting at her side, head bowed, like a man drawing with his finger in the sand.

'How'd you make it through the lines, old boy?' Donohue enquired above the rumble of traffic, while he sipped his coffee. 'Little bird told me you were in Saskatchewan couple of days ago.'

'Safari package,' said Justin.

'Via London?'

'Amsterdam.'

'Big group?'

'Big as I could find.'

'As Quayle?'

'More or less.'

'When did you jump ship?'

'In Nairobi. Soon as we'd cleared customs and immigration.'

'Smart lad. I misjudged you. Thought you'd use one of the land routes. Slip up from Tanzania or whatever.'

'He wouldn't let me fetch him from the airport,' Ghita put in protectively. 'He came here by cab in the dark.'

'What do you want?' Justin asked from another part of the darkness.

'A quiet life, if you don't mind, old boy. I've reached an age. No more scandal. No more lifting of stones. No more chaps sticking their necks out, looking for what isn't there any more.' His craggy silhouette turned to Ghita. 'What did you go up to Loki for, dear?'

'She went for my sake,' Justin's voice cut in, before she had thought of a reply.

'And so she should,' Donohue said approvingly. 'And for Tessa's sake too, I'm sure. Ghita's an admirable girl.' And to Ghita again, more forcibly, 'And you found what you were looking for, did you, dear? Mission accomplished? I'm sure it was.'

Justin again, faster than before. 'I asked her to check on Tessa's last days up there. To make sure they were doing what they said they were doing: attending the gender seminar. They were.'

'And you agree with that version of events, do you, my dear?' Donohue enquired, back to Ghita.

'Yes.'

'Well, good on you,' Donohue remarked and took another sip of his coffee. 'Shall we talk turkey?' he suggested to Justin.

'I thought we were doing that.'

'About your plans.'

'What plans?'

'Precisely. For example, if it were ever in your mind to have a quiet word with Kenny K. Curtiss, you'll be wasting your breath. I can tell you that for no fee.'

'Why?'

'His bully boys are waiting for you, that's one reason. For another, he's out of the race, if he was ever completely in it. The banks have taken his toys away. ThreeBees' pharmaceutical interests will go back to where they came from: KVH.'

No reaction.

'My point being, Justin, that there's not a lot of satisfaction to be had from firing bullets into somebody who's already dead. If it's satisfaction you're looking for. Is it?'

No answer.

'As to the murder of your wife, much as it pains me to have to tell you this, Kenny K was not, repeat not, *complicit*, as we say in court. Neither was his sidekick Mr Crick, though I've no doubt he'd have leaped at the opportunity if it had been offered to him. Crick was under standing instructions to report Arnold's and Tessa's movements to KVH, naturally. He made ample use of Kenny K's local assets, notably the Kenyan police, to keep an ear and an eye out for them. But Crick was no more *complicit* than Kenny K. A watching brief doesn't make him a murderer.'

'Who did Crick report to?' Justin's voice asked.

'Crick reported to an answering machine in Luxembourg that has since been disconnected. From there, the fatal message was passed down the line by means that you and I are never likely to establish. Until it reached the ears of the sensitive gentlemen who killed your wife.'

'Marsabit,' Justin said, from nearby.

'Indeed. The celebrated Marsabit Two, in their green safari truck. They were joined en route by four Africans, bounty hunt-ers like themselves. The purse for the job was a million dollars to be divided at the discretion of their leader, known as Colonel Elvis. All we can be sure of is that his name is not Elvis and he never rose to the dizzy rank of colonel.'

'Did Crick report to Luxembourg that Tessa and Arnold were heading for Turkana?'

'That, dear boy, is a question too far.'

'Why?'

'Because Crick won't answer it. He's afraid. As I could wish you were. He's afraid that if he is too liberal with his information, and with the information of certain friends of his, he'll get his tongue chopped out to make room for his testicles. He may be right.'

'What do you want?' Justin repeated. He was crouched at Donohue's side, staring into his blackened eyes.

'To dissuade you from doing whatever you intend to do, dear boy. To tell you that whatever it is you're looking for, you won't find it, but that won't prevent you from getting killed. There's a contract out on you as soon as you set foot in Africa and here you are in Africa with both feet. Every renegade mercenary and gang boss in the business dreams of getting you in his sights. Half a million to make you dead, a million to make it look like suicide, the preferred way. You can hire yourself all the protection you want, it won't do you a blind bit of good. You'll probably be hiring the very people who are hoping to kill you.'

'Why does your Service care whether I live or die?'

'At the business level, it doesn't. At the personal level, I'd prefer not to see the wrong side win.' He took a breath. 'In which context, I'm sorry to tell you that Arnold Bluhm is as dead as a dodo and has been for weeks. So if you're here to save Arnold, I'm afraid that, once again, there's nothing to save.'

'Prove it,' Justin demanded roughly, while Ghita swung silently away from them and buried her face in her forearm.

'I'm old and dying and disenchanted and I'm telling you tales out of school that would get me shot at dawn by my employers. That's all the proof you can have. Bluhm was knocked senseless, shoved in the safari truck, driven into the empty desert. No water, no shade, no food. They tortured him for a couple of days in the hope of finding out whether he or Tessa had thought to make a second set of the disks they'd found in the four-track. I'm sorry, Ghita. Bluhm said no, they hadn't made a second set, but why should anybody take no for an answer? So they tortured him to death to be on the safe side and because they enjoyed it. Then they left him to the hyenas. And that, I am afraid, is the truth.'

'Oh my dear God.'

It was Ghita, whispering into her hands.

'So you can cross Bluhm off your list, Justin, together with Kenny K. Curtiss. Neither of them is worth the journey any

451

more.' He rode on remorselessly. 'Meanwhile, hear this. Porter Coleridge is fighting your corner in London for you. And that's not just top secret. That's eat before reading.'

Justin had disappeared from Ghita's vision. She searched the darkness and discovered him close behind her.

'Porter is calling for Tessa's case to be reassigned to the original police officers, and for Gridley's head to be placed on a charger next to Pellegrin's. He wants the relationship between Curtiss, KVH and the British government to be the subject of a cross-party enquiry and he's chipping away at Sandy Woodrow's feet of clay while he's about it. He wants the drug to be assessed by a team of independent scientists, if there are any left in the world. He's discovered there's something called the Ethical Trials Committee of the World Health Organization that might serve. If you go home now, you might *just* be able to tip the balance. So that's why I came,' he ended happily and, having drained the last of his coffee, stood up. 'Getting people out of countries is one of the few things we still do well, Justin. So if you'd rather be smuggled out of Kenya in a warming-pan than brave the hells of Kenyatta airport a second time, not to mention Moi's watchers and everybody else's, have Ghita give us the wink.'

'You've been very kind,' said Justin.

'That was what I was afraid you'd say. Goodnight.'

*   *   *

Ghita lay on her bed with the door open. She was staring at the ceiling, not knowing whether to weep or pray. She had always assumed that Bluhm was dead, but the vileness of his death was worse than anything she had feared. She wished she could return to the simplicities of her convent school, and recover her belief that it was God's will that man should rise so high and stoop so low. On the other side of the wall, Justin was back at her desk, writing by pen because pen was what he liked although she had offered him her laptop. The plane to Loki was due to leave Wilson at seven which meant he would be gone in an hour. She wished she could share the rest of his journey, but knew that no one could. She had offered to drive him to the airport but he preferred to take a taxi from the Serena Hotel.

'Ghita?'

He was knocking on her door. She called, 'It's all right,' and rose to her feet.

'I'd like you, please, to post this for me, Ghita,' Justin said, handing her a fat envelope addressed to a woman in Milan. 'She's not a girlfriend, in case you're curious. She's my lawyer's aunt' – a rare smile – 'and here's a letter for Porter Coleridge at his club. Don't use the Field Post Office, if you don't mind. And no courier service or anything. The normal Kenyan mails are quite reliable enough. Thank you immeasurably for all your help.'

At which she could restrain herself no longer, and threw her arms round him, and herself against him, and held him as if she were holding onto life itself until he prised himself free.

CHAPTER TWENTY-THREE

Captain McKenzie and his co-pilot Edsard sit in the Buffalo's cockpit, and the cockpit is a raised platform in the nose of the Buffalo's fuselage, with no dividing doors to shield the crew from their cargo – or the cargo, for that matter, from the crew. And directly below the platform, one step down from it, some thoughtful soul has provided a low russet-coloured Victorian armchair of the sort an elderly family retainer might pull up before the kitchen fire on a winter's evening, and clamped its feet to the deck by means of improvised iron shoes. And that is where Justin sits, with a headset over his ears and frayed nylon ribbons like a child's walking harness round his belly, while he receives the wisdom of Captain McKenzie and Edsard and occasionally removes his headset to take questions from a white Zimbabwean girl called Jamie who has made herself comfortable amid a tethered mountain of brown packing cases. Justin has tried to offer her his chair but McKenzie has stopped him with a firm, 'You're here.' At the tail end of the fuselage, six Sudanese women in robes crouch in varying attitudes of stoicism or stark terror. One of them is vomiting into a plastic bucket kept handy for the purpose. Quilted panels of shiny grey line the plane's roof, red launch-lines dangle from a cable beneath them, their metal-lined tips dancing to the thunder of the engines. The fuselage grunts and heaves like an old iron horse dragged back for one more war. There is no sign of air-conditioning or parachute. A blistered red cross on a wall panel indicates medical supplies. Below it runs a line of jerry-cans marked 'Kerosene' and tied together with twine. *This is the journey Tessa and Arnold made and this is the man who flew them. This is their last journey before their last journey.*

'So you're Ghita's friend,' McKenzie had observed, when Sudan Sarah brought Justin to his *tukul* back in Loki, and left them alone together.

'Yes.'

'Sarah tells me you had a travel document issued to you by the South Sudanese office in Nairobi, but you've mislaid it. That right?'

'Yes.'

'Mind if I take a look at your passport?'

'Not at all.' Justin hands him his Atkinson passport.

'What's your line of country, Mr Atkinson?'

'Journalist. The London *Telegraph*. I'm writing a piece on the UN's Operation Lifeline Sudan.'

'That's a real pity just when OLS needs all the publicity it can get. Seems silly to let a little piece of paper stand in the way. Know where you lost it?'

'I'm afraid I don't.'

'We're ferrying mostly cases of soya oil today. Plus a few care packages for the boys and girls in the field. Pretty much the normal milk round, if you're interested.'

'I am.'

'Do you object to sitting on the floor of a jeep under a pile of blankets for an hour or two?'

'Not in the least.'

'Then I think we're in business, Mr Atkinson.'

And thereafter McKenzie has clung doggedly to this fiction. On the plane, as he might for any journalist, he describes the workings of what he proudly calls the most expensive anti-starvation operation ever mounted in the history of mankind. His information comes in metallic bursts that do not always rise above the din of the engines.

'In South Sudan we have calorie rich, calorie middle, calorie poor and plain destitute, Mr Atkinson. Loki's job is to measure the hunger gaps. Every metric tonne we drop costs the UN thirteen hundred US dollars. In civil wars, the wealthy die first. That's because, if someone steals their cattle they can't adjust. The poor stay pretty much the way they were. For a group to survive, the land around it has to be safe to plant. Unfortunately, there's not a lot of safe land around. Am I going too fast for you?'

'You're doing admirably, thank you.'

'So Loki has to assess the crops and measure where the hunger gaps will appear. Right now, we're on the verge of a new gap. But you've got to get the timing right. Drop food when they're due to harvest, you mess with their economy. Drop it too late, they're already dying. Air's the only answer, by the way. Transport the food by road, it gets hijacked, often by the driver.'

'Right. I see. Yes.'

'Don't you want to take notes?'

If you're a journalist, behave like one, he is saying. Justin opens his notebook as Edsard takes over the lecture. His subject is security.

'We have four levels of security at the food stations, Mr Atkinson. Level four means abort. Level three is red alert, level two fair. We got no zero-risk areas in South Sudan. OK?'

'OK. Understood.'

McKenzie comes back. 'The monitor will tell you when you arrive at the station what level they've got today. If there's an emergency, do what he tells you. The station you're visiting is in territory technically controlled by General Garang, who gave you the visa you lost. But it's under regular attack from the north as well as rival tribes from the south. Don't think this is just a north–south thing. The tribal groupings change overnight

456

and they'd as soon fight one another as fight Muslims. Still with me?'

'Absolutely.'

'Country of Sudan is basically a fantasy of the colonial cartographer. In the south we've got Africa, green fields, oil and animist Christians. In the north we've got Arabia and sand and a bunch of Muslim extremists intent on introducing shariah law. Know what that is?'

'More or less,' says Justin who in another life has written papers on the subject.

'Result is, we've got everything we need for pretty much perpetual famine. What the droughts don't achieve, civil wars do and vice versa. But Khartoum's still the legal government. Ultimately, whatever deals the UN cuts in the south, it's still got to pay its dues to Khartoum. So what we've got here, Mr Atkinson, we've got a unique triangular pact between the UN, the boys in Khartoum and the rebels they're beating the living daylights out of. Follow me?'

'You going up to Camp Seven!' Jamie the white Zimbabwean girl bellows in his ear, crouching becomingly beside him in her brown denims and bush hat and cupping her hands to her mouth.

Justin nods.

'Seven's the hot one right now! Girlfriend of mine got hit by a level four up there just a couple of weeks ago! Had to trek eleven hours through marshland, then wait another six hours without her pants for the pick-up plane!'

'What happened to her pants?' Justin yells back at her.

'You have to take them off! Boys and girls! It's the chafing! Wet hot steaming trousers! It's unbearable!' She rests for a while then returns her hands to his ear. 'When you hear cattle moving out of a village – run. When the women follow them – run faster. We had a guy once ran fourteen hours on no water. Lost eight pounds. Carabino was after him.'

'Carabino?'

'Carabino was a good guy till he joined the northerners. Now

457

he's apologised and come back to us. Everybody's very pleased. Nobody asks him where he's been. This your first time?'

Another nod.

'Listen. Statistically, actuarially, you should be pretty safe. Don't worry. And Brandt's a real character.'

'Who's Brandt?'

'The food monitor at Camp Seven. A great guy. Everybody loves him. Crazy as a bedbug. Big God man.'

'Where does he come from?'

She shrugs. 'Calls himself a washed-up mongrel like the rest of us. Nobody has a past up here. It's practically a rule.'

'How long's he been there?' Justin yells, and has to repeat himself.

'Six months, I guess! Six months in the field non-stop is a lifetime, believe me! Won't come down to Loki even for a couple of days R and R!' she ends regretfully, and flops back exhausted by her yelling.

Justin unbuckles himself and goes to the window. *This is the journey you made. This is the spiel they gave you. This is what you saw.* Below him lies emerald Nile swamp, misted by heat, pierced with jigsaw-shaped black holes of water. On higher ground cellular cattle pens are packed tight with animals.

'Tribesmen never tell you how many cattle they've got!' Jamie is standing at his shoulder, yelling in his ear. 'The food monitors' job is to find out! Goats and sheep get the centre of the pen, cows outside, calves next to them! Dogs go in with the cows! At night they burn the cow dung in their little houses in the perimeter! Wards off the predators, keeps the cows warm and gives them God-awful coughs! Sometimes they put the women and kids in there as well! Girls get good food in Sudan! If they're well fed, they fetch a better marriage price!' She pats her stomach, grinning. 'A man can have as many wives as he can afford. There's this incredible dance they do – I mean *honestly*,' she exclaims, and puts her hand over her mouth as she bursts out laughing.

'Are you a food monitor?'

'Assistant.'

'How did you get the job?'

'Went to the right nightclub in Nairobi! Want to hear a riddle?'

'Of course.'

'We drop grain here, right?'

'Right.'

'Because of the north–south war, right?'

'Go on.'

'Big part of the grain we drop is grown in North Sudan. That's whatever the US grain farmers don't dump on us from surplus. Work it out. The aid agencies' money buys Khartoum's grain. Khartoum uses the money to buy arms for the war against the south. The planes that bring the grain to Loki use the same airport that Khartoum's bombers use to bomb the South Sudanese villages.'

'So what's the riddle?'

'Why is the UN financing the bombing of South Sudan and feeding the victims at the same time?'

'Pass.'

'You going back to Loki after this?'

Justin shakes his head.

'Pity,' she says, and winks.

Jamie returns to her seat among the soya oil boxes. Justin stays at the window, watching the gold sunspot of the plane's reflection flitting over the twinkling marshes. There is no horizon. After a distance, the ground colours merge into mist, tinting the window with deeper and deeper tones of mauve. *We could fly for all our lives*, he tells her, *and we'd never reach the earth's hard edge*. With no warning the Buffalo begins its slow descent. The swamp turns brown, hard ground rises above the water level. Single trees appear like green cauliflowers as the plane's sunspot whips across them. Edsard has taken the controls. Captain McKenzie is studying a brochure of camping equipment. He turns and gives Justin a thumbs-up. Justin returns to his seat, buckles up and glances at his watch. They have been flying three hours. Edsard banks the plane steeply. Boxes of toilet paper, fly spray and chocolate shoot down the steel deck and thump against the raised daïs of the cockpit close to Justin's feet. A cluster of rush-roofed huts appears at the end of the wing-tip. Justin's headset is full of atmospherics like classical music being played at the wrong speed. Out of the cacophony he selects a gruff Germanic voice giving details of the state of the ground. He makes out the words 'firm and easy'. The plane starts to vibrate wildly. Rising in his harness Justin looks through the cockpit window at a strip of red earth running across a green field. Lines of white sacks serve as markers. More sacks are strewn over one corner of the field. The plane straightens and the sun hits the back of Justin's neck like a douche of scalding water. He sits down sharply. The Germanic voice becomes loud and clear.

'Come on down here, Edsard, man! We made a fine goat stew for lunch today! You got that layabout McKenzie up there?'

Edsard is not so easily wooed. 'What are those bags doing out in the corner there, Brandt? Has someone made a drop just recently? Are we sharing space with another plane up here?'

'That's just empty bags, Edsard. You ignore those bags and come on down here, you hear me? You got that hotshot journalist with you?'

McKenzie this time, laconically. 'We got him, Brandt.'

'Who else you got?'

'Me!' yells Jamie cheerfully above the roar.

'One journalist, one nymphomaniac, six returning delegates,' McKenzie intones as calmly as before.

'What's he like, man? The hotshot?'

'You tell me,' says McKenzie.

Rich laughter in the cockpit, shared by the faceless foreign voice from the ground.

'Why's he nervous?' Justin asks.

'They're all nervous down there. It's the end of the line. When we touch down, Mr Atkinson, you stay with me, please. Protocol

460

requires I introduce you to the Commissioner ahead of everybody else.'

The airstrip is an elongated clay tennis court, part overgrown. Dogs and villagers are emerging from a clump of forest and heading towards it. The huts are rush-roofed and conical. Edsard makes a low pass while McKenzie scans the bush to either side.

'No bad guys?' Edsard asks.

'No bad guys,' McKenzie confirms.

The Buffalo banks, levels out and rushes forward. The airstrip hits it like a rocket. Clouds of flaming red dust envelop the windows. The fuselage sags left, then further left, the cargo howls in its moorings. The engines scream, the plane shudders, scrapes something, moans and bucks. The engines die. The dust subsides. They have arrived. Justin is staring through the falling dust at an approaching delegation of African dignitaries, children and a couple of white women in grubby jeans, dreadlocks and bracelets. At their centre, clad in a brown Homburg hat, ancient khaki shorts and very worn suède shoes, strides the beaming, bulbous, gingery and undeniably majestic figure of Markus Lorbeer without his stethoscope.

*   *   *

The Sudanese women clamber from the plane and rejoin a chanting cluster of their people. Jamie the Zimbabwean is hugging her companions to whoops of mutual pleasure and amazement, and hugging Lorbeer also, stroking his face and pulling off his Homburg and smoothing his red hair for him while Lorbeer beams and pats her bottom and chortles like a schoolboy on his birthday. Dinka porters swarm into the rear of the fuselage and unload to Edsard's instructions. But Justin must remain in his seat until Captain McKenzie beckons him down the steps and leads him away from the festivities, across the airstrip, up a small mound to where a cluster of Dinka elders in black trousers and white shirts sit in a half-circle of kitchen

461

chairs under a shade tree. At their centre sits Arthur the Commissioner, a shrivelled, grey-haired man with a hewn face and intense, sagacious eyes. He wears a red baseball cap with Paris embroidered on it in gold.

'So you are a man of the pen, Mr Atkinson,' says Arthur, in faultless archaic English, when McKenzie has made the introductions.

'That's correct, sir.'

'What journal or publication, if I may make so bold, is fortunate enough to retain your services?'

'The *Telegraph* of London.'

'*Sunday* *Telegraph*?'

'Mostly the daily.'

'Both are excellent newspapers,' Arthur declares.

'Arthur was a sergeant in the Sudanese Defence Force during the British mandate,' McKenzie explains.

'Tell me, sir. Would I be correct in saying you are here to nourish your mind?'

'And the minds of my readers, too, I hope,' says Justin, with diplomatic unction, as out of the corner of his eye he sees Lorbeer and his delegation advancing across the runway.

'Then, sir, I pray that you may also nourish the minds of my people by sending us English books. The United Nations provides for our bodies but too seldom for our minds. Our preferred authors are the English master storytellers of the nineteenth century. Perhaps your newspaper would consider subsidising such a venture.'

'I'll certainly propose it to them,' says Justin. Over his right shoulder, Lorbeer and his group are approaching the mound.

'You are most welcome, sir. For how long shall we have the pleasure of your distinguished company?'

McKenzie answers on Justin's behalf. Below them, Lorbeer and his group have come to a halt at the foot of the mound and are waiting for McKenzie and Justin to descend.

'Until this time tomorrow, Arthur,' says McKenzie.

'But no longer, please,' says Arthur, with a sideways glance at his courtiers. 'Do not forget us when you leave here, Mr Atkinson. We shall be waiting for your books.'

'Hot day,' McKenzie observes as they descend the mound. 'Must be around forty-two and rising. Still, that's the Garden of Eden for you. Same time tomorrow, OK? Hi, Brandt. Here's your hotshot.'

*   *   *

Justin has not reckoned with such overwhelming good nature. The gingery eyes that in the Uhuru Hospital refused to see him radiate spontaneous delight. The baby face, scalded by the daily sun, is one broad, infectious grin. The guttural voice that sent its nervous mutterings into the rafters of Tessa's ward is vibrant and commanding. The two men are shaking hands while Lorbeer speaks, Justin's one hand to Lorbeer's two. His grasp is friendly and confiding.

'Did they brief you down there in Loki, Mr Atkinson, or did they leave the hard work to me?'

'I'm afraid I didn't have much time for briefings,' Justin replies, smiling in return.

'Why are journalists always in such a hurry, Mr Atkinson?' Lorbeer complains cheerfully, releasing Justin's hand only to clap him on the shoulder as he guides him back towards the airstrip. 'Does the truth change so fast these days? My father always taught me: if something is true, it is eternal.'

'I wish he'd tell my editor that,' says Justin.

'But maybe your editor does not believe in eternity,' Lorbeer warns, swinging round on Justin and raising a finger in his face.

'Maybe he doesn't,' Justin concedes.

'Do *you*?' The clown's eyebrows are hooped in priestly inquisition.

Justin's brain is for a moment numb. *What am I pretending to be? This is Markus Lorbeer, your betrayer.*

'I think I'll live a while before I answer that one,' he replies awkwardly, at which Lorbeer lets out a roar of honest laughter.

'But not too long, man! Otherwise eternity come and get you! You ever see a food drop before?' A sudden lowering of the voice as he grabs Justin's arm.

'I'm afraid not.'

'Then I show you one, man. And then you will believe in eternity, I promise. We get four drops a day here and it's God's miracle every time.'

'You're very kind.'

Lorbeer is about to deliver a set-piece. The diplomat in Justin, the fellow sophist, hears it coming.

'We *try* to be efficient, here, Mr Atkinson. We *try* to get food into the right mouths. Maybe we oversupply. When customers are starving, I never saw that as a crime. Maybe they lie to us a little, how many they got in their villages, how many are dying. Maybe we make a few millionaires in the black market in Aweil. Too bad, I say. OK?'

'OK.'

Jamie has appeared at Lorbeer's shoulder, accompanied by a group of African women bearing clipboards.

'Maybe the foodstall-keepers don't love us too much for screwing up their trade. Maybe the poor spearmen and witch doctors in the bush say we do them out of business with our Western medicines. Maybe with our food drops we create a dependency. OK?'

'OK.'

A gigantic smile dismisses all these imperfections. 'Listen, Mr Atkinson. Tell this to your readers. Tell it to the UN fat-arses in Geneva and Nairobi. Every time my food station gets one spoonful of our porridge into the mouth of one starving kid, I've done my job. I sleep in God's bosom that night. I earned my reason to be born. You tell them that?'

'I'll try.'

'You got a first name?'

'Peter.'

'Brandt.'

They shake hands again, for longer than before.

'Ask anything you want, OK, Peter? I got no secrets from God. You got something special you want to ask me?'

'Not yet. Maybe later, when I've had a chance to get the hang of things.'

'That's good. You take your time. What's true is eternal, OK?'

'OK.'

*   *   *

It is prayer time.

It is Holy Communion time.

It is miracle time.

It is time to share the Host with all mankind.

Or so Lorbeer is pronouncing, and so Justin affects to write in his notebook, in a vain effort to escape the oppressive good spirits of his guide. It is time to watch 'the mystery of man's humanity correcting the effects of man's evil', which is another of Lorbeer's disconcerting soundbites, delivered while his gingery eyes squint devoutly into the burning Heaven, and the great smile beckons down God's benison, and Justin feels the shoulder of his wife's betrayer nudge affectionately against his own. A line of spectators is drawn up. Jamie the Zimbabwean and Arthur the Commissioner and his courtiers are the closest. Dogs, groups of tribesmen in red robes and a subdued crowd of naked children arrange themselves around the airstrip's edge.

'Four hundred and sixteen families we feed today, Peter. For a family you got to multiply by six. The Commissioner over there, I give him five per cent of everything we drop. That's off the record. You're a decent guy so I tell you. Listen to the Commissioner, you'd think the population of Sudan was a hundred million. Another problem we got, that's rumour. Takes one guy to say he saw a horseman with a gun and ten thousand people run like hell, leave their crops and villages.'

He stops dead. At his side, Jamie is pointing one arm to

Heaven while her spare hand discovers Lorbeer's and gives it a covert squeeze. The Commissioner and his retinue have also heard it, and their response is to raise their heads, half close their eyes and stretch their lips in tense and sunny smiles. Justin catches the far rumble of an engine and makes out a black spot lost in a burnished sky. Slowly the spot becomes another Buffalo like the one that flew him here, white and brave and solitary as God's own cavalry, clearing the treetops by a hand's breadth, flickering and bobbing as it jockeys for line and height. Then vanishes, never to return. But Lorbeer's congregation does not lose faith. Heads remain lifted, willing it back. And here it comes again, low and straight and purposeful. A lump rises in Justin's throat and tears start to his eyes as the first white shower of food bags, like a trail of soapflakes, issues from the plane's tail. At first they drift playfully, then gather speed and spatter onto the drop zone in a wet tattoo of machine-gun fire. The plane circles to repeat the manoeuvre.

'You see that, man?' Lorbeer is whispering. There are tears in his eyes also. Does he weep four times a day? Or only when he has an audience?

'I saw it,' Justin confirms. *As you saw it and like me, no doubt, became an instant member of his church.*

'Listen, man. We need more airstrips. You put that in your article. More airstrips and closer to the villages. The walk's too long for them, too dangerous. They get raped, they get their throats cut. Their kids get stolen while they're away. And when they get here, they find they've screwed up. It's not the day for their village. So they go home again, and they're confused. A lot of them, they die of the confusion. Their kids too. You gonna write that?'

'I'll try.'

'Loki says more airstrips means more monitoring. I say, OK, we have more monitoring. Loki says, where's the money? I say, spend it first, then find it. What the hell?'

A different silence grips the airstrip. It is the silence of apprehension. Are marauders lurking in the woods, waiting to steal

God's gift and run? Lorbeer's great hand is again clutching Justin's upper arm.

'We got no guns here, man,' he is explaining, in answer to the unspoken question in Justin's mind. 'In the villages they've got Armalites and Kalashnikovs. Arthur the Commissioner over there, he buys them with his five per cent and gives them to his people. But here in the food station, all we got is a radio and prayer.'

The moment of crisis is judged to have passed. The first porters advance shyly onto the strip to stack the bags. Clipboards in hand, Jamie and the other assistants take up their positions among them, one to each heap. Some bags have burst. Women with brushes zealously sweep up the loose grain. Lorbeer clutches Justin's arm while he acquaints him with 'the culture of the food bag'. After God invented the food drop, he says with a rich laugh, He invented the food bag. Broken or whole, these white synthetic fibre sacks stamped with the initials of the World Food Programme are as much a staple commodity of South Sudan as the food they bring:

'See that windsock? – see that fellow's moccasins? – see his headscarf? – I tell you, man, if ever I get married, I'm gonna dress my bride in food bags!'

From his other side Jamie lets out a hoot of laughter which is quickly shared by those next along from her. The laughter is still running high as three columns of women emerge from different points along the treeline on the other side of the airstrip. They are Dinka tall – six feet is not exceptional. They have the stately African stride that is the impossible dream of every fashionable catwalk. Most are bare-breasted, others are in copper cotton dresses drawn strictly across the bosom. Their impassive gaze is fixed on the stacks of bags ahead of them. Their talk is soft and private to themselves. Each column knows its destination. Each assistant knows her customers. Justin steals a glance at Lorbeer as one by one each woman gives her name, grasps a bag by the throat, chucks it in the air and settles it delicately on her head. And he sees that Lorbeer's eyes are now filled with tragic disbelief, as if he were the author of the women's plight, not of their salvation.

'Is something wrong?' Justin asks.

'The women, they're the only hope of Africa, man,' Lorbeer replies, still in a whisper while he continues to stare at them. Does he see Wanza among them? And all the other Wanzas? His small, pale eyes peer so guiltily from the black shadow of his Homburg hat. 'You write that down, man. We give food only to the women. The men, we don't trust those idiots across a road. No, sir. They sell our porridge in the markets. They have their women make strong drink with it. They buy cigarettes, guns, girls. The men are bums. The women make the homes, the men make the wars. The whole of Africa, that's one big gender fight, man. Only the women do God's work around here. You write that down.'

Justin obediently writes as he is asked. Needlessly, because he has heard the same message from Tessa every day. The women file silently back into the trees. Guilty dogs lick up the uncollected grains.

*   *   *

Jamie and the assistants have dispersed. Paddling himself on his tall staff, Lorbeer in his brown Homburg has the authority of a spiritual teacher as he leads Justin across the airstrip, away from the hamlet of *tukuls* towards a blue line of forest. A dozen children vie with one another to stay on his heels. They tweak at the great man's hand. They take a finger each and swing on it, utter loud growls, kick their feet in the air like dancing elves.

'These kids think they're lions,' Lorbeer confides to Justin indulgently as they pull and roar at him. 'Last Sunday we are having Bible School and the lions gobble up Daniel so fast that God got no chance to save him. I tell the kids: no, no, you gotta let God *save* Daniel! That's in the Bible! But they say the lions are too damn hungry to wait. Let them eat up Daniel first, and afterwards God can do his magic! They say otherwise, those lions die.'

They are approaching a line of rectangular sheds at the far end of the airstrip. To each shed a rudimentary enclosure like a paddock. To each enclosure a miniature Hades of the desperately sick, the parched, crippled and dehydrated. Stooped women hunching stoically upon themselves in silent torment. Fly-laden babies too sick to cry. Old men comatose with vomiting and diarrhoea. Battle-weary paramedics and doctors doing their best to cajole and gentle them into a crude assembly line. Nervous girls standing in a long queue, whispering and giggling to each other. Teenaged boys locked in frenzied combat while an elder whacks at them with a stick.

*   *   *

Followed at a distance by Arthur and his court, Lorbeer and Justin have reached a thatched dispensary like a country cricket pavilion. Tenderly pushing his way through clamorous patients, Lorbeer leads Justin to a steel screen guarded by two stalwart African men in Médecins Sans Frontières T-shirts. The screen is pulled open, Lorbeer darts inside, removes his Homburg hat and hauls Justin after him. A white paramedic and three helpers are mixing and measuring behind a wooden counter. The atmosphere is of controlled but constant emergency. Seeing Lorbeer enter, the paramedic looks up quickly and grins.

'Hi, Brandt. Who's your handsome friend?' she asks, in a brisk Scots accent.

'Helen, meet Peter. He's a journalist and he's going to tell the world you're a lot of lazy layabouts.'

'Hi, Peter.'

'Hi.'

'Helen's a nurse from Glasgow.'

On the shelves, many-coloured cartons and glass jars are packed roof high. Justin scans them, affecting a general curiosity, hunting for the familiar red and black box with its happy logo of three gold bees, not finding one. Lorbeer has placed himself before the display, assuming once more the rôle of lecturer. The paramedic and her assistants exchange raw smiles. Here we go again. Lorbeer is holding up an industrial jar of green pills.

'Peter,' he intones gravely. 'Now I show you the other lifeline of Africa.'

Does he say this every day? To every visitor? Is this his daily act of contrition? Did he say it to Tessa too?

'Africa has eighty per cent of the world's Aids sufferers, Peter. That's a conservative estimate. Three-quarters of them receive no medication. For this we must thank the pharmaceutical companies and their servants, the US State Department, who threaten with sanctions any country that dares produce its own cheap version of American-patented medicines. OK? Have you written that down?'

Justin gives Lorbeer a reassuring nod. 'Keep going.'

'The pills in this jar cost twenty US dollars apiece in Nairobi, six in New York, eighteen in Manila. Any day now, India's going to manufacture the generic version and the same pill will cost sixty cents. Don't talk to me about the research and development costs. The pharmaceutical boys wrote them off ten years ago and a lot of their money comes from governments in the first place, so they're talking crap. What we got here is an amoral monopoly that costs human lives every day. OK?'

Lorbeer knows his exhibits so well he doesn't need to search for them. He replaces the jar in the shelves and grabs a large black and white box.

'These bastards have been peddling this same compound for thirty years already. What's it for? Malaria. Know why it's thirty years old, Peter? Maybe a few people in New York should get malaria one day, then you see if they don't find a cure pretty damn quick!' He selects another box. His hands, like his voice, are trembling with honest indignation. 'This generous and philanthropic pharma in New Jersey made a donation of its product

470

to the poor starving nations of the world, OK? The pharmas, they need to be loved. If they're not loved, they get scared and miserable.'

And dangerous, Justin thinks, but not aloud.

'Why did the pharma donate this drug? I'll tell you. Because they have produced a better one. The old one is superfluous to stock. So they give Africa the old one with six months of life left in it, and they get a few million dollars' tax break for their generosity. Plus they are saving themselves a few more millions of warehousing costs *and* the costs of destroying old drugs they can't sell. Plus everybody says, look at them, what nice guys they are. Even the shareholders are saying it.' He turns the box over and scowls contemptuously at its base. 'This consignment sat in a customs house in Nairobi for three months while the customs guys waited for somebody to bribe them. A couple of years back the same pharma sent Africa hair restorer, smoking cures and cures for obesity, and collected a multi-million-dollar tax-break for their philanthropy. Those bastards got no feeling for anything but the fat god Profit, and that's the truth.'

But the full heat of his righteous anger is reserved for his own masters – *those lazy bums in the aid community in Geneva who roll over for the big pharmas every time.*

'Those guys who call themselves humanitarians!' he protests, amid more grins from the assistants, as he unconsciously evokes Tessa's hated H-word. 'With their safe jobs and tax-free salaries, their pensions, nice cars, free international schools for their kids! Travelling all the time so they never get to spend their money. I seen them, man! In the fine Swiss restaurants, eating big meals with the pretty-boy lobbyists from the pharmas. Why should *they* stick their necks out for humanity? Geneva's got a spare few billion dollars to spend? Great! Spend it on the big pharmas and keep America happy!'

In the lull that follows this outburst, Justin ventures a question.

'In what *capacity* did you see them exactly, Brandt?'

Heads lift. All but Justin's. Nobody before, apparently, has thought to challenge the prophet in his wilderness. Lorbeer's gingery eyes widen. A hurt frown creases his reddened forehead.

'I seen them, man, I tell you. With my eyes.'

'I don't doubt you've seen them, Brandt. But my readers may. They'll be asking themselves, "Who was Brandt when he saw them?" Were you in the UN? Were you a diner in the restaurant?' A small laugh to signal the unlikely circumstance: 'Or were you working for *the Forces of Darkness*?'

Does Lorbeer sense the presence of an enemy? Do the Forces of Darkness sound threateningly familiar to him? Is the blur that was Justin in the hospital less of a blur? Lorbeer's face has become pitiful. The child-light drains out of it, leaving a hurt old man without his hat. Don't do this to me, his expression is saying. You're my pal. But the conscientious journalist is too busy taking notes to be of assistance.

'You want to turn to God, you gotta be a sinner first,' Lorbeer says huskily. 'Everybody in this place is a convert to God's pity, man, believe me.'

But the hurt has not left Lorbeer's face. Nor has the unease. It has settled over him like an intimation of bad news he is trying not to hear. On the walk back across the airstrip he ostentatiously prefers the company of Arthur the Commissioner. The two men walk Dinka-style, hand in hand, big Lorbeer in his Homburg and Arthur a spindly scarecrow in a Paris hat.

*   *   *

A wooden stockade with a log boom for a gateway defines the domain of Brandt the food monitor and his assistants. The children fall away. Arthur and Lorbeer alone escort the distinguished visitor on a mandatory tour of the camp's facilities. The improvised shower cubicle has an overhead bucket with a string attached to tilt it. A rainwater tank is supplemented by a stone-age pump powered by a stone-age generator. All are the invention of the great Brandt.

'One day, I apply for the patent on this one!' Lorbeer vows, with a too-heavy wink that Arthur dutifully returns.

A solar panel lies on the ground at the centre of a chicken run. The chickens use it as a trampoline.

'Lights the whole compound, just with the day's heat!' Lorbeer boasts. But the zest has gone out of his monologue.

The latrines are at the edge of the stockade, one for men, one for women. Lorbeer beats on the men's door, then flings it open to reveal a foul-smelling hole in the ground.

'The flies up here, they develop resistance for every disinfectant we throw at them!' he complains.

'Multi-resistant flies?' Justin suggests, smiling, and Lorbeer casts him a wild glance before he too manages a pained smile.

They cross the compound, pausing on their way to peer into a freshly dug grave twelve feet by four. A family of green and yellow snakes lies coiled in the red mud at its base.

'That's our air-raid shelter, man. The snakes in this camp, they got bites worse than the bombs,' Lorbeer protests, continuing his lament against the cruelties of nature.

Receiving no reaction from Justin, he turns to share the joke with Arthur. But Arthur has gone back to his own kind. Like a man desperate for friendship, Lorbeer flings an arm round Justin's shoulder and keeps it there while he marches him at light-infantry speed towards the central *tukul*.

'Now you gonna try our goat stew,' he announces determinedly. 'That old cook, he makes stew better than the restaurants in Geneva! Listen, you're a good fellow, OK, Peter? You're my friend!'

Who did you see down there in the grave among the snakes? he is asking Lorbeer. Was it Wanza again? Or did Tessa's cold hand reach out and touch you?

*   *   *

The floor space inside the *tukul* is no more than sixteen feet across. A family table has been banged together from wooden pallets. For seats there are unopened cases of beer and cooking oil. A rackety electric fan spins uselessly from the rush ceiling, the air stinks of soya and mosquito spray. Only Lorbeer the head of the family has a chair, which has been wrested from its place in front of the radio that sits in stacked units under a bookmaker's umbrella next to the gas stove. He perches in it very upright in his Homburg hat, with Justin on one side of him and on the other Jamie, who seems to occupy this place by right. To Justin's other side is a ponytailed young male doctor from Florence; next to him sits Scottish Helen from the dispensary, and across from Helen a Nigerian nurse named Salvation.

Other members of Lorbeer's extended family have no time to linger. They help themselves to stew and eat it standing, or sit only long enough to gulp it down and leave again. Lorbeer spoons his stew voraciously, eyes flicking round the table as he eats and talks and talks. And though occasionally he targets a particular member of his audience, nobody doubts that the principal beneficiary of his wisdom is the journalist from London. Lorbeer's first topic of conversation is war. Not the tribal skirmishes raging all around them, but 'this damn big war' that is raging in the Bentiu oilfields of the north and spreading daily southwards.

'Those bastards in Khartoum, they got tanks and gunships up there, Peter. They're tearing the poor Africans to pieces. You go up there, see for yourself, man. If the bombardments don't do the job, they got ground troops to go in and do it for them, no problem. Those troops rape and slaughter to their hearts' content. And who's helping them? Who's clapping from the touchlines? The multinational oil companies!'

His indignant voice is holding the floor. Conversations round him must compete or die and most are dying.

'The multis *love* Khartoum, man! "Boys," they say, "we respect your fine fundamentalist principles. A few public floggings, a few hands cut off, we admire that. We want to help you any which way we can. We want you to use our roads and our airstrips just as much as you like. Just don't you go letting those lazy African bums in the towns and villages stand in the

474

way of the great god Profit! We want those African bums ethnically cleansed out of the way just as bad as you boys in Khartoum want it! So here's some nice oil revenues for you, boys. Go buy yourselves some more guns!" You hear that, Salvation? Peter, you writing this down?'

'Every word, thank you, Brandt,' says Justin quietly to his notebook.

'The multis do the Devil's work, I tell you, man! One day they will end up in Hell where they belong, and they better believe it!' He cringes theatrically, his great hands shielding his face. He is acting the part of Multinational Man facing his Maker on the Day of Judgment. ' "It wasn't me, Lord. I was only obeying orders. I was commanded by the great god Profit!" That Multinational Man, he's the one who gets you hooked on cigarettes, then sells you the cancer cure you can't afford to pay for!'

He's the one who sells us untried medicines too. He's the one who fast-streams clinical trials and uses the wretched of the earth as guinea pigs.

'You want coffee?'

'I'd love some. Thank you.'

Lorbeer leaps to his feet, seizes Justin's soup mug and rinses it with hot water from a thermos as a prelude to filling it with coffee. Lorbeer's shirt is stuck to his back, revealing billows of trembling flesh. But he doesn't stop talking. He has developed a terror of silence.

'Did the boys down in Loki tell you about the train, Peter?' he yells, drying the mug with a piece of tissue plucked out of the rubbish bag beside him. 'This damned old train that comes south at walking speed like three times a year?'

'I'm afraid not.'

'It comes down the old railway that you British laid, OK? The train does. Like in the old movies. It's protected by wild horsemen from the north. This old train resupplies every Khartoum garrison on its route from north to south. OK?'

'OK.'

Why is he sweating so? Why are his eyes so haunted and questing?

What secret comparison is he making between the Arab train and his own sins?

'Man! That train! Right now it's stuck between Ariath and Aweil, two days' hike from here. We got to pray God to make sure the river stays flooded, then maybe the bastards don't come this way. They make Armageddon wherever they go, I tell you. They kill everyone. Nobody can stop them. They're too strong.'

'Which bastards are we talking about here exactly, Brandt?' Justin asks, jotting again in his notebook. 'I lost the plot there for a moment.'

'The wild horsemen are the bastards, man! Do you think they get paid for protecting that train? Not a bean, man. Not a drachma. They do it for free, out of the goodness of their kind hearts! Their reward, that's the killing and the raping their way through the villages. It's the setting fire to them. It's kidnapping the young guys and girls to take back north when the train is empty! It's stealing every damn thing they don't burn.'

'Ah. Got it.'

But the train isn't enough for Lorbeer. Nothing is enough if it threatens to bring silence in its wake, and expose him to questions he dare not hear. His haunted eyes are already searching desperately for a sequel.

'They told you about the plane then? – the Russian-made plane, man, older than Noah's ark, the plane they keep down in Juba? Man, that's some story!'

'Not the train, not the plane, I'm afraid. As I said, they didn't have time to tell me anything.'

And Justin waits once more, pen obediently poised, to be told about that old Russian-made plane they keep in Juba.

'Those crazy Muslims in Juba, they make dumb bombs like cannon-balls. They take them up, then they roll them down the fuselage of that old plane and drop them on Christian villages, man! "Here you are, Christians! Here's a nice love letter from your Muslim brothers!" And these dumb bombs are very effective, you better believe me, Peter. Those boys have mastered the art of aiming them very straight. Oh yes! And those bombs are so volatile that the crew make damn sure they get rid of them before they land their old plane back in Juba!'

From beneath the bookmaker's umbrella the field radio is announcing the approach of another Buffalo. First comes the laconic voice of Loki, then the captain in the air, calling in for contact. Hunched to the set, Jamie reports good weather, firm ground and no security problems. The diners hastily depart but Lorbeer remains in his place. With a snap, Justin closes his notebook and under Lorbeer's gaze feeds it into his shirt pocket alongside his pens and reading spectacles.

'Well, Brandt. Lovely goat stew. I've a few special-interest questions, if that's all right by you. Is there somewhere we could sit for an hour without being interrupted?'

Like a man leading the way to his place of execution Lorbeer guides Justin across a patch of trodden grassland strewn with sleeping tents and washing lines. A bell-shaped tent is set apart from them. Hat in hand, Lorbeer holds back the flap for Justin and contrives a hideous grin of servility as he lets him go first. Justin stoops, their eyes meet and Justin sees in Lorbeer what he has seen already when they were in the *tukul*, but now with greater clarity: a man terrified by what he resolutely forbids himself to see.

CHAPTER TWENTY-FOUR

The air inside the tent is acrid and compressed and very hot, the smells are of rotten grass and stale clothes that no amount of washing can get clean. There is one wooden chair and in order to free it Lorbeer must remove a Lutheran Bible, a volume of Heine's poetry, a baby-style fleecy sleeping suit and a food monitor's emergency backpack with radio and protruding beacon. Only then does he offer the chair to Justin, before squatting himself on the edge of a bony camp bed six inches from the ground, ginger head in hands, damp back heaving as he waits for Justin to speak.

'My paper is interested in a controversial new TB cure called *Dypraxa* – manufactured by Karel Vita Hudson and distributed in Africa by the House of ThreeBees. I notice you don't have it on your shelves. My paper thinks your real name is *Markus Lorbeer* and you're the good fairy who saw the drug onto the market,' Justin explains, as he once more opens his notebook.

Nothing about Lorbeer stirs. The damp back, the ginger-golden head, the sodden pressed-down shoulders remain motionless in the aftershock of Justin's words.

'There's a growing clamour about Dypraxa's side-effects, as I'm sure you know,' Justin goes on, turning a page and consulting it. 'KVH and ThreeBees can't keep their fingers in the dam for ever. You might be wise to get your word in ahead of the field.'

Sweat pouring off them, two victims of the same disease. The heat inside the tent so soporific that there is a risk in Justin's mind they will both succumb to it, and fall into a sleeping sickness, side by side. Lorbeer embarks on a caged prowling of the tent's circumference. This is how I endured the confinement of the lower ground, thinks Justin, as he watches his prisoner pause and startle himself in a tin mirror, or consult a wooden cross pinned to the canvas above his bedhead.

'God Christ, man. How the hell did you find me?'

'Talked to people. Had a bit of luck.'

'Don't bullshit me, man. Luck nothing. Who's paying you?'

Still pacing. Shaking his head to free it of sweat. Swinging round as if he expects to find Justin on his heels. Staring at him with suspicion and reproach.

'I'm freelance,' Justin says.

'To hell you are, man! I *bought* journalists like you! I know all your rackets! Who bought you?'

'Nobody.'

'KVH? Curtiss? I made them *money*, for Christ's sake!'

'And they made money for you too, didn't they? According to my paper, you own one third of forty-nine per cent of the companies that patented the molecule.'

'I renounced it, man. Lara renounced it. It was blood money. "Take it," I told them. "It's yours. And on the Day of Judgment, may God preserve you all." Those were my words to them, Peter.'

'Spoken to whom exactly?' Justin enquires, writing. 'Curtiss? Someone at KVH?' Lorbeer's face is a mask of terror. 'Or to Crick, perhaps. Ah yes. I see. Crick was your link at Three-Bees.'

479

And he writes down *Crick* in his notebook, one letter at a time, because his hand is sluggish from the heat. 'But Dypraxa wasn't a *bad* drug, was it? My paper thinks it was a good drug that went too fast.'

'*Fast?*' The word bitterly amuses him. '*Fast*, man? Those boys in KVH wanted trial results so fast they couldn't wait till tomorrow breakfast.'

A huge explosion stops the world. First it is Khartoum's Russian-made plane from Juba dropping one of its dumb bombs. Then it is the wild horsemen from the north. Then it is the savage battle for the Bentiu oilfields that has arrived at the food station's gates. The tent shakes, sags and braces itself for a new attack. Guy-ropes wince and sob as sheets of water crash onto the canvas roof. Yet Lorbeer seems not to have noticed the attack. He stands at the centre of the tent with one hand pressed to his brow as if he has forgotten something. Justin pulls back the tent flap and through sheets of rain counts three tents dead and two more dying before his eyes. Water is spouting from the washing on the lines. It has made a lake of the grass and is rising in a tide against the wooden walls of the *tukul*. It is crashing in freak waves over the rush roof of the air-raid shelter. Then, as suddenly as it arrived, it stops.

'So Markus,' Justin proposes, as if the thunderstorm has cleared the air inside the tent as well as out. 'Tell me about the girl Wanza. Was she a turning-point in your life? My paper thinks she was.'

Lorbeer's bulging eyes remain fixed on Justin. He makes to speak but no words come.

'Wanza from a village north of Nairobi. Wanza who moved to Kibera slum. And was taken to the Uhuru Hospital to have her baby. She died and her baby lived. My paper believes she shared a ward with Tessa Quayle. Is that possible? Or Tessa Abbott, as she sometimes called herself.'

And still Justin's voice is even and dispassionate, as becomes your objective reporter. And this dispassion is in many ways unfeigned, for he does not take easily to having a man at his mercy. The responsibility is more than he wishes. His instincts for vengeance are too weak. A plane zooms low overhead on its way to the drop zone. Lorbeer's eyes lift to it in feeble hope. They have come to save me! They haven't. They have come to save Sudan.

'Who are you, man?'

It has taken him a lot of courage to get the question out. But Justin ignores it.

'Wanza died. So did Tessa. So did Arnold Bluhm, a Belgian aid worker and doctor and her good friend. My paper believes that Tessa and Arnold came up here to speak to you just a couple of days before they were killed. My paper also believes that you confessed yourself to Tessa and Arnold on the matter of Dypraxa and – this is only supposition, of course – as soon as they had gone, betrayed them to your former employers in order to reinsure yourself. Perhaps by means of a radio message to your friend Mr Crick. Does that ring any bells at all?'

'Jesus God, man. God Christ.'

Markus Lorbeer is burning at the stake. He has seized the central tent pole in both arms and with his head pressed to it is hugging it to himself as if to shelter from the onslaught of Justin's remorseless questioning. His head is raised to Heaven in agony, his mouth whispers and implores inaudibly. Rising, Justin carries his chair across the tent and sets it at Lorbeer's heels, then takes him by the arm and lowers him into it.

'What were Tessa and Arnold looking for when they came here?' he enquires. His questions are still formulated with a deliberate casualness. He wishes for no more sobbing confessions, and no more appeals to God.

'They were looking for my guilt, man, my shameful history, my sin of pride,' Lorbeer whispers in reply, dabbing his face with a sopping piece of rag hauled from the pocket of his shorts.

'And they got it?'

'Everything, man. Every last bit, I swear.'

'With a tape recorder?'

'With two, man! That woman had no faith in one alone!' With an inward smile, Justin acknowledges Tessa's legal acumen. 'I abased myself totally before them. I gave them the naked truth before the Lord. There was no way out. I was the last link in the chain of their investigations.'

'Did they say what they intended to do with the information you had given them?'

Lorbeer's eyes opened very wide but his lips remained closed and his body so motionless that for a second Justin wondered whether he had died a merciful death, but it seemed he was only remembering. Suddenly he was speaking very loudly, his words mounting to a scream as he fought to get them out.

'They would present it to the one man in Kenya they trusted. They would take the whole story to Leakey. Everything they had collected. Kenya should solve Kenya's problem, she said. Leakey was the man to do it. That was their conviction. They warned me. She did. "Markus, you better hide yourself, man. This place is not safe for you any more. You got to find yourself a deeper hole, or they will kill you to pieces for betraying them to us."'

It is hard for Justin to recreate Tessa's actual words from Lorbeer's strangled voice, but he does his best. And certainly he has no problem with the general drift of what she must have said, since Tessa's first concern would always have been for Lorbeer rather than herself. And 'kill you to pieces' was undoubtedly one of her expressions.

'What did Bluhm have to say to you?'

'He was right down to earth, man. Told me I was a charlatan and a traitor to my trust.'

'And that of course helped you to betray him,' Justin suggests kindly, but his kindness is in vain, for Lorbeer's weeping is even worse than Woodrow's – howling, alienating, infuriating tears as he pleads for himself in mitigation. He *loves* that drug, man!

It does not *deserve* to be publicly condemned! A few more years and it will take its place among the great medical discoveries of the age! All we've got to do, we've got to check the peak levels of toxicity, control the rate at which we admit it to the body! They're already working on that, man! By the time they hit the United States market, all those bugs will have disappeared, no problem! Lorbeer loves Africa, man, he loves all mankind, he is a good man, not born to bear such guilt! Yet even while he pleads and moans and rages, he contrives to raise himself mysteriously from defeat. He sits up straight. He draws back his shoulders and a smirk of superiority replaces his penitent's grief.

'Plus look at their *relationship*, man,' he protests, with ponderous insinuation. 'Look at their *ethical behaviour*. Whose sins are we speaking of here, precisely, I ask myself.'

'I don't think I quite follow you,' says Justin mildly, as a mental safety screen between himself and Lorbeer begins to form inside his head.

'Read the newspapers, man. Listen to the radio. Make up your own mind independently and tell me, please. What is this pretty married white woman doing travelling about with this handsome black doctor as her constant companion? Why does she call herself by her maiden name and not by the name of her rightful husband? Why does she parade herself at her lover's side in this very tent, man, brazenly, an adulteress and hypocrite, interrogating Markus Lorbeer about his personal morality?'

But the safety screen must have slipped somehow, for Lorbeer is staring at Justin as if he has seen death's very angel come to summon him to the judgment he so dreads.

'God Christ, man. You're him. Her husband. Quayle.'

*   *   *

The last food drop of the day has emptied the stockade of its workers. Leaving Lorbeer to weep alone in his tent, Justin sits himself on the hummock beside the air-raid shelter to enjoy the evening show: first the pitch-black herons, swooping and circling as they announce the sunset. Then the lightning, driving away the dusk in long, trembling salvoes, then the day's moisture rising in a white veil. And finally the stars, close enough to touch.

CHAPTER TWENTY-FIVE

Out of the finely steered gossip of Whitehall and Westminster; out of parroted television soundbites and misleading images; out of the otiose minds of journalists whose duty to enquire extended no further than the nearest deadline and the nearest free lunch, a chapter of events was added to the sum of minor human history.

The formal elevation *en poste* – contrary to established practice – of Mr Alexander Woodrow to the estate of British High Commissioner, Nairobi, sent ripples of quiet satisfaction through white Nairobi, and was welcomed by the indigenous African press. 'A Quiet Force for Understanding' ran the sub-headline on page three of the Nairobi *Standard*, and Gloria was 'a breath of fresh air who would blow away the last cobwebs of British colonialism'.

Of Porter Coleridge's abrupt disappearance into the catacombs of official Whitehall, little was said but much implied. Woodrow's predecessor had been 'out of touch with modern Kenya'. He had 'antagonised hard-working ministers with his sermons on corruption'. There was even a suggestion, cleverly not enlarged upon, that he might have fallen foul of the vice he so condemned.

Rumours that Coleridge had been 'hauled before a Whitehall disciplinary committee' and invited to explain 'certain embarrassing matters that had arisen during his stewardship' were dismissed as idle speculation but not denied by the High Commission spokesman who had initiated them. 'Porter was a fine scholar and a man of the highest principle. It would be unjust to deny his many virtues,' Mildren informed reliable journalists in an off-the-record obituary, and they duly read between the lines.

'FO Africa Tsar Sir Bernard Pellegrin', an uninterested public learned, had 'sought early retirement in order to take up a senior managerial post with the multinational pharmaceutical giant Karel Vita Hudson of Basel, Vancouver, Seattle and now of London' where, thanks to Pellegrin's 'fabled skills at networking', he would be at his most effective. A farewell banquet in the Pellegrins' honour was attended by a glittering assembly of Africa's High Commissioners to the Court of St James and their wives. A witty speech by the South African delegate observed that Sir Bernard and his Lady might not have won Wimbledon, but they had surely won the hearts of many Africans.

A spectacular rise from the ashes by 'that latter-day Houdini of the City' Sir Kenneth Curtiss was welcomed by friend and foe alike. Only a minority of Cassandras insisted that Kenny's rise was purely optical and the break-up of House of ThreeBees nothing less than an act of daylight sandbagging. These carping voices did not impede the great populist's elevation to the House of Lords where he insisted upon the title of Lord Curtiss of Nairobi and Spennymoor, the latter being his humble place of birth. Even his many critics in Fleet Street had to concede, if wryly, that ermine became the old devil.

The *Evening Standard*'s 'Londoner's Diary' made amusing weather of the long-awaited retirement of that incorruptible old crime-stopper Superintendent Frank Gridley of Scotland Yard, 'known affectionately to the London underworld as Old Grid-iron'. In reality, retirement was the last thing that lay in store for him. One of Britain's leading security companies was poised to snap him up just as soon as he had taken his wife on a long-promised holiday on the island of Majorca.

The departure of Rob and Lesley from the police service received by contrast no publicity at all, though insiders noted that one of Gridley's last acts before leaving the Yard had been to press for the removal of what he termed 'a new breed of unscrupulous careerists' who were giving the Force a bad name.

Ghita Pearson, another would-be careerist, was not successful in her application for acceptance as an established British foreign servant. Although her examination results were good to excellent, confidential reports from the Nairobi High Commission gave cause for concern. Ruling that she was 'too easily swayed by her personal feelings', Personnel Department advised her to wait a couple of years and reapply. Her mixed race, it was emphasised, was not a factor.

No question mark at all, however, hung over the unhappy passing of Justin Quayle. Deranged by despair and grief, he had taken his own life at the very spot where his wife Tessa had been murdered only weeks before. His swift loss of mental balance had been an open secret among those entrusted with his welfare. His employers in London had gone to every length short of locking him up in an effort to save him from himself. The news that his trusted friend Arnold Bluhm was also his wife's murderer had dealt the final blow. Traces of systematic beating around his abdomen and lower body told their own sad story to the tightly knit group of insiders who were privy to the secret: in the days leading up to his death, Quayle had resorted to self-flagellation. How he had come by the fatal weapon – an assassin's short-barrelled .38 pistol in excellent condition with five soft-nosed bullets remaining in the chamber – was a mystery unlikely to be resolved. A rich and desperate man bent upon his own destruction is sure to find a way. His final resting-place in Langata cemetery, the press noted with approval, had reunited him with his wife and child.

The permanent government of England, on which her transient politicians spin and posture like so many table dancers, had once more done its duty: except, that is, in one small but irritating respect. Justin, it seemed, had spent the last weeks of his life composing a 'black dossier' purporting to prove that Tessa and Bluhm had been murdered for knowing too much about the evil dealings of one of the world's most prestigious pharmaceutical companies which so far had contrived to remain anonymous. Some upstart solicitor of Italian origin – a relation of the dead woman to boot – had come forward and, making free use of his late clients' money, retained the services of a professional troublemaker who hid behind the mask of Public Relations Agent. The same hapless solicitor had allied himself with a firm of supercharged City lawyers famous for their pugnacity. The house of Oakey, Oakey & Farmeloe, representing the unnamed company, challenged the use of clients' funds for this purpose, but without success. They had to content themselves with serving writs on any newspaper that dared take up the story.

Yet some did, and the rumours persisted. Scotland Yard, called in to examine the material, publicly declared it 'baseless and a bit sad' and declined to forward it to the Crown Prosecution Service. But the lawyers for the dead couple, far from throwing in the sponge, resorted to Parliament. A Scottish MP, also a lawyer, was suborned, and tabled an innocuous parliamentary question of the Foreign Secretary concerning the health of the African continent at large. The Foreign Secretary batted it away with his customary grace, only to find himself grappling with a supplementary that went for the jugular.

Q: Has the Foreign Secretary knowledge of any written representations made to his department during the last twelve months by the late, tragically murdered Mrs Tessa Quayle?

A: I require notice of that question.

Q: Is that a 'no' I'm hearing?

A: I have no knowledge of such representations made during her lifetime.

Q: Then she wrote to you posthumously, perhaps? *(laughter)*

In the written and verbal exchanges that followed, the Foreign Secretary first denied all knowledge of the documents, then protested that in view of pending legal actions they were *sub judice*. After 'further extensive and costly research' he finally admitted to having 'discovered' the documents, only to conclude that they had received all the attention they merited, then or now, 'having regard for the disturbed mental condition of the writer'. Imprudently, he added that the documents were classified.

Q: Does the Foreign Office regularly classify writings of people of disturbed mental condition? *(laughter)*

A: In cases where such writings could cause embarrassment to innocent third parties, yes.

Q: Or to the Foreign Office, perhaps?

A: I am thinking of the needless pain that could be inflicted on the deceased's close relatives.

Q: Then be at peace. Mrs Quayle had no close relatives.

A: These are not however the only interests I am obliged to consider.

Q: Thank you. I think I have heard the answer I was waiting for.

Next day a formal request for the release of the Quayle papers was presented to the Foreign Office and backed by an application to the High Court. Simultaneously, and surely not by coincidence, a parallel initiative was mounted in Brussels by lawyers for friends and family of the late Dr Arnold Bluhm. During the preliminary hearing, a racially varied crowd of mischief makers dressed in symbolic white coats paraded for television cameras outside the Brussels Palace of Justice and brandished placards bearing the slogan 'Nous Accusons'. The nuisance was quickly dealt with. A string of cross-petitions by the Belgian lawyers ensured that the case would run for years. However, it was now common knowledge that the company in question was none other than Karel Vita Hudson.

* * *

'Up there, that's the Lokomorinyang range,' Captain McKenzie informs Justin over the intercom. 'Gold and oil. Kenya and Sudan been fighting about it for well on a hundred years. Old maps give it to the Sudan, new ones give it to Kenya. I reckon somebody slipped the cartographer a backhander.'

Captain McKenzie is one of those tactful men who knows exactly when to be irrelevant. His chosen plane this time is a Beech Baron with twin engines. Justin sits beside him in the co-pilot's seat, listening without hearing, now to Captain McKenzie, now to the banter of other pilots in the vicinity: 'How are *we* today, Mac? Are we above the cloud level or below?' – 'Where the hell are you, man?' – 'A mile to your right and a thousand feet below you. What's happened to your eyesight?' They are flying over flat brown slabs of rock, darkening into blue. The clouds are thick above them. Vivid red patches appear where the sun breaks through to strike the rock. The foothills ahead of them are tousled and untidy. A road appears like a vein among the muscles of the rock.

'Cape Town to Cairo,' McKenzie says laconically. 'Don't try it.'

'I won't,' Justin promises dutifully.

McKenzie banks the plane and descends, following its path. The road becomes a valley road, weaving along a ridge of snaking hills.

'Road to the right there, that's the road Arnold and Tessa took, Loki to Lodwar. Great if you don't mind bandits.'

Coming awake, Justin peers deeply into the pale mist ahead of him, and sees Arnold and Tessa in their jeep with dust on their faces and the box of disks bobbing between them on the bench seat. A river has joined the Cairo road. It is called the

Tagua, McKenzie says, and its source is high up in the Tagua mountains. The Taguas are eleven thousand feet high. Justin politely acknowledges this information. The sun goes in, the hills turn blue-black, menacing and separate, Tessa and Arnold vanish. The landscape is again godless, not a man or beast in any direction.

'Sudanese tribesmen come down from the Mogila range,' McKenzie says. 'In their jungle they wear nothing. Coming south they get all shy, wear these little bits of cloth. And *boy*, can they run!'

Justin gives a polite smile as brown treeless mountains rise crooked and half buried from the khaki earth. Behind them he makes out the blue haze of a lake.

'Is that Turkana?'

'Don't swim in it. Not unless you're very fast. Fresh water. Great amethysts. Friendly crocodiles.'

Flocks of goat and sheep appear below them, then a village and a compound.

'Turkana tribesmen,' McKenzie says. 'Big shoot-out last year over livestock thefts. Best to steer clear of 'em.'

'I shall,' Justin promises.

McKenzie looks squarely at him, a prolonged, interrogative stare. 'Not the only people to steer clear of, they tell me.'

'No, indeed,' Justin agrees.

'Couple of hours, we could be in Nairobi.'

Justin shakes his head.

'Want me to stretch a point and take you over the border to Kampala? We've got fuel.'

'You're very kind.'

The road reappears, sandy and deserted. The plane reacts violently, nosing left and right like a plunging horse, as if nature is telling it to go back.

'Worst winds for miles around,' McKenzie says. 'Region's famous for 'em.'

The town of Lodwar lies below them, set small among cone-shaped black hills, none more than a couple of hundred feet

491

high. It looks neat and purposeful, with tin roofs, a tarmac airstrip and a school.

'No industry,' McKenzie says. 'Great market for cows, donkeys and camels if you're interested in buying.'

'I'm not,' says Justin with a smile.

'One hospital, one school, lot of army. Lodwar's the security centre for the whole area. Soldiers spend most of their time in the Apoi hills, chasing bandits to no effect. Bandits from Sudan, bandits from Uganda, bandits from Somalia. A real nice catchment area for bandits. Cattle-thieving is the local sport,' McKenzie recites, back in his rôle of tour guide. 'The Mandango steal cattle, dance for two weeks till another tribe steals them back.'

'How far from Lodwar to the lake?' asks Justin.

'Give or take, fifty kilometres. Go to Kalokol. There's a fishing lodge there. Ask for a boatman called Mickie. His boy's Abraham. Abraham's all right as long as he's with Mickie, poison on his own.'

'Thanks.'

Conversation ends. McKenzie overflies the airstrip, waving his wing-tips to signal his intent to land. He climbs again and returns. Suddenly they are on the ground. There is nothing more to say except, once more, thanks.

'If you need me, find someone who can call me on the radio,' McKenzie says as they stand sweltering on the airstrip. 'If I can't help you, there's a guy called Martin, runs the Nairobi School of Flying. Flying for thirty years. Trained in Perth and Oxford. Mention my name.'

Thanks, says Justin again and, in his anxiety to be courteous, writes it down.

'Want to borrow my flight bag?' McKenzie asks, making a gesture with the black briefcase in his right hand. 'Long-barrelled target pistol, if you're interested. Gives you a chance at forty yards.'

'Oh, I'd be no good at ten,' Justin exclaims, with the kind of self-effacing laugh that dates from his days before Tessa.

'And this is Justice,' McKenzie says, introducing a grizzled philosopher in a tattered T-shirt and green sandals who has appeared from nowhere. 'Justice is your driver. Justin, meet Justice. Justice, meet Justin. Justice has a gentleman called Ezra who will be riding point with him. Anything more I can do for you?'

Justin draws a thick envelope from the pocket of his bush jacket. 'I'd like you please to post this for me when you're next in Nairobi. Just the ordinary mail will do fine. She's not a girlfriend. She's my lawyer's aunt.'

'Tonight soon enough?'

'Tonight would be splendid.'

'Take care then,' says McKenzie, slipping the envelope into his flight bag.

'Indeed I will,' says Justin, and this time manages not to tell McKenzie he's been very kind.

*   *   *

The lake was white and grey and silver and the overhead sun made black and white stripes of Mickie's fishing boat, black in the shadow of the canopy, white and pitiless where the sun shone freely on the woodwork, white on the skin of the fresh water that popped and bubbled with the rising fish, white on the misted grey mountains that arched their backs under the sun's heat, white where it struck the black faces of old Mickie and his young companion the poisonous Abraham – a sneering, secretly angry child, McKenzie was quite right – who for some unfathomable reason spoke German and not English, so that the conversation, what there was of it, was three-cornered: German to Abraham, English to old Mickie and their own version of kiSwahili when they spoke between themselves. White also whenever Justin looked at Tessa, which was often, perched tomboy-style on the ship's prow where she was determined to sit despite the crocodiles, with one hand for the boat the way her father had taught her and Arnold never far away in case she

493

slipped. On the boat's radio an English-language cookery pro-gramme was extolling the virtues of sun-dried tomatoes.

At first it had been difficult for Justin to explain his destination in any language. They might never have heard of Allia Bay. Allia Bay didn't interest them in the least. Old Mickie wanted to take him due south-east to Wolfgang's Oasis where he belonged, and the poisonous Abraham had hotly seconded the motion: the Oasis was where Wazungu stayed, it was the first hotel in the region, famous for its film stars and rock stars and millionaires, the Oasis without a doubt was where Justin was heading, whether he knew it or not. It was only when Justin drew a small photograph of Tessa from his wallet – a passport photograph, nothing that had been defiled by the newspapers – that the purpose of his mission became clear to them, and they became quiet and uneasy. So Justin wished to visit the place where Noah and the Mzungu woman were murdered? Abraham demanded.

Yes, please.

Was Justin then aware that many police and journalists had visited this place, that everything that could be found there had been found, also that Lodwar police *and* the Nairobi flying squad had separately and together decreed the place to be a forbidden area to tourists, sightseers, trophy-hunters and anybody else who had no business there? Abraham persisted.

Justin was not, but his intention remained the same, and he was prepared to pay generously to see it fulfilled.

Or that the place was well known to be haunted, and had been even before Noah and the Mzungu were murdered? – but with much less conviction, now that the financial side was settled.

Justin vowed he had no fear of ghosts.

At first in deference to the gloomy nature of their errand, the old man and his helper had adopted a melancholy pose, and it took all Tessa's determined good spirits to bounce them out of it. But as usual, with the help of a string of witty comments from the prow, she succeeded. The presence of other fishing boats further up the sky was also a help. She called out to them – what have you caught? – and they called back to her – this many red fish, this many blue, this many rainbow. And so infectious was her enthusiasm that Justin soon persuaded Mickie and Abraham to put a line out themselves, which also had the effect of diverting their curiosity into more productive paths.

'You are all right, sir?' Mickie asked him, from quite close, peering like an old doctor into his eyes.

'I'm fine. Fine. Just fine.'

'I think you have a fever, sir. Why don't you relax under the canopy and let me bring you some cold drink.'

'Fine. We both will.'

'Thank you, sir. I have to attend to the boat.'

Justin sits under the canopy, using the ice from his glass to cool his neck and forehead while he rides with the motion of the boat. It is an odd company they have brought with them, he has to admit, but then Tessa is absolutely *wanton* when it comes to extending invitations, and really one just has to bite one's lip and double the number one first thought of. Good to see Porter here, and you too, Veronica, and your baby Rosie always a pleasure, no – no objections *there*. And Tessa always seems to get that bit more out of Rosie than anybody else can. But Bernard and Celly Pellegrin a total mistake, darling, and how absolutely typical of Bernard to include *three* rackets, not just one, in his beastly tennis kit. As for the Woodrows – honestly, it's time you overcame your laudable but misplaced conviction that even the most unpromising among us have hearts of gold, and you're the one to prove it to them. And for God's sake stop peeking at me as if you're about to make love to me at any moment. Sandy's going half crazy from looking down your shirt front as it is.

'What is it?' Justin asked sharply.

At first he thought it was Mustafa. Gradually he realised that Mickie had taken a fistful of his shirt above his right shoulder blade and was shaking it to wake him.

'We've arrived, sir, on the eastern shore. We are close to the place where the tragedy happened.'

'How far?'

'To walk, ten minutes, sir. We will accompany you.'

'That's not necessary.'

'It is most necessary, sir.'

'*Was fehlt dir?*' Abraham asked, over Mickie's shoulder.

'*Nichts.* Nothing. I'm fine. You've both been very kind.'

'Drink some more water, sir,' Mickie said, holding a fresh glass to him.

They make quite a column, clambering over the slabs of lava rock here at the cradle of civilisation, Justin has to admit. 'Never realised there were so many civilised chaps around,' he tells Tessa, doing his English bloody fool act, and Tessa laughs for him, that silent laugh she does when she smiles delightedly and shakes and generally does all the right things but no sound issues. Gloria leads the way, well, she would. With that royal British stride of hers and those elbows she can outmarch the lot of us. Pellegrin bitching, which is also normal. His wife Celly saying she can't take the heat, what's new? Rosie Coleridge on her dad's back, having a good sing in Tessa's honour – how on earth did we all fit into the boat?

Mickie had stopped, one hand held lightly on Justin's arm. Abraham was standing close behind him.

'This is the place where your wife passed away, sir,' said Mickie softly.

But he need not have bothered because Justin knew exactly – even if he didn't know how Mickie had deduced that he was Tessa's husband, but perhaps Justin had informed him of this fact in his sleep. He had seen the place in photographs, in the gloom of the lower ground and in his dreams. Here ran what looked like a dried river bed. Over there stood the sad little heap of stones erected by Ghita and her friends. Around it – but spreading in all directions, alas – lay the junk that was these days inseparable from any well-publicised event: discarded film cassettes and boxes, cigarette packets, plastic bottles and paper plates. Higher up – maybe thirty or so yards up the white rock slope – ran the dust road where the long wheelbase safari truck had pulled alongside Tessa's jeep and shot its wheel off, sending the jeep careering down this same slope with Tessa's murderers in hot pursuit with their pangas and guns and whatever else they were carrying. And over there – Mickie was silently pointing them out with his gnarled old finger – were the blue smears of the Oasis four-track's paintwork left on the rock face as it slid into the gully. And the rock face, unlike the black volcanic rock surrounding it, was white as a gravestone. And perhaps the brown stains on it were indeed blood, as Mickie was suggesting. But when Justin examined them, he concluded they might as well be lichen. Otherwise he observed little of interest to the observant gardener, beyond yellow spear grass and a row of doum palms that as usual looked as though they had been planted by the municipality. A few euphorbia shrubs – well, naturally – making themselves a precarious living among chunks of black basalt. And a spectral white Commiphora tree – when were they *ever* in leaf? – its spindly branches stretched to either side of it like the wings of a moth. He selected a basalt boulder and sat on it. He felt light-headed, but lucid. Mickie handed him a water bottle and Justin took a pull from it, screwed the top back on and set it at his feet.

'I'd like to be alone for a little while, Mickie,' he said. 'Why don't you and Abraham go and catch a fish and I'll call to you from the shore when I'm done?'

'We would prefer to wait for you with the boat, sir.'

'Why not fish?'

'We would prefer to remain here with you. You have a fever.'

'It's going now. Just a couple of hours.' He looked at his watch. It was four in the afternoon. 'When's dusk?'

'At seven o'clock, sir.'

'Fine. Well, you can have me at dusk. If I need anything I'll call.' And more firmly, 'I want to be alone, Mickie. That's what I came here for.'

'Yes, sir.'

He didn't hear them leave. For a while he heard no sounds at all, except for the odd popping of the lake, and the putter of an occasional fishing boat. He heard a jackal howl, and a lot of backchat from a family of vultures that had commandeered a doum palm down on the lakeside. And he heard Tessa telling him that if she had it all to do again, this was still where she would want to do her dying, in Africa, on her way to heading off a great injustice. He drank some water, stood up, stretched and wandered over to the paint marks because that was where he knew for a surety that he was close to her. It didn't take much working out. If he put his hands on the marks he was about eighteen inches from her, if you discounted the width of the car door. Or maybe twice that much if you imagined Arnold in between. He even managed to have a bit of a laugh with her because he'd always had the devil's own job persuading her to wear her seat belt. On potholed African roads, she had argued, with her usual stubbornness, you were better off hanging loose: at least you could weave and dodge around inside the car instead of being plonked like a sack of potatoes into every bloody crater. And from the paint marks he made his way to the bottom of the gully and, hands in pockets, stood beside the dried-up river bed, staring back at the spot where the jeep had come to rest and imagining poor Arnold being hauled senseless from it, to be taken to his place of prolonged and terrible execution.

Then, as a methodical man, he returned to the boulder he had chosen as his sitting place when he first came here, and sat down on it again, and devoted himself to the study of a small blue flower not unlike the phlox that he had planted in the front garden of their house in Nairobi. But the problem was, he was not absolutely sure the flower belonged to the place where he was seeing it, or whether in his mind he had transplanted it from Nairobi or, come to think of it, from the meadows surrounding his hotel in the Engadine. Also his interest in flora generally was at a low ebb. He no longer wished to cultivate the image of a sweet chap passionately interested in nothing except phlox, asters, freesias and gardenias. And he was still reflecting on this transition in his nature when he heard the sound of an engine from the direction of the shore, first the little explosion of it as it sprang to life, then its steady chugging as it faded into the distance. Mickie's decided to have a go after all, he thought; for your true fisherman, rising fish at dusk are an irresistible temptation. And after that, he remembered his attempts to persuade Tessa to go fishing with him, which invariably ended with no fish but a lot of undisciplined love-making, which was perhaps why he was so keen on persuading her. And he was still humorously contemplating the logistics of making love in the bottom of a small boat when he had a different idea about Mickie's fishing expedition, namely that it wasn't happening.

Mickie didn't mess about, change his mind, give in to whims. That wasn't Mickie at all.

The thing about Mickie that you knew the moment you set eyes on him, and Tessa had said the same, was that this fellow was your born family retainer, which was why, to be honest, it was easy to confuse him with Mustafa.

So Mickie hadn't gone fishing.

But he'd gone. Whether he'd taken the poisonous Abraham with him was a moot point. But Mickie had gone, and the boat had gone. Back across the lake – that boat's engine had faded and faded.

So why had he gone? Who had *told* him to go? *Paid* him to go? *Ordered* him to go? *Threatened* him if he didn't go? What message had Mickie received, over his boat's radio, or man to man from another boat or somebody on the shore, that had persuaded him, against all the natural lines of his good face, to walk out on a job when he hadn't been paid for it? Or had Markus Lorbeer the compulsive Judas taken out some more insurance with his friends in the industry? He was still mulling over this possibility when he heard another engine, this time from the direction of the road. The dusk was falling quickly by now, and the light already fickle, so he might have expected a passing car at this hour to put on its sidelights at the very least, but this one – car or whatever – hadn't done so, which was a puzzle to him.

One thought he had – probably because the car was moving at a snail's pace – was that it was Ham, driving at his habitual five miles an hour below the speed limit, come to announce that Justin's letters to the ferocious aunt in Milan had been safely received, and that Tessa's great injustice would shortly be righted on the lines of her oft-stated conviction that the System must be forced to mend its own ways from within. Then he thought: it's not a car at all, I've got it wrong. It's a small plane. Then the sound stopped altogether which almost succeeded in convincing him it had been an illusion in the first place – that he was hearing Tessa's jeep, for instance, and any second it was going to pull up just above him on the road there and she was going to hop out wearing both Mephisto boots, and come skipping down the slope to congratulate him on taking over where she'd left off. But it wasn't Tessa's jeep, it didn't belong to anyone he knew. What he was looking at was the elusive shape of a long wheelbase jeep or four-track – no, *safari truck* – either dark blue or dark green, in the fast-vanishing light it was hard to tell, and it had stopped in exactly the spot where he had just been watching Tessa. And although he had been expecting something of the kind ever since he had returned to Nairobi – even in a remote way wishing for it, and had therefore regarded Donohue's warning to him as superfluous – he greeted the sight with an extraordinary sense of exultation, not to say completion. He had met her betrayers, of course – Pellegrin, Woodrow, Lorbeer. He had rewritten her scandalously discarded memorandum for her – if in a piecemeal form, but that couldn't be avoided. And now, it seemed, he was about to share with her the last of all her secrets.

A second truck had pulled up behind the first. He heard light footsteps and made out the fast-moving shapes of fit men in bulky clothes crouching at the run. He heard a man or woman whistle and an answering whistle from behind him. He imagined, and perhaps it was true, that he caught a whiff of Sportsman cigarette smoke. The darkness grew suddenly deeper as lights came on around him and the brightest of them picked him out, and held him in its beam.

He heard a sound of feet sliding down white rock.

Author's Note

Let me rush to the protection of the British High Commission in Nairobi. It is not the place I described, for I have never been inside it. It is not staffed by the people I have described, for I have never met nor spoken to them. I met the High Commissioner a couple of years back, and we had a ginger beer together on the verandah of the Norfolk Hotel and that was all. He bears not the least resemblance, externally or otherwise, to my Porter Coleridge. As to poor Sandy Woodrow – well, if there were a Head of Chancery at all in the British High Commission in Nairobi as I write, you may be sure he would be a diligent and upstanding man or woman who never covets a colleague's spouse or destroys inconvenient documents. But there isn't. Heads of Chancery in Nairobi, as in many other British Missions, have fallen to the axe of time.

In these dog days when lawyers rule the universe, I have to persist with these disclaimers, which happen to be perfectly true. With one exception nobody in this story, and no outfit or corporation, thank God, is based upon an actual person or outfit in the real world, whether we are thinking of Woodrow, Pellegrin, Landsbury, Crick, Curtiss and his dreaded House of

ThreeBees, or Messrs Karel Vita Hudson, also known as KVH. The exception is the great and good Wolfgang of the Oasis Lodge, a character so imprinted upon the memory of all who visit him that it would be ridiculous to attempt to create a fictional equivalent. In his sovereignty, Wolfgang raised no objection to my traducing his name and voice.

There is no Dypraxa, never was, never will be. I know of no wonder-cure for TB that has recently been launched on the African market or any other – or is about to be – so with luck I shall not be spending the rest of my life in the law courts or worse, though nowadays you can never be sure. But I can tell you this. As my journey through the pharmaceutical jungle progressed, I came to realise that, by comparison with the reality, my story was as tame as a holiday postcard.

On a happier note, let me warmly thank those who helped me and are willing to have their names mentioned, as well as others who helped me and for good reasons are not.

Ted Younie, a longtime and compassionate observer of the African scene, first whispered pharmaceuticals in my ear and later purged my text of several solecisms.

Dr David Miller, a physician with experience of Africa and the Third World, first suggested tuberculosis as the way, and opened my eyes to the costly and sophisticated campaign of seduction waged by pharmaceutical companies against the medical profession.

Dr Peter Godfrey-Faussett, a senior lecturer at the London School of Hygiene and Tropical Medicine, gave me precious expert advice, both at the outset, and again at the manuscript stage.

Arthur, a man of many trades and son of my late American publisher Jack Geoghegan, told me horrendous tales of his time as a pharma man in Moscow and Eastern Europe. Jack's benign spirit presided over us.

Daniel Berman of Médecins Sans Frontières in Geneva provided me with a briefing that was three-star Michelin: worth the whole journey.

BUKO Pharma-Kampagne of Bielefeld in Germany – not to be confused with Hippo in my novel – is an independently financed, under-manned body of sane, well-qualified people who struggle to expose the misdeeds of the pharmaceutical industry, particularly in its dealings with the Third World. If you are feeling generous, please send them some money to help them continue their work. As medical opinion continues to be insidiously and methodically corrupted by the pharma-giants, BUKO's survival assumes ever greater importance. And BUKO not only helped me greatly. They actually urged me to extol the virtues of responsible pharmaceutical companies. For love of them, I tried here and there to do as they asked, but it wasn't what the story was about.

Both Dr Paul Haycock, a veteran of the international pharma industry, and Tony Allen, an old Africa hand and pharma consultant with a heart and an eye, gave me freely of their advice, knowledge and good humour, and graciously suffered my assaults on their profession – as indeed did the hospitable Peter, who prefers to remain modestly in the shadows.

I received help from several sterling individuals in the United Nations. None had the smallest notion of what I was about; nevertheless I suspect it is tactful not to name them.

With sadness, I have also decided not to name the people in Kenya who generously gave me their assistance. As I write, news is coming in of the death of John Kaiser, an American priest from Minnesota who worked in Kenya for the last thirty-six years. His body was found in Naivasha, fifty miles north-west of Nairobi. It had a bullet wound to the head. A shotgun was found close by. Mr Kaiser was a longtime outspoken critic of the Kenyan government's human rights policies, or lack of them. Accidents like that can happen again.

In describing the tribulations of Lara in chapter eighteen, I drew on several cases, particularly in the North American continent, where highly qualified medical researchers have dared to disagree with their pharmaceutical paymasters and suffered vilification and persecution for their pains. The issue is not about whether their inconvenient findings were correct. It is about individual conscience in conflict with corporate greed. It is about the elementary right of doctors to express unbought medical opinions, and their duty to acquaint patients with the risks they believe to be inherent in the treatments they prescribe.

And lastly, if you should ever chance to find yourself on the island of Elba, please do not fail to visit the beautiful old estate that I appropriated for Tessa and her Italian forebears. It is called La Chiusa di Magazzini, and is the property of the Foresi family. The Foresis make red, white and rosé wines and liqueurs from their own vineyard, and an immaculate oil from their own olive orchard. They have a few cottages that you may rent. There is even an oil room where those in search of answers to life's great riddles may seek temporary seclusion.

John le Carré
December 2000